D0938021

HANGMAN

_ _ _ _ _ _ _ _ _

HANGMAN

A NOVEL

JACK HEATH

HANOVER
SQUARE
PRESS

HANOVER
SQUARE
PRESS

ISBN-13: 978-1-335-06291-8
ISBN-13: 978-1-335-00566-3 (International Trade Paperback Edition)

Hangman

Copyright © 2018 by Jack Heath

For questions and comments about the quality of this book, please contact us at CustomerService@Harlequin.com.

Library of Congress Cataloging-in-Publication Data has been applied for

HanoverSqPress.com
BookClubbish.com

Printed in U.S.A.

For Venetia, with love

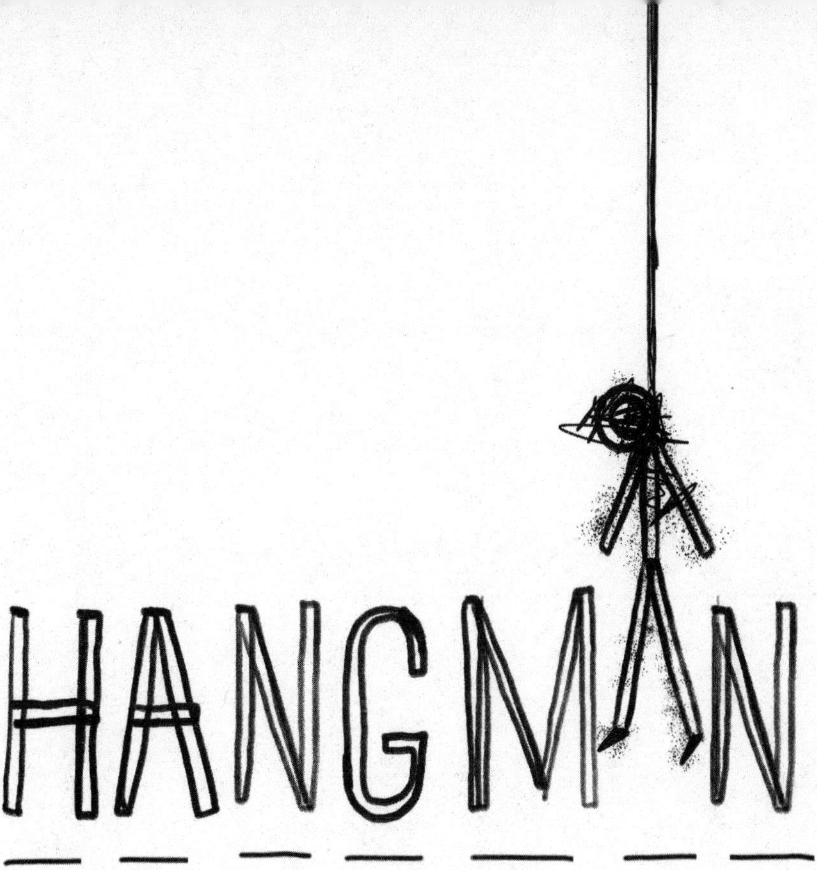
HANGMAN

CHAPTER 1

**THE MORE OF ME YOU TAKE,
THE MORE YOU LEAVE BEHIND.
WHAT AM I?**

THE BLOOD IS STICKY AND SOUR BETWEEN MY teeth.

"You can't be here, sir," the FBI agent says, blocking the doorway. "Move on."

I chew on my fingertip, tearing out another chunk of the nail. "I work for you," I say. "I'm a civilian consultant."

The agent looks at my sneakers from Walmart, my stained jeans, my tattered sweater.

"You got ID?" she asks.

I left my credentials at home, expecting to know the agent on the door. Around here, people get shot just for saying the word "cop."

The house has green patches where the graffiti couldn't be scrubbed away. The mailbox has been mangled by a baseball bat. A coyote-wolf hybrid—coywolves, they're called—limps around an overturned trash can up the street. His chewed-off foot would be in a bear trap somewhere.

Some white teenagers in hoodies sip cheap beer nearby. Grinning like a jack-o'-lantern, one boy crushes his empty can and hurls it at the coywolf, which leaps back. The kids cackle but keep their distance as the creature hobbles away between two crumbling fence pickets.

Footsteps from within the house. Raised voices. I need to be in there.

"Please," I say. "The field office—"

"Unless you have ID," the agent says, "you gotta leave."

"The field office director called me."

A few strands of hair come loose from her cap and fall into her eyes. She determinedly ignores them. She's black, about five foot eight—same height as me—with no makeup and no wedding ring. Attractive in a tough, unsmiling sort of way. Her lanyard reads *Agent R. Thistle, Houston Field Office*.

"What's his name?" she asks. "The field office director."

"Peter Luzhin," I say.

She looks me up and down again, reassessing.

"You want his Social Security number too?" I ask.

"You shouldn't know the director's Social Security number."

I shouldn't, but I do. I broke into his house and found it on his water bill. The trick to memorizing long numbers is to convert each digit into a consonant and then fill in the vowels with whatever makes a memorable image. The director's Social Security number—404 62 5283—becomes RZR BN FNHS, which becomes RaZoR BoNe FuNHouSe. I remember it by picturing Peter Luzhin shaving his cheeks with a straight razor until all his flesh is gone and the bone is exposed, and then calmly examining his handiwork in a fun house mirror.

"I was kidding," I tell the FBI agent.

There's no more nail or loose skin to chew on this finger. I start on my thumb. This compulsion permanently damages my cuticles and teeth and puts parasites in my mouth. But I can't stop.

Another agent appears at the top of the stairs. He's a white, skinny smoker with the mashed-up ears people get from wrestling or boxing. His jacket is faded on the left side from hours of driving in the Texas sun. He's not wearing a lanyard, but I've met him before. His name is Gary Ruciani. The other agents call him "Pope," because he's Italian.

"Hey, Pope," I say. "Let me in."

The woman steps forward to obscure my view. "Sir—"

"Oh," Ruciani says as he trots down the stairs. "It's you." Being remembered isn't usually a relief.

"Collins and Richmond are upstairs in the bedroom," he tells me. To Thistle, he says, "Let him through. Luzhin must have given up."

I get a faint whiff of Thistle's perfume as I push past. She shrinks away. There's a Greek myth about a guy who wanted to marry a Spartan princess but was exiled to an island because his wounded foot got infected and started to stink. Eventually the army came back for him because they realized they needed his poisoned arrows. He helped win the war—he was with them inside the wooden horse—but everyone still hated him. The way Ruciani avoids my gaze makes me feel like that guy.

The floorboards squeak as I enter the kitchen, passing a leaning tower of grimy dishes. Oswald Collins vanished eight days ago. His wife, Billie, apparently hasn't done any washing-up since then. In the fridge are three half-loaves of supermarket bread and two open cartons of milk. They don't put photos of missing children on the cartons anymore, but it's not because kids have stopped disappearing. If they had, I'd be out of a job.

A crumple of aluminum foil holds five cocktail weenies. I eat one and drop the rest into my pocket for later.

The bedroom door is open. Billie Collins sits on the bare mattress, her head in her hands. Her hair has gone gray at the roots, and her legs look prickly. Her shorts are unraveling where she has tugged at the seams.

Agent Richmond looks up as I walk in. He has a spork in one hand and a cup of noodles in the other, almost empty. Droplets of soup cling to the stubble around his chin. "Blake," he says. "Where have you been?"

I'm a civilian, so I'm not supposed to visit crime scenes or talk to witnesses without supervision. Richmond is my baby-sitter. Fortunately, he's lazy, and he doesn't know me as well as he thinks he does.

"Agent Thistle wouldn't let me in," I say. "Where were you?"

He waves a fat-knuckled hand toward Billie, who flinches and stares at me uneasily. Richmond wants us both to think that he stayed here to comfort her, but "comfort" isn't the right word. He suspects Oswald Collins is dead. He's hoping to catch Billie on the rebound.

"Mrs. Collins," I say, "I'm Timothy Blake. We met last week."

She nods. Her red-rimmed eyes focus on my mouth. "You're bleeding."

The blood is from my fingernails. I lick my lips. "I've been looking for your husband and your mom for five days. I can't find any trace of them."

She doesn't look surprised. "Warner wouldn't want them found."

Oswald Collins is a drinker with a habit of gambling away other people's money. He borrowed eight thousand dollars from Charlie Warner, who bankrolls most of the crime in Houston. Then he disappeared, along with Billie's mother.

Billie is talking as though Oswald and her mom are dead, but her body language is all wrong. Grief and relief both slacken the shoulders and the neck. Billie is all tensed up, gripping the mattress as though bracing herself for a plane crash. She's scared.

"Warner *would* want him found," I say. "With his head cut off, or his eyes ripped out. To send a message: *This is what happens to people who don't pay me what they owe.*"

Richmond winces. Cops are taught to be gentle with the families of victims. But I'm not a cop.

"So I thought Oswald might have escaped," I continue.

"But then his car would be missing. Or there'd be a record of him buying a ticket out of town. Even if he paid cash, he would've shown up on the CCTV at the bus station."

There are ways to travel off the grid. But Oswald wouldn't know them.

"Warner took him," Billie says, louder.

"I talked to Warner's enforcers," I say. "They're as keen to find Oswald as you are. Keener, in fact."

"Whoa." Richmond raises his palms, begging me to stop. He turns to Billie. "What Mr. Blake is saying…"

"They're lying," Billie says to me.

"No, ma'am. I can tell when I'm being lied to."

I hold her gaze until she looks away.

"Gangs don't kidnap the person who owes them," I continue. "They don't take the mother-in-law either. They take a child, or a spouse."

"You're saying I'm in danger?"

"Is your husband violent?"

"No." Billie shifts on the mattress. "No, of course not."

Even if I hadn't seen her shrink back when Richmond raised his hand, I would still know she wasn't telling the truth. Oswald Collins has priors for aggravated assault and armed robbery.

"But he doesn't plan very far ahead, right?" I say.

She says nothing.

"He's the kind who will bet his paycheck, lose and borrow more to chase the loss. He'll start a loaf of bread before the last one is finished, and he won't throw the old one out. He won't wash his dirty dishes, even when he's supposed to be hiding."

"I'd like you to leave," Billie says.

Richmond is staring at me, unsure why I'm antagonizing her.

"Why?" I ask.

"Because you're not gonna find him sitting here talking!" As she says *find him*, she points at her bedroom door. It's a subconscious gesture, not deliberate. Every level of her mind wants me out of here.

"Actually," I say, "I think I will."

She stands up. "Get out."

"No one took your husband," I say. "He's hiding until after Charlie Warner's trial. He told you to report him missing. You said his plan was stupid, so he threatened to kill your mom if you didn't do it. How many times has he visited you since then? Two? Three? Is he sleeping here?"

"Holy shit," Richmond says. He's dropped his spork.

"I never said that!" Billie screeches. "I never said any of that!"

"If you had, this would be over by now." I realize I'm chewing my thumb again. I stuff my hands into my pockets. "Listen, he can't kill your mom. Once he does, he has no leverage. So just tell me where—"

Billie Collins is looking over my shoulder, terror in her eyes.

"You goddamn bitch," says a voice from behind me.

I turn to see the police mug shot I've been looking at for a week. Oswald Collins has a squid's face—wide-set eyes and a flat nose, with a hairline that has receded since his most recent arrest. He's pointing a scratched-up Beretta 3032 Tomcat at his wife's chest.

An old woman stands in front of him. Oswald is holding her by the collar of her flannel pajamas. She smells like one of the youth shelters where I grew up. Her eyes are wet but alert. Mary-Sue McGinness. Billie's mother.

"You told!" Oswald hisses at Billie.

"I didn't!"

"Whoa now," Richmond says. "Take it easy."

"Shut your mouth," Oswald says.

It's a small handgun, but with five of us crammed into this tiny room, Oswald is sure to hit someone. The weapon takes seven .32 ACP cartridges. Enough to kill us all.

"You heard!" Billie says. "I didn't say a thing!"

I raise my hands and step in between them, blocking Oswald's shot.

The old lady glares. Her breaths are fast and quiet.

"Hey, asshole," Oswald says to me. "You want to mind your own business?"

"You're outnumbered four to one," I tell him. "And there are more FBI agents outside. It's over. You'd be an idiot not to put the gun down."

Veins pulse in his neck. He knows there are only two ways out: in handcuffs, or in a body bag. But he's been in a Texas prison before, so he isn't sure which is worse.

"It's okay," I tell him. My heart is thudding against my lungs, but I keep my voice calm. I nod gently, hoping he'll start nodding too. "We can cut a deal. Just put the gun down, and we'll talk it out. Okay?"

Oswald's finger relaxes on the trigger. His arm starts to descend.

Richmond whips out his SIG, takes aim and yells, "Drop the—"

Oswald shoots him.

The room fills with noise and Richmond goes down like he's been kicked in the gut, wheezing on the floor. The SIG thumps against the carpet and Oswald stomps on it, stopping Richmond from making another attempt.

He needn't have worried. Richmond's face is going purple. He's wearing Kevlar, but the bullet may have broken a rib. He can't breathe.

Oswald yells something, but my ears are ringing too loudly to decipher it. Spit explodes outward from his lips like spider silk.

McGinness has wriggled out of his grip. She's poised like a gargoyle in the corner of the room, ready to leap aside should the gun turn her way. But Oswald is trying to line up a shot on his wife. He doesn't seem to care that I'm still in the way. The hammer rises as he puts more and more pressure on the trigger.

I look over his shoulder, toward the door. "Take the shot!" I shout.

Oswald falls for it. He whirls around, looking for the other FBI agents. I lunge at him, hooking one arm across his throat and grabbing the gun with my other hand.

He staggers backward, his free hand clawing at his throat, tearing some skin off my elbow. As he tries to point the gun back over his shoulder at me, I force it upward and press his trigger finger. The gun blows *one, two, three* holes in the ceiling before I feel it click empty.

The noise messes with the fluid in my ears, and the floor tilts. I cling to Oswald, my forearm still crushing his neck. He gurgles in my grip. If the blood is getting to his brain, he could be conscious for three minutes or more. If it's not, he'll go down in just a few seconds.

"Let him go." The voice is barely audible over my whining eardrums. For a second I think it's Billie, but then I see Agent Thistle—the pretty black agent from downstairs. She's in the doorway, aiming her service revolver at me.

I drop Oswald and stagger sideways. He hits the floor. I raise my hands.

"Don't shoot," I say. "I'm one of the good guys."

Thistle spins me around and binds my wrists with flex-cuffs. Perhaps, like me, she can sense when she's being lied to.

It doesn't matter. I solved the case, so I get my reward. My mouth is already dry with anticipation.

Ruciani pins Oswald to the floor and tells him that if he cannot afford an attorney, one will be provided for him by the state. Oswald doesn't seem to hear. He's looking up at McGinness, Billie's mother. In the confusion, she's picked up the Beretta and is pointing it at him. Her eyes are rich with hatred.

"Don't," he says.

McGinness's lip curls. She lines the gun up on Oswald's face and tugs on the trigger.

Click.

CHAPTER 2

WHAT IS SO FRAGILE THAT YOU CAN BREAK IT JUST BY SAYING ITS NAME?

THE AMBULANCE KILLER SHUFFLES INTO THE concrete room, chains clinking around his ankles as though he's wearing boots with spurs. His hair is matted on one side, but he's clean-shaven. I can see scraps of his final meal between his square teeth. His knuckles are bruised evenly on both hands from push-ups on the concrete floor of his cell. His name is Nigel Boyd.

I watch him from behind the thick glass. It's like visiting an aquarium. A rep from the TDCJ—the Texas Department of Criminal Justice—is a few seats away from me, playing with her phone. Boyd's lawyer sits next to her, trying in vain to catch her eye and start a conversation. There's only one other person here: a white woman with graying hair clutching a leather-bound journal. Probably a reporter, although executions don't get much coverage these days.

Normally the family of the killer and the families of the victims would sit in adjacent viewing galleries, unable to see each other. As he's bound to the gurney with thick straps, the condemned man can look at both groups side by side, dressed in their best clothes and kept separate, like the guests at a wedding. But none of Nigel Boyd's living relatives are here. His sister changed her name, and his cousins moved to Kansas. His father put a shotgun in his mouth. So this time the victims' families took one gallery and I joined the paper-pushers in the other.

This part of the Huntsville prison is creatively nicknamed the Death House. It's the busiest execution chamber in the USA. They kill so many people here that it's hard to keep enough lethal chemicals on hand, especially since the European manufacturers now refuse to sell the drugs to the TDCJ. Tennessee has the same problem—they've gone back to using the electric chair. There's talk of doing that here too.

Five guards follow Boyd into the room. They're called "the tie-down team." The man in charge is a beanbag-shaped guy with a squashed chin and a name badge that says *Woodstock*.

The guards lead Nigel Boyd over to a green rubber bench covered with leather straps and brass buckles. They fold two rectangles out from the sides to go under his arms, then they tie his wrists to them like it's a crucifixion. Boyd is sweating, but he doesn't fight the guards as they strap him to the gurney. The doomed men never seem to struggle, even though they have nothing to lose.

Soon Nigel Boyd is immobilized. He spent years driving a stolen ambulance around Houston and knocking people out with an ether-soaked dishrag. He used the ambulance like a mobile surgery, cutting up his victims and selling their organs on the black market. The director thinks Charlie Warner got a lung transplant from him, but he couldn't prove it. Six years later, it's Boyd's turn on the gurney.

"Raise the curtain," Woodstock tells one of the other guards as he tightens the final strap.

"It's already up."

"Shit." Woodstock looks over at the two windows that are supposed to be covered with a curtain while the inmate is strapped down. He sees me watching and quickly looks away.

The woman with the gray hair and the journal notices this. She sidles over and sits next to me.

"Hey," she says gently. "Are you doing okay?"

Definitely a reporter. Warming me up for an interview.

I nod, giving her nothing.

"Is he your..." She gestures to Boyd, waiting for me to fill in the blank.

"He's not my anything," I say.

The warden enters the execution chamber, along with a priest. The warden is a thin guy in a gray suit. His shaved head and long nose make him look like a bald eagle. He's new. The priest I've seen many times before. He's an old man with sad eyes, who staggers into the room as though he's the one in leg-irons. He puts a pillow under Boyd's head.

There's a moment of silence. The priest lays his hand on Boyd's leg. Everyone in the execution chamber is watching the clock.

"You never get used to it," the reporter says. "This is my twenty-first execution, and it still chills me to the bone."

I grunt.

"You're family?" the reporter guesses.

"I'm just the driver. I take the body to the disposal facility after."

She deflates. "Oh. They make you watch the executions?"

"Hey, are you a reporter?" I ask. "I got lots of stories. My whole family's crazy. My brother, when he's been drinking, he does some funny shit."

"Excuse me a second," the woman says. She pulls out her phone and moves to a different seat. Reporters don't usually want to talk to anyone who wants to talk to them.

I go back to watching Boyd. He's hypnotic. So big, so muscular. The veins in his neck are pulsing, but his cheeks have gone gray. Maybe he didn't think it would go this far. The Supreme Court rejected his last appeal days ago, but he might have been waiting for a presidential pardon.

In the dark subways of their unconscious minds, some people believe that no one else is real—that it's all just a single-player video game, and the other characters don't matter.

Nigel Boyd can't believe that he, the most important man in the universe, is about to die. Sometimes I wonder if I'm one of those people.

The phone inside the execution chamber rings.

The warden strides over to answer it. While everyone's distracted, Woodstock adjusts the bag of IV fluid. His back is blocking the view from the window, but I know what he's doing. He's swapping the pentobarbital for a bag of suxamethonium chloride.

Suxamethonium is harmless if swallowed, but it paralyzes the victim when injected—and it works even if the needle misses the vein. Doctors can't perform lethal injections because of the Hippocratic oath, so the job is left to prison guards, who aren't good at calculating doses or finding veins.

Woodstock looks at me and gives a faint nod.

I turn to see if the reporter noticed. She didn't—she's doodling in her journal. Her "chilled to the bone" remark must have been for my benefit.

The warden hangs up the phone. He's gone gray too. He looks at Boyd and shakes his head.

"Oh, fuck," Boyd says. "Oh, Jesus."

Tears well up in his eyes. He's breathing hard and fast, as though trying to squeeze a lifetime of air into his last few minutes.

"Proceed," the warden tells Woodstock.

"Wait," Boyd says. "Please."

Woodstock won't look him in the eye. He pushes the needle into Boyd's radial artery.

Boyd screams, so loud that the sound rattles the windows. Even the jaded reporter flinches.

The bag of suxamethonium slowly deflates as the fluid is pumped into Boyd's body. Boyd runs out of air and tries to scream again, but he can't. The paralytic is already taking

effect. His face goes slack. In half a minute, he's gone completely still.

His lawyer lets out a long, relieved sigh. He thinks it's over.

The priest is muttering something inaudible. The new warden looks like he's about to throw up. Woodstock places a
finger to Boyd's throat, apparently checking for a pulse.

"Time of death," he says, checking the clock, "eleven forty-
seven p.m."

Only he and I know that Boyd's heart is still racing. He's
completely conscious, but the paralytic has frozen his lungs.
He's silently suffocating on the gurney.

Woodstock and the other guards start loosening his straps.
The reporter follows the lawyer and the bureaucrat out.

I watch for a minute more, fascinated by Boyd's limp form.
Dead outside, alive and screaming inside. It's the opposite of
how he was before—dead within, alive on the surface. The
drug has turned him inside out.

The corridors of the Death House are designed so that the
families of the victims don't have to exit the same way as the
families of the killers. But I see a few old people in the parking lot—still surrounded by the huge red walls of the Huntsville prison—who I figure are the moms and dads of Boyd's
victims. A man with a vest and a walker is sobbing. A woman
in a frilly dress and a flower in her hair is leaning against a
car. She looks faintly concussed. Another woman is talking
to the reporter, who nods sympathetically while holding a
phone up to record the audio.

"It's not enough," the grieving woman says. "It was so
peaceful. My daughter didn't die like that. It's not enough."

I know how she feels. It's never enough for me either.

As the last of the parents leaves, Woodstock emerges
through a big set of double doors. He rolls out a different
gurney with a body bag on it. The bag is made of white fabric so thin that I can see the shape of Nigel Boyd's frozen

face through it. The suxamethonium makes it impossible to tell if he's still alive.

I open the back of the windowless van. Haz-chem symbols are painted on both sides. Woodstock helps me fold up the legs of the gurney and slide it into the van. He hands me a sheaf of papers. If anyone were watching—and I don't think anyone is—they would assume these were authorization forms to get the body into the disposal facility.

Woodstock doesn't speak and doesn't meet my gaze. He just turns around and hurries back into the Death House.

I shut the van door, sealing the Ambulance Killer inside.

CHAPTER 3

WHAT BELONGS TO YOU,
BUT IS USED MOSTLY BY OTHERS?

IT'S SIX DAYS LATER. I BRAKE AT THE STOP SIGN, check left and turn right from Hackett onto Jester, my beaten-up Mitsubishi casting a long shadow on the blacktop. I drive northwest until the building emerges from behind the pine trees—an obelisk of tinted-glass windows, ten stories high, with the American and Texas flags billowing on twin poles out front.

The radio bellows at me, advertising new phones, plastic surgery and kitchen renovations. I can't afford any of those things, but I keep the volume way up. I'm not in the mood to hear myself think.

The Mitsubishi is cheap, common and new enough to be in good repair. I found it in an outdoor lot near a Walmart. A doorstop and a coat hanger opened the door; a flat-head screwdriver and a hammer smashed the locking pins in the ignition. I put the dings in myself with a wrench so the old owners wouldn't recognize it. I also switched the plates with another car—a purple Volkswagen with lots of bumper stickers, whose driver probably won't notice the change.

Even so, I'm careful. I never speed and I always signal. I decelerate gradually so no one rear-ends me. And I always park in places the cops wouldn't think to look for a stolen car. Such as the Houston Field Office of the FBI.

I switch the stereo off before I stop the engine. The battery's half-dead, so the car won't start if the radio is on, or the headlights, or the AC. I leave the window partway open so the interior won't become an oven in the sun. I put the civilian consultant lanyard around my neck. Seven minutes later I'm opening the door to Peter Luzhin's office.

Luzhin is a forty-eight-year-old man, nicknamed "Mr. Burns" because of the sideburns bristled down his cheeks. Six foot three, with wide shoulders and thick arms. A little flabby around the gut, the way ex-junkies sometimes are.

He's hunched over a laptop but looks up as I enter. "Oh. It's you."

I close the door behind me and sit on a barely cushioned chair.

The nameplate on his desk reads *Director, Houston Field Office, Federal Bureau of Investigation*, just in case I missed the plaque on the door. As usual, the framed photo of his family is facedown so I can't see them, or maybe so they can't see me.

"New case," he says. "Cameron Hall, fourteen years old, last seen at four o'clock yesterday afternoon. There was a ransom call."

"Real?"

"As far as we can tell."

"Rich parents?"

"Parent." Luzhin taps the touch pad, trying to wake up the computer. Eventually he gives up. "His mother inherited some land from an uncle," he says. "Sold it to a health club in San Antonio. Used the money to buy a few upmarket houses around Houston, and she's renting them out. Probably takes home about two hundred grand per year."

Lucky her. I inherited diddly-squat from my family.

"Where's the kid's dad?" I ask.

"Pennsylvania. The mom—Annette Hall is her name—says it wasn't his voice on the ransom call."

"He got a record?" I say.

"Still waiting to confirm that. The kid is clean. His mom got snagged for tax evasion two years back. Suspended sentence."

"Maybe Warner is fund-raising for the trial." I'm spit-balling, but if the kidnapper isn't the dad, it's statistically likely to be someone in Charlie Warner's organization.

Luzhin lifts his eyebrows. "Warner posted bail with a million dollars in cash."

"All the more reason to kidnap a rich kid."

"It's not Warner."

"How do you know?"

Luzhin hesitates.

"You have someone on the inside," I guess. "If Warner gave the order, you would have heard it."

He won't admit it, but his flaring nostrils tell me I'm right. I wonder how he got a volunteer. The last agent to go under-cover in Warner's gang was found hanging by his wrists from a tree branch over a river. His skin was slashed up—not enough to kill, but enough to bait the alligators below. By the time the cops got there, everything below his ribs was gone.

"Stay away from Warner," Luzhin says. "I don't want you messing up the trial."

"Fine. Who saw the kid last?"

"Guy named Crudup. Music teacher at North Shore Middle School. The vic finished class, got on his bike, never made it home. The ransom demand came in around six last night. Annette Hall called 911 right after."

"Did the kidnappers tell her not to?" I ask.

"Of course. But we have plainclothes agents near the house. No one's watching her except us."

"When's she gotta pay by?"

"Six tonight."

Twenty-four hours after the call is typical. Too short for a thorough search, but long enough to get a lot of money together. The clock on Luzhin's wall reads 09:22. I have eight hours to figure this out.

"You should've called me last night."

"I hoped I wouldn't need you," he says.

"You tapped the mom's phone, right?"

"Vasquez did it at eight p.m. No calls since then."

"No existing leads?"

Luzhin turns one of his hands over, like a magician, showing it to be empty.

"You got a picture of the kid?" I ask.

He slides a folder across his desk. I pick it up and flick through the file until I find a photo. It's a selfie, taken at a house party. In the background, kids drink out of red plastic cups. Cameron grins at me, jaw wide, eyebrows up. He's Caucasian, with dirty-blond hair and dark eyes.

People go missing all the time in Houston. The cops don't have the funding to find them all, so they focus on the ones that'll get media attention. I'm not surprised my new case is a rich white kid.

"Who's my reward?" I ask.

Luzhin glances at the door, checking that it's closed. His voice is low. "Foreign guy. Tanzanian. Forty-three. Convicted of a triple homicide eleven years ago. No family in the States."

"He speak English?"

"Christ. Why does that matter?"

I shrug.

Luzhin isn't a good guy. In his early days he wasn't against hitting a suspect to make him confess, and he still turns a blind eye to the cops who do the same. He forges documents, bullies witnesses and bribes Woodstock—or blackmails him, I'm not sure which. But whenever he looks at me, there's disgust in his eyes.

"Before you go," he says, dodging the question, "Richmond

still hasn't been cleared for duty since Oswald Collins shot him.
I've assigned you a new partner."

"Who?"

"Special Agent Reese Thistle."

The one who wouldn't let me into Billie Collins's house
and then handcuffed me after I saved Billie's life. "No," I say.
"I'll choose the new one."

"That's not the deal."

"Our *deal* doesn't say anything about who's looking over
my shoulder."

"I make the rules, not you. You got a problem with that,
feel free to terminate our arrangement, along with all its perks.
But if you stay, you can't choose your own partner. Thistle
already knows she's been assigned to you."

"So what?" I say. "Afraid of disappointing her?"

"If I choose someone else because you threw a tantrum,
she'll find out. When the other agents hear that the field office director reshuffled his staff at your request, they'll start
asking questions. You want that?"

He's got me, and he knows it.

"Stop wasting time," he says. "Find Cameron Hall." He
turns back to his computer, which has finally woken up.

As I walk out the door, I hear a clack as he puts the family
photo back where it belongs.

"Mr. Blake."

I turn to see Agent Thistle hovering nearby. She's not in
uniform this time—she's wearing a dark gray pantsuit over a
maroon blouse, with flat leather shoes she can probably run in.

"Good to see you again," she says without enthusiasm. "I'll
be assisting you on this investigation."

She means supervising. Monitoring. Her tone suggests she's
reading from a script and isn't happy about her new assign-
ment. That makes two of us.

"On behalf of the Bureau, I want to thank you for—"

"Yeah, yeah, yeah," I say. "There'll be time for this on the way."

"Sure. Where are we headed?"

"Cameron Hall's house."

"Agents have already swept it." She gestures to the file in my hand. "There's a complete report."

"I want to see the house anyway."

"What do you think we'll find?"

"If I knew, I wouldn't need to go."

Thistle's car is a standard FBI-issue Ford Crown Victoria sedan. White. Several years old, but clean—on the outside, at least. I can smell old vomit on the back seat. My guess is Thistle arrested a drunk driver. The perp was probably from Louisiana, because if they hadn't crossed state lines, it would have been a case for the Houston PD, not the FBI.

Thistle turns the key and the Georgia Satellites start howling out of the speakers. She twists the volume down to zero. Dust blankets the built-in cigarette lighter.

So, Reese Thistle is an unmarried nonsmoker who likes eighties blues-rock. The car is running low on gas, so she must live in Houston—no commuter from farther away than Liberty would let the needle fall below a quarter of a tank.

Now that I'm seeing her side-on, I can tell she's a violinist, and she plays left-handed. The callus on her neck from the instrument's body is on the wrong side. This probably means she's self-taught, since most left-handed violinists play to the right anyway. She's a couple of years older than me, judging by her face. Mid-thirties. No kids, judging by her breasts.

"Something wrong?" she says without looking at me.

I turn back to the windshield. "Nothing."

"I'm sorry about last week." She twists the wheel, and the car zooms out of the parking lot. "I wasn't sure what was going on, and I made a snap decision. Now I know the handcuffs were unnecessary."

"Don't sweat it."

She waits for me to say more. I don't.

The air is soupy inside the car. I push my sleeves up my arms. Thistle glances over at the scar tissue that covers me from wrists to elbows, then looks back at the road. She probably thinks the wounds are old oil burns.

Cameron Hall lives with his mother in Cloverleaf, about a half hour's drive east. The squad car has GPS, but Thistle doesn't switch it on. She takes a right off Jester onto the North Loop service road and merges into the I-610 with the confidence of someone who's lived in Houston a long time.

She's rubbing her ring finger with her thumb, as though something used to be there. Divorced, probably.

I wonder what she's into. Drugs, booze, gambling, frequent flyer miles. Everyone's addicted to something, especially people in high-stress jobs. If I work out what her thing is, I can eventually manipulate her into leaving me alone. The FBI is hopelessly corrupt. Everyone has a price.

"So what's your deal?" Thistle asks, as if she can read my mind.

My heart skips a beat. Was she listening outside Luzhin's door? "My deal?"

"All the other agents are out there looking for this kid," Thistle says. "I could be helping—I've been with the Bureau twelve years—but instead I'm watching you. Want to tell me why?"

She must be tough. Twelve years ago, life wasn't easy for young, black, pretty women in the Bureau. I started consulting three years ago, and even then some senior officers still referred to female agents as "breast-feds."

I say, "I've helped out on a few missing person cases."

She nods. "Yessir, I heard that. Figured you for a felon who got busted and struck a bargain with Luzhin—trading on your underground connections. But if that's the case, why are we going to the kid's house?"

"All police got the same training," I say. "On any case, every pair of eyes is looking at it in the same way. Sometimes they miss things."

"Right," she says slowly. "So you're, what—a psychic?"

I smile. "No, ma'am. Just good eyesight."

"And you're using it to help us out."

She doesn't believe me. I shrug.

"Why not become a cop, then?"

"Never finished high school," I say.

"You could be a PI."

"And spend my time following cheating husbands?" I watch Houston scroll past outside the window—long stretches of grassy nothing interrupted by warehouses the size of city blocks. My stomach growls. Not even 10:00 a.m. and I'm already hungry.

"If you bullshit me," Thistle says, "I can only be so much help."

"Just take me to the kid's place. That's all the help I need."

The address turns out to be a gated community with a wrought-iron fence and a lawn you could play golf on. Thistle doesn't have a key to the front gate, so she pushes a buzzer next to it. After a minute, an old man with a moustache and a stoop emerges from a distant guardhouse. He shuffles up to us, glances at Thistle's ID, unlocks the gate and waves the car through without saying a word.

The house itself sits atop a hill right up the end of the drive. It's sprawling and old, with recently painted boards and lots of big windows. The front garden grows with the kind of precision that requires constant encouragement.

We park by the curb and get out. Thistle locks the Crown

Vic with a *chup-chup* and the pea gravel crackles under our shoes as we walk up the path to the porch. I put a foot too far back on one of the steps, resting a little too much weight on my crooked toe, and suck some air through my teeth as the pain zaps up my leg.

I'm clumsier than I was in my twenties. Someone once told me the poor age in dog years, which would make me more than two hundred years old.

I reach for the doorbell. Thistle gets there first. *Ding-dong.* The message is clear—this is an FBI investigation; I'm a civilian, she's in charge.

Whatever. I turn to face the other houses. They're far enough away that it would be tough to spy on the Halls unless you had a telescope or a drone.

The door opens behind me. "Ms. Hall," Thistle says. "I'm Agent Reese Thistle, this is my associate Timothy Blake. Can we come in?"

I turn around. Annette Hall is a looker; white, five foot four, a hundred and thirty pounds and approaching thirty-six years of age. Pretty young to be the mother of a fourteen-year-old. She has her son's full lips and his upturned nose. There's a ring on every finger except the one that counts.

Her eyes are red, and her strawberry-blond hair is a little wet, like she showered half an hour ago. She looks faintly suspicious of Thistle—maybe she doesn't like cops—but when she turns to me, her expression is scared and hopeful at the same time.

She looks familiar. We've never met in person, and I've never seen her photograph, so it must be TV. Not the news, not a movie, not a talk show…a soap. That's it. She had a couple lines in an episode of *Days of Our Lives*, which I saw in a diner six years back.

I give her a nod and a polite half smile that says *Sorry we had to meet under these circumstances.*

"Have you…" Hall crosses her arms over her chest. "Have you found Cam?"

Not a Texas accent. She sounds like one of the million teen girls who moved to California to be famous actresses, and got too old before they landed major roles.

"Not yet, ma'am," Thistle says. "But we got the whole force out looking for him."

That was the wrong thing to say. "No!" Hall says. "They told me not to call the police! If there are cops everywhere, they'll—"

"They're plainclothes agents in unmarked vehicles, ma'am. Not identifiable as police officers in any way. May we come in?"

Hall stands aside, keen to get us out of sight. We walk into her foyer.

The inside matches the front—big, neat, expensive. A few paintings on the walls that look original. Floorboards recently oiled. There's a keypad for an alarm system next to the front door. The ink has partly worn away on the numbers two, five, eight and nine. If she uses her birthday for the code like most people do, she was probably born on either the fifth of September or the ninth of May in 1982.

"Your housekeeper here today?" I ask.

"I sent her home." Hall is staring at my shoes. They're cheap, even by cop standards. "Sorry, who are you?" she asks.

"Timothy Blake, ma'am," I say. I move toward the staircase.

"Uh, mind if we look around, Ms. Hall?" Thistle says quickly.

"What? Why?"

"Just procedure. In cases like this, the perpetrator typically has met the victim at least once, so—"

"The other agents already searched the house," Hall says. "What exactly are you looking for?"

I get to the top of the staircase. Glance back down. "Won't know until I find it." Then I walk up the hall to the bedrooms.

I keep one hand on the wall as I move around, and listen to the echoes of my footsteps. I take deep breaths of the faintly perfumed air. I'll be able to remember the layout of the house in much more detail later if I make it a multisensory experience now. Nine-tenths of memorization is just about paying attention. People forget where they parked their cars because they were thinking about something else when they did it. I always focus on where I am. This isn't just about memory. When my mind wanders, I don't like where it goes.

The first bedroom is Annette's. Queen-size bed, unmade. The room hasn't been tidied, which is good—a woman's mess says more than her facade. A vase of posies, three or four days old, is on a credenza by the window. A cordless phone on a charger. A Bible next to it, with two pages folded at the corners. One is Leviticus 18—all that stuff about not having sex with animals or with menstruating women. The other is Luke 12. *Fear him who, after your body has been killed, has the authority to throw you into hell.*

I find a framed photo of an eighteen- or twenty-year-old boy in clothes that went out of fashion a decade ago. Could be Cameron's father—Philip Hall, according to the file—as a young man. Looks like a college campus in the background. He's got a slightly annoyed smile, like whoever took the picture had interrupted him.

No photos of Cameron himself. Maybe the other agents took them away.

In the corner of the en suite is the most spacious shower I've ever seen. It doesn't even have a door; just an opening at one end and a long pane of glass to stop the toilet getting splashed. I pull back the mirror to look at Annette's collection of pills. Xanax, Tylenol, Valium. Nothing exotic. I could steal some

Xanax to sell to my roommate, but he has his own suppliers. It isn't worth the trouble. I close the mirror.

Up the other end of the hall, I find Annette and Thistle in the kid's bedroom. It's about what you'd expect of a fourteen-year-old boy. The duvet cover is branded with some movie or video game called "Uncharted 4." A Batman poster hangs crooked on the wall. A trumpet is perched on a stand in the corner, with a silver mute.

"He never made it home," Annette says. "Why aren't you at his school, asking questions there?"

Thistle is looking under the bed. "Did Cameron have problems at school?"

"No. He's a good boy. But the other kids... Cameron belongs with a better class of people."

"What do you mean by that?" Thistle asks casually.

"But he wanted to go there," Annette continues, ignoring her, "and God help me, I didn't feel like I could say no."

A camera rests on Cameron's bedside table. Looks expensive. Kids can take pictures with their cell phones, so the fact that he wants something more sophisticated probably means he's into photography. The bookshelf holds mostly comics, a few novels alphabetized by series title. There's a small wooden box, in which I find a couple of condoms and some loose change. The kid was sexually active, or expected to be soon.

"You think he fell in with a bad crowd?" Thistle asks.

"No, no. But the student population is very mixed. The teachers too. Have you met Mr. Crudup, the music teacher?" Annette doesn't wait for an answer. "Some people have no work ethic. So they steal, or take handouts from the government. It's a cultural thing. And anyone could see that Cameron came from money."

I don't point out that Annette inherited her fortune and then tried to hide it from the IRS. Instead, I hold up one of the condoms.

Hall turns pink. "He's a good boy," she says. "Is it really necessary to dig through his things like this?"

"He have a girlfriend?" I ask.

"No." But the answer comes too quick. Her arms are crossed defensively over her chest, her gaze locked onto me like she thinks I'll doubt her if she looks away.

Thistle hasn't missed these cues. "You sure? Any girls you see around here regularly?"

"No."

"Boyfriend?" I ask.

"Absolutely not. At his school they teach sex ed, not abstinence. That's probably where he got those things."

"Was there someone he was interested—" I stop talking. Turn back toward the trumpet. It shouldn't be here. Not if his music teacher saw him last.

"He wasn't abducted on his way home," I say. "He was taken from here."

CHAPTER 4

**I'M AS BIG AS YOU ARE, BUT I WEIGH NOTHING.
I FOLLOW YOU AROUND ALL DAY,
BUT AT NIGHT I AM INVISIBLE.
WHAT AM I?**

AGENT THISTLE DOESN'T WASTE TIME ASKING how I know. In an instant her phone is up against her ear.

"This is Thistle. I need a forensic team at the Hall residence ASAP."

"What? Forensic—what? What do you mean, *here*?" Hall is turning from me to Thistle and back to me again.

"Your boy had music class yesterday," I say, "but his trumpet is right there. Did he have two trumpets?"

"He could've forgotten it," Hall says uncertainly.

I nod. The music teacher probably would have mentioned that, but I'll have to make sure someone asked. "Nice camera. Does Cameron print out his favorite photos?"

Hall turns around, looking at empty spots all over the walls. The color drains from her cheeks.

"But...his backpack is gone. And..."

"Someone wanted it to look like he didn't come home," I say. "Are there security cameras in the house?"

"No. We like our privacy."

"What about at the front gate?"

"There's a guard."

But no camera. Even if there had been one, the kidnapper could have avoided the gate and climbed over the fence without much trouble.

Thistle snaps her phone shut. She says, "Why take the photos away if they wanted it to look like they were never here?"

"We'll find out when we see the picture. Maybe he photographed them doing something they shouldn't have done. Maybe that was the reason they took him. The ransom could be a distraction."

If it is, they'll probably kill Cameron even if Annette pays up. Thistle doesn't say this, but I can see her thinking it.

"Or maybe they knew him," she says, "and they're in one of the pictures."

"Can you access his social media profiles?" I ask Hall.

"I gave his laptop to the other FBI agents."

"They already downloaded his photo stream," Thistle says. "Nothing unusual."

"I want to see them," I say.

"You think Cameron knew the perp?"

"No forced entry. Nothing broken in the house. The kid might not even know he's been kidnapped."

Thistle turns to Hall. "Have you seen Cameron's father lately?"

Most kidnappings are the result of a custody battle, although the perp rarely bothers to fake a ransom call.

Hall shakes her head. "Like I told the other agents, he moved to Pennsylvania when I got pregnant. I haven't seen him since, except...except in Cam." Her lip quivers. "He looks so much like his daddy."

The resemblance between the photos of Philip and Cameron seemed superficial, but I don't say so.

"Tell me about Cameron's other friends," Thistle says.

Hall starts naming the kids she's most suspicious of. The surnames sound mostly Latin or black. I'm starting to realize what she meant by *a better class of people*, and why she looked uncomfortable at the sight of Thistle on her doorstep.

I leave them and go back down the corridor toward the stairs.

If Cameron knows the people he's with, his phone would be useful. And if he was taken from here, he might have left it behind. According to the file, Maurice Vasquez—the field office tech guru—couldn't trace it, so it must be switched off or broken.

I duck into Ms. Hall's bedroom. Take the cordless phone off the charger and scroll through her speed dial. *Cam* is number two, after *Mom + Dad*.

Note to self: check out the grandparents. Could they have taken Cameron to get him away from his bigoted mother?

A weak hypothesis without more evidence. Children tend to be less prejudiced than their folks, so the grandparents are probably worse than Hall.

I select *Cam* and hit the call button.

It's ringing. So, not switched off, not broken. Then where is it?

A distant chiming from somewhere else in the house. I leave the bedroom and walk downstairs.

Separating a teen from his phone requires force. Cameron must know he's been kidnapped.

There's a hamper in the shadows of the laundry. A pair of faded jeans is buried under a couple of gray blouses. I pull the phone out of the pocket and hit Reject.

I go back upstairs to the bedroom. Thistle is saying, "Was there a teacher, or maybe another parent from the school, who knew Cameron better than the others?"

Hall stares helplessly at her son's bed.

Another theory has been bubbling up to the surface of my mind—that it might be a hoax. Maybe Annette Hall killed her son, buried him in the yard and faked the ransom demand to divert suspicion.

But she looks desperate to help. And she wasn't that good

on *Days of our Lives*. She might be racist, but I don't think she's a murderer.

"We're done here," I tell Thistle.

I walk down the stairs as Thistle feeds Annette some platitudes. Things like *We're doing everything we can*, and *We'll call as soon as we know anything*.

On my way to the front door I glance into the kitchen and see the knife.

It gleams on the granite counter, slivers of onion clinging to the stainless-steel blade. But it wasn't designed for vegetables. It's a carving knife, made to strip flesh from bone. The handle is cold and just heavy enough to balance the blade. It's not until I make these observations that I realize the knife is in my hand.

I should put it down. But I don't.

The edge, shining with potential, curves up to a harsh point. My finger, when it touches the blade, isn't cut. The knife just dimples my skin.

Disappointed, I push harder. A droplet of blood grows fat on my fingertip and a tingle rushes up my spine.

"Blake?"

I slam the knife down on the bench. Thistle is staring at me.

"Ready to go?" I ask.

"You're bleeding," she says.

I put my finger in my mouth. "It's nothing. Let's go."

She doesn't say anything as we leave the house, walk over to her car and get in.

When we reach the gate, we have to stop and wait for the old security guard to amble over.

Thistle flashes her ID again. "You see anything unusual over the last few days?"

"Define unusual," the guard says. He sounds younger than he looks. His gums have receded, exposing yellow teeth.

"Any people or vehicles you haven't seen before?"

"Just you guys. But I'm not the only guard."

"You keep a record?" Thistle asks. "Of who comes and goes?"

"If I have to unlock the gate for someone, I write down their license plate. But anyone who lives here has their own key. They don't get recorded."

"You'd see them, though. Right?"

"Not necessarily," the guard says.

"Any nonresidents come through between four and six p.m. yesterday?"

"No."

"Are you an ex-cop?" I ask. Plenty of security guards are. And unlike most civilians, this guy isn't falling over himself trying to be helpful.

He nods slowly. "Seventeen years with the Houston PD."

"Do any of the residents look familiar from your time in the force?"

"Can't say that they do."

The wind sweeps across the perfect grass and ruffles his gray hair.

"Well, thanks for your help," Thistle says.

"Anything for my hardworking colleagues at the Federal Bureau of Investigation." The guard opens the gate for us, smiling faintly. Thistle rolls up the window and drives through. I can feel the guard watching us as we turn onto the street.

"I'll track down the other guards," she says. "See if they're more useful. You really think our kidnapper might be one of the other residents?"

"No," I say, and point west. "Head that way. I want to meet Cameron's music teacher."

At the group home I grew up in, meat loaf was served every Friday night. Steaming ground shoulder roast, with

Vidalia onions and apple cider vinegar sauce. Fat and juicy. Most weeks, that meat loaf was all I could think about.

Meals were served in the garage, which was the only place big enough to fit all the kids. We ate at two trestle tables, which meant some kids sat back to back under the fluorescent lights. The floor was sealed concrete. After dinner we would sweep it, and Mrs. Radfield would hose it down.

One Friday night a skinny black girl named Arty sat next to me. I didn't know her well—she hadn't been at the home as long as I had. She was always humming, with perfect pitch but no rhythm, like wind chimes. She also had a knack for finding the best clothes in the donation bin. She was often wearing a floral dress, or some cool jeans.

Arty wolfed down her meat loaf in seconds, not taking the time to suck out the juices and appreciate the flavor like I did. Then she grabbed my bread roll and threw it onto the floor.

"Hey!" I picked it up, and when I turned back to put it on my plate, my meat loaf was gone. I was confused at first. Arty couldn't possibly have snatched it up and eaten it so quickly. Then I realized she'd switched our plates around. She was gulping down my meat loaf, and I was left with a lump of potato and a dirty roll.

A smarter kid would have solved this problem verbally. Talked her into giving me back the rest, threatened her, gone to get Mrs. Radfield, whatever. But I was watching my favorite dish disappear, bite by bite, and I wanted a solution that would get it back before it was all gone.

My solution was to hit her.

I belted her in the cheek, and she collapsed sideways off the bench. I slid over, grabbed the meat loaf and stuffed it into my mouth. But I didn't have time to swallow before she reared up behind me, crushing my throat with her forearm. I choked, precious gobs of meat splattering the table, and then grabbed a fistful of her hair and yanked at it. She screamed and let go of me.

Meanwhile, someone else had done the smart thing and gone for help. All us kids wore soft slipper-like shoes, but I could hear a pair of hard rubber soles striking the path outside the garage, getting closer. *Tock, tock, tock.* We were all wired to listen out for that noise.

Arty and I let go of one another. I neatened my hair, smoothed my shirt, wiped the food and drool off my lips, trying to look responsible and innocent. But when I glanced at Arty, she was doing the exact opposite. She'd scruffed up her hair, poked herself in the eye to bring out some tears and kicked off one of her shoes, exposing a yellowed sock.

Mrs. Radfield saw us, Arty looking helpless and me looking sensible. Then Arty got a pat on the head and a third helping of meat loaf, while I was sent to the Prayer Room.

Later I learned that she'd gone hungry at lunch because someone had pulled the same trick on her. That was what gave her the idea. So I forgave her for stealing my food—but not for the hour I spent in the Prayer Room. I was supposed to spend it thinking about what I'd done, but instead I spent it telling myself that nobody was ever going to outsmart me again.

"Sorry, sir," the lady in the drive-thru says. "We don't have meat loaf."

"In that case," I say, "I'll have a double-shot latte with three sugars, a packet of salt and a straw."

"Pardon me?"

I repeat the order.

"You're not gonna eat?" Thistle says. "Uncle Sam's paying. Director's orders."

Luzhin is a notorious miser, but he makes sure I'm well-fed. "I packed a lunch," I say.

Thistle orders a black coffee and a blueberry muffin. Then

we drive to the pay window. I unwrap my lunch—a thick slice of defrosted meat. Nothing else.

"What is that, ham?" Thistle asks.

"Yeah."

"You know, traditionally, a ham sandwich would have bread."

"I'm on the paleo diet," I say, my mouth already full.

"Uh-huh. You know a latte has milk in it, right?" Thistle digs through her purse for change. "Mr. Burns is pretty stingy," she says. "I've never seen him pay for a consultant's meals before."

"Part of my fee."

She hands some coins to the guy in the booth. He thanks her, and she drives on.

"You don't get a fee," she says.

"Where'd you hear that?"

"I used to work in payroll. We don't have the budget to pay civilian consultants. You work for free."

She looks both admiring and suspicious.

"How much is the ransom?" I ask, changing the subject.

"Twenty K." Thistle takes the paper bag with her food in it, hands it to me and drives back out onto the highway. "Hall's already withdrawn it from the bank. She's supposed to drop it in a dumpster behind the Walmart on the Northwest Freeway. Unmarked bills, two hundred twenties, a hundred and twenty fifties, and one hundred hundreds. Are you really putting that in your coffee?"

I tear open the salt packet and pour it into my latte. "I like it how I like it. Does twenty grand seem low to you?"

"Probably means they need the money for something specific."

"So they're amateurs."

"Yep," Thistle says. "Especially since they gave her the

drop location this far in advance, and they took Cameron's printed photos even though we can easily get digital copies."

If they're not professional kidnappers, they'll be easier to catch. But it means Cameron is less likely to survive.

I pass the muffin to Thistle and take another bite out of the meat. It's salty, warm from the car, and does little to put out the hungry flames in my gut.

"Did they make the usual threats about what they'd do if she won't pay?" I ask.

"Worse than usual. Said they'd nail him to the basement wall by his eyelids, nostrils and lips. Then they'd leave him to starve."

Imaginative. Makes my extracurriculars look tame.

"Probably exaggeration," Thistle says. "If Hall doesn't cough up the cash, they'll get mad and ask again. Maybe for more this time. Then, if they don't get that, they'll just shoot him and dump him in Galveston Bay. No need for sadistic bullshit."

"So we're looking for someone with a violent imagination, but no follow-through."

Thistle takes a bite out of her muffin and swallows. "Maybe we should arrest Quentin Tarantino."

"Those aren't real blueberries," I say. "Just blobs of glucose, dyed blue, set in dough made out of wood pulp."

"It's not a fucking celery stick," she says. "I'm not eating it for my health. Mind your own business, Mr. Ham-and-nothing-else-for-lunch."

She takes another bite of the muffin. I suck my latte through the straw in short pulses. *Sip-sip. Sip-sip.*

"Of course, they might have shot him already," Thistle says. "Proof of life is eighteen hours old. You know the stats."

I do. A kid goes missing every forty seconds in the USA. Most kidnappings are committed by family members of the victims, but 4,600 people every year are abducted by strangers or loose acquaintances. And three out of four kidnap deaths occur within three hours of the abduction.

Cops don't say "deaths" when they cite these statistics. They say "tragic outcomes."

I tell myself I'm worried for Cameron's safety. But that's not the whole truth. If the kid dies, I don't get my reward. And without it, who knows what I might do?

Thistle's phone chimes. She glances at the screen. "Mr. Burns says the housekeeper's alibi checks out. The other agents all got nothing so far. It's like the kid just vanished."

"Maybe we should see if he's at Area 51," I say.

"Area 51 is an urban legend," Thistle says, apparently not aware that I was kidding. "Like Slender Man, or the guy who eats death row inmates."

I choke on my latte.

"You okay?" Thistle asks.

"Yeah," I say, but my heart is racing. "What did you say?"

"Area 51. It exists, but it's just a normal air force base. They test new planes there."

"Not that part. The death row thing."

Thistle flashes a wicked smile. "Oh, you haven't heard that one? The government struck a bargain with a cannibal, and they use him to dispose of bodies after executions."

"Who told you that story?" I ask, trying to sound casual.

"The supermax prisoners use it to scare each other up in Huntsville. Better watch your step or a man from the government will come and eat you." She shrugs. "It doesn't make much sense, but conspiracy theories never do."

"Right. It's probably bullshit."

Thistle laughs. "Probably?"

"Definitely bullshit," I clarify. Then I take another bite out of Nigel Boyd's thigh.

CHAPTER 5

WHAT HAS MANY KEYS,
BUT CANNOT OPEN ANY DOOR?

I WAS ELEVEN WHEN AN OLDER BOY DECIDED to beat me up because he didn't like the way I was looking at him. It was the same way I looked at everybody—sideways and hungry—and probably lots of kids didn't like it, but he decided to do something about it.

He used to play basketball barefoot, his shoes side by side like spectators on the edge of the court. I rarely saw anyone playing with him. He would be alone, hurling the ball directly at the ground to see how high he could get it to bounce. One time it swished through the hoop on the way back down, and he beamed as if he'd put a grand on a winning greyhound. Until he saw me staring.

"What?" he said.

I looked away quickly.

He was walking over. "What the fuck you looking at?"

"Nothing."

He knocked me down on the asphalt and started kicking me. Aimed for my face when I covered my chest, and my gut when I covered my head. Since I was the weird boy from the refuge system, draped in piss-smelling donation-bin clothes, it was a while before anyone intervened. People were too scared to grab him, and too hygiene-conscious to grab me.

When a teacher finally pulled the kid off, she sentenced us both to half an hour in "the sorting-out room." He and I sat in silence on opposite sides of an empty classroom for twenty-two minutes while a different teacher read a magazine. I was dizzy, my nose bleeding like a gut-shot fox. Then we were released back into the playground, where he pushed me down again and emptied a trash can on my face. He yelled something at me too, but I don't know what it was. I was completely deaf until three weeks after the beating.

My hearing's fine now, but my nose is still crooked, and my arm sometimes aches where he broke it. My tongue has stopped searching for the missing tooth behind my right canine, which couldn't be replanted because the root dried out. I still can't afford a fake.

At the time, I hated that teacher for not suspending or expelling the other boy. But now I realize that as an adult, kids look harmless—skinny arms and big eyes and innocent grins. How could they hurt anyone? They're so cute. A few playground scrapes are nothing to worry about. Boys will be boys.

I look out the office window at the students chasing one another around the football field. Maybe they're beating on each other when I'm not looking, and the skin under their shirts is black and blue. Or maybe this is a better school than the one I went to.

"Cameron isn't in trouble, is he?" the principal asks Thistle and, to a lesser extent, me.

Not the kind of trouble she's thinking, I'll bet.

"We'd just like to ask him a couple of questions," Thistle says. Her tone implies that Cameron was witness to something rather than the perpetrator or the victim. That's important—she can't lie, but nor can she reveal that he's missing. There's a list of people who are cleared to know about the kidnapping, and the principal isn't on it. The truth might create a panic that would get Cameron killed.

The principal is a small white woman with hair like gray cotton candy and a blouse buttoned so high the collar might just choke her. I could snap her narrow, flimsy bones with my bare hands.

I close my eyes, forcing the image away. It's the drone of the air-conditioning, sapping my focus.

Outside in the corridor there are framed photographs of every principal who ever served here, all sitting on the same wooden throne. According to her plaque, she's had the job for fifteen years. She didn't have a wedding ring in the picture, but she does now.

The principal's office is not so different from Luzhin's. Computer, filing cabinet, family photos. Maybe the more authority you have, the less important it is where you have it. Your office starts to look the same as that of every other bank manager and town mayor and colonel in the country.

Cautiously, the principal says, "This a drug thing?"

"Not that we know about."

Her shoulders sag with relief. Some things haven't changed since my school days—the staff don't care how many fights break out, but if a kid gets busted with weed or shrooms, all hell breaks loose. Suspensions, firings, reporters hanging around the campus.

"Is he a good student?" Thistle asks.

The principal nods. "Yeah, he's really sharp. Hard worker too."

The compliment sounds automatic. She probably barely knows him.

"His music teacher is Mr. Crudup, right?"

"Uh..." The principal turns to her computer. She types fast, but clumsy. Every third tap is the backspace key, because her nails are too long for accuracy.

"Yes, Harold Crudup," she says. "You want to have a word with him?"

"That'd be great. Where is he?"

"He should be in the staff room. He's tall, African American, bald."

"Harry Crudup?" I ask. "From the Smooth Candies?"

"That's the one," the principal says. "But you might not want to bring that up."

"A band?" Thistle guesses.

"Yeah," I say. "Had a couple of hits fifteen years ago."

"And Mr. Crudup doesn't like talking about it?"

"The opposite," the principal says. "Get him started on his glory days, and you won't be able to stop him."

On the field, two boys are getting up after a tackle. One of them throws the ball at the other's face, point-blank. The other ducks and shouts as it bounces off his helmet. The coach blows the whistle, and everyone retreats to their sides.

Harry Crudup smiles like a grocery bagger: tired and distracted. His fingers tap out a rhythm on the arm of his chair. His keys are on his desk and have a miniature piano attached. Strange—I thought he was a guitarist. There's no music in the air, but his head is bobbing as though there is.

I'm focused on a different beat. A pronounced vein pulses on his temple. I can almost hear the thumping of his heart.

"Harold Crudup?" Thistle asks.

The bobbing of his head turns into a nod.

Thistle holds up her badge. "I'm Special Agent Reese Thistle, this is Timothy Blake. We want to ask a couple of questions about one of your students."

"Sure." Crudup gestures to a few empty chairs. We're the only ones in the music staff room.

It's a weird thrill, being this close to a semi-celebrity. When I was fifteen, I found a Discman in a trash can near a shelter. The CD was still in it—a self-titled album by the Smooth Candies. I spent the afternoon walking around Houston with the headphones in my ears, pretending I was a rich kid dressing down rather than an orphan dressing up. All the while

Harry Crudup's voice crooned in my head: *He can't do the things I can, but, baby, I ain't your man.*

Now that same voice is saying, "Nice to meet you." He talks deeper than he sings.

"You know Cameron Hall?" Thistle asks.

"Yeah. Is he okay?"

This is a hard question to dodge, but she manages it. "You got any reason to believe he wouldn't be?"

"His mom called yesterday," Crudup says. "Asked if I'd seen him. I said sure, he finished class an hour ago and went home, far as I know. Then some FBI guy calls me, asks the same thing. I tell him what I told her. Now you're here."

"Ms. Hall called you direct?"

"She called the school switchboard. They put her through. I was just about to leave for a lesson at home."

"You do private lessons? What instrument?"

"Any instrument." He smiles, revealing the gap between his front teeth. "Want to learn?"

"You teach Cameron privately?"

"No. What's this about?"

"Nothing you need to worry about," Thistle says. "But we do need to speak with Cameron."

I speak up for the first time. "Is he any good? On the trumpet, I mean."

Thistle shoots me a sideways look. She doesn't know how that's relevant. Nor do I, but it doesn't hurt to ask.

"Yeah," Crudup says. "He's better than most."

"Who does he hang out with?" Thistle asks.

"He's by himself mostly. He's a quiet kid."

"Secretive?"

"Quiet," Crudup says.

"The kids choose their own seats? In the band?"

"They're grouped by instrument. Other than that, sure."

"So who does he sit with?"

Crudup stares up at the ceiling, thinking, index finger extended. "The kid on his right would be Chrissie Porter," he says. "Sax player. To the left he'd have Jim Epps, on the trumpet. He'd be more friendly with Jim—the instrument sections tend to stick together."

"We'll need to speak with Jim," Thistle says.

"Can't help you. Talk to reception, that's their thing."

I'm picking up an anxious vibe off Crudup, but not anxious enough for him to be the kidnapper. Most people get nervous talking to cops. Maybe he has some pot stashed in his desk.

"Mr. Crudup?" There's a girl in the doorway.

"You'll have to wait a minute, Pam," Crudup says.

"I need another copy of the permission slip for next week."

"What happened to the one you got?"

She shrugs.

Crudup sighs and digs through a pile of papers. He puts a sheet in her outstretched hand.

"That's the original," he says. "Xerox it and bring it back."

"Yeah, sure," she says, and leaves.

Crudup sighs. "She's not coming back."

"You ever notice anyone making fun of Cameron?" Thistle says. "Pushing him around?"

"No. Don't see a lot of that these days. The kids don't give wedgies or steal lunch money anymore—too busy staring at their phones. He might have been getting a hard time online, I guess."

I ask, "Any girlfriend that you know of?"

"I never saw him with any girls. But he came to school with a hickey one time."

Hall wasn't telling the truth. I knew it. But why?

"How about a boyfriend?" Thistle suggests.

"I don't think so. Like I said, he was always on his own."

There's a pause. I get the feeling Crudup has outlived his usefulness, and not just in this interview.

Thistle feels it too. She stands up, hands him a business card. "Call us if you remember anything else."

Crudup digs out his phone. He snaps a photo of the card, scribbles his cell number on the back and hands it back. "Call *me*," he says, "when you know he's okay."

"Will do."

Thistle walks out. I stop in the doorway.

Crudup is staring out the window at the footballers. His gaze doesn't move when they do, so I don't think he's seeing them. Maybe he's remembering the days when folks looked up to him. Ex-presidents keep their titles, their security teams, their pensions. Ex–rock stars get nothing.

"One more thing," I ask. "Did Cameron have his trumpet with him when you saw him last?"

Crudup nods. "Some kids forget their instruments a lot—or pretend to, when they don't know their parts. But he pretty much always had his horn."

"Thanks." I leave him to his thoughts.

As we walk up the corridor, Thistle holds up the card with Crudup's number on it. "That strike you as a performance?" she asks.

"With guys like that, everything's a performance."

On our way back to reception, the bell rings, and suddenly we're surrounded by laughing, yelling kids. One of them is Pam, who's sharing a soda with a friend and has no obvious intention of returning the permission slip to the music staff room.

I saw a timetable on Crudup's wall—the bell goes at two o'clock.

We have four hours left, and we're still nowhere.

We wait for Jim Epps in the sick bay. It smells of iodine and disinfectant. The CPR posters are ten years out of date—they still have the mouth-to-mouth instructions on them.

"You know they don't teach it that way these days," I say, pointing.

"What way?"

"The mouth-to-mouth stuff. It's not necessary. It's better to keep doing the chest compressions."

Thistle frowns. "You're shitting me."

"Nope."

"Don't people need to breathe?"

"Not as much as they need a pulse, I guess," I say.

"Well, thanks, Dr. Blake," she says. "I'll just forget everything they taught me at Quantico, shall I? I'm sure you know best."

"Quantico was more than twelve years ago."

"The human body hasn't changed."

I look down at my stiff knees and the shrunken muscles in my arms. "Mine has," I grumble.

She stifles a laugh.

Something about her is distracting me. It's not just the uneasy feeling I always get from cops. Nor is it my usual painful fascination with pretty women. She feels like a puzzle piece. Or one of those internet cables under the ocean—an invisible connection between two distant things.

"So," she says, "your magic powers telling you anything?"

I rub my eyes. "Lots about Cameron. Not much about his kidnapper."

"Kidnapper? You think there's only one?"

"Twenty grand isn't much split two or three ways," I say. "But that doesn't narrow down our suspect pool. Anyone who's been to his house would know his mom has money."

"Only close friends would have been to his house. He doesn't strike me as the kind of kid to have big parties."

"Someone could have followed him back to the gated community."

"Why would they," Thistle asks, "if they didn't already know about the money?"

I keep coming back to the house. If Cameron went willingly, how did the kidnapper steal the photos and get Cameron to leave his phone behind? And if he went unwillingly, why weren't there signs of a struggle?

I close my eyes and do a mental walk-through of Cameron's house. But just like last time, I see nothing out of the ordinary. Which means...

"He came back," I say.

"What?"

"The kidnapper. He came back. Cameron went with him willingly, he was taken to the hideout, and then the kidnapper returned to Cameron's house with his keys and his alarm code so he could take the backpack and the photos and leave the phone in the laundry. And then he went somewhere else to make the ransom call."

"How'd the kidnapper get through the gate?"

"I'm guessing he climbed the fence to get in the first time, and got Cameron to let him out when they left together. Then he came back with Cameron's gate key."

Thistle nods slowly. "Makes sense. So Cameron definitely knows the kidnapper."

"Not just that," I say. "Where was the ransom call made from?"

"Pay phone on Wood Bayou Drive."

"That's, what, fifteen minutes from the house?"

"More like ten," Thistle says.

"And when did Hall get home?"

"Five-forty, so she said."

"Then we just narrowed our search radius," I say. "The kid finished school at four. We know he made it home, probably around four-thirty. Whoever picked up the backpack was gone by the time Hall arrived..."

"So there was only an hour and ten minutes to grab the kid, take him to the hideout, go back to the house, dump Cameron's phone, grab the photos and get out again," Thistle says. "Meaning that the hideout has to be within about thirty minutes' drive of the house."

"And probably much closer."

Thistle gets out her phone and starts dialing a colleague. Eighty percent of the force is searching outside the zone. The quicker she fixes this, the better our chances of finding Cameron.

But that still leaves the FBI with five thousand square miles to search, and less than four hours to do it.

There's a knock at the door. Thistle's busy, so I call out, "Come in."

A boy opens the door—he's white, acne-scarred, and has gelled hair that tries to make him look taller, and fails. But his shoe size suggests that he's still growing. His school file says he's just turned fourteen and shares two classes with Cameron.

He looks at us, sees we're neither teachers nor his parents and says, "Um..."

"Jim Epps?" I ask.

"Yeah."

"Take a seat."

We're sitting in the only chairs, so he sits down on the bed.

"You know Cameron Hall?"

The color fades from his face. He looks at Thistle's pant-suit and her phone, then back at me. "What's happened?" he demands. "Did his mom hurt him?"

He thinks we work for children's services. Or he thinks Thistle does—I probably look more like a children's psychologist. Using her tactic, I say, "You got any reason to believe she might have?"

He looks confused now. "Um," he says again, "I don't know. Why else would you be here?"

My original thought was that Hall had killed her son and
buried him in the garden. I might have to revisit the idea.
She does, after all, live within a thirty-minute drive of her
own house.

"We're with the FBI," I say. "We'd like to ask Cameron a
few questions, but we can't find him."

Thistle has finished her phone conversation and seems
slightly nervous, probably worried I'll reveal too much. But
I don't. I just look expectantly at Epps and, after a moment,
so does she.

"He's not at school?"

The kid looks honestly surprised. He's not as close to Cameron as we expected.

"No," Thistle says. "Who does he hang out with when
he's here?"

"I don't know. I don't have many classes with him. We
sometimes see each other at lunch, but he's not the kind of
guy you want to be seen with, you know?"

The last statement stinks of teen bravado. "We heard you
were close," Thistle says.

Epps blanches. "Really? Well, you know how sometimes
somebody just latches on to you, like, starts calling you a
friend, telling you their secrets, and they just won't take a
hint?"

"What kind of secrets?"

Epps is looking at the floor, the door, the posters on the
walls—anywhere but at us.

I ask, "He have a girlfriend?"

The kid's Adam's apple bobs. "Uh, I don't think so. I'm
not sure."

He's lying, just like Hall was—and he looks scared. Lots of
boys Cameron's age have girlfriends. What's so special about
this one?

"Sure he does," I say. "He came to school with a hickey on his neck."

Epps's hands are bunching up the bedsheets. "I never saw nothing like that."

"You know what the penalty is for lying to the FBI, Jim?"

"I don't know anything about any girlfriend!" His voice has risen to a terrified squeak.

Thistle says, "Cameron could be in trouble, Jim. We can't help him if we don't know all the facts."

"I want an attorney," Epps says.

Thistle and I look at each other.

"You don't need an attorney," she says. "You're not accused of anything."

He points at me. "He just said I was lying."

"He asked if you knew the *penalties* for lying." Thistle's lips are drawn back over clenched teeth. "He didn't say you were."

"I want an attorney and you can't stop me. That's the law."

If I had two minutes alone with this kid, I could make him tell me everything he knows. Nothing is so secret that the right amount of pain and fear won't tease it out. But Thistle won't give me that chance. That's why Luzhin put her here.

No point asking Epps more questions. By the time his lawyer gets called, shows up, tells him his rights and then lets us talk to him again, it'll be so close to six that it won't matter what we know.

"Fine," says Thistle. "You're free to go."

Epps blinks. "What?"

"Get your ass back to class," she says. "And hope you haven't just killed your friend."

Annette Hall is wearing a strapless full-cup bra and some black elastic panties. Plenty of skin is on display. I can see straight through it to the soft muscles, the tangled veins, the smooth shafts of bone. She looks delicious.

"Remember," the special agent in charge is saying as she tapes a tiny microphone to Hall's sternum, "Cameron's safe as long as you have the money. So don't let go of it until you can see him, got it?"

Hall nods, eyes shut.

The SAC is on loan from the Critical Incident Response Group in Virginia. They always send a few agents in kidnapping cases. The other agents call them "rent-a-goons." The goons themselves don't seem to mind. This one has half-closed eyes, shiny black hair and one hand that always seems to be a fist. Her voice echoes around the concrete floor of the storeroom.

Boxes of juicers, kettles and microwaves are stacked on pallets in the corners. I came in through the roller door out the back, so I don't know what the SAC told the store manager to get us in and to get the staff out. But she seems confident that we won't be interrupted. It's a good spot—about a ten-minute walk from the Walmart where Hall is supposed to drop the money.

Thistle is outside, phoning in our progress to Luzhin. Probably getting yelled at: first for not having solved the case, second for leaving me alone. Not that she's given me enough freedom to enjoy, given that she's right outside the door. She probably didn't want Hall to overhear her saying we know basically nothing.

"They'll want you to put the money in the dumpster and walk away," the SAC continues. She sticks another piece of tape to Hall's belly, pinning down the cord. "They want you to trust them. But you won't. Okay?"

"Okay," Hall says. Her fear-chewed lips are starting to scab.

"So when you get to the dumpster, just stand there. They'll call you. They'll be angry. They'll make threats. Don't listen. Just tell them they'll get their money when you can see Cameron."

"Okay." She's practically crying.

"You're not alone," says the SAC. "We'll hear every word you say, and every word they say to you. Here."

She holds out a pink lump of rubber. Hall shifts so both her breasts are covered by one arm before taking it with her free hand. I watch.

Call me a monster if you want. You'll find plenty of evidence to back you up. But I haven't seen a naked woman in a long time.

When I was seventeen, I spent a lot of time at Houston Community College. It was a place where would-be actors staged plays attended only by other would-be actors, and where fistfights regularly erupted over whether rap counted as poetry. I wasn't enrolled; I hung out there because the large meatball pizza was only three bucks. The real students were living without their folks' money for the first time in their lives, so I fit right in. Most were too busy or too high to notice I never had a textbook or went to a lecture.

One afternoon I was sleeping on a bench when something tickled my hand. A husky had trotted up and was slurping at my fingers. There was no one else around, so I said, "Get lost," and shooed it away.

It sniffed at the bushes for a few seconds and then came back, staring at me with tar-black eyes. I got up and walked to another bench, but it followed me.

I checked the tags and led it to the owner, who turned out to be a grateful nineteen-year-old geology major with a thing for quiet, scruffy boys. She hugged her dog first, then me. Her hair was dyed brown and smelled like watermelon.

She bought me the best dinner of my life. She did the talking while my mouth was full of burrito—how she'd just moved here from St Louis, how her only brother was eight years older but still lived with her folks, how she used to have a boyfriend but she ditched him after he made her try meth.

"I felt itchy," she said, nose wrinkled. "Like, itchy inside my head."

After, she led me back to her room—I was better-looking than I am now. She mixed me a drink with some of her room-mate's whiskey. When she kissed me, some new urges got mixed up with some I'd had all my life. And when she took off her clothes, instinct took over. My pulse was too loud in my ears, sweat erupted all over me and my body moved like someone else was driving it.

What I did scared me almost as much as it scared her.

Since then, I'm afraid to be alone with a woman—with al-most anyone, in fact. I don't date, not that anyone ever asks. I don't go to strip clubs or brothels, because somewhere out there is a woman with a scar that proves I can't control myself.

The only reason I'm here, staring at Hall's quivering flesh, is that I have less than three hours to find her son, and I still need to ask her some questions. She's safe from me as long as the SAC is here. I think.

When I can't sleep, I fantasize about meeting that girl again—the geology major. I imagine getting served by her at the welfare office, or sitting next to her on the bus. I look at her, nod, offer an apologetic half smile. And she looks back at me without a trace of recognition.

Forgotten isn't forgiven. But it's the closest I'll ever get.

Hall is staring at the rubber lump like a teenager looking at her first tax return—confused, frightened, sinking into despair.

"For your ear," the SAC explains. "Narrow end first, pin-hole facing the front."

Hall pushes it in, squirming like a cornered cat.

"We'll only talk to you if we have to. But if we do, don't touch the plug. It'll feel weird, it'll sound weird, but it's im-portant that you pretend it's not there."

"They'll see it," Hall says.

"No, they won't. It's invisible from about five feet. And no one will get closer than that—we have snipers in the windows of several surrounding buildings. The second this guy comes into sight, we'll drop him."

"No! You'll hit Cam!"

"The snipers are damn good, ma'am. They won't fire without a clear shot."

I say, "Ms. Hall, can you tell me about the ransom call?"

The SAC glares at me—she wants Hall focused—but lets her answer.

"I already told the other agents," she whimpers. "It was distorted."

Luzhin hadn't mentioned that. "Tell me anyhow. Did the guy have an accent?"

"I don't know."

"What about the choice of words? Did he sound educated?"

"I don't know."

"You don't know if he sounded educated, or you don't remember what he said?"

Hall shoots me a venomous glance. I'm starting to feel unwelcome. "I remember every word of what he said."

"So tell me. You be the kidnapper, I'll be you. *Ring ring.*" I mime reaching for a phone.

She stares like she thinks I've gone mad. Or maybe she thinks she has. "I can't."

"Sure you can. I want his exact words, his accent, everything. *Ring ring.*"

"Mr. Blake," the SAC says, "we don't have time for this."

She's right, but I ignore her. *"Ring ring."* I pick up the invisible telephone. "Hello?"

"Annette," Hall says. Her eyes are closed. "I want you to listen very carefully."

Her voice has become deeper, harsher. There's a phlegmy

crackle in it. Her accent hasn't changed, but clearly she's learned a lot since *Days of Our Lives*.

"Who is this?" I ask. I don't know if that's what she said to the kidnapper, but she doesn't correct me.

"Mom! Please, help me!" Her voice trembles like a weather vane, but she pushes through. "Someone's got—"

She interrupts herself, switching back to the growling voice. "Right now, your son is safe. How long he stays that way is up to you. If you tell the police about this call, he will be nailed to a basement wall by his eyelids and nostrils and lips and left to starve. If you tell anyone else about this call, he will be nailed to a basement wall by his eyelids and nostrils and lips and left to starve. And if you don't fill a Walmart bag with twenty thousand dollars in unmarked bills—one hundred hundreds, a hundred and twenty fifties, and two hundred twenties—and put it in the dumpster behind the Walmart on the Northwest Freeway at six p.m. tomorrow, he will be nailed to a basement wall by his eyelids and nostrils and lips and left to starve. You have twenty-four hours."

"Anything else?" I ask.

"I'll repeat that," Hall says, still in the kidnapper's voice. "A Walmart bag. Twenty thousand dollars. Unmarked bills. One hundred hundreds, a hundred and twenty fifties, and the rest in twenties. The dumpster behind the Walmart on the Northwest Freeway. Six p.m. tomorrow, or Cameron dies."

Silence.

The SAC hands Hall her clothes without a word. Hall starts putting them on, head bowed.

The choice of words is telling. Clear, direct—the kidnapper sounds like he was reading from a prepared speech. Possibly a professional. He probably didn't expect Hall to call the cops. I'm surprised she did.

I ask, "What did you say that I didn't?"

"I said, 'Please don't hurt my son.' He didn't reply."

She stares me down, not blinking, not looking away. She's hiding something, and trying to look like she's not.

"Did he listen?" I ask.

"How should I know?"

"Was there a pause?"

She thinks about it. "No."

"What else?" I say. "I'm trying to save your son's life. What are you not telling me?"

"That's enough," the SAC snaps at me. "We have to focus. I want you out."

Hall's cell phone rings.

She pulls it out of her pocket. "Private number," she says.

"Shit," says the SAC.

Hall stares down at her phone like it's a live tarantula. "Oh God. It's him, isn't it?"

"You got a speakerphone setting on that thing?" I ask.

"Um..." She fiddles anxiously. "Yeah, I do."

"Blake..." the SAC warns.

"Switch it on," I say.

Hall does. The SAC clamps her mouth shut.

Hall lifts the phone to her ear. "Hello?"

There's a pause.

"Hello, Annette," a voice says.

It's running through a filter that removes all changes in pitch. The man sounds like a robot from a cheesy old sci-fi show, but it's a very effective disguise. It could be my own voice, and I wouldn't even know.

"The arrangement has changed," he says. "You will drop the money in the dumpster at four p.m., not six."

Only fifty minutes away.

"What? But—"

"Mom?" It's Cameron's voice, not distorted. "Don't let—"

He's cut off again by the kidnapper. "You already know what will happen to him if you're not there."

He could be changing the time because he needs the money more urgently. But probably he wants her to be less prepared. He doesn't want her to have time to set up a trap.

"I'll do whatever you want!" Hall cries. "Just please, don't hurt him!"

"The location remains the same. The dumpster behind the Walmart on the Northwest Freeway."

"Excuse me," I say.

Hall and the SAC whirl around to face me, shock splattered across their faces.

"I'm the kid's father," I say. "I've got the money. But how do I know you'll release my boy once we're paid up?"

The voice keeps talking over the top of me. "Be there by four p.m. or you'll never see him again."

The line goes dead.

The SAC grabs the front of my shirt and pins me to the wall. I can smell her coconut shower gel and feel the heat from her body. I haven't been this close to a woman in years. My heart is racing.

"What the fuck do you think you're doing?" the SAC demands, her breath on my face.

I can feel my lips peeling back to expose my teeth. I shut my eyes, trying to get back in control.

"He couldn't hear me," I say. "It was a recording. That's why he ignored her the first time, that's why there was a pause after she answered and that's why his voice was distorted but Cameron's wasn't. It's been edited."

Hall looks like an earthquake is happening beneath her. "What does that mean?"

"It means he could have made that call from anywhere," I say. "Not necessarily his hideout. And it also means—"

"He could have recorded it yesterday." The SAC lets go of me. "There's no proof of life."

I nod.

"Shit," she says again.

"I'm being punished," Hall says behind me.

I turn around to ask what she means, but I'm too late. With the clap of skin against concrete, she collapses to the floor.

CHAPTER 6

WALK RIGHT THROUGH ME, NEVER SEE ME, DIE WITHOUT ME. WHAT AM I?

THE ROOFTOP HAS SOAKED UP THE DAY'S HEAT like an old dishcloth. The concrete reeks of it. My toes, my thighs, my stomach, my forearms—every part of me touching the roof is wrapped in sweat.

"Five minutes," Thistle says, mostly to herself. We're lying on top of an office building about two hundred yards from the Walmart, which is a mustard-brown building big enough to house passenger planes. A McDonald's logo glows on one wall, and a sign says **PHARMACY DRIVE-THRU**. An American flag droops from a pole on top of the Walmart. Hundreds of pigeons are perched on the edge of the rooftop, watching pedestrians come and go. The parking lot is as big as a football field. Stadium lights fizz quietly, their shine competing with the late-afternoon sun. People wander to and from their cars at a lazy pace.

Through Thistle's binoculars I can see Hall sitting in her car down below, digging nervously at an invisible blemish on the back of her hand. Her face is strangely calm. It's been that way since she woke up on the floor of the storeroom. She's probably in shock and needs treatment, but we can't take her to a hospital. If she doesn't make the drop, her son is as good as dead.

Then again, it's likely he's floating facedown in the bay already. That's why she's in shock.

My mouth is gritty with chewed-up fingernails. I swallow the remains and start on another. Tiny seams of blood are appearing around my cuticles.

I pan left. Another McDonald's. Earlier, the SAC said it was strange to have one McDonald's inside the Walmart and another one right outside. Maybe she hasn't been to Texas before. A sniper in SWAT gear lies on the roof of the second McDonald's, eye to the scope, as still as any statue of Ronald. In the Bureau, they call the SWATs "ninjas."

Another is crouched on the roof of the Walmart itself. The SAC is in this building somewhere below me, her gun barrel resting on the frame of an open window. Yet another sniper is around the other side of the Walmart, watching the back of the building from above a cabinetmaker's shop.

Thistle and I have the highest and most distant vantage point, but we don't need to be closer. We're looking, not shooting.

Luzhin's voice crackles on Thistle's radio. "All units. Any sign of hostiles?"

The snipers sign off one by one.

"Negative, sir."

"Negative."

"That's a negative here too."

The SAC says, "All negative this side."

Thistle is last to reply. "Sorry, sir," she says. "We got nothing."

"Well, stay sharp," Luzhin says. "No children are going to die today."

He's in an unmarked van somewhere on the other side of the Walmart. The other agents may wonder why he's taking a personal interest in this case. They don't know he's here to watch me.

It's one thing to let me read files, question witnesses and even interrogate suspects, but this is a ransom drop, which is much more volatile. Luzhin won't let me near something like this without someone there who knows who I am and what I do. And since he can't tell anybody, it has to be him.

I'm tense. The muscles in the back of my neck are knotted around my spine. Most of me wants to see Hall pay the ransom, the kidnapper drop Cameron off and the FBI shoot him dead. The kidnapper, that is, not the kid—although that sort of screwup does happen from time to time.

But if it goes down that way, everything I did was useless. Working out where Cameron was taken from, who he's close to, why the ransom calls weren't interactive—none of it means anything if he gets returned right now.

One body for every life I save. That's my deal with Luzhin. If my input leads directly to a rescue, I get to feed my addiction with a death row inmate. If Cameron dies, or if he shows up without my help, I get nothing. And there's a Tanzanian triple murderer I'm just dying to meet.

Figure of speech. He's the one who will be dying.

I should hate myself for wanting the drop to go wrong. But a pound of guilt is worth an ounce of lust.

Annette Hall pushes the car door open. She wobbles on her pumps as she hurries across the lot toward the dumpster. I would have worn something easier to walk in if I were her. Maybe it's a confidence thing.

"Three minutes," Thistle mutters. "You noticed anything?"

"Like what?"

"Like whatever the fuck you were supposed to notice while I was babysitting you all day."

"There are two hundred and thirty-eight cars down there in six hundred and four spaces," I say. "Twenty-three of the cars have vanity plates. At this moment, seventeen pedestrians are headed toward Walmart, and twelve are going back to their cars. Of those twenty-nine people, twenty-one are women, and nine are under twenty years old. Fourteen of them are black, three are Asian. The rest are Caucasian."

Thistle says nothing.

"That all means," I say, "our suspect isn't here."

"How so?"

"Statistics tell me he'll be a white male between twenty and forty. Experience tells me that he won't be walking into or out of Walmart. He'll be standing still, pretending to read a newspaper or talk on a cell phone or smoke a cigarette. A hoodie would be conspicuous in this heat, so he'll be wearing a baseball cap and maybe sunglasses too. And his clothes will be old, faded, badly fit. He'll want to look homeless when he's searching the dumpster for the bag."

"How do you know he'll be standing? What if he's in one of the cars?"

"He'll want a direct line of sight to the dumpster. Only the cars closest to the Walmart have that, and they're all empty."

Thistle stares at me for a long time and then says, "Blake, were you a kidnapper?"

"What?"

"No one knows that shit except cops, ex-cops, PIs and kidnappers. I suppose judges and lawyers and psychologists might know parts of it, but if you didn't finish high school, you never went to college."

Sure I did. I bought pizzas there.

"Kidnappers typically get twenty years," I say. "Do I look old enough to have done that kind of time?"

"Maybe you didn't get caught. Maybe Mr. Burns knows you did it but can't prove it, so now he's using you."

That's worryingly close to the truth. "I never kidnapped anybody," I say.

We're interrupted by a ringing phone. It takes me a moment to realize that the sound is in my earplug.

I look down through the binoculars. Hall is fumbling with her handset, searching for the accept button.

"He's not here," I say. "I would've seen him."

Hall answers, "Yes?"

"Then why is he calling?" Thistle asks.

My mind is racing. Maybe he left something here—like a car with the keys in it, to take her to yet another location, somewhere we can't monitor her. If he did, we're in deep trouble.

The kidnapper starts talking. "Annette, for Cameron's sake, I hope that bag contains twenty thousand dollars."

I'm searching the parked cars, looking for one with missing plates or a patchy paint job, and suddenly I see something. On the back seat of a white Toyota Camry, nowhere near the Walmart, there's something hay-colored. Blond hair, maybe. Could be a boy slumped against the window. Cameron. Unconscious...or dead.

Or it could be something else—a golden retriever, asleep on the back seat. The angle makes it impossible to tell. I wriggle sideways without taking my eyes off it, but it's too far away to get a better view.

"The money's all there," Hall tells the kidnapper, just in case it's not a recording this time. "Where's Cam?"

A car pulls out of its spot, giving me a clear line of sight.

That's no dog.

I yell, "The kid!" Then I'm running across the roof, toward the stairwell door.

Thistle cries out, "Wait! Wait, damn it!"

But the kidnapper's not here, I'm sure of that. No reason for me to stay hidden. Every reason to get to the boy as fast as possible. If he's unconscious, that means drugged. And I doubt the kidnapper is a professional anesthesiologist.

I race down two flights of stairs, soles slapping the cement, and shove open a fire door. Office workers stare at me as I sprint down the corridor to the elevators and stab the call button.

The voice is still going. "You're going to put it in the dumpster and start walking back to your car."

"Don't do it," the SAC reminds her.

Hall screams, "Not until I see my son!" Her voice overloads the mic. The plug crackles in my ear.

The ten seconds it takes the elevator to arrive feel like an hour. Finally the doors open and I dive through them. I hit the button marked G, and then the one that's supposed to close the doors.

Thistle slips through, blocking them. "Blake, just what the hell do you think you're doing?"

I stab the button again. "The kid's in a white Camry in the parking lot."

"Alive?"

The doors slide closed. "I don't know."

The kidnapper says, "If you don't comply, you will be killing Cameron."

"Okay, okay," Hall says. I hear the thump of the bag dropping into the dumpster. "It's done. Just please don't hurt him. Please."

The SAC says something I don't catch.

I can see Thistle's jaw clenching as the floors hum past. She says, "You can't go out there. He might be watching."

"He's not. I'd have seen him."

"You don't know that."

"Reese," I say. *"Trust me."*

She bites her lip. Then she mutters, "Christ," and grabs her radio.

"This is Thistle, calling all units. I have an unconfirmed sighting of Cameron in a white Toyota Camry. Registration number…"

She looks at me. I recite the plates from memory.

Thistle repeats the number into the radio. "Heading down to check it out," she says.

Luzhin's voice comes on immediately. "Stand down, Agent—the kidnappers could be here."

"With all due respect, sir, your boy Blake says they're not."

There's a pause. "Then get out there," Luzhin says finally. "Everyone else, eyes on the Camry. The suspect may be inside."

The kidnapper is still talking to Hall. "Keep walking toward the dental clinic up the other end of the lot. There's a white Toyota Camry parked on the end of the row. It's unlocked."

"He's releasing Cameron," Thistle says.

"That doesn't make sense," I say. "He's not here to collect the ransom."

The elevator doors open again. Thistle and I run out, past the reception desk, headed for the fading daylight.

We reach the door. Thistle says, "You stay here."

Not likely. I follow her out.

Ahead of us, Annette Hall has nearly reached the Camry. Her eyes widen as she sees the boy in the back seat. She starts running. Thistle and I sprint toward the car from the other side.

We all reach it at the same moment. Hall pulls open the rear door.

A shop-window mannequin tumbles out. One plastic arm gets caught in the frame on the way, and it spins like a ballerina before hitting the ground with an ugly crack. The blond wig slithers off.

"No!" Hall cries.

Thistle says, "Fuck." She holds up the radio again. "That's a negative on contact. We don't have Cameron. Repeat, we do not have Cameron."

There's a stab mark in the dummy's abdomen. The cheap T-shirt it wears has been torn, and the plastic split. Blood surrounds the fake wound.

Real blood. I can smell it.

The kidnapper resumes talking. "You shouldn't have called the cops, Ms. Hall. I'm willing to give you another chance, but the discount has expired. You have now paid zero point five percent of the total ransom. Think of it as a down payment on your son's life."

They want more money. That figures.

Hall is sobbing hysterically. Thistle leans in closer to the stab wound. "What's that?" she says.

"As a gesture of good faith," the kidnapper continues, "I have returned zero point five percent of Cameron."

Thistle flicks open a pocketknife and pries the wound open with the blade. Brittle plastic cracks, revealing the slick lump of flesh inside.

"What *is* that?" she says again.

Hall screams.

I recognize the body part. It's a human kidney.

People are yelling. I don't listen. Point five percent of the money. That means they want a total of four million dollars.

Except that the kidnapper didn't take the twenty grand Hall brought with her. He didn't even show up—the dummy could have been sitting in that car for hours. So what did he mean by down payment?

I look over at the dumpster.

A man is walking away from it.

He's wearing sunglasses, a baseball cap and a tattered overcoat. He's talking on a cell phone.

And he's carrying a dark green Walmart bag.

The dummy was a distraction. So he could grab the ransom when no one was looking.

I snatch Thistle's radio out of her hand. "The kidnapper is here! Heading toward the southeast corner of the Walmart."

It's a long way from this side of the parking lot to the

Walmart. I start running, but it's hopeless. He'll disappear around the corner before I can get there.

"Describe him," one of the snipers says.

"White male." The words squeeze out between ragged breaths. "At least six feet tall. Two hundred pounds. Baseball cap, sunglasses, brown coat. Can't see his face."

"Too many people around. I don't have a clear shot."

"I have one," another sniper says. "Do we have a kill order?"

"No!" Luzhin says. "Hold your fire. Blake, how do you know it's him?"

The guy is nearly at the corner. He hasn't turned to look at me, but he seems to be moving quicker. He's still on the phone, so he must be working with accomplices.

"He's carrying the ransom bag," I puff.

"It's a normal Walmart bag! Give me something concrete!"

"Do I take the shot?" the sniper says.

"Don't shoot," Luzhin says. "Blake, can you see a weapon?"

I could lie. I'm sure this is the guy. But I need Luzhin's trust. "No," I say, and keep running.

If I catch him, the feds will make him talk. He'll tell them where the kid is in exchange for a reduced sentence, Cameron will be returned to his mom and I'll get to celebrate with one of the few people on this earth worse than me. Everybody wins.

But if I *don't* catch him, then Hall has to find four million dollars before Cameron goes into septic shock. You can live with one kidney—but only under a doctor's supervision. It also helps if the other one was removed by an actual surgeon.

An engine roars behind me. I turn to see Thistle's sedan hurtling across the lot—she must have jumped in when I started running. As it zooms past, sirens wailing, I hear her voice on the radio.

"I'm in pursuit," she says, as though we might not have noticed. I keep sprinting through the cloud of exhaust as the Crown Vic rockets toward the kidnapper, who changes direction and slips between two cars.

I half expect Thistle to ram the cars, but she slams on the brakes instead. The Crown Vic spins to a screeching halt and she tumbles out the door, somehow lands on her feet and starts running. Faster than me. Faster than the kidnapper. He's almost within her reach.

He whirls around and stabs her in the throat.

Thistle crumples like a controlled demolition, limbs instantly limp as though her spine has been snipped. She disappears behind a parked car. I get a quick glimpse of the kidnapper's face—saggy, pallid, older than I would have thought—before he keeps running toward the east corner of the Walmart.

The rational move would be to keep chasing him. If Thistle's dead, she's dead. But my body seems to have made the decision without my brain, and I'm already almost at the fallen agent, my heart pounding in my ears.

"Agent down!" one of the snipers is saying. "Agent down!"

Running past the car, I almost trip over her. She's dragged herself into a sitting position and has one hand pressed against her neck.

"Get after him," she rasps.

I crouch down next to her.

"I'm fine!" she says, and shoves me with her other hand. "Go! Now!"

Thinking I imagined the knife, I look for blood and see none. The other agents are right behind me, so I do as she says and start running again. As I watch, the kidnapper disappears around the side of the Walmart.

"I've lost him," one of the snipers says.

"Ninjas, stay at your posts," Luzhin says. "All other units, head for the east side of the Walmart. Go!"

I round the corner. I'm on the east side of the Walmart.

The man with the bag is gone.

I scan the crowd of Walmart shoppers. A few baseball caps, but in the wrong colors. A couple of coats, but too short.

I can see the SAC and a couple other agents appearing from around the northeast corner. Luzhin is already here, looking utterly perplexed. "Can anyone see him?" he yells. "Can anyone fucking see him?"

I turn to look at the Walmart. Maybe the guy went inside to hide. But as I start to move toward the sliding doors, something catches my eye. A gray-brown lump, stuffed between a dumpster and the wall.

It's a coat, and a baseball cap. No sign of the bag—he probably hid it inside a different bag as soon as he was out of sight.

Cars are already leaving the lot. People are walking toward nearby fast-food chains. No way to seal off the area. We've lost him.

Luzhin looks at me, fists clenched. "You were closest. Did you see his face?"

I shake my head. "Wouldn't have mattered. He was wearing a mask."

Luzhin pulls out the coat and, sure enough, there's a floppy lump of rubber inside it, too wrinkly to be real skin. He unfolds it and stares into the empty eyeholes. The mask leers at us all.

The SAC says, "Don't worry, sir. We'll get him."

We will. *I* will. I have to. The smell of the kidney has lodged itself in my throat like a fishbone and the need is rising faster than usual.

"Yes," I say. "Don't worry."

CHAPTER 7

I ALWAYS RUN BUT NEVER WALK,
OFTEN MURMUR BUT NEVER TALK.
I HAVE A BED BUT NEVER SLEEP,
AND HAVE A MOUTH BUT NEVER EAT.
WHAT AM I?

I ALMOST DON'T SEE THISTLE OUTSIDE THE FO-
rensic pathologist's office. She's sitting on a plastic chair behind a fake fern, her head pressed between her palms like
she's trying to crush it. When I listen, I can hear her breathing shakily through her nose.

I usually don't ask—I have my own problems—but I find
myself saying, "You okay?"

Her head snaps up. "Yeah. Fine. Ready to go in?" She tucks
her hair behind her ears and glares, challenging me to comment on her composure.

"Let's wait for Luzhin," I say, and sit down beside her.

"Sure." She leans back in her chair and stares at the opposite wall.

"How's your neck?"

She tilts her head from side to side. The kidnapper's Taser
left twin puncture wounds, like a vampire bite. "It's okay,"
she says. "I've had worse."

This doesn't sound like bravado. But she still looks distressed.

"Really?" I ask.

"Sure. I've been stabbed, shot. You should see my scars.
The governor gave me the FBI star for bravery, even though

it wasn't like I *chose* to take a bullet." She looks down. "But that kidney… I guess it was a shock."

"It gets easier," I tell her after a pause. "Finding a body, or part of one, or whatever."

She takes a deep breath. "You remember Beaumont?" she says. "The guy who went undercover in Charlie Warner's gang?"

"And got turned into alligator food," I say. "Yeah. He and Luzhin were friends, so I met him a couple times. Nice guy." He wasn't, but it feels wrong to say so. "Did you know him?"

"Not until I found him. Half of him." She picks a speck of lint off her pants.

"I'm sorry," I say, not sure why she's brought this up.

"If Cameron Hall is dead, I can accept that and focus on the perp. If he's alive, I can promise myself I'll save him." She sighs. "What kills me is not knowing one way or the other."

"You been in yet?" Luzhin asks.

I look over to see him approaching, a manila folder in his hand. "No."

"Well, let's do it."

He knocks on the door. Thistle gets out of her chair as the door opens.

The forensic pathologist is almost as tall as Luzhin—six foot one, maybe. And she looks like the sort who'd seem to be looking down on us even if she wasn't gigantic. She holds her head so high that I can see straight up her nose. I feel like I'm in a petri dish.

The morgue isn't as gloomy as people probably assume. Brown floor tiles, lots of lights. The steel drawers are painted cream. It all looks a bit like the locker room of the pool I used to sneak into for a wash when I was homeless.

I don't like doctors—not since meeting Dr. Fallun at Fort Sam. Pathologists are different from shrinks, but knowing that isn't enough to smother my unease.

"Director," the pathologist says, ignoring me and Thistle.

"Dr. Norman," he says, and hands her the manila folder. "Here's your blood work."

"Have you looked at it?"

"It doesn't mean anything to me—you'll have to translate it. Have you had a look at the kidney?"

"That I have," Norman says. She leads us over to a steel slab, flicking through the folder as she goes. The kidney sits in a Ziploc bag on what looks to me like a baking tray. Rosy ice crystals have appeared where the flesh touches the plastic. I button up my jacket and breathe onto my palms.

"Can it be reattached?" I ask.

She points at me and addresses Luzhin. "Who is this?"

Thistle says, "He's helping us with our inquiries. Same as you."

Her voice is about as warm as the kidney. The doctor looks intimidated for a second, but then the facade is back.

"No," she says. "The kidney can't be reattached. It's so shredded that I wasn't even sure it was human at first. Plus, it was left sitting in a hot car for hours, which turned it from a healthy organ into a lump of rotten meat."

"Was Cameron alive when it was taken?" Thistle asks.

"That's complicated. Do any of you have medical training?"

We all shake our heads. I don't have *training*, per se. I guess you could call me self-taught.

"A kidney removal is called a nephrectomy," the doctor says. "The surgeon has to cut through the renal artery, the ureter—which connects the kidney to the bladder—and a whole lot of fat tissue. On this kidney, a lot of that tissue is still attached. In theory, the blood saturation of that tissue would tell me if the patient was alive when the operation was performed. In practice…" She spreads her palms wide. "The hours in the car make it impossible to tell. The sun dried out most of the tissue."

"What about the time frame?" Thistle asks.

"Same deal. I couldn't say with any certainty when it was removed."

Luzhin asks, "Was the kidney removed with skill?"

"Great skill," the doctor says. "Your kidnapper has medical training, or is working with someone who does."

"So the boy could have survived the operation."

"Yes. Although——" she turns to a particular page in the folder and holds it up, as though it should mean something to us "——there was no anesthetic in the blood."

"Jesus," Thistle says.

Silence falls. We're all imagining what it would be like to be fully conscious while someone cuts a kidney out of us.

"I've heard of people undergoing surgery with hypnosis instead of anesthetic," Thistle says. "Is that legit?"

"It's not really my field," Dr. Norman replies. "From what I understand, it's quite effective on some people, especially since your internal organs don't feel much pain to begin with. But it depends on making the patient feel very relaxed, which would be difficult if you kidnapped them."

So we're probably not looking for a hypnotist. "You sure it belongs to Cameron?" I ask.

"We took a DNA sample from Annette Hall," Luzhin puts in. "The lab techs ran it against the blood from the kidney. The results should be in the folder."

The pathologist turns to a different page. "Yes," she says. "These two samples match."

"What about the mask?" Thistle asks. "Get any prints off it?"

"Just the cops who handled it. The kidnapper must have worn gloves."

My training has left me ignorant in one area. "How long can a person survive with only one kidney?"

"As long as anybody else, if they eat right, don't drink, et cetera. But that's assuming the surgeon didn't give him an infection or damage any other organs while he was in there. There's a good chance the kid's bleeding into his abdomen through a nicked artery as we speak. He could be dead in hours. Could be dead already."

Luzhin shakes his head. "Cameron's his meal ticket. The kidnapper wouldn't have taken the kidney if he wasn't sure he could do it without killing the boy."

"Being sure doesn't make him smart," the doctor says.

"No," Luzhin says. "But he is."

He turns to me. "That all you need?"

I nod.

"Thistle?"

She says, "Yes, sir."

"Thanks for your help, Doc."

Norman picks up the tray and puts it back in the freezer. "Always a pleasure, Peter," she says. But she's looking at me. Wondering, guessing, calculating.

I don't look away. *Whatever you're thinking, lady, you're way off.*

She smiles faintly, as if she can hear my thoughts. Then she shuts the freezer, peels off her latex gloves and sits down at her desk.

"What about the security cameras outside the Walmart?" Thistle asks.

We're back in Luzhin's office. This time he hasn't put the family photos facedown. His wife smiles at me. Brunette, with a heart-shaped face and a nose ring. She's holding a confused-looking baby in a pink onesie. Luzhin is in the picture too, forcing a smile, looking about ten years younger.

Real-life Luzhin shakes his head. "The feed cut out just as the kidnapper rounded the corner. He was using some kind of frequency jammer."

"Are those hard to get?"

"A dozen stores in Houston sell them. I have a team asking around."

"You should check if any of Annette Hall's contacts have medical training," I say.

"Vasquez is working through the list." He drums his fingers on the desk. "What else you got?"

"Nada," I say.

He frowns. "Really?"

"Yep. Sorry. But it sounds like you got it under control."

Luzhin is suspicious. He's never known me to give up so quickly. But he can't ask me what I'm up to, not in front of Thistle.

I try to look innocent. I've had a lot of practice.

"Okay," he says. "Agent Thistle, escort Mr. Blake back to his car."

He thinks it's over. So does she. So does the doctor. Everyone but me.

We leave.

Thistle and I walk in silence through the corridors to the elevator, then from the elevator to the lobby to the parking lot. It's not until I roll my sleeves up again that she says, "Fleas, right?"

"What?"

"Your scars." She points. "Fleabites."

When I was a kid, I used to think group homes were made to support fleas rather than children. At the one I was in, every mattress, every bedsheet and every pillow had a colony living in it. Fortunately, the blankets were like sandpaper, which made scratching easy.

Mrs. Radfield—a spindly old woman with wide, wet eyes—told me that fleas were God's way of telling me to wash more regularly. I believed her and stood shivering in the communal showers four times a day, but I always woke up with blood under my fingernails and a throbbing in the skin of my forearms, my calves, my scalp, my crotch.

Most of the staff, if they caught me scratching, would make me kneel and pray in front of the other children. As well as being the currency with which we bought food and sleep, prayer was also used to fine us for wrongdoing. Not Mrs. Radfield, though. If she caught me scratching at the fleabites that covered my body, a stiff hand would swoop out of her summer dress and crack across my face, leaving my ears ringing and my nose beginning to run. To this day, I can't scratch a mosquito bite without a guilty glance each way.

"Hands off, or they won't heal!" she'd hiss. Decades later, and my arms and legs are proof that she was right.

"No," I tell Thistle. "Oil burns."

She nods sympathetically, without believing me.

As we get to my car, she hands me a pen and paper. "I'll need your number," she says. "In case a new lead comes up."

It seems unlikely, but I scribble the number down anyway and hand it back to her.

"How about a cell?" she says.

"Don't have one," I say. "I heard they give you cancer."

She looks down at the paper doubtfully.

"I work from home," I say. "That number is enough."

"Okay," she says, and pockets it. "I'll see you."

She holds out her hand to shake. I take it. It's soft, in the way all women's hands somehow are. A tingle ascends my spine, and I let go as if scalded.

She turns away without another word, and I climb into the car and start the engine as though I have somewhere important to be. I do—but not until nightfall. For now, I'm headed home.

Leather handbag. Knee-high boots. A red plastic shopping basket hanging from her elbow, filled with cans and bottles.

At a distance, the woman looks like an ordinary grocery shopper—if you ignore the dirt in her hair, the dusty highway she walks alongside, the hopeful thumb jutted out at traffic.

The car up ahead of me, the only other one on the road, slows down. The hitchhiker looks hopeful at first, and then grateful, but the car speeds up again with a growl. She stares down at the blacktop through eyes dulled by the glare of the sun.

Maybe the driver thought she was pretty until he got close. It happens.

There's no one else around. She could be stuck out here for hours if I don't give her a ride. It's been a long time since I've walked down mile after mile of highway with my thumb out, but not so long that I don't remember the sweaty brow and the aching feet and the pounding head.

I slow down.

An idea rises, uninvited: if she didn't make it home, no one could trace it back to me.

That thought carries my foot from the brake to the accelerator. A ride with me could do much more damage than a few hours plodding through the heat. But I saw her disappointment when the last car passed her, and I don't want to see it again. I pull up onto the shoulder a few yards ahead of her.

"She'll come to no harm," I tell myself. A direct order.

She runs up to the window, a smile on her cracked lips.

"Where you headed?" I ask.

She points a Browning .45 at me. "Out of the car." Her voice is croaky as a crow's.

"Oh, hell," I say.

She waggles the gun. I don't move. She points it at the sky and pulls the trigger. The gunshot booms around the empty desert, and then she points it at me again.

"You just cost me a bullet," she says. "Two's my limit."

I unbuckle my seat belt and open the door. She might shoot

me anyway, drag me into the shrubbery and leave me to feed the coywolves so that I can't report the carjacking and get her caught. That would be the smart thing to do.

But she might have a conscience. "I tried to help you," I say.

Her expression doesn't change. "Cry me a river."

I circle around the front of the car. So does she, and we meet in the middle.

"Give me your phone," she says.

"Those bullets aren't big," I reply.

She pokes my chest with the hot muzzle. Too close to miss if I try anything. "Big enough."

"They'll kill me, that's for sure," I say. "But it won't be quick. Even if you use up the seven rounds you have left, I'll stay up for five seconds, maybe ten. Enough to snap your little neck."

She holds my gaze. We're both thinking hard.

"Give me your fucking phone," she says again. Stalling.

"I don't have a phone," I say. "See?"

Carefully, I turn out my pockets. Some dollar bills fall to the road. She looks down at them, giving me an opportunity to grab her hair and peel off her scalp. I don't take it.

"The car's yours," I say. "The money's mine. Don't shoot me, and I won't strangle you." Not the most eloquent treaty, but clear enough.

"Turn around."

"No."

After a pause, she nods. Edges around toward the driver's-side door. I follow her. If I give her too much space, I'm no longer dangerous and she can shoot me safely.

She gets in. Closes the door. I run back behind the car, putting the rear windshield between us. It won't stop a bullet, but it might stop her pulling the trigger. A stolen car isn't worth much with a smashed window.

She floors the accelerator and the car zooms off, tires

crackling. I watch her spin the steering wheel and swerve into a U-turn, and then I realize what she's doing and start running.

The fender rushes past, just missing me as I throw myself off the highway and land hard on the dirt. The car skids to a halt, and I roll sideways as the woman opens fire out the window. Five bullets kick up the dust beside me before the gun clicks empty.

I lie still, holding my breath, my eardrums strumming. If she thinks I'm dead, she may get out to hide the body, giving me a chance to reclaim my ride.

No such luck. The car roars away and I get to my feet, coughing up dust, in time to watch it disappear over the horizon.

She's driving fast. Maybe she'll get pulled over and discover that the car was reported stolen by its actual owner months ago.

Maybe not. I'll never know. I start walking along the highway and stick out my thumb.

The guy who stops is a big black bowling ball of a man, driving a car that's three decades old and hasn't gotten any better with age. The paint job is the same color as the mud on the fender, and the faux-wood covering is peeling off the plastic on the inside.

"Now just what in hell do you think you're doing?" the bowling ball asks, a cigarette waggling in his mouth.

"Walking," I say. My voice is hoarse.

"*Walking?* No one's walked in Texas since Jesse James, buddy. Get in."

He opens the door. I'm suspicious of him—mostly for his lack of suspicion about me. I don't want to get in a car that would have me as a passenger. But that attitude won't get me far, and he's the first person to stop in the two hours I've been walking.

I get in.

As he pulls back out onto the highway, he asks where I'm headed. I tell him, and he says he can get me the whole way there. Then he wants to know how I got to where he found me without a car.

"Broke down," I say. "About three miles back." He strikes me as the kind of guy who might insist on calling the cops for me if he finds out I've been jacked.

"I didn't see your car," he says. "But I can turn around. I used to be a mechanic—maybe I can fix it."

"Thanks," I say, "but it'll need to be towed. Fan belt snapped and the radiator burst."

"Shit. Why didn't you hitch a ride with the tow truck?"

"Never called one. No phone."

"Mine's in the glove compartment," he says. "Want to call one now?"

I shake my head. "My roommate has a car trailer. I'll borrow it when I get there."

"Well, it's your call. Or lack thereof." He laughs.

Talking hurts my throat, so I ask him what he's been doing since he gave up auto repair. He says he drives a cement mixer, which is easy work so long as you get the truck to its destination less than ninety minutes after it's been loaded up. The job, he says, only gets hard if the concrete does. His name is Walter Bouchet.

Before he started working on cars, he was a preacher. I ask why he gave that up, and he tells me he wasn't very good at it. His congregation kept right on lying and stealing no matter what he did.

"Are you supposed to stop them?" I ask. "I thought you were just supposed to forgive them."

"That's more a Catholic thing," he says. "I was a Baptist."

"Oh."

Bouchet tells me that after one man sprayed a swastika on the church wall and blamed it on his own son when he was accused, he quit. "To hell with them," he says. "Literally."

He laughs again, and I humor him. Literally.

It's getting dark by the time his car squeaks and rumbles to a halt in my driveway. My roommate's van is parked on the grass, but I doubt it'll be here long. He works nights.

"Where's the trailer?" Bouchet asks.

"Around the back."

"Need a hand hooking it up?"

"No, thanks."

"Well," he says, "nice to meet you."

I shake his hand and tell him never to pull over for a woman carrying a shopping basket. He chuckles as though I've made a pun, then drives away into the twilight.

I walk to the front door and jam a key into one rusted lock, then another, then another. The door groans open. I walk in.

My roommate is on the sofa, staring at the TV like it's a hypnotist's watch. His pupils are the size of pennies. Based on the sweat on his brow and the way he's stroking the couch next to him, I'd say he's had a couple of tablets of ecstasy.

Perhaps he has a new supplier. I've heard him bragging that he never sells anything unless he can personally vouch for the quality. Then again, I've also heard him claiming to be "the almighty butterfly king." Whoever the new supplier is, I bet they buy from—or work for—Charlie Warner, just like the old one did.

My roommate and I first met in the cramped waiting room of a real estate agent who specialized in overcharging people for scummy share houses after they'd run out of better options. I introduced myself. The man who became my roommate didn't. I asked him what his name was, and he thought about it, then said, "John." When, later, the agent wanted a last name to put on the rental agreement, he said, "Johnson," and glared at the man, as if daring him to question it.

Despite the drugs and the paranoia, John's not the worst roommate I've ever had. The one before him was a fast-talking pyromaniac named Jesse, who used to kidnap the neighbors' cats and bury them in the backyard.

With a shock, I realize the guy talking on the TV is Luzhin, standing in front of the field office. There's a picture of Cameron in the corner of the screen. "If anyone has seen Cameron or has any other information, we urge you to come forward," Luzhin says, squinting against the sun. "Also, if you'd like to contribute funds to our missing person investigative team, you can donate cash at any branch office, or with a credit card by calling..."

I guess the kidnapper knows what Annette Hall told us, so Luzhin figures we may as well get the public on our side.

"I can feel it in my feet," my roommate says suddenly.

"Uh-huh," I reply, and leave him to it.

Someone called for him yesterday, but I won't give him the message now. He wouldn't remember, then he'd claim I didn't tell him, call me a liar and tell one of the hundreds of junkies dependent on him to attack me while I slept.

Johnson doesn't like me writing things down—he sees it as surveillance—but today it seems like the best option. I pick up a newspaper and tear off a strip, write *Gemma called* on it and stick it to the fridge door under a magnet that advertises a carpet cleaner I can't ever imagine calling, since the house has no carpet. Then I open the fridge to grab some stale bread.

There's a big chest freezer on the other side of the kitchen. The meat inside no longer resembles the Ambulance Killer. The pieces are softball-sized, too small to be recognizable as human. The head, hands and feet are distinctive, so I keep them taped up in a cardboard box under everything else in the freezer.

Since he no longer looks human, I have to make him *taste* human. I put a tiny bit of salt on the filets along with some ground-up pregnancy vitamins. These include copper, which will make the filets taste bloody again. I microwave them for forty-eight seconds.

While I wait for the microwave, I munch on the stale bread. This stops me from getting sick—a person can't live on meat alone.

When the filets are heated to exactly ninety-eight degrees, I unlock my bedroom door and go inside. Stepping over the maze of half-finished jigsaw puzzles, I make my way over to the mattress on the floor and sit down, chewing as I go. The springs creak under me.

A pile of jumbled Rubik's Cubes looms beside the bed. I pick up the one on top and start working on it. People assume only geniuses can solve Rubik's Cubes, but all you need is pattern recognition and a good memory. You have to see which squares are already in the right places, and remember which sequences of turns will end up moving only the others.

It takes me about two minutes to solve the cube. I would have done it quicker, but the mechanism inside is rusty, and I won't get paid if I break it.

Three years ago I went to an internet café and set up a profile on a social networking site. My username was *hangman*—*puzzlesolver* was taken—and in the *About me* section I wrote that I could solve any puzzle in two weeks. Anyone who wanted to use this service could post the puzzle with a self-addressed, stamped envelope and a twenty-dollar bill to my PO box. If I couldn't solve it, I'd send double their money back on receipt of the solution.

This started out as a money-laundering operation. The FBI wasn't paying me, so I survived by selling credit card numbers on Russian web forums. The puzzles were only supposed to make me look legit if the IRS ever came knocking.

I didn't expect to have any actual customers, and for the first few months I was right. But word got around, and now I get sent three or four puzzles a week. Jumbled Rubik's Cubes are quite common. Jigsaw puzzles too—I glue the pieces in place before I mail them back. Sometimes I get those weird metal and wood things where the goal is to disassemble them. And I get a huge number of riddles.

I put down the solved cube and take a handful of paper scraps off another pile. The first one reads: *Who is my son's only sister's only husband's only mother-in-law's only husband's only mother-in-law?*

Another reads: *Each morning I lie at your feet, every morning and afternoon I follow no matter how fast you run, yet I abandon you at noon. What am I?*

A third reads: *You may find me in the sun, and yet I'm never out of darkness. I am the beginning of sorrow and the end of sickness. You cannot express happiness without me, nor misery. I am always in risk, yet never in danger. What am I?*

I pick up a pen, scribble on my palm until the ink starts flowing, and then I write on each sheet of paper. *Your mother. A shadow. The letter* S. Too easy.

I'll never get rich doing this. But it pays about a third of my rent, fills the cars I steal with gas and runs my space heater in winter. It sure beats begging, sleeping on benches and living on scraps from trash cans, like I used to do.

Sometimes I find myself wondering what I'll do in the long-term. I live so close to the edge that an illness or a car accident would push me off. But my lethal hobby is all-consuming. I can't spend much time thinking about anything before my mind is tugged back toward the Death House like a dog on an ever-tightening leash.

I solve a few more riddles and two more Rubik's Cubes, and I start another jigsaw. None of these tasks are urgent. I've still got at least a week to return each of them to the owners. I'm just killing time, waiting for night to fall.

In the shadows creeping from the east, people are eating dinner, watching those interchangeable crime shows that come on at nine, then switching off their TVs and going to bed. They're reading, taking Valium, turning over. The windows on my street go dark, one by one.

It's time to go.

In the front room I find Johnson still on the sofa, but he's stopped groping it. He must be coming around. And he has company.

Harry Crudup, the music teacher, has a tourniquet around his arm and a teaspoon in his hand. He looks at me, as motionless as a startled deer.

"Uh, hi there," I say.

He nods curtly.

"What a coincidence, you two being friends."

"Fuck off," Johnson says.

I hold Crudup's gaze for a moment longer. *I never saw you if you never saw me.* Then I take a plastic bottle from the cupboard and fill it with water, trying to shake off a sense of disappointment. I shouldn't judge him. His addiction is probably safer than mine.

I make a cup of coffee with cream, three sugars and a teaspoon of salt. I do it noisily, partly so I can pretend I don't hear what they're doing, partly so they both notice that I'm not up to anything suspicious. A drug dealer and an addict aren't a good alibi, but they're better than nothing.

A hand falls on my shoulder.

I spin around to see Crudup, too close. I raise my hand to grab his throat and then realize he's not threatening me—the drugs have messed up his sense of personal space.

"If you were me," he says, "then you'd be me."

This sounds like typical user nonsense, so I say, "Yeah."

"No," he says. I can smell tobacco on his breath. "You don't get it. You think you're better than me."

Even genocidal dictators at least believe themselves to be doing the right thing, which makes them better men than me. "I don't," I say.

"Damn right you're not," he says, mishearing me. "You ever put a project off until the last minute? Ever give up on a diet? If you've ever hit your fucking snooze button, then you could be an addict. You would be, if someone offered you the drugs and you were unhappy enough to take them."

I pick up the coffee mug and take a sip. It burns my lips, and I set it back down.

"It's not about drugs," Crudup continues, a longing in his voice. "It's about willpower. There's no such thing as an addict. Just a man in difficult circumstances. Now all I have is the guitar and the needle."

"I forgive you," I tell him, since that seems to be what he's asking for.

He offers his worn-out smile and says, "How can you? I can't forgive myself."

He doesn't say anything more after that, so I pick up the steaming mug and the bottle and squeeze past him. Carrying them back to my bedroom, I leave them on the floor, close the door almost all the way and watch Crudup's shadow.

He stands where I left him for more than a minute. Then he shuffles out of the kitchen and back into the living room.

I wait for the creaking of the sofa's springs before I tiptoe back down the corridor to Johnson's bedroom. He's surprisingly neat, at least compared to his clients. The CDs by the stereo aren't alphabetized, but they are squared away between a pair of bookends. The clean clothes are in the lowboy, the dirty ones in a laundry basket.

The shelves are crammed with books, but I'm not fooled. At least ten percent of those volumes have been hollowed out to hold cash or drugs. One of the others is an address book. The rest are just camouflage. Several are in Spanish, which Johnson doesn't speak as far as I know.

Silently, I remove and open a few books. It doesn't take long to find what I need. Hundreds of white tablets, twelve in each packet, circular, innocuous, a cross in the center. The label, printed at a hospital in Ecatepec, says *Flunitrazepam*.

Addicts take these to make a fix of smack seem more potent, or to ease the crash after a night of coke or meth. But flunitrazepam is most famous for a different purpose, and under a different name.

Rohypnol. The date-rape drug.

I steal a whole packet. A missing packet is less obvious than a missing pill.

Making sure the bookshelf is as I found it, I sneak back out into the corridor and go back into my bedroom, where I close the door and lock it.

The coffee has cooled down now. I slurp it up greedily and put the empty mug back on the floor. Then I take the water bottle, open the window—slow, quiet—and climb out.

I close the window behind me and run across the dry grass, past the van, over the curb, onto the road. I reach the end of my street and turn the corner. As I get farther from my house, I become less concerned about speed and silence, so I slow down to a jog, shoes slapping the asphalt. Just another night runner with a water bottle. No, Officer, I didn't get a good look at his face.

As I run, I open the water bottle, pop a roofie out of its packaging and drop it in. Then I put the lid back on and shake the bottle until the pill has dissolved.

The full moon hangs directly above me, spilling a faint glow across the street. As a child, I once asked Mrs. Radfield where the moon came from, and she told me God had made it so we could see at night. This sounded a lot like her answers to all my other questions, so in high school I looked it up myself at the library.

One theory is that Earth once didn't weigh enough to attract an atmosphere. But about five billion years ago, a planetary embryo called Theia crashed into it. Theia was obliterated, but the shattered pieces added enough mass for Earth to acquire air and become habitable. The impact also carved out a chunk of our planet, which spun off into space and became the moon. The book added that we still don't really know how many planets are in our solar system, since the area past Mercury is too bright to see and the void beyond Uranus is too dark. There could be another Theia out there.

Since reading that, I find it hard to look up without imagining a giant ball of stone hurtling down out of the darkness, ready to crush our petty little lives into ash.

The houses get taller and taller as I run. The beat-up trucks and vans fade, replaced by sporty two-seaters and gleaming minivans. Dead trees become angular hedges. Soon I'm in the right suburb. Then I'm on the right street. Then I'm staring up at the right house, wondering which room is the one I want.

The only second-floor window on this side of the house has purple beaded curtains, shut. A girl sleeps there. Wrong room.

There's no front fence, which means no dog. But there could be a security light, so I identify a bush I can take cover behind before I start moving.

The light clicks on as I sprint toward the side of the house and dive between the bush and the neighbor's fence. I'm careful not to break any branches. The smell of fresh fertilizer tells me that the house has an attentive gardener.

I crouch, still as a photograph, and wait. I open my mouth

as wide as it goes so my breaths don't whistle through my teeth or my nostrils.

I can't hear anything moving in the house. The light goes off.

No windows on this side. Makes sense—if there were, they would be overlooking the neighbor's yard. Rich people like to pretend their neighbors don't exist.

I circle around to the back of the house, where a spacious yard hosts some big dogwood trees. A basketball hoop is nailed to the side of the garage. Two more second-floor windows. Through one of them I see a poster stuck to the ceiling inside. Not an adult's bedroom. I've found what I'm looking for.

I shove the water bottle into my pocket and clamber up a tree. A few blossoms shake themselves loose from the branches. They fall as slow and silent as snowflakes. A couple of old nails are stitched into the bark, and a perfect dent runs alongside them. There used to be a tree house here.

Soon I'm high enough to step across onto the roof. The tiles are still warm through my shoes. Carefully, I walk across to the window so I'm standing right above it. I crouch, grip the gutter and reach down.

The hinges are on the left, so I pull the right-hand side of the window. It's not locked. Second-floor windows rarely are. I tug it open, inch by inch, listening for any squeaks. Soon it's perpendicular to the wall.

I take a deep breath. Turn so my back is to the edge. Then I step backward off the roof.

For a split second I'm in free fall. Then I grab the gutter as I drop past, swinging off it like a kid on a jungle gym, and fly through the window.

I hit the floor softly, but not softly enough. I hear bedclothes shift suddenly, and a voice says, "What the fuck?"

I lunge toward the sound and slap a palm over Jim Epps's mouth before he's awake enough to scream. I hold him down against the bed. He tears at my hand, trying to pry it off, but he can't. I'm adjusting to the dark—I can see his eyes, huge and terrified.

"Make a sound and I'll kill you," I whisper.

He lets out a muffled groan.

I grab his hair with my other hand and pull. "Now, what did I just say?"

His legs flail under the blankets. I let go of his hair, grab the water bottle and unscrew the cap. I take my hand off his lips and pinch his nose shut. As he gasps for air, I shove the bottle into his mouth.

He chokes, gags, swallows, coughs, swallows some more. Tears spill from his eyes. I keep pouring until all the drugged water is gone. Then I cover his mouth again.

"Listen close, Jim," I say. "I'm gonna let go of you. If you scream, I'll throw you out the window and be gone by the time your parents hear the thump. But if you answer my questions, truthful and quiet-like, I'll go back out the window, and then, as far as you're concerned, I may as well have been a bad dream. Blink twice if you understand me."

I won't actually kill him. If he screams, I'll just climb out the window, and his parents will assume it was a nightmare, especially when he becomes sleepily incoherent ten minutes from now. But I really hope he believes me. I need to know what he knows.

He blinks twice.

I take my hand off his face. He doesn't make a sound. He just lies there, shaking.

"You remember me?" I ask.

He nods.

"Are you going to be more forthcoming this time?"

He nods again. He starts to cough, then chokes it back.

"Okay. Were you and Cameron close?"

"No." His voice is faint, croaky. But he's not lying.

I rephrase the question. "Was anyone at school closer to Cameron than you?"

He sniffles. "I don't think so."

"Did you ever go to his house?"

"No."

"You know anyone who did?"

"No."

"He tell you his family was rich?"

Epps looks surprised. "He didn't dress like he was rich."

"How'd he dress?"

He shrugs. "Geeky. Old clothes. Like his…" He looks away.

I lean forward. "Like his what?"

"Like his mom dressed him," he said.

Something's straining against its bonds at the edge of my consciousness. It's been growing since I did those riddles this afternoon, and now it's too big to ignore.

I voice the question I came here to ask. "Who's Cameron's girlfriend?"

Epps says nothing.

I grab his hand and wrap my palm around his index finger. I bend it back, like I'm going to break it off. "Wrong answer, Jim."

"Wait!" he hisses. "Just wait, okay?"

I don't let go of his finger.

"One time I saw Cameron's mom drop him off at school." Epps's lip is quivering. "It was early. No one else was around yet. She got out of the car and gave him a hug—*my* mom hasn't done that since elementary school. And I knew Cameron from band, so when he came up to me, I said I thought his mom was hot. Because she totally is. You should see her ass."

"Get to the point."

"I thought he'd get all defensive, but he just smiles and says, 'I know.' And then he *winks*."

The riddle is back in my head. *Who is my son's only sister's only husband's only mother-in-law's only husband's only mother-in-law?*

"Like he knew. Like he was hitting that, man. And I didn't know what to say, so I just stared at him, and then it's like he realizes what he's done, and he looks all nervous. He says, 'Bro, I'm just kidding. Jesus.' But I knew he wasn't, and he knew I knew it. And then he just walks off. He never talked to me again."

I hit the rewind switch inside my head, re-listen to the first conversation I had with Annette Hall. Her voice chills me now. *He looks so much like his daddy.*

I think of that big, luxurious house on top of the hill in the gated community. Private. Safe. Separated from the rest of the world and its rules.

I'm being punished, she said.

The Bible by her bedside was earmarked at Leviticus 18. *She is thy mother; thou shalt not uncover her nakedness.*

"You think Cameron's mother raped him?" I ask.

He shakes his head miserably. "I think he wanted it."

He's too young to understand that it's still rape. Cameron probably doesn't understand it either.

Epps's eyes are already becoming bleary as the drug kicks in. He's no longer capable of lying to me. "I never saw him look at a girl like he looked at her that day. And the way she hugged him—it wasn't a mom hug."

This must be why Epps thought we were from children's services. He figured Cameron had told someone else, and that they had informed the cops.

"You told anybody else about any of this?" I ask.

He shakes his head slowly. "I never... Nobody."

Soon he'll be too dopey to interrogate. And I still don't know who kidnapped Cameron. Knowing that his mother molested him doesn't help me. Did the kidnappers find out somehow and figure she was less likely to go to the police? Or did she have a fight with Cameron, kill him and fake the kidnapping, with the help of a male accomplice? At first I thought she seemed truthful, but that was before I saw her recite the ransom call. She's a hell of an actress. Most sociopaths are.

Or maybe it's a coincidence. Maybe the abuse has nothing to do with the kidnapping.

I slap Epps across the cheek. "Stay awake! Has anyone else been asking about Cameron?"

"Asking," he slurs. "Cam-ron."

Questions don't work so well on someone who's been roofied. They respond better to instructions.

I say, "Tell me who's been asking about Cameron."

His eyes are closed now. His breaths are slow and shallow. "Nobody," he says.

I grip his shoulders and shake him. "Who kidnapped Cameron Hall?"

Epps doesn't reply. I pry his eyelids open, but the pupils won't focus. He stares up through the ceiling like a sex doll. Lifelike, but not alive.

I wipe the tainted water off his face with his bedsheet, like a parent cleaning drool from a baby's chin. Tomorrow he'll be sick, but he won't remember a thing.

It's looking less and less likely that Cameron will be rescued and I'll be permitted to indulge my dark urges.

But there's a human being right in front of me, warm and defenseless.

The death row inmates suffocate before I get the chance to eat them. I haven't had a live victim in a long time.

I find my eyes tracing the road map of veins beneath Epps's skin. My hands peeling back his blanket.

A creak from downstairs. I freeze.

A footstep. The parents are coming.

I quickly roll my sleeve across the windowsill to smudge my fingerprints, then jump out. I swing off a dogwood branch, land in a crouch on the lawn and sprint out onto the street.

Somewhere behind me, the security light clicks off.

I get a block away before I collapse in the gutter, shaking with relief—but also with disappointment so strong it feels like grief.

Deep breaths. Inhale the damp blacktop, the congealed trash. Don't think about Epps. Don't think about his parents, who don't know they just saved his life.

Focus on the case. These FBI investigations feed my addiction, but they're also my only distraction from it.

I jog home, listening to my footfalls and my heartbeat. Occasionally a car sweeps past—an office cleaner returning home, a drinker kicked out at closing time, a waitress on her way to the diner.

I want to know what Thistle thinks about this new information, but I can't tell her about it. So I have a conversation with a hypothetical Thistle:

We should look at the mother again, she says. *If she was abusing Cameron, she might have killed him and made up a story about a ransom demand.*

You saw her, I say. *She was genuinely frightened.*

Maybe that was because she was being questioned by a pair of cops. Plus, she was an actress. She can fake it.

I'm not a cop.

Imaginary Thistle's teeth gleam as she smiles. *You're smart enough to be one,* she says. *And brave, breaking into that boy's house, even when you knew you could be caught. You're handsome too, in a rough sort of way.*

I abort the fantasy, not liking where it's going.

Johnson's van is gone when I arrive home. He'll be in the clubs, offering pills to twenty-one-year-old girls who don't know any better and thirty-year-old men who want to look and feel as young as them. No need to climb back in through my bedroom window. I walk in the front door and triple-lock it behind me.

The TV's playing an infomercial for an inflatable mattress that somehow doubles as a sofa. I flick it off, wash and dry the bottle in the kitchen, then head for my room. Now the only thing linking me to the doped-up teenager across town is the packet of pills in my pocket. With one missing, I can't put the pills back in Johnson's room. I'll toss them in a dumpster tomorrow.

I unlock my bedroom door. The room has been trashed.

The pile of Rubik's Cubes has been kicked over, the jigsaws shoved aside. The mattress has been slit open and propped up against the wall, exposing the floor. Johnson has been in here, looking for his drugs.

Riddles waltz around the floor in the breeze. The window is still open from when I sneaked out. I slam it closed and stare at the wreckage.

He won't rat me out to the cops for stealing his Rohypnol; somehow I doubt he has a convincing prescription. But he does have guns, friends and a brain so drug-warped that killing me might seem like a reasonable option. Coke makes you paranoid and steroids make you angry. He uses both.

I grab my other outfit—I have only two—and stuff it into a plastic bag. I might need to leave in a hurry. As usual, my bank account is empty. Every dollar I own is already in my pocket, since I've never trusted Johnson. My body is safer than any hiding place in my house. I have enough cash for a night or two at a cheap hotel, but after that I'll need something more permanent.

Wait. The window.

I'm pretty sure I closed it on my way out.

Did I? Yeah, I did.

Johnson wouldn't have come in through the window. He would have smashed through the lock on the door, and he would have been waiting to attack me when I came back.

Every house I've ever lived in has been broken into at least once. One robber even pissed on the carpet on his way out. But this time, the intruder trashed only *my* room. They were looking for something specific, something of mine.

I don't own anything worth taking. My possessions are limited to my clothes, my mattress and a ton of other people's puzzles, which are no good to anybody.

I kick idly at another riddle as it blows past my feet. There's a paradox here. Anyone who knows me knows that my possessions are worthless, but anyone who doesn't know me has no motive to break in.

Perhaps it's someone who only knows *of* me. A secret friend or relative of one of the people I ate, maybe. Or someone who remembers me from the group home.

Or the man in the baseball cap and sunglasses.

A finger of fear strokes my heart. While the SAC, Luzhin and I were all staring into the crowd looking for the kidnapper, he could've been looking right back at us. With his coat, hat and mask gone, he could have been anybody.

I was the only one not in an FBI windbreaker. He might have wondered who I was. But how would he find me here? And what do I have that he could possibly want? What could he *think* I have?

A riddle rustles past, taunting me.

Maybe he wasn't after something I owned at all. Maybe he was after *me*.

Wait. I already closed the window, and I'm not moving. What is disturbing the scraps of paper?

I whirl around, but not quickly enough. A damp cloth is shoved over my face, covering my mouth and nose and eyes. Ether, or chloroform. *Don't breathe.*

The slit mattress thumps to the floor, springs rattling. He must have been hiding behind it. I should have checked. Stupid.

My heart pounding, I try to peel the cloth off my face, but a hand grabs the corners of the cloth behind my skull and pulls it tight. My head is completely cocooned.

I swing a punch backward, but the angle makes it impossible; my fist doesn't hit anything. Then my attacker grips my elbow and yanks it back over my shoulder, holding my forearm against my bicep.

I cry out as a tendon snaps, and then, purely on reflex, I breathe in. The cloth sucks inward against my lips, and I'm overwhelmed by a pungent smell—like rotting fruit dipped in disinfectant.

My last thought is *Yep, that's ether, all right.*

And then I'm gone.

CHAPTER 8

WHEN IS A DOOR NOT A DOOR?

IT'S HOT, DARK AND CRAMPED. I'M CURLED UP like a baby in the womb, my chin pressed against my thighs. The electrical tape that binds my hands has made them heavy and swollen. Something dry and crackly is packed into my mouth, and I can't spit it out—tape is stretched across my lips. The air quivers and roars around me, as though a rocket is taking off with me inside.

Trunk. I'm in the trunk of a car.

I've barely finished that thought before my throat clenches up and my guts heave and suddenly I'm twisting desperately, pulling my feet over my wrists so I can reach the tape and tear it off and spit out the ball of paper before—

I puke sideways all over the floor. Sludgy chunks of Nigel Boyd splatter the carpet. The ether will leave me nauseated for hours. If I live that long.

I've been unconscious for longer than five minutes. Even a skilled kidnapper couldn't truss me up and get me into the trunk quicker than that. Less than twelve hours, though, since my stubble doesn't feel longer.

Twelve hours' driving could get me seven hundred miles out of Houston. But I'm sure the kidnapper is a local. Whatever he wants to do—execute me, torture me, hold me for ransom—he'll do it nearby. I don't have much time to come up with a plan.

If I scream for help, someone on the street or in another car might hear. But so would the kidnapper.

He doesn't know I'm awake and ungagged. Surprise is just about the only thing in my favor right now. I don't want to waste it.

Tape is harder to wriggle out of than rope. I start gnawing on the sticky plastic. Ether, vomit, electrical tape—my mouth is a symphony of flavors.

It takes me about ten minutes to realize that I won't be able to break the tape. It just compresses into a hard, thin cord. But the more I chew, the more it stretches. Soon it's slack enough to tear off, ripping out the hairs on my wrists.

I search for a weapon. A gun, a tire iron—even a phone book might do. But there's nothing in here.

The car swerves right and I lurch sideways, hitting my shoulder on the roof. I clench my teeth to choke back a grunt. Can't let him know I'm awake.

I roll toward the lock as the car goes over a bump and up a slope. We're slowing down. The brakes groan.

Wherever we're going, I think we just arrived.

I brace one arm under me, ready to spring out when the trunk opens. My other fist is clenched. If he's smart, he'll open the trunk with the remote, standing at a safe distance with a gun in his hand. But if he lifts the lid from up close, expecting to find me sleeping and bound, I'll crack his skull.

The engine rumbles to a stop. I hear the door open. The car tilts as the driver's weight is lifted. The door closes again. I listen for footsteps, but they're muffled by the metal.

I'm blinking sweat out of my eyes. I haven't drawn breath since the car stopped moving.

Come on, pal. I'm just a helpless, sleepy, trussed-up turkey. Come and get me.

Still no audible footsteps. Every passing second makes it less likely that he will be unprepared.

I wait. This is going to be the strongest punch of my life.

He waits too. Hoping I'll get tired? Hoping I'll go back to sleep? Maybe he's just checking the safety is off on his gun.

Five minutes pass. Ten.

Maybe he's gone. Maybe the plan is to leave me in the trunk all night, suffocate me. He could leave me here all day tomorrow too. The midday heat would finish me off.

Fifteen minutes now.

Screw this. I'm coming out.

Most trunks have a release catch on the inside to stop kids from getting themselves killed in their parents' cars. I fumble around in the darkness and discover that this one doesn't. I'll have to get out the old-fashioned way.

I press my foot against the roof, right near the lock. Trunks are designed to take a lot of pressure from the outside, but from within, they're fragile. The metal creaks, the hinges groan and the lock cracks. I kick the trunk open and sit up, arms raised.

No one is here.

The car is parked near the middle of an empty lot. A chain-link fence stands to my right, crawled under so many times that the bottom is twisted and broken. On my left is a graffiti-scarred warehouse sitting in a halo of broken glass.

I'm somewhere in Houston's industrial district. No one of sound mind comes here at night. A sex worker will throw herself out of a moving car if the driver takes an exit toward here. I could shout until I was hoarse and nobody but the kidnapper would come running.

I climb out of the trunk, close it softly and crouch beside the sedan. The car is empty, so he must be in the warehouse. I peep in the driver's-side window. The keys are not in the ignition.

I could run. I might get away. But the kidnapper would still know where I live, and I don't even know what he looks like. If Luzhin can't afford police protection for witnesses against Charlie Warner, he isn't going to fork out for a scum-bag like me.

I emerge from behind the car and sneak toward the ware-house, staying low. The roller door is slightly open. I creep up and stand near the gap, listening.

Silence inside. This could be his hideout, and he's gone to sleep somewhere within. Or he might have seen me coming and be waiting.

I take a deep breath and step through the gap.

No bullet hits my chest. No lead pipe swings out of the darkness and slams into my nose. So far, so good.

There's just as much broken glass on the floor inside as out. I don't know where he is, and he probably doesn't know where I am. A crunching footstep could shift that situation in his favor.

I can't see anything, so I close my eyes. The air currents and the minute echoes of distant traffic give me a sense of enormous space. The roof feels high—I don't think there's a second floor. And the far wall seems to be a long way away, so the warehouse probably isn't divided into separate rooms. There are no barriers to separate me from the kidnapper.

I build a mental map of the warehouse and walk through it with my arms outstretched, ready to attack if I bump into him. I can't shake the fear that he's watching me through night-vision goggles, chuckling to himself at the clumsy green apparition.

A sudden intake of breath to my left.

Could have been a stifled sneeze, could have been some-one lifting something heavy. Could have been my imagina-tion. Now that the echoes are gone, there's no proof I ever heard him.

Guessing he'll expect me to head toward the noise, I back away. Sensing a wall behind me, I reach out to touch it. Cor-rugated iron, with a power cable running along it.

I follow the cable along the wall. Rivets hold it in place every three feet or so. Soon I reach a light switch. I turn to face the kidnapper, or where I think I heard him, and descend into a sprinter's crouch. He'll be dazzled by the lights for a second or two at the most. I'll have to move fast.

I flick the switch.

Nothing happens.

I'm already wondering whether he heard the click and if that will lure him over here when suddenly the lights *do* come on—old fluorescent bulbs that take a few seconds to warm up. I run, fist raised, ready to exploit his confusion—

But no one is here. Just roaches scratching across the walls and trash blowing around the floor. Machine parts, so rusted and broken that their purpose is opaque, have been swept to the sides of the warehouse. Mold-slimed jars are stacked in one corner.

Correction. Someone *is* here. Naked, facedown on a stained mattress, one hand cuffed to a pipe on the wall. An ugly fence of stitches sits just above his ass.

He's missing a kidney.

It's like a present. A nude, helpless, wounded, breathing gift, just for me. I want to grab his scrawny arms and twist them off, popping the joints and leaving his arteries trailing from his shoulders like spaghetti.

Instead, I roll the kid over and slap a hand over his mouth. His eyes flutter open.

"Stay quiet," I whisper.

He stares at me with growing terror. He looks worse than his picture—thinner, with less color in his face. But for a kid who's just had a nephrectomy with no anesthetic, he looks pretty good.

"I don't know how far he's gone," I say. "We gotta be real quiet. Okay?"

He nods. I take my hand off his face.

"You're Cameron Hall, right?"

He hesitates and then nods again.

"I'm Timothy Blake," I say. "I'm here to help you. Where's the handcuff key?"

"He keeps it on him." His voice is dry, croaky.

I don't have the tools to pick the lock or a phone to call the cops. A small office with empty window frames has been constructed near the roller door. Maybe I can use something in there to cut the chain. I stand up.

"Don't leave me!"

"I'm just looking for something to get the cuff off," I say. "Stay quiet."

The boy bites his lip.

I move over to the office. The door is locked, so I climb in through one of the windows and start opening drawers.

The drawers are empty of everything except cobwebs and cigarette butts. The place looks like anything useful would have been looted long ago.

A sledgehammer, too heavy to steal easily, leans against the wall. Maybe I can smash the chain. But that'll be loud.

An engine rumbles outside.

I freeze, listening. The car I arrived in pulls slowly out of the lot. The kidnapper must have picked something up from around the back of the warehouse, and now he's leaving again. But when he realizes I'm not in the trunk, he'll hightail it back here. We may not have much time.

I drag the sledgehammer over to Cameron, leaving a trail of lime dust. "Hold still," I tell him.

I raise the hammer and let it fall. *Thunk.* The chain looks unaffected.

I lift the hammer higher and bring it down harder. The metal looks scratched, but the damage is only cosmetic.

I hit the chain a few more times and succeed in denting

it—but then I notice that the head of the hammer is dented almost as much.

I can't leave Cameron here. By the time I've found a pay phone, the kidnapper will have come back and moved him. But I can't get him out of the cuffs either. The metal is stronger than the hammer.

I swing the sledge against the pipe, trying to crack it. But the way the impact thrums up my arms tells me that it's not going to work; the pipe is too solid. How can I get him out of here?

I look at Cameron's hand, limp and thin on the floor. An idea is taking shape.

I push a couple of pills out of the Rohypnol packet and give them to Cameron. "Take these."

"Why?"

"Because this is going to hurt."

He looks up at the sledgehammer, then down at his cuffed hand. "Oh shit," he says. "No way, man!"

"Sorry," I say, meaning it. "But it's the only way."

"No! Don't!"

"Take the goddamn pills!"

"No way!"

I raise the hammer, and he changes his mind immediately. The tablets vanish down his throat faster than a mouse when a cat shows up. I lower the hammer again. The drugs will need a minute to kick in.

I've been knocked out and tied up, I've vomited and I've drugged two teenage boys. Even by my standards, this is a bad night out.

"Don't break my hand, mister," he says. "Please."

"Bite down on the mattress, Cameron."

"Cameron," he repeats. His voice is already blurred and distant. He weighs less than Epps, and the double dose is taking its toll. "Cameron's not…"

"Bite the mattress."

He chews at the foam sleepily, like a grazing cow. Every passing second brings the kidnapper closer.

I slam the hammer down on Cameron's hand. It hits him at the base of the thumb, and there's a cruel snap as the bones splinter beneath the skin. He moans.

"Nearly over now," I tell him. Then I take his hand and squeeze it so the cuff will slide over it. It's like handling a water balloon filled with broken glass.

"Uhh-oow," he mumbles.

"Don't worry. We'll be out of here soon."

Finally the cuff is loose. I say, "Okay, stand up," because Rohypnol makes people obedient, and I'm an optimist at heart. But Cameron doesn't move.

I grab him under the armpits, haul him to his feet and throw him over my shoulder like a rolled-up rug. He doesn't weigh much—he's a pound or two lighter than a kid with two kidneys, just for starters. But I won't be able to run with him on top of me. If the kidnapper sees us, I'll have to leave Cameron behind, or die by his side.

I carry him to the roller door and peek out. The night is dark and silent and hopefully empty.

It's harder than before to avoid the noisy shards of broken glass as I carry Cameron through the parking lot. My eyes are still adjusted to the light inside the warehouse, which I've just realized I left on. Too late to go back now. Got to keep moving.

Gritting my teeth, I lug Cameron along the fence line until I find the driveway, then carry him out to the road. The lights of the city are to my left, so I turn that way, starting the long trek to civilization.

After walking for about ten minutes, it occurs to me that when the kidnapper comes back, there's a good chance he'll be coming up this very road, and he'll see me carrying his meal ticket away. So I turn at a narrow alley between two half-assembled buildings and then turn again at the other end.

The howl of a coywolf carries on the breeze. Hunting and deforestation has left wolves nearly extinct in Texas, but coyotes are more adaptable. They have taken over the harsh new terrain and bred with the survivors. Coywolves are bigger than coyotes and not as shy as wolves.

Not many people get mauled by them. But not many people are running long distances in the middle of the night. Getting eaten by a wild animal would be an oddly fitting end for me. Cameron doesn't deserve it, though.

It takes an hour and a half to jog back to the city. I don't see another soul the whole time. I'm so tired. I've walked or run at least sixteen miles today, six of them with a teenage boy on my back. My calf muscles burn. My joints creak. Every step triggers a throb of pain in my swollen feet.

An emergency station stands up ahead like a computer in sleep mode, dull lights glowing all around it. Two fire engines loom behind big windows, waiting for someone to dial 911. Ambulances are parked in the dark beyond. No cop cars— those are dispatched from the police precinct.

I stagger up to the windows and slap a palm on the glass. "Hey!"

No response. I hit the glass harder. I'm sweaty, with dried puke on my face. Cameron is still limp and naked, his stitches exposed, his broken fingers swollen up like a giant foam hand at the Super Bowl. To anyone watching, we would look like zombies.

A firefighter shuffles out of the darkness inside. Her face goes from half-asleep to wide-awake in a split second. She stares at me like I'm an elephant who escaped from the zoo.

"What happened?" she asks. "What's going on?"

"Call the fucking FBI," I gasp.

Then my legs buckle under me and I hit the concrete.

CHAPTER 9

**A PERCHING BARREL, FILLED WITH MEAT,
TAKES HITS FROM LEAPS AND DIVES.
LOOK INSIDE, BUT DO NOT EAT—
THE MEAT IN THERE IS STILL ALIVE!
WHAT IS IT?**

I'M TELLING MY STORY FOR THE FIFTH TIME.

The first was to some beat cops who showed up at the emergency station. They were understandably suspicious. I looked more like an abductor than an abductee. While paramedics loaded Cameron into an ambulance, they put me in the back of their squad car—handcuffed—and drove me to their precinct.

They put me in an interview room that looked and smelled like a prison cell, except a cell would have a bed at least. Several times they asked if I wanted a lawyer. They ignored me when I asked which hospital Cameron had been taken to.

Eventually they figured out I was telling some version of the truth, so they called the FBI. The second time I told my story was to a balding, wet-eyed agent named Butten, who seemed less concerned with Cameron's well-being and more with the ass-kicking he would get from Luzhin for waking him up. It took me fifteen minutes to convince Butten to make the call—or maybe he just thought 4:20 a.m. was a more acceptable hour than 4:05.

The third time was to Luzhin himself, who demanded to speak to me as soon as Butten told him my name. He spent twenty minutes grilling me about what I'd seen at the warehouse. Where was it? How far did I have to drive to get there? Did I get a better look at the kidnapper? Might anyone else have seen him at my house? Did I hear his voice? What kind of car was I moved in? Did I remember the license plate? I gave it to him, and he hung up without saying goodbye.

The fourth was to a trauma counselor, who asked me the same questions, but in a more soothing tone of voice. He was a tall, hairy-armed guy who hung his head low like a stegosaurus. I tried to look shaken, as a normal person would be. It wasn't hard, since counselors and psychologists scare me. I worry that my face or voice will remind them of the serial killers they studied at college.

When the counselor was done with me, I asked him where Cameron had been taken. After expressing his shock that no one had told me already, he said Cameron was at Park Plaza Hospital. I hitched a ride there with Butten, whose grumbling stopped me from dozing off in the passenger seat. When he dropped me off, I stumbled into the waiting room and found Reese Thistle swearing at a coffee machine.

"Cream and three sugars, thanks," I grunted.

"Blake!" She spun around and opened her arms as if to hug me. Then she changed her mind and clasped my shoulder with one hand instead. "You okay? What the hell happened?"

That was when I collapsed onto a sofa that wasn't as soft as it looked and started recounting the events of the evening for the fifth time.

Cops ask the same questions repeatedly for a few reasons. One is so the initial investigator's report doesn't bias subsequent lines of questioning—everyone on the case gets the chance to form their own opinions. The other is to check for inconsistencies, see if a witness is telling the truth. Since I'm lying my ass off, that's the part that concerns me.

"How was Cameron's demeanor when you found him?" Thistle asks as she hands over my coffee.

I take a sip and swill it around inside my mouth before swallowing it. "Naked and unconscious."

I can't admit I talked to him. When his tox screen comes back with traces of Rohypnol, I want the kidnapper to be blamed. Hopefully Cameron won't remember enough to contradict that.

"Oh, right," she says. "Well, we'll be able to question him soon. The doctors have him on some kind of drip that's supposed to help wake him up. What about you? How are you feeling?"

"I'm okay."

"You don't look okay. You're limping, and favoring one arm. Your eyes are bloodshot. Have you slept?"

"Sure. The kidnapper knocked me out."

"You should get a doctor to take a look at you."

"I don't like doctors. Anyway, I want to talk to Cameron when he's conscious."

"It's over, Blake," she says. "You've done your job."

"For all we know, the kidnapper is choosing another victim as we speak."

"We have an APB out on his license plate."

"Doesn't matter. It was a stolen car."

"How do you know?"

It was the kind of car that I would steal. Old but common. Cheap but not distinctively so. "Just a feeling," I say.

Thistle digs a hair tie out of her bag and starts pulling her hair into a ponytail. I feel a weird thrill at the realization that she hasn't finished getting dressed.

"Either way," she says, "Luzhin brought you in to find the kid, and you've done that. We'll take it from here. What do you think happened to Cameron's hand?"

"There was no key to the cuffs," I say. "And I couldn't just leave him there."

"So you did…what, exactly?"

"I broke his bones with a sledgehammer."

She gapes. "Christ!"

I say, "There was no other way."

"I know, I'm just— Most people wouldn't have done that."

"How would most people have got him out?"

"They wouldn't have. They'd have left him."

She's looking at me with something resembling respect. It makes me uncomfortable.

"And he didn't wake up?" she says. "Even when you were smashing his hand in?"

I shrug. "I tried to wake him first. I assume he'd been drugged with something."

"Well, the doctor says he'll be playing the trumpet again in no time."

"And by no time, you mean…"

"Three months, give or take. But he couldn't play it for at least a month even if you hadn't smashed his hand, because of the missing kidney. Puts too much stress on the diaphragm, or something."

"Plus, he'd be dead, possibly."

"Good point."

There's a pause.

"Well," she says, "you did real well. You found him less than eighteen hours after they put you on the case."

"Sixteen. But I only found him by getting kidnapped myself. I doubt they'll give me a medal."

She puts her hand on my shoulder. "You got the kid—and yourself—out of there in one piece. That's what counts."

"Three pieces," I say. "Me, him and his kidney."

She laughs before she can stop herself. Richmond, my old babysitter, never laughed at my jokes. I think he found me morbid.

We're approached by someone who looks just old enough

to be a doctor, but not old enough to be one whose judgment I would trust. "Cameron's regained consciousness," he says.

"Can we talk to him?" Thistle asks.

He shakes his head. "Not without parental consent. He's a minor."

"Can you tell us if he's okay?"

"No sign of internal bleeding. Whoever removed the kidney did a damn fine job, and the surgical scar has healed right quick. You said the surgery was less than forty-eight hours ago?"

"Less than thirty-six," Thistle says.

"Incredible. I've never seen a wound heal that fast. The kid's Wolverine, basically. Anyway, he wants to see you."

"You just said—"

"Not you, I'm afraid." He points at me. "Just you. You're the guy who saved him, right?"

I feel a stab of unease. How much does Cameron remember? What if whatever the doctors injected him with reversed the memory-loss effects of the Rohypnol?

Thistle sighs. "Go on, then. I'll be here."

I leave her sitting on the sofa and follow the doctor through the maze of disinfectant-scented halls. Thick doors, shatter-proof glass, hard neon lights. I'm right at home. Park Plaza Hospital resembles the Death House, and not just on the surface. Many of the people here will die before they leave, gurneys under them, catheters in their arms.

The doctor leads me to a private ward in the north wing. There's a uniform outside the door. He says, "Morning."

The doctor holds up his ID.

The uniform looks disappointed that we're not pausing to chat. It's almost 6:00 a.m.—injured drunks have stopped coming in, visiting hours haven't started yet, the patients are all asleep, the nurses are gliding around silently and invisibly.

There's no one for him to talk to, nothing to keep him awake. But he waves us through.

Cameron's head is slumped back against the pillow. An oxygen mask smothers his face. His hand is splinted and bandaged. A pulse monitor is perched on his fingertip like a thimble. His eyes are open, rolling from side to side. They settle on me.

I wait, tense. Does he recognize me?

The doctor says, "Cameron? This is Mr. Blake. The guy you asked for."

"Oh," Cameron says.

There's a pause.

"Thanks," he adds.

Whatever drug they put him on, it's not helping much.

"Can you…" He lifts a hand slowly, carefully, and pushes his mask up onto his head. "Can you give me a minute with Mr. Blake? Alone?"

The doctor looks at me and says, "Sure. But you gotta keep this on, okay?"

He puts the mask back on Cameron's face. "Just hit the call button if you need me," he says, more to me than to Cameron. Then he leaves.

"So I guess I owe you a thank-you," Cameron says, but he doesn't sound sure.

Now that the doctor's gone, I can't think of a reason not to just ask. "How much do you remember?"

"From the kidnapping?"

"From the rescue."

"Rescue?" he repeats. "Nothing."

I can't tell if he's lying. Maybe he really doesn't remember anything. Or maybe he just wants me to think so, because he realizes how dangerous I am—because he remembers everything.

I say, "Sorry about your hand."

He stares down at the cast. "Can't feel it. What happened?"

"You were handcuffed. I couldn't find the key."

"Oh." He still looks confused, but not confused enough to ask for more details. "So you're a cop?"

"No. But I work with the FBI sometimes."

He looks like he's struggling with a tough decision, like he doesn't know whether to trust me or not. Maybe to his conscious mind I'm a stranger, but to his subconscious, I'm a sledgehammer-wielding demon.

"Mr. Blake," he says, "I need—"

Footsteps behind me. A voice. "Cameron?"

I turn around. It's Annette Hall, tears on her cheeks, looking so vulnerable you could forget she's a racist child molester.

"It's me," she says. "Your mother."

That strikes me as strange—does she think he won't recognize her? But he reacts the same way. "Mom?" Like he's not sure.

She approaches him like a lover just returned after years abroad, not sure where she stands. She places a hand on his head and says, "I'm so glad you're okay."

I can't tell anyone what I know about Cameron and his mother, because then I'd have to explain how I know it. Even if I did, what good would come of it? He'd grow up in foster care like I did, but worse, thanks to the journalists and their cameras. KIDNAP VICTIM'S MOTHER CHARGED WITH RAPE—no way would the media leave such good clickbait alone. And I'd find myself behind bars. FBI CONSULTANT DRUGGED VICTIM'S FRIEND.

Trying to help people gets you shot at and stranded in the middle of nowhere while someone re-steals your car. Sorry, Cameron. I have my own problems.

But there's a dark, guilty ache in my guts. Maybe the next time Cameron goes missing, we *will* find him buried in the backyard. Eleven percent of murder victims are killed by family members, and twenty-three percent are killed by their lovers. Annette Hall is both.

Hall turns to face me. "Did you want something?" Her voice wobbles angrily.

Not the thank-you I expected. I guess the damage I did to her son's hand outweighs the saving of the rest of him.

"No," I say, and leave.

Thirty-six hours later I'm in the Huntsville prison parking lot. Huntsville is known as the Walls, which are its most distinctive feature. They're made of bricks as red as blood and they stretch all the way up to the sky, where bored guards sit in distant watchtowers cradling assault rifles.

When Woodstock eventually emerges through the double doors of the Death House, he's struggling to push the gurney. The dead guy was six foot five and two hundred and twenty pounds. It took four minutes for the suxamethonium to take effect, immobilizing his limbs and cutting off his air supply.

It feels like I'm paralyzed too. I keep forgetting to breathe. My heart is jumping. I'm always twitchy when I'm about to get my reward.

The dead man came over here from Tanzania in 1997 and moved into a quiet suburb in Austin, where his neighbors, if you'd asked them at the time, would have told you he was a polite, funny guy who mostly kept to himself. And he was.

If you asked those same neighbors now, they'd say they always knew there was something a bit off about him, and that they found him creepy at times. They didn't, but nobody wants to believe that a guy who was dismembering and eating people in his basement could go to the local market and smile and wave and no one would suspect a thing.

Anyone who lives in a big city has walked past at least one murderer. And they didn't get chills. They didn't look twice. They kept walking.

I've never eaten a cannibal before. I'll have to be extra careful to avoid the brain and the pituitary gland, which could give me kuru—the human equivalent of mad cow disease. At least his last physical said he didn't have HIV or hepatitis.

The dead man was christened "The Witch Doctor" by Fox News after it came out that he was using the body parts of albino people in a potion that was supposed to bring good luck. Doesn't look like it worked.

Woodstock gives me the paperwork. I'll be handing the same papers back to him, unchanged, when I return in a couple of hours. It's a receipt from the disposal center, supposedly proving that I dropped off a body there. Luzhin must have someone working for him at the other end, but I've never met them.

Woodstock helps me load the gurney into the van. Through the body bag, I can feel that the Witch Doctor's body is still warm. If I start eating soon, I can pretend he's still alive. It took about half an hour for Boyd's body to cool after his suffocation, but he was smaller.

Woodstock and I are both puffing by the time the dead body is in the van.

"He took a long time to go down," I say.

"Shut up," Woodstock says, looking around for someone who might overhear us. Then he remembers who he's talking to, and looks scared.

"Sorry," he says. "I gotta go."

He runs back into the Death House. I get in the van and drive it through the prison gates. The guards sweep a mirror underneath to check that no escaped prisoners are clinging to the underside. They're supposed to check inside too, but they don't bother.

I take 11th Street toward the I-45. Yesterday I went to Walmart and bought two big plastic tubs with airtight lids and stole a 1983 Chevrolet Malibu from the parking lot. I hid the tubs in a forest just off the interstate, halfway between here and Houston. I'll be there in half an hour. Then I'll eat for about forty-five minutes before I drive the empty van back, return the dummy paperwork to the prison, pick up the Malibu from the Huntsville lot and drive it back to pick up the tubs.

I check the side mirrors. It doesn't look like I'm being followed. I never have been so far, but it's hard to shake the feeling that someday Luzhin or Woodstock will turn on me.

I look in the rearview mirror just in time to see the body bag sit upright.

"Motherfucker!" I slam my foot on the brake. The van skids off the road and bumps across the dirt toward a ditch. A strap comes loose, and the body bag rolls off the gurney. It slams into the wall, and the Witch Doctor makes a muffled grunt.

The van stops just in time to avoid toppling into the ditch. I scramble out of my seat into the back of the van, my heart racing.

The Witch Doctor is trying to tear open the body bag from inside. The material is thin, but the paralytic is making him clumsy. Woodstock must not have used enough of the poison for a man of this size. He might be brain damaged, but he's very much alive.

I try to grab him. He punches me through the bag—a blow to my ribs that leaves me wheezing. One of his kicking feet hits the handle of the back door. It pops open and he flops out onto the grass.

He screams something that sounds like "Uniokoe!" I don't know if it's a Tanzanian swearword or a plea for mercy or what. I leap out of the van and land on top of him. Still wrapped in the bag, he pushes me off and rolls sideways into the ditch.

Approaching headlights illuminate the open van. Someone is coming.

I pray that the car won't stop. It's a red Cadillac Escalade with a mud-spattered bumper. The brakes squeak as it approaches.

I look down at the ditch. The Tanzanian is out of the driver's sight line, but not out of earshot.

The side window of the Escalade rolls down to reveal an apple-cheeked white guy in a trucker cap. He flashes a friendly smile.

"You need help?" he asks.

I force a laugh, hoping the Witch Doctor will stay silent at the bottom of the ditch. "No, thanks, pal. Just stretching my legs."

"Long drive?"

"All the way from Little Rock." It's a dumb lie—now he probably thinks I'm headed for the Mexican border. "Almost home, though," I add. "I'm fine."

"All right, then." He tips his hat. "You stay safe now." He closes the window and zooms back onto the highway.

I exhale. That was too close. As soon as he's out of sight, I jump down into the ditch.

The Witch Doctor is gone. The empty body bag lies trampled in the mud.

"Shit, shit, shit." I look around. He's not anywhere along the shoulder of the highway, which means he ran into the forest.

I give chase. I can't see him, but I can make myself think like him. He didn't try to flag down a car, because he doesn't want to go back to Huntsville. So his plan is to hide. He'll run for a while, heading for lower ground where the trees are thickest, and then, when he thinks he's lost me, he'll sneak into the darkest shadows he can find and stay there.

I can't let him get away. Someone will eventually find him and realize who he is. That will lead them to Woodstock, who will turn me in. Then it'll be me at the Death House getting the needle.

I run deeper and deeper into the woods. Moths buzz around me. Leaves scrape my face. The smell of rotting vegetation is thick in the air.

Suddenly I see the Tanzanian. Stumbling down the hill, one leg dragging. He's naked except for his tighty-whities, which are clearly visible in the dark.

I try to sneak up on him, but he hears me coming and turns. His eyes are wide with terror.

"Is this hell?" he asks.

"It's Texas," I say.

Recognition flashes across his face. He must have noticed me behind the glass at his execution. He snatches up a rock and hurls it at my head.

I catch the rock. It's big and sharp—the impact jars my wrist. I hurl it right back at him, and it hits him in the throat. His Adam's apple makes a crunching noise and he falls over backward, gurgling.

It's a fatal blow. I can hear the blood crackling in his lungs. But I don't wait for it to kill him. I pick up the rock and hit him again, hard. His skull caves in and he goes limp.

The adrenaline seeps away. I fall onto my hands and knees, exhausted. Invisible insects chitter in the gloom around me. The moon peeks between the trees. I can hear the distant highway.

I'm miles away from my plastic tubs. The Tanzanian is too heavy to carry back to the van in one piece, and I don't have my hacksaw with me. I'll have to go back to the van, drive to the tubs, collect them and bring them back here.

Hard work on an empty stomach. I peel off my clothes so they don't get blood on them, and then I lick my lips and get started.

CHAPTER 10

I'M A BUTCHER.
I'M SIX FEET TALL, WITH SIZE NINE SHOES.
WHAT DO I WEIGH?

I WAKE UP ON THE COUCH. NOT LYING DOWN. Sitting.

This sometimes happens. At age twenty-one, I was fired. A couple weeks later I couldn't make rent. I left without complaint when the real estate agent's letter told me to and slept on a squeaky mattress in a roadside motel for a few nights before I couldn't afford that either. The homeless shelters were full, and I wasn't yet ready to sleep on the sidewalk. I felt sure that things would pick up before it came to that. Someone would hire me. I'd find another place to live. Things would balance out again.

That's why they call it a death spiral, not a death slope or a death line—or even a death row. The trajectory is curved, which means if you look only in the direction you're facing, you won't see where you're actually going.

I caught the overnight Greyhound to Dallas, because the bus was cheaper than a motel. I slept in my seat, or tried to. The next night, I caught the same bus back. By the third journey, I had no trouble sleeping while sitting upright—I was too tired not to.

During the day, I sat on fiberglass chairs in corridors, ten other desperate people on either side of me. We'd all somehow lost our jobs when the housing market collapsed, even though none of us worked in real estate. Washington rescued the banks, but not us.

When my name was called, I'd get up and step into the silence of the office, where I told the HR manager or recruitment officer or whoever that I hadn't finished high school and that my only job experience was in fast food, but that I was loyal and polite and eager to work.

Every day, they said they'd let me know.

After the sixth bus ride, I ran out of money. The following night I slept on the dead grass under an overpass as cars rumbled past overhead. After those six nights on the bus, the engine noise didn't keep me awake.

And now I sleepwalk. I climb from my bed, unlock my bedroom door and trudge through my house to the couch. Hours later, I wake up to find myself sitting there with my hands in my lap, as though I'm on a bus.

I check that the front door is still locked and the curtains are closed. My bedroom is a mess, but there's no sign that the kidnapper has been back, or that Johnson has been snooping around.

The blood stuck to my teeth brings back memories of last night. The terror on the Witch Doctor's face. The sound of his skull cracking.

I used to feel guilty. After eating my first inmate, I punished myself with a brick, which didn't leave me with a clear conscience—just a crooked toe.

Guilt fades. Unfortunately, so does satisfaction. I ate last night until I was fit to burst, and already I'm hungry again.

You're losing control. The thought flits across my mind like a small bird before I push it away.

Five days later the sun is grilling me from the top down, the sidewalk hot under my feet, when I see it. A letter-size sheet of paper stapled to a telephone pole with **HAVE U SEEN**

THIS BOY??? scrawled on it, and a phone number. There are posters like this all over Houston, probably all over the world, but something about this one stops me mid-step.

The photo is a cheap black-and-white Xerox of a teenage boy, white, with dark eyes and blond hair. It's a goofy photo—he's at a party with a handful of popcorn halfway to his mouth, surprised to see the camera.

He looks just like Cameron Hall.

I'd assume they were brothers, or even the same person, except that Cameron is an only child and nobody put up posters like that when he went missing. So who is this?

It's not an unbelievable coincidence. If every person in Houston was a half-inch jigsaw piece, the resulting puzzle would be more than sixty feet wide and sixty feet deep. Almost eight thousand pieces would represent blond, dark-eyed teenage boys.

But the photograph looks so much like him. Maybe his kidnapping wasn't about the money at all. Perhaps the ransom demand was just a smoke screen, and the real motive was more sinister. Now that Cameron has escaped, the kidnapper has found a new plaything—one who fits his type.

Only half the Witch Doctor is left in the freezer. I'm ready for a new case.

I tear the poster off the pole, turn around and jog toward the FBI office.

I'm on the couch outside the director's office, my civilian consultant lanyard around my neck, holding the torn piece of paper and listening to Luzhin's boss from Washington yell at him.

"Who the fuck said you could go on TV and ask for donations?" the boss roars.

"It worked," Luzhin says. "We got more than fifty grand

in one night. Heaps of cash donated to field offices, plenty of credit card donations over the phone—"

"I don't care if Bono showed up and did a concert. The FBI isn't a goddamn charity."

The boss has flown down here just to have this shouting match. I think he enjoys it. Maybe once you've done enough press conferences, you get a thrill out of saying what you actually think.

"I had no choice! We didn't have the resources to—"

"That's the point, shithead. When the FBI's Houston Field Office director tells the media that the Bureau doesn't have the money to find missing kids, CNN asks why the FBI isn't better funded. Someone suggests increasing the budget, someone else says that'll lead to a tax hike and suddenly the public says, *Hold your horses—I want kidnapped kids found, but not if it means paying more taxes!* And God help us if someone asks Trump what he thinks. I have no clue what he'll say, but whatever it is, it'll become my problem."

"Are you suggesting I should have let that kid die, just to help out you and your friends in Washington?"

"The kid's not dead, and it has nothing to do with your little stunt. You found him without spending a dime!"

"Blake!" Agent Thistle says.

I look up, wondering how obvious my eavesdropping was. But Thistle is smiling. She hasn't caught me.

"Howdy," I say.

"How are you holding up?" She sits down next to me. "You sleeping?"

For a second I worry that I called her while sleepwalking. "Not well."

"It's hard, after some asshole's been in your house."

Actually, I've been kind of hoping the kidnapper might come back. Next time I'll be ready. It'll be like a guilt-free delivery of takeout.

I don't like being this close to Thistle. Not just because she's attractive, but because she seems to trust me now. I prefer it when people keep their distance. If the other person's guard is up, I don't have to worry so much about my own.

"What about you?" I ask. "How you doing?"

Thistle raises a stack of papers with one hand and a cup of instant coffee with the other. "Living the dream," she says. "My neck's better. I'm cleared for active duty."

"Great."

There's a pause.

"How's Cameron?" I ask. "Heard anything?"

"With his mama. They both seem pretty shook up, but they'll be all right. It's all over for them, unless we catch the guy and Cameron has to ID him. So what brings you in?" She sees the bit of paper in my hand. "Huh. That looks a bit like—"

"Yeah."

"So Luzhin called you in?"

"No. I came to ask why he hadn't."

Thistle stares at me. "Probably because a week ago you got drugged and locked in a car trunk, then had to carry a hostage five miles."

"Six. So what?"

What I mean is, Luzhin won't care what I've been through. He withholds or gives me cases based on how much he needs my help, nothing else. But I can tell by the look on Thistle's face that she's misunderstood.

"That's incredible," she says. "You're not going to let a single child down. Not on your watch, huh?"

I shrug. She looks even more impressed by my modesty.

"Well, you just give me a call if you need anything. I'll do whatever I can."

That could be very useful. Luzhin does things for me, but being aware of what I am, he's suspicious when I ask. Having someone to call on who thinks I'm selfless could have all kinds of benefits. "Thanks."

"No problem. Don't hesitate to ask either. My ex-husband, he—"

She winces. I've seen that expression on other people's faces. It's the *I promised myself I wouldn't mention my ex* look.

"You ever been married, Blake?" she asks abruptly.

I stifle a laugh. "Uh, no. Your ex—he didn't like asking for help?"

"Not him, me. He had money, and I didn't. After the divorce, he offered me alimony, but I was too proud—and I've had plenty of opportunities to regret that."

Standing up, she says, "Anyway, the point is, don't be proud." She points at the picture. "You get stuck on this one, you call me."

"I'll do that," I say.

"I should get back to work. See you, Blake."

"See you."

She disappears, with only a quick glance back.

Luzhin's boss is still shouting. "As of right now, you no longer take donations. This office is going to solve every case assigned to it without spending a penny more than it gets from Washington, or your head is on the chopping block."

"If I had a dollar for every time you said that," Luzhin says, "I'd have more than the FBI's annual budget."

"I fucking mean it. If you want to keep your job—and if you want to be able to find another one when you leave—you'd better do as you're told."

"When I *leave*? I built this department!"

"That doesn't mean you own it, asshole," the boss says. "It belongs to Uncle Sam."

With that, Luzhin's boss storms out, adjusting his tie. I can hardly see the knot under his flabby neck. He doesn't notice me staring as I imagine ripping out his hamstrings and chewing off the fatty tissue.

I catch the office door before it closes and slip inside. Luzhin raises an eyebrow.

"Blake!" he says. "How good to see you again so soon."

His tone is convincing, but his expression lets him down. He looks terrible. Bags under his eyes, his hair hastily combed. With Washington on his back and Charlie Warner's trial looming, he probably isn't getting much rest.

I shut the door.

"What are you doing here?" he says.

I don't waste time. "You got a problem. There's a serial rapist in town."

He scratches his sideburns. "Hundreds, probably. Not my jurisdiction."

I hold up the poster, and he stares at it for a long time.

"Where did you get that?" he asks finally.

"Telephone pole on Main Street. Look familiar?"

He doesn't reply, just keeps staring.

"We were wrong about Hall's kidnapping," I say. "The motive was sexual. The money was only incidental. And now that Cameron's free, the perp has found a replacement."

Luzhin doesn't look convinced. "Cameron was fully examined at the hospital. No signs of sexual trauma. What's this theory based on?"

Not all kinds of trauma show up in an examination. "The timing," I say. "The condition I found Cameron in. Oh yeah, and the fact that the two kids look *exactly the same*."

"The condition you found Cameron in?"

"Naked."

"I think it's a fair bet that the perp had to take his clothes off to take out his kidney."

"But he didn't put them back on afterward?"

"The doctors found Rohypnol in Cameron's bloodstream. You wouldn't know anything about that, would you, Blake?"

He's caught me by surprise. We never discussed it, but I think he knows what my roommate does for a living. He must have put two and two together.

"The date-rape drug?" I say. "Well, that sure suits my serial rapist theory, doesn't it?"

He looks at me. I look at him.

I say, "What?" He can't prove anything.

"You got any idea who this kid is?" he asks, pointing at the picture. "Or who put up the poster?"

"I haven't called the number yet. I wanted to make sure I'd be properly compensated."

Luzhin glowers at me. "No deal. I choose the cases, not you."

"You going to risk this kid's life over your pride?"

"Since nobody brought this case to my attention, I can assume the FBI's already dismissed him as a runaway. It's not worth your price."

"Would they have reached that conclusion if they knew how much he looked like Cameron Hall?"

There's a pause. Luzhin is in a jam. He won't be able to live with himself if he doesn't investigate this, but his boss will fire him if he does, because it'll stretch the budget until it snaps. I'm his only way out.

Eventually he says, "Fine. But no FBI help. Not until you have good reason to believe he's in danger and not just on a bus to San Antonio. Got it?"

I nod. Too easy.

"And no reward unless you find him and his life is being threatened. By someone other than you, obviously. Are we clear?"

I nod again.

"Call me when you know something. Me, no one else. Understood?"

Once, Luzhin gave me a body to eat and I found a bullet in it. I'd assumed he was a death row inmate, but later I saw the guy's face on the news—he'd just been found not guilty of sex trafficking. Everyone thought he'd moved to London after the verdict.

With this kidnapper, it sounds like Luzhin may wish to use one of his "unofficial solutions." Arresting people is expensive, and the conviction doesn't always stick. Killing them is cheap and permanent. Thanks to his skill with paperwork, Luzhin can make it look like they never existed.

"Understood," I say, and walk out.

When I get back to the front desk, I ask the receptionist—a muscular woman with enough makeup to look like a porcelain doll—if I can use her phone, and she hands it over. I don't need to take the poster back out of my pocket. Phone numbers are even easier to memorize than credit card numbers.

Someone answers on the third ring. "Hello?" A quiet, uncertain voice. Female.

"Saw your poster," I say. "I might have seen the kid you're looking for."

"Really? Where? When?" She sounds too young to be the boy's mother. Sister, or girlfriend.

"Cloverleaf," I say. If it really is the same kidnapper, then it makes sense that the new victim would live near Cameron. "About a week ago, I think."

"Can we meet?" she says. "Today?"

Exactly what I was hoping she'd say. "Sure. Where?"

"What about Jenny's Diner on Beechnut Street? Near the freeway?"

I run some quick calculations. An hour to get home, then another thirty to drive to the diner. But I want to get there before she does.

"I can be there in two hours," I say.

"Okay. Did...did he look okay?"

"As far as I could tell," I say.

"Okay," she says again. She sounds hurt. Maybe I just accidentally gave her the impression that her brother did run away. "See you soon."

She hangs up.

I ask the receptionist, "Mind if I make another call?"

She shrugs.

I dial Annette Hall. If I'm right about the kidnapper having a thing for blond teens, it's likely Cameron was abused while he was being held captive. Nothing turned up in his debriefing or his examination at the hospital, but maybe he wasn't asked the right questions. People don't like admitting they've been sexually assaulted, especially boys.

No answer. Cameron and his mom could well be home but just not picking up—if I was Annette Hall, I'd be scared to ever answer the phone again.

Or maybe they can't hear it ringing over the sound of squeaking bedsprings.

I shiver and hand the phone back to the receptionist.

"You all right, Mr. Blake?" she says.

"Thanks, I'm fine. You take care now."

"You too."

I walk back out into the sunshine, trying to ignore the hunger already growing in my stomach. I've been living off the frozen dregs of the Witch Doctor. I want something fresh.

Soon, I tell myself. *Solve the case, find the kid, get the reward. Do your job, and keep the food on the table.*

A van marked *Miami Personal Security* pulls into the parking lot. Eight guys in sunglasses and pressed gray uniforms climb out and walk past me, smelling of Axe body spray and laundry powder.

Personal security means bodyguards. Now that the kidnapper knows where I live, maybe I should hire one to hang out at my place. But these guys are from out of town, and they look premium—I probably can't afford them. Plus, they might object to me eating the kidnapper.

I wonder what they want.

Uneasy but unsure why, I get into my stolen Chevy and start the engine.

Just like every other diner in Houston, the sign out front of Jenny's advertises "world famous chicken-fried steak." Inside there are sticky vinyl seats, a tired-looking clientele and food that comes in big portions and tastes only slightly better than it looks. Just about every other customer has one of those Bluetooth earpieces.

I sit in a booth, order a coffee, fill it with sugar, cream and salt, and drink it through a straw. *Sip-sip, sip-sip.* Like a vein pumping directly into my mouth. Someone has left a newspaper on the table. Charlie Warner is descending the courthouse steps in a blurry photo, staring straight ahead. The headline is **ALLEGED CRIME BOSS SWAPS LAWYERS BEFORE TRIAL.** The article below doesn't say this, but Warner is stalling. Buying more time to find and kill the state's witnesses.

A guy on a stool is staring at me. When I look up from the newspaper, he turns away. It takes me a moment to place him, since it's the first time I've seen him out of uniform. It's Woodstock, Luzhin's man inside Huntsville.

I can see a word forming on his lips: *Hangman.* He doesn't know my real name.

He glances back at me, sees that I'm still looking and turns away again. Then he comes over to the booth.

"Did you follow me here?" I say.

He shakes his head. "My house is just around the corner." He raises his hand to point and then changes his mind. Doesn't want me knowing where he lives.

"Can I sit down?" he says. Hash browns and bacon on his breath. He's been having breakfast before the night shift.

Bacon is the meat that tastes most like human flesh. This is a piece of trivia I have accidentally almost shared on several occasions.

"We shouldn't be seen together," I say.

He doesn't go away. Instead, he sits at the booth behind mine, so we're back to back.

His voice reaches my ears. "When's your next visit?"

"That's not up to me. Why?"

"I'm rostered on. Next week."

Guards at Huntsville take turns at executing the prisoners. They receive training beforehand, learning to manage the straps and buckles and needles and machines. When the night arrives, they bring the inmate his last meal. Sometimes it's lobster or caviar, but more often it's a chicken-fried steak from whichever diner was closest to the inmate's childhood home. After they're done eating, the inmates usually cry. We have that in common.

Execution duty is well-paid, but it's not uncommon for the guard to donate the paycheck to their church. Buying their souls back.

"I can't do it again," Woodstock says. "Not after last time."

I say nothing.

"How would you like a live one?" he asks.

My mouth goes dry.

"I can put one in solitary and sneak you in. Afterward, we can say there was a fight with one of the others."

I wonder if Luzhin suspects his man on the inside is losing his nerve. Woodstock is happy to lead the inmates into a room where I will kill them. But he doesn't want to be the one who looks him in the eyes and pushes the button.

"Please," he says. "I can't sleep. I can't eat. I feel it in my gut every day. Don't make me do it again."

Him and me, back to back. He doesn't want to kill, but he
has to. I want to, and I can't.

"Get out of here," I say. "Before somebody sees you."

After a moment, the leather seat creaks and he walks past
me without a word. The door jingles as he leaves.

I lounge there with my coffee for another ten minutes before the girl arrives, which makes her twenty minutes early.
And it is a girl, not a woman. I doubt there's nine months between her age and that of the boy in the picture. Twin sister?
They have a similar body type, and while her hair is brown, it
looks like it's dyed. She wears a dark dress that is too wide in
the hips and too loose in the chest to be anything but a hand-
me-down. She looks like she's here for her first job interview.

I hold up my hand, and she comes over. Her hopeful look
fades as she looks me up and down. I'm used to that.

"You the one who put up the posters?" I ask.

She nods. "I'm JJ. Can you take me to where you saw
Robert?"

Robert. "Robert got a last name?"

"Shea. *EA*, not *AY*."

"*You* got a last name?"

"Austin, like the city. Can you take me there or not?"

Not his sister, then. And since I never saw Robert, I can't
take her anywhere that will be any use. "I told you, it was
in Cloverleaf. Andorra Lane. Does Robert live near there?"

Austin shakes her head. "He's from Westside. He goes to
Paul Revere Middle School, catches the same bus as me."

Catches the bus, not driven. Probably means his parents
aren't as rich as Cameron's. Different neighborhoods, different levels of wealth—I'm struggling to find more than a
superficial link between the two boys.

I say, "If your last name is Austin, why do you call yourself JJ?"

"My real name's Jane."

"Jane Austin?"

"Right. So I go by JJ. When exactly did you see Robert?"

"I don't know, about a week ago." I like not having an FBI-appointed babysitter. It means I can lie as much as I want.

Austin scrunches a napkin into a ball. Her cheeks look deliciously puffy—I shut my eyes and exhale slowly. I've eaten only recently, but like any addiction, feeding the craving only makes it stronger.

"Weekday, weekend?" she is saying. "What time of day?"

"Mid-afternoon. Weekday. Must have been Friday. When did he go missing?"

"Just before that," she says. "He didn't come to school on Thursday."

I rescued Cameron about one o'clock Thursday morning. If it's the same kidnapper, he must have gone hunting for a replacement pretty much as soon as he discovered Cameron was gone. He probably grabbed Robert from the bus stop on his way to school.

"How do you know him?" I ask.

"I'm his girlfriend."

"How long have you been together?"

"What's that got to do with anything?"

I shrug. "It could show how likely he is to run off without telling you."

Her face goes cherry red. "Two years," she says. Like a challenge.

Always be suspicious of round numbers, Mrs. Radfield once told me. *They're usually made up.*

"No," I say. "How long have you *really* been going out with him?"

She looks away. "Fine—almost three months. But I know him, all right? I know everything about him."

"What does he do on school nights?"

"Jujitsu on Mondays and Wednesdays. Bass lessons on Fridays."

I'd like to push her further, but she already looks suspicious that I'm asking so many questions. "Okay," I say. "You got a better picture of him?"

She shakes her head. "Just the one from the poster, but I have it in color."

"Got it with you? On your phone, maybe?"

"No."

"Who are his other friends?"

Her eyes narrow. "Why?"

"They might have a better picture."

She shrugs. "He's popular. He gets along with everyone. So, you're not sure it was him that you saw?"

I've learned all I can from this girl. And she's just handed me an excuse to leave.

"No," I say. "In fact, I'm pretty sure it was somebody else."

Then, before the shock can register on her face, I get up and walk out, leaving her to pick up the check.

I feel bad about it—but this way, she thinks I just used her for a free coffee. She won't go telling people I was asking about Robert.

She looks out the window at me. Not angry; hurt and confused, like a kicked dog. But she'll cheer up when I find him.

School is done for the day, so I can't track down any of Robert's friends. And I have no way of knowing where he gets his bass lessons, so my first stop would be his jujitsu class. There can't be many of them in this town, right?

Wrong. It takes me almost half an hour to find a pay phone—there aren't many around these days—and the phone book inside lists a dozen gyms that offer jujitsu classes. It would take days to go to each one pretending to know Robert, asking if anyone is close to him, and questioning them if they are. But I can't just call and ask if Robert trained there.

Gyms clam up when someone asks about that, same as any other private institution…

Unless they're talking to a cop.

I put a quarter in the pay phone and dial Thistle. Her phone rings twice, and then I hang up. The quarter jingles into the change box, and I put it back in my pocket.

The phone booth smells like piss. It reminds me of the youth shelters I used to hang around in, where pregnant girls would come to cry and drunks would shit on the bathroom floor.

I have to wait only a few seconds before the pay phone rings. I answer it. "Thistle, it's Blake."

"Calling me and hanging up? Creepy," she says, but she doesn't sound like she means it.

"Didn't have much change," I say. "Listen, I need a favor."

"Shoot."

"The missing kid's name is Robert Shea. He does jujitsu on Mondays and Wednesdays, and I want to find out where."

"There can't be that many gyms that—"

"That's what I thought, but there's at least twelve. I was thinking you could maybe call them, ask for a membership list."

"Under what pretext?"

I shrug. "Whatever. Surveying for new recruits?"

"Okay, I'll work that bit out on my own. But you gotta do something for me."

"What?"

"Let me take you out to dinner sometime," she says.

I hesitate. I can just hear her soft, quiet breaths.

"To congratulate you for finding Cameron," she says. "And hopefully Robert by then."

I don't like giving people too many opportunities to work out my secrets. The less time I spend with Thistle, the safer I am. But…

"Come on," she says, sounding almost nervous. "You look like you could use a decent meal."

And I'm thinking, *You got no idea.*

"Okay," I say. "I'd like that. You choose the place."

"Great. Day after tomorrow? I'll call you when I've made a reservation."

"Or if you've found Robert's gym."

"Sure."

"One more thing—officially, this isn't a case. I'm not supposed to be working on it."

"My lips are sealed," she says.

I open my front door to find a fist-sized hole in the living room wall. John Johnson is staring out the window with an old Colt .45 clenched in his hand. His knuckles are bleeding, but he doesn't seem to notice.

Most people who take AAS, anabolic-androgenic steroids, do it because they want to look like Schwarzenegger. But a few people—the kind who buy from my roommate—just like the high. It makes you feel like a superhero, like you could just pick up a car and chuck it over a house if you wanted to.

AAS is basically fake testosterone. In small doses it makes you bigger, stronger, hairier. Your voice gets deeper. But take too much, and the dark side of masculinity starts to appear. You start to get hostile, paranoid, violent. They call it roid rage, and this is what it looks like. It also makes your balls shrink, which just makes you even more angry and paranoid.

Johnson drips on the carpet, the blood blossoming into a rosy stain on the floor.

"Tim," he says. "Where the fuck have you been?"

Whatever I say, he'll find some reason to get mad about it. But ignoring him will piss him off even more. I decide to give him the least possible ammunition.

"Working," I say.

"Well, while you were out working, guess who came by?" He pauses, apparently expecting me to know.

"The cops?"

His head whips around so fast I'm surprised his neck doesn't snap. "Cops? You've seen cops hanging round here?"

"No," I say. "Sorry, just guessing."

"Why would you guess cops?" he snarls. Veins bulge in his arms.

"What? No, man, I said 'Cox.' You know, Dudley Cox? From college?"

There's no such person, and people with roid rage are easily confused. Just as I'd hoped, he rewinds the conversation back to before I made my clumsy guess. "Patrick," he says. He turns back to the window. "Fucking Patrick was here."

I have no idea who Patrick is. "Shit," I say noncommittally.

He says nothing. Then, just as I'm retreating toward my room, "What the hell is that in the freezer?"

Damn it. He must have unwrapped the Witch Doctor. Fortunately, not much of him is left. I've eaten the face and the chest and gnawed the flesh off the hands, feet and one of the arms. I put his digestive tract and his brain down the garbage disposal—those parts are poisonous.

"It's bear," I say. "Don't tell anyone. They're endangered."

He looks impressed. "You killed a *bear*?"

I shake my head. "Not me. My uncle. He got off a lucky shot, then wasn't sure what to do with the body. Asked if I wanted it. You want to try some?"

He wrinkles his nose. "Bear meat? No, thanks."

He'll swallow pills that have been cut with powdered acid, but he won't try bear meat. More for me. I go into my room and close the door, wondering where I can hide my next victim.

CHAPTER 11

**I AM BROWN.
I HAVE A HEAD AND A TAIL BUT NO BODY.
WHAT AM I?**

FIVE YEARS AGO, I PEERED THROUGH THE WIN-
dow of a clothes store and saw a living skeleton. He wore
paint-stained slacks and gloves that were leopard-spotted with
holes. His skin was cracked by the heat like an old sidewalk,
and his eyes were swollen with hunger. His body was wasting precious energy to grow a tangled beard.

The man turned out to be my reflection in the window.

I hadn't eaten since last Friday, when I found a stack of
pizza boxes beside a dumpster. No pizza in them, but strips
of cheese, ketchup smudges, a few bacon chips. My body was
already eating itself. It had finished the fat and started on the
muscle, desperate to feed my heart and brain. I was slightly
less hungry than I had been yesterday, and I could still think
clearly enough to know this was a bad sign. My stomach was
shriveling up, leaving less empty space to ache with. My breath
had gone bad like old milk.

When the clothes shop closed, I drifted to the nearest cross
street, looking for somewhere with more pedestrians. But foot
traffic was rare in this part of Houston at this time of night. I
was shivering even though it was the middle of summer, and
I had a dirty sleeping bag. You're much more likely to catch
the flu when you're starving.

"Spare change?" I held out my cup as a woman approached.
"Please."

The woman kept her eyes straight ahead, hands jammed in her pockets, sparkling heels striking the pavement like a ticking clock. Perhaps she was a sex worker—one of Charlie Warner's brothels was just around the corner. Then again, she might just have been lost. Soon she was gone, and the street was empty again but for the wind and me.

Sometimes, when you have nowhere to live and nothing to eat, you start to wonder if you're dead. Maybe when you slept on that bench, you never woke up. The cops took your body away in the night, and now you're just a ghost, haunting a street corner, asking for change from people who can't see or hear you. Homeless people talk to themselves because nobody else will.

But tonight, the hunger didn't let me believe I was dead. A ghost wouldn't feel this much pain.

I'd counted the pennies and nickels in my cup so many times I could tell them all apart by their scratches and stains. Only a dollar and twenty-nine cents, after two days. Yesterday, nine people told me to get a job. Like I hadn't thought of that. Like I had chosen to starve myself, out of laziness. Like anyone would ever hire a homeless guy who looked and smelled like I did.

Just one more quarter would be enough for a burger at the Jack in the Box two blocks over.

Somebody else appeared farther up the street, headed my way. "Spare change?" I asked, though the guy didn't look the type to give anything. His teeth were chipped, his shirt grimy, his shoes peeling—only a couple of rungs above me on the poverty ladder, so he probably couldn't afford to give much. But he didn't look away or cross to the other side of the street. Sometimes the poor folks were the most sympathetic.

He approached me, reached into his pocket and pulled out a 9mm Luger.

"Hand it over," he said.

More confused than scared, I said, "Hand *what* over?" I didn't own anything.

His voice was quiet. "The cup."

I looked around. No sign of anyone else coming. Nothing and no one to stop him taking whatever he wanted.

"Come on, man," I said. "I'm starving."

"You don't think I'll shoot you?" he said. He pressed the barrel to my forehead. When I was a kid, I used to play a game where I'd push a penny against that exact spot, let go and see how far I could run before it fell off.

"I will fuck you up," he was saying. "I will blow your brains out if you don't give me that fucking cup."

I looked down at the dollar and twenty-nine cents I'd collected.

He screamed at me, "Fucking hand it over, asshole!"

I pushed the gun aside and lunged at him. The gun went off next to my ear as I chomped down on his throat.

He was a human fire hose—the blood just sprayed out of him, covering us both. His hands fumbled at my chest like those of a clumsy lover. Just one bite and the fight was already draining out of him, his shocked eyes getting that blank emptiness that only comes with death. The blood slowed to a trickle as he staggered and fell into a puddle, where he lay still among the scattered coins.

I snatched up his gun and pointed it at him, fighting to keep the barrel steady. After a minute, I crept closer and prodded his shoulder with my foot. He moved like a sack of beans.

It didn't feel real. Even as I stared down at the body, I wasn't sure it was there. Because if it was, then I was a killer.

Killers were bad people. And I was just a decent guy down on his luck. Wasn't I?

"What the fuck?"

I whirled around to see another man pointing a gun at me—this one bigger and better-dressed than the mugger. He looked at the dead man's ripped throat, and then at the blood dribbling down my chin. His eyes were bulging like he was in space without a helmet.

"Don't move," he said. "Don't… Holy shit. Don't move."

I didn't. I'm not sure I could have if I wanted to. A fugue of sensations swept over me, the street unnaturally bright and loud.

The big man, recovering from the shock, said, "Turn around. Get on your knees and interlace your fingers behind your head."

I didn't. My eyes drifted back down to the dead man. I was still so hungry.

"Turn around," the big guy said again, edging closer. Droplets of sweat were weaving down through his sideburns.

But I couldn't stop looking at all the delicious redness.

My nose exploded across my face as the big man pistol-whipped me. I fell backward, the world spinning like it was on a Tilt-A-Whirl, but before he could grab me, I pointed the mugger's gun at him.

"Back off," I roared.

He stepped back but kept his pistol trained on my head.

"Drop the gun," he said.

"No," I replied.

There was a pause.

I didn't want to hurt him. But if I lowered the 9mm, he could shoot me without fear of me shooting back.

When he opened his mouth, things got much worse.

"I'm arresting you under suspicion of first-degree murder," he said. "You have the right to remain silent. You have the right to an attorney. If you cannot afford an attorney, one will be provided for you by the state. Do you understand these rights as I have read them to you?"

"You're no cop," I said. But he had spoken quickly enough to have said those words hundreds of times before.

"I fucking am. Put the gun down."

"Let's see your badge."

He reached into his pocket, slowly, and pulled out a cell phone.

"If you *are* a cop," I said, "then you really don't want to make that call."

"Shut up," he said, and dialed with his thumb.

The words tumbled from my mouth. "You're not in uniform. You're off duty. When your bosses ask what you were doing without your badge or your cuffs, half a block from the busiest brothel in Houston, what are you going to say?"

"I'm thinking they'll be more interested in you, somehow." But he didn't hit the call button. Prostitution is illegal in Texas.

"What about your wife? Will she be more interested in me?"

It was a lucky guess. He wasn't wearing a wedding ring, but married men usually don't when they hire sex workers.

"I took a drive," he said. "It's a free country."

"It is until they lock you up. You know how many cops survive prison? Not many. The ones who do sometimes wish they hadn't."

"I'm not going to prison," he scoffed, and hit the call button.

"Not for visiting a brothel, maybe," I said. "It's the cocaine that will put you away."

He hung up. "What the fuck did you just say?"

I was sure I was right. His nostrils were pink. He'd been sniffing in between sentences. His veins stuck out, like he had blood pressure problems. Plus the scabs on his wrists— he'd been scratching and scratching.

"How many times have you raided the evidence locker for a fix?" I asked. That would be the easiest way for a cop to get drugs. "You've been with the force for ten years." Another guess, based on his age. "That's a lot of convictions to overturn when they put you away."

Now he was looking at me like I could read minds. "You can't prove anything," he said.

"There's white powder on your collar."

"No, there isn't."

"Sure there is. At least, that's what I'll tell the public defender. Then he'll get a warrant to test your hair. Traces last thirty days, or so I heard."

"You're going to prison no matter what your attorney finds. You got blood all over you. How are you gonna explain that?"

"I found the guy on the ground, tried to stop the bleeding, gave him CPR. Hell, I might've succeeded if you hadn't shown up and arrested me. In a way, *you* killed him."

"Not one person in this whole county will believe that," he said.

"Maybe not," I replied. "But they'll still lock you up for the cocaine and release all your collars. Unless you let me go."

The cop's finger was on the trigger, ready to end my life in an instant.

"You shoot me, I shoot you," I reminded him.

"You killed a man," he said.

"Self-defense."

"You were eating him."

"Self-defense again. I was starving."

It wasn't as simple as that, and we both knew it. There was something wrong with me, something that made me attack the mugger with my teeth rather than my fists, something that might rise to the surface again at any moment.

But it was also something that made me unnaturally observant. I'd worked out his darkest secret just by looking at him.

"It was him or me," I said. "Don't make it me or you."

The silence was the longest of my life, before he started walking backward. He kept the gun trained on me, but there was shame in his eyes—disgust at his own cowardice. Faced with divorce, prison time and a bullet, he had decided it was easier to let a cannibal go free.

A minute later he was gone. Forever, I thought. But what I didn't realize was that this cop would someday become the director of the Houston Field Office of the FBI—and that he was already thinking about a use for me.

I dragged the mugger into a nearby alleyway, leaving a trail of blood not unlike the smears on the bottom of the pizza box.

"I'm thinking pizza," Thistle says.

I find myself back in the real world. "What?"

She exits the revolving door behind me. "For dinner tomorrow night. Or would you rather a steak house? I know a good place."

"Steak sounds good," I say.

The gym smells like air freshener and sweaty rubber. I expected to see a boxing ring, but there isn't one—just a faded blue jigsaw of thick mats on the floor. Two kids are rolling around on it, one of them a girl of maybe fifteen, the other a boy of fourteenish. Other students are sparring, doing crunches or just jogging on the spot. As I watch, the two wrestlers twist into pose after pose, like they're trying to do the whole Kama Sutra in under a minute.

A man in a sleeveless shirt bashes at a speed bag in the corner. It thumps against the ceiling in perfectly even triplets—you could dance to the beat. Is this Robert's coach?

I watch his bulging biceps, already seasoned by the salty moisture trickling from under his arms.

"What can I do for you?" he asks Thistle, who doesn't look impressed.

She holds up the picture of Robert Shea. "Looking for this boy," she says. "This his class?"

The coach nods. "That's Bobby. Used to train here."

"With you?"

"Yeah."

"Used to?" I say.

"He quit last week."

"Why?"

He shrugs. "Canceled his membership online, so I didn't get the chance to ask. I'm sorry to lose him, but it happens." He looks me up and down. "Always thought you FBI guys had to wear suits and earpieces."

I open my mouth to tell him I'm not FBI, but Thistle gets there first. "The Bureau's dress code isn't as strict as it used to be," she says. She can't directly state that I'm a cop, but she wants him to take me seriously.

She's bending a few rules for me. When she called with the address of the gym, I told her I'd check it out on my own.

She said, "You sure this kid's in danger?"

"Pretty sure."

"Then I'm coming with you."

"Luzhin won't—"

"Luzhin can't tell me what to do on my sick days," she said, and coughed theatrically.

Richmond wouldn't have called in sick so that he could search for a kid who wasn't officially missing. But I'm starting to realize that Thistle isn't Richmond. She cares more about her cases than her paycheck. The only other person I know who shares that devotion is Luzhin himself, who would—now that he's sober—give up his life if the job called for it. He's already given up his soul.

Thistle is asking the coach if any of these kids are close to Robert.

"Uh…" He turns to face the group. The wrestling boy is facedown on the floor, the girl sitting on his ass, facing his feet, pulling one of his legs up in a stretch that Hitler would have described as inhumane.

"Clarke, get over here," the coach says.

The boy taps out—he can't reach any part of the girl, so he slaps his hand twice against the blue rubber instead. She releases his foot, and he comes over to join us. He's taller and skinnier than me, with a face that seems squashed and crooked.

"Yeah?" he says.

"Clarke, this is—"

"Timothy Blake," I say, not giving him a chance to directly call me a cop. "And that's Agent Reese Thistle, FBI. We're investigating the disappearance of Robert Shea. Mind if we ask you a couple of questions?"

"Disappearance?" Clarke looks at his coach. "I thought he just quit."

"He *did* quit," the coach says. "He probably disappeared since then. Right?"

"When did he last show up for training?" Thistle asks.

Clarke says, "Last week," and at the exact same moment, the coach says, "Wednesday."

Clarke adds, "Yeah, Wednesday." As I watch, his face is becoming less mangled, realigning itself where the floor pushed it sideways.

The body odor is making me hungry. "He tell you why he was quitting?"

Clarke shakes his head. "Didn't even tell me he was going to. After all I did for him."

"What did you do?"

"Introduced him to his girlfriend. And he was crazy about her—like, obsessed."

Jane Austin seemed crazy about him too. My theory that he ran off without telling her is looking less likely.

Thistle asks, "Do you know any of Robert's other friends?"

"He and Gracie are pretty tight. Gracie Dunn. She plays in his band."

Robert takes bass lessons—I should have guessed that he would be in a band. "Who else plays with them?"

"Nobody. She does drums. He plays bass and sings. They're called Easy Lies."

"Got a phone number for this Gracie Dunn?"

Clarke runs over to his locker to get his cell phone. The coach says to Thistle, "You'll tell us if you learn anything, won't you? I genuinely liked that kid."

He used the past tense. Could mean he thinks Robert is dead. And "genuinely" is a word people use when they're trying to seem honest, rather than when they actually are.

I say, "Does the name Cameron Hall mean anything to you?"

He frowns. "Don't think so. Why?"

He didn't hesitate, which means he didn't think about it very hard. Either he's lying or he doesn't care about my investigation. "Never mind," I say.

Clarke returns with the phone. Thistle gets out her pen and paper.

"You ready?" he asks, and she says, "Go ahead."

He reads out the number. I ask for his as well, and his full name, which turns out to be Clarke McGoughny.

"Hey," the fifteen-year-old girl calls. "We're not finished, Clarke."

Clarke sighs. It strikes me as a performance—I think he secretly likes wrestling with the girl.

"Are we done here?" he asks.

I nod. He jogs back over to the girl, bumps fists with her, and they resume their battle.

"And what's your name and number?" Thistle asks the coach.

He looks reluctant.

"So we can contact you," she says, smiling. Her teeth shine in the fluorescent light. "You know, if we find anything."

"Henrik Morse," he says, and recites his number. Thistle writes it down.

"Thanks for your help, Mr. Morse," I say. "We'll be in touch."

Across the room, the girl has spun Clarke into a head-lock, crushing his face against her right breast. He pretends to struggle.

"What do you think?" I ask Thistle as we enter the same compartment of the revolving door. Her shoulder is warm against mine. I force myself not to look at the bare skin of her neck.

"I don't think Morse is all that worried about Shea," she says as we step out into the afternoon light.

"He strike you as having anything to hide?"

She chews her lip. "Can't tell," she says finally.

"Let's call the drummer and see what she says."

Thistle takes her phone out of her pocket. I repeat Dunn's number from memory to save her the trouble of getting out her notepad. She dials and puts the phone to her ear.

"Voice mail," she says after a few seconds.

"Don't leave a message."

"You think I'm an idiot?"

"Sorry," I say. When cops leave messages, the call back usually comes from an attorney.

"You been to Shea's house yet?"

"No."

Thistle's car key is already in her hand.

Thistle finds Shea's address in the police database. Turns out that Robert has a record. It's sealed, so we don't know what he did. But there's another photo, in which he looks even more like Cameron Hall.

Thistle calls the house. No one picks up. Some people

never answer the phone on principle, so we decide to go out there anyway.

We stop at Cameron Hall's place on the way. The guard waves us through the gate. I still want to know if the kidnapper raped Cameron, to give some credibility to my theory. But Annette's car isn't in the drive, and no one answers the door.

Robert's house in Westside is newer, crappier. Small, one-story, window cracks repaired with adhesive tape. I'm reminded again that he and Cameron are from completely different worlds. Their only connection seems to be what they look like. This supports my theory, except that I can't work out how the kidnapper could have known them both.

Empty driveway. The bell—a sharp, buzzing sound like a prison door—echoes into oblivion, indicating an empty house. I press my ear to the door.

"Anything?" Thistle asks.

"No." I try the handle. Locked. There's a cat flap by my feet. Also locked.

If Thistle wasn't here, I'd probably break in. Instead, I'll have to see what I can deduce from the outside.

"Let's walk the perimeter and look in the windows," she suggests. "You go that way, I'll go this way."

I'm not sure why we're splitting up—we're in no hurry, and the yard isn't big—but I nod and start circling the house counterclockwise.

The weeds are tall enough to require a machete. Pushing them aside, I peer through the dirty glass into the house.

Something moves inside.

I duck and listen.

The only sound is distant traffic and the faint ringing of wind chimes. I rise again and see the chimes themselves through a window on the opposite side of the room, throwing swaying shadows across the floor inside. That's probably what I saw. Probably.

"Blake," Thistle calls.

I release the weeds and jog back. "What's up?"

"The front door's unlocked," she says.

I open my mouth to contradict her. Then I realize she must have sent me away so that she could find the spare key or pick the lock without incriminating us both.

"Technically, we still can't go in," she says. "Not without permission or a warrant."

"We won't get one," I say. "Not until the kid is officially declared missing."

"I know. I'm just saying, whatever we find in there, it's inadmissible. We're looking for clues, not evidence. Got that?"

I nod, and we step inside.

"Hello?" Thistle calls out.

Silence.

No keypad by the door, which means no motion-activated alarm. A dog would have gone crazy when we rang the bell. We're probably safe, for now.

The living room has a cheap sofa, an old TV and a glass case filled with small ceramic cows—bovine scuba divers and ballet dancers and Hell's Angels. A couple of small paintings hang on the walls. Landscapes, not original. No photos.

The fridge in the adjoining kitchen is empty, and the cupboard holds nothing but cans of tomatoes and chunky chicken soup; food bought based on price and expiration date, not on taste or nutritional value. I look under the sink and see that the trash has recently been taken out.

Robert's girlfriend reported him missing, not his parents. Why? Where are they?

The shower in the bathroom is just a detachable spray gun and a curtain in the corner of the room. Enough water has leaked out from under this curtain to make the bath mat moldy. No toothbrushes on the vanity, no razor.

I join Thistle in the second bedroom, which belongs to an

adult woman. Maybe a man too—interior decoration–wise, that can be harder to detect. A full-length mirror leans against the wall, along with a dresser and a bowl of potpourri that looks ready to add milk and eat. I open the dresser and find some folded men's shirts, but not a full wardrobe's worth. Some clothes seem to be missing.

"No cell phone chargers," Thistle says, pointing at the outlets.

"Meaning what?"

"Meaning maybe Shea's parents are both out of town."

I squat and stare at the two square dustless patches under the bed where suitcases maybe used to be.

I head back out to the living room and find the answering machine. Twenty-two new messages.

I hit Play. The machine reads out the caller's number like a female Stephen Hawking before playing the message: *"Hey, Celine. I'm sorry to hear about your mama. Give me a call when you get back from Chicago."*

The second message is similar. *"Hi, Larry. Just wanted to let you know that I'll save your spot at the warehouse while you're gone. You just take care of the missus and Bobby."*

"Shit," Thistle says behind me. "The kid isn't even missing. He's gone to Chicago so his folks can organize his grandma's funeral or nursing home or whatever."

"Then why didn't he tell his girlfriend?" I ask.

The answering machine plays the next message. *"What the fuck, Bobby? I tried your cell. Call me. Oh yeah—it's Gracie."*

The drummer. She sounds pissed.

I stop the machine, and after a bit of fiddling, I mark the three messages we heard as new. It'll be like we were never here.

"Sorry, Blake," Thistle says, "but the only crime that's been committed here is breaking and entering. We have to go."

"No pictures anywhere," I say. But there are spots on the walls where they might have been.

Thistle looks around. "Maybe they took them along. For the funeral."

"Do you smell that?"

Thistle sniffs. "Potpourri?"

"No." A period of starvation leads to an incredible sense of smell, which doesn't seem to go away. The brain reshapes itself into a searchlight, the olfactory cortex swelling to hunt for even the tiniest morsel of food.

But this isn't food.

"I think we have a body," I say.

Thistle's eyes widen. Her hand twitches toward her hip, reaching for a gun that isn't there.

"Where?" she asks, quite reasonably. We've searched the whole house.

I looked under the bed before, but that's where the smell is coming from, so I check again.

No suitcases, no forgotten clothes, no baseball bat. Just dust and shadows, which slowly become transparent.

Something is hiding in the corner, next to the dresser. Something small, crumpled, withered. Ribs are visible under matted fur.

"So they went to Chicago," I say, "but they left their cat to starve to death?"

Thistle crouches down to look. "Poor thing," she says. "The cat flap was locked, right?"

"Right."

Her phone rings, and we both jump. She checks the screen. "Gracie Dunn," she says.

I hold out my hand for the phone. She gives it to me, and I answer.

"Hello?"

"Yeah," Dunn says. "I got a missed call from this number. Who's this?"

"My name's Timothy Blake," I say. "I heard you needed a new bass player."

CHAPTER 12

**THE FIRST IS DEAD AND SLOWLY SHRINKS.
THE SECOND IS ALWAYS EATING
AND WILL NEVER BE FULL.
ONCE THE THIRD IS GONE, IT NEVER RETURNS.
WHAT ARE THEY?**

THE SIGN SAYS **NO SMOKING**, BUT AT LEAST TWO out of every three people in this joint are doing it anyway. The haze is so thick it feels as if I could run headlong into the wall without getting hurt. It's like cotton wool.

Smokers taste pretty good. Cigarettes make those bitter organs shrivel away until all that's left is the tasty fat and muscle—that's why smoking makes people lose weight. The meat is flavored too. Like the ham on a wood-fired pizza.

Inside the doorway, a teenage boy with a greasy pony-tail holds out an ice cream container half filled with change. "Money for the band—suggested donation, five dollars."

I say, "Suggestion noted," and push past him.

On stage are two guitarists, one keyboardist, one drummer and one saxophonist, all about sixteen years old. One of the guitarists is singing. He plays better than he sings.

A group of middle-aged folks are watching intently. Law-yers, middle managers, upper-class types. Five women, four men. I figure they're parents. The kids aren't old enough to be in here, but the bar staff wouldn't want to refuse them entry, not with their folks willing to drink the bar dry of expensive wines and liqueurs.

Thistle walked in two minutes before I did. I can already

see her at the back with a beer in her hand, chatting with a balding stranger. She's here just in case someone needs to be arrested.

The man is laughing. I feel an unexpected throb of jealousy. The balding man doesn't look at all suspicious. If a woman as attractive as Thistle approached me in a bar, I'd assume she was trying to score some cheap weed. There's no other reason to go near someone who looks like me.

A girl sits on her own near the front, same age as the band. Braided hair, nose ring. I've never liked piercings—they break my teeth. Both her feet are tapping and her hands are slapping her thighs to complicated rhythms. Imaginary drums.

I sidle up to her. "Gracie?"

She turns. Looks me up and down. "Timothy?" she says doubtfully.

"Yeah," I say. I shake her hand and nod to the stage. "Friends of yours?"

"She is." Dunn points at the keyboardist. "I only kind of know the others."

"They're pretty good."

"Sure. But they'll never get big unless they ditch the saxophone."

The saxophonist is one of the better players, and I say so.

"He doesn't fit with the genre. Record companies need a genre to sell their product—labels love labels, so they say. This group, they got together because they were friends, not because of their skills." She appraises me again. "You're older than I expected."

She seems serious about a music career, so the best way to play her is to outdo her.

I fix her with a critical eye and say, "I was told you were looking for a professional. Think you're going to find it in a teenager?"

"I wasn't doubting your professionalism. I just think you'll be tough to market."

Charming. "Well, the bass player isn't exactly the front man. So why did your last one quit?"

She glares at her drink—a tall glass of water, no ice. "Fucked if I know. Didn't show up for rehearsal, then I got an email from him saying he was going to Chicago. Sick grandma or some shit."

My stomach rumbles. I'm getting really hungry. "Doesn't sound like it was his fault."

"Rule one: show up for rehearsal. He could be in the hospital with a broken neck and I still would have kicked his ass out of the band."

"Especially since he probably couldn't play bass anymore," I say. She doesn't laugh. "Did he ever mention his grandma's health problems?"

"Nah, never even told me he had family in Chicago." She frowns. "What are you suggesting?"

I shrug. "Nothing. You guys close? How long's the band been together?"

"Two years," she says.

Unlike Robert's girlfriend, Dunn has no reason to make that number up. It's probably true.

I say, "So you'd have a decent-size set list, then."

"Yeah, about twenty originals, thirty covers. I brought a demo." She digs around in her bag and pulls out a thumb drive with magic marker on it. "You got yours?"

I could have compiled a bunch of tracks from obscure bands and pretended I played bass on them, but it's simpler just to bluff. "No offense, but I want to hear yours first."

Dunn looks resentful and impressed at the same time.

The band hits the last note of an overblown twelve-bar standard and bows, to thunderous applause from their parents. The other patrons remain oblivious.

An MC gets up on the stage to back-announce the band. The lighting is so bad that I don't recognize him until I hear his voice. It's Harry Crudup, Cameron's music teacher.

"That was Rumble in the Box," he booms. "Ladies and gentlemen, let's give them another big hand!"

Not many heroin addicts can hold down two jobs. Crudup must have been living with his habit a long time to manage life as a teacher by day, open mic host by night.

I sink lower into my seat, hoping he doesn't spot me, and ask Dunn if Easy Lies has been going well lately—if there are big gigs or record deals or anything on the horizon. If I'm wrong about Robert being taken by the same kidnapper as Cameron, there could be a motive here. Maybe some other bass player killed him with the intention of taking his spot before the band hit the big-time.

But Dunn says, "No. So you'll have lots of time to learn the songs. Assuming I like your demo."

"Have you talked to Robert's other friends about him going to Chicago?"

The first hint of suspicion is growing in her eyes. "Why are you asking so many questions about Bobby?"

"Just worried he might show up wanting his place in the band back."

"He's not coming back. His girlfriend said he was going to be gone a long time. She's here—want to meet her?"

I shake my head. "No, thanks." I glance around, looking for Jane Austin. If she sees me, my cover is blown.

But Dunn is beckoning to a different girl—one of the guitarists from the band. She's tallish, blondish, and wears a necklace of big black beads. Not much meat on her. It'd take three or four of her to make the same size meal as the Witch Doctor.

"Hey, Portia," Dunn says, bumping fists with the girl. "Kick-ass set."

"Thanks." The guitarist looks at me expectantly.

"This is Timothy Blake. Bobby's potential replacement."

Portia looks confused, and a little bit hurt. Like, *Why are you telling me this?*

Dunn continues, "Timothy, this is Portia, Bobby's girlfriend. Tell me, Porsh, did he sound like he was coming back?"

"I already told you, no."

I say, "You're Robert Shea's girlfriend?"

Portia bites her lip and says, "I was. Sorry, who are you again?"

"And you're a friend of Clarke McGoughny's?"

"Clarke? What's Clarke got to do with anything?"

Dunn says, "Wait, what the fuck? How do you know Bobby's last name?"

"Shut up," I say. "This is really important. Does the name Jane Austin mean anything to either of you?"

They look at each other.

"Duh," Dunn says. "She's, like, famous."

"Austin with an *i*," I say. "Girl about your age. Goes by JJ."

Dunn looks baffled.

"I don't know any Jane Austin," says Portia. "What is happening right now?"

I stand. It's time to go. Because if *this* is Robert's girlfriend, then who is the girl I met in the diner?

"Hey," Dunn says from behind me. "Where are you going?"

Thistle slides off her bar stool. The bald guy tries to hand her his phone, presumably so she can type her number into it. She declines with a polite wave.

I don't wait for her. As I walk out, Crudup is shouting, "Ladies and gentlemen, it's a pleasure, a real pleasure to be able to introduce this next act to you tonight. Put your hands together for a very talented bunch of boys from—"

The door closes behind me, cutting him off.

A few seconds later, Thistle emerges. "Get any answers?" she asks.

"Just more questions." I drag my fingers through my hair. "Can you give me a ride home?"

"Okay," Thistle says, working the accelerator and the clutch like she's on a StairMaster. "So what do we know?"

"Jane Austin says Robert Shea disappeared immediately after Cameron Hall," I say. "But she also said she was his girl-friend, which now doesn't seem to be the case."

"This whole *case* doesn't seem like a case," Thistle says. "Shea's other friends say he just went away to visit a sick or dead relative. The fact that his parents are gone too seems to fit with that."

"But none of them have heard from him in person," I say. "Or even on the phone. Just email and the grapevine. Also, they left their cat to starve. Turn left here."

"I'll make some calls," Thistle says. "If he's gone to Chi-cago, there'll be flight records."

I can see her calculating, considering, contemplating. Cir-cling the case the way a mover might circle a heavy piece of furniture, looking for a handhold.

"You enjoy this," I say. "The chase."

She glances over at me as though she'd forgotten I was there. "I do," she admits. "Some people think it's inappro-priate to enjoy police work. In an ideal world we wouldn't even need cops. But for me it's like math. You any good at math, Blake?"

"Basic math, sure."

"I mean the kind where there's a whole lot of informa-tion, and a whole lot of variables designed to trip you up, but only one right answer to find at the end of it all. Some-thing you could never guess on your own, but it's inevita-ble if you follow all the steps. And once you've found the answer, you see it can't be any other way." She nods to herself. "I love that."

I don't like math, but I know the feeling she's describing. It's the same sense of progression I get from Rubik's Cubes and jigsaw puzzles. Taking something chaotic and making it orderly, step by step.

"Those calls," I say. "Can you make them tonight?"

A curl of hair slips loose from behind her ear as she shakes her head. "I could, but I wouldn't get an answer until all the relevant people got into their offices tomorrow morning. May as well do it then."

My driveway is coming up on the right. No sign of Johnson's van. "Stop here," I say.

She pulls over, switches off the engine and looks around, trying to guess which house is mine.

"We'll pay Austin a visit tomorrow," I say. "She's a liar, but not for the fun of it. She knows something."

"Okay," Thistle says.

Silence fills the car. It takes me a moment to realize she's waiting for me to invite her in. It takes her a moment to realize I'm not going to. No matter how much I enjoy her company, no matter how much I'm drawn to her, I can't have an FBI agent snooping through my things.

"What time should I pick you up tomorrow?" she says.

"I'll meet you at Austin's school. Eight-thirty a.m."

"I can come here," she says.

I'd rather not drive there, but I don't want Thistle near my house—specifically, the dead body in my freezer.

"I'll be in the neighborhood anyhow," I say. "I'll see you tomorrow."

"Sure."

As I'm getting out of the car, she says, "Are we still on for dinner after?"

I never forget a meal. "Can't wait."

She grins, and I close the door. The car pulls away as I walk up the drive; she waited just long enough to see which house is mine. Is she figuring out what I am, or is it just natural cop curiosity?

I open the door, step inside and lock it behind me. I'm not safe anywhere, but this house feels especially threatening since Cameron's kidnapper broke in. I walk through every room, opening every closet.

No indication that the kidnapper has been here. No sign of John Johnson either—but he's usually out much later than this.

When I'm sure I'm alone, I open the freezer and grab the Tanzanian's leg.

A carving knife is attached to a magnetic strip on the wall. I pull it free and use it to slice a chunk off the thigh. It's best to do this while the body's frozen, otherwise the tendons are too slack to cut. I put the meat in the microwave and switch it on.

I'm starving, but I know the meat won't help much. Even if the temperature is perfect, even if the amount of salt is exactly right, I can't pretend it's not dead. This kind of hunger goes away only after a really fresh meal.

There's a soft rattle at the front door. Someone is checking if it's unlocked.

If Thistle suspected me of a crime, she could have parked her car around the corner and walked back to snoop around. But I think she trusts me, so the person at the door is probably Johnson, back unexpectedly early. Or it could be one of his customers.

Or the kidnapper.

In none of these scenarios would it be good for the person to walk in while I'm holding a chewed human thigh bone. I throw it back into the freezer and bury it under other things. Then I slam the lid just as the door bursts open.

CHAPTER 13

**THE FIRST ROOM IS ON FIRE,
THE SECOND CONTAINS ASSASSINS WITH
LOADED GUNS AND THE THIRD IS FULL OF LIONS
THAT HAVEN'T EATEN IN THREE YEARS.
WHICH ROOM IS SAFEST TO ENTER?**

IT'S JOHNSON, AND HE'S NOT ALONE. HIS ARM is draped across the shoulders of a white woman in her early twenties. Bleach-blonde, with skinny legs sprouting from a tiny skirt. She's drunk, staggering on her stilettos. A silver bracelet with a bicycle charm jangles around her wrist. Her hair has fallen into her eyes, and she's pawing at it ineffectively.

Johnson drags her inside and kicks the door shut with his heel. Then he presses his lips against hers.

She doesn't kiss him back. She barely seems aware of what's happening. Maybe Johnson slipped something into her drink.

Johnson pulls away and leads her over to the sofa. She looks at it like she's never seen one before.

Then Johnson sees me.

"Fucking pervert," he says. "Go to your room."

The hypocrisy of the first sentence and the parental-ness of the second clash so confusingly in my head that I just stand there.

Johnson has already turned his attention back to the woman. He tugs her top down and the bra with it, exposing breasts that are smaller than they looked.

"Shit," he says. Then, "Hell, it'll do."

The woman stares at the wall, hypnotized, as he hikes up her skirt.

I'm not a good guy. I kill, I steal, I lie. But no matter how convenient it would be to go to my room and pretend this isn't happening, I can't.

Johnson drops his pants, his belt clacking against the floor, his buttocks freckled with track marks. I grab him by the hair and pull him off the semiconscious woman.

He topples over and crab-walks backward. "Hey! What the hell, man?"

I let go of him. "Get up."

"You son of a bitch." He stands up.

I'm in real danger here. When I fought the Witch Doctor, he was naked and still half-paralyzed. He'd been softened by years in a cage, like a lion at the zoo. But Johnson is a wild animal, pumped full of steroids and coke.

"Pull your pants up."

He doesn't. His erection bobs obscenely at me. "This isn't your business," he says.

"You're making it my business."

"Oh, am I?" He reaches down to pull up his jeans—and tugs a short-barreled revolver out of his pocket instead.

I duck around the corner into the kitchen just as he pulls the trigger. The shot is deafening. A puff of wood chips and sawdust explodes out of the ceiling.

"It's your business now, asshole!" Johnson crows from the living room.

The dogs up the street are howling. The neighbors will have heard the shot, but it's not an uncommon sound in this neighborhood. No one's likely to investigate. There's no help on the way.

The knives on the wall would make effective weapons, but I'd have to cross the doorway to reach them. I don't know if Johnson would miss a second time.

Footsteps. He's coming after me.

I open the freezer and wrench out the Tanzanian's thigh bone. I wrap both hands around one end of it, like a batter stepping up to the plate. The cold burns my palms.

Johnson rounds the corner, and I swing the bone sideways. The knobbly joint cuts through the air and slams into his ear with a wet crunch.

The gun goes off again, smashing the kitchen window as he tumbles sideways. I hit him a second time, this time on top of the head, and he moans like a lost cow. He tries to point the gun at me, but slowly, like his limbs won't obey him. I grab his wrist to divert his aim, then bite his exposed forearm, puncturing an artery.

He's too concussed even to scream. His lips droop like a stroke victim's as he bleeds out. His eyes—baffled, frightened—lock onto mine.

"Uhhyeeummm?" he says. He holds my gaze for a long time, and then I realize he's dead. "John Johnson" is no more.

The woman is limp, but still breathing. I don't know what he gave her. Maybe Rohypnol, maybe GHB, maybe something else. I don't know if there's anything I can do.

I stare at her naked skin and warm flesh. She wouldn't be as chewy as Johnson.

I quickly pull her panties back up and her skirt back down, covering as much flesh as I can. Rolling her over, I drag her bra and top back over her chest. I need to get her out of here, fast.

I wipe my face with a kitchen towel. Then, wondering why all my nights seem to end this way, I lift the unconscious woman over my shoulder and carry her out to the Chevy. I put her in the passenger seat, attach her seat belt and go around to the other side.

Her wallet is in her handbag. The address on her driver's

license is 16231 Jones Road, Cypress. Her name is Cynthia Greene.

She doesn't start to groan until we're out on the highway. I take it as a good sign. Whatever he gave her must be wearing off.

I can't just take her home. When she wakes up, there'll be a black spot in her memory, and she'll realize someone spiked her drink. That black spot will haunt her.

Rape survivors often came to the youth shelters where I spent my teenage years. They'd stay in the corners, watching everyone, cheeks swollen from the tears, rubbing their arms like they were scrubbing with soap. And those were the lucky ones—some just switch off, stare at the walls, don't even realize you're talking to them. In both cases, it can be weeks before they start acting normal again, and even then you can tell they're only acting.

I head for Park Plaza Hospital. I'll tell the doctors I saw a man dragging Greene out of a bar, and that he ran when I confronted him. The doctors can treat her for the drugs and confirm that she wasn't raped. She'll think she had a lucky escape, but she won't realize just how lucky.

My fingers twitch as I drive. There are two dead bodies with my tooth marks on them, in a house that recently called attention to itself with gunshots and sounds of breaking glass. I need to clean up the mess before I'm due to meet Thistle at 8:30 a.m.

"Who are you?" Greene asks when we pull into the hospital parking lot. She speaks slowly, eyes closed.

"I'm no one," I say. "Come on."

I get home at 5:00 a.m. No cop cars out front. I guess no one called.

Inside, Johnson lies in a lake of blood, stretched out like

he's trying to backstroke toward the shore. The wound in his forearm shines at me.

I take off my clothes and hurl them into the corner of the room. Falling to my knees, sending ripples through the puddle, I reach for the mutilated arm—

And see the gun still in his hand.

The grimy mirror beside the TV reflects a naked man, dribbling, covered in blood, preparing to eat a dead body. This scene wouldn't have horrified me a week ago. But suddenly I find myself seeing it through Thistle's eyes. For a fraction of a second, I catch a glimpse of what I really am—a monster.

My reflection lifts the revolver and presses it to his temple. The barrel has cooled to room temperature. My finger trembles outside the trigger guard.

I could end this right now. No more hunger. I'm smart enough to know that I'm criminally insane, so killing myself might save lives in the long run. And to do it without finishing the feast in front of me would prove that I still have some humanity left.

My suicidal urges are rare, and they evaporate quickly. If I don't act right now, my life will end on someone else's terms. A bullet from a cop, or a lethal injection at the Death House, or a battle with AIDS after eating the wrong body.

I move my finger to the trigger. My shaky breaths form clouds of condensation in front of my face. This house is always cold. I feel the absurd urge to stick my fingers in my ears, even knowing that I'll be dead before I hear the shot.

The hungry man in my brain, the cannibal, screams at me to drink all that delicious blood.

"Fuck you," I tell him, and pull the trigger.

The hollow *click* is deafening. My heart skips a beat, goose bumps rise on my arms and the world warps around me as my eyes fill with tears.

"Fuck you!" I scream again, this time at Johnson, who didn't buy enough bullets, and at the God that I don't believe in, and most of all at myself. Then I fall forward and start to eat.

The army recruiter looked like he was barely out of high school—a thick-browed boy with forearms like legs of ham. He was dubious at first, seeing my sun-hardened skin and my hollow cheeks. I eased his worries by seeming like I wasn't sure I wanted this. Made it about him convincing me, not me convincing him. Played hard to get.

I wasn't here to serve my country. I wasn't here to kill people. I just liked the sound of three meals a day and a bed every night. People said life in the army was tough, but I figured it couldn't be tougher than sleeping on the sidewalk.

A good recruiter isn't looking for a guy like me. He wants someone who's just finished high school. Someone who's good at football, but not so good that he got a college scholarship. Smart, but not so smart that he's already locked into another career.

I was already twenty-four years old, but I had cleaned myself up. I dug through somebody's trash until I found a disposable razor, then shaved carefully—most discarded razors are just dirty rather than blunt. I cut my hair short. The only suspicious thing about my clothes was that they stank, so I threw myself into Buffalo Bayou and swam a couple of laps. Then I dragged myself out and walked around in the summer heat until I was baked dry.

When I signed the recruiter's forms, he told me to show up to Fort Sam on assessment day. So I stole a respectable car and drove to San Antonio.

I sat on a bench alongside twenty other recruits, mostly men, mostly young, mostly black. The guy next to me was all three and seemed nervous. He tried to strike up a conversation with me but gave up after a handful of one-word replies.

When they called my name, I was led into a room that

looked like the inside of a Styrofoam brick, where a doctor who didn't introduce himself told me to take off my clothes and asked me questions as I did. Was I asthmatic? No. Was I diabetic? No. Was there anything else he should know? No.

He made me stand on a set of scales, which said I was only a hundred and thirty pounds. Looking at my ribs, he said, "You're very thin."

"I've lost almost twenty pounds this last year," I said proudly.

He seemed to buy it. "Well, you can stop now. Much thinner and I couldn't let you in."

He stuck a needle in the inside of my elbow and gave me a stress ball to squeeze while he siphoned off my blood into a vial. I watched, fascinated. Then he pointed me to the bathroom, gave me a cup and told me to fill it with urine.

After I was done with that, he told me to put my clothes back on, and then I had to do a few more tests. Could I read the smallest letters on this chart? What about with this eye covered? With these headphones on, could I hear the beeping sound? Could I walk while squatting? "Recruits call this the duck walk," the doctor said as I waddled around.

Eventually he sent me out. I thought I was done, but it turned out there was one more test: a psych exam.

The shrink was a middle-aged man with a moustache like Stalin and a missing finger on his left hand.

"Mr. Blake?" he said. "I'm Dr. Fallun. Take a seat."

I did.

"I'm going to ask you some questions," he said. His voice was quiet, soothing. "Then I'm going to use your answers to see if you're psychologically fit for duty. It's important for you to know that we're not looking for perfect people, but we are looking for honest people. Don't try to impress me—if you do, I'll know, and this exam will be considered invalid. You understand?"

"Yes, sir."

"Why do you want to join the army?" he asked.

"To serve my country," I said. "Sir."

"That's one," he replied without hesitation. "Lie to me again, and you're out of here. Again, why do you want to join the army?"

Honesty. Fine. "Nothing else to do," I said.

He nodded. "You married?"

"No."

"Ever?"

"No."

"Girlfriend?"

"No."

"What did your parents do for a living?"

"They died when I was one."

"Sorry to hear that. But it's not what I asked."

"My pop worked at an electronics store. My mama was a train conductor, but she gave it up when I was born."

"How did they die?"

"Is this relevant?" My feet were sweaty inside my shoes.

"I need to hear your answers to judge their relevance, Mr. Blake. How did it happen?"

"They were killed during a home invasion."

"Beaten? Raped?"

"Just shot." I swallow. "I'm told it was quick."

"Did the cops catch the perpetrator?"

"No."

"You ever think about what you'd do to him if you met him?"

"No. I was too young to understand, and when I got older, I didn't really remember my folks."

The shrink stared for a while, then said, "So killers should only be punished if you remember the victims?"

"No," I said. "I just don't think about it, is all."

"Where were you when they died?"

"I was there."

"Where exactly?"

"In my mama's arms."

His questions started to get very specific after that. Had I ever engaged in self-harm, cutting, burning? No. Did I find it difficult to control my anger? No. Were my relationships often intense and unstable? I had no relationships. Did I suffer from chronic feelings of boredom or emptiness? No.

He asked if I engaged in reckless activities, such as dangerous driving, spending more than I could afford, risky sex, drugs. I said no to all until he asked about binge eating, and then I paused for too long.

"Sometimes I eat too much," I said. "Everyone does that now and then, right?"

But I always did. I ate everything I could find. I hadn't eaten any people yet, but I'd thought about it. His questions changed direction again, and my honesty diminished. If I told the truth to these questions, I'd definitely fail the psych report.

"Do you induce vomiting when you feel uncomfortably full?"

"No." False.

"Do you wear baggy clothes because you worry about your body shape?"

"No." True.

"Do you worry that you've lost control of your eating habits?"

"No." True—I'd lost control, but I'd stopped worrying.

"Would you say that food dominates your life?"

"No." False.

"Ever used laxatives to lose weight?"

"No." True.

"Do you count calories?"

"No." True.

"After you eat, do you feel disgusted with yourself?"

"No." False.

I think at first he thought I had borderline personality disorder, which I don't. At most, I have borderline borderline
personality disorder.

Then he thought I was bulimic. But I didn't quite fit that
mold either. Yes, I ate compulsively, sometimes to the point of
puking afterward, but it had nothing to do with body image.
I rarely thought about how fat or thin I was—I rarely thought
about myself at all. I was just a seashell being dragged around
by the ravenous crab inside.

Fallun seemed to have run out of questions. He stared at
me, scratching his moustache. I stared back. His expression
went from puzzled to thoughtful to unnerved.

"Well," he said finally, "I guess that'll be all, Mr. Blake."

"Did I pass?"

He leaned back in his chair and glanced at the computer on
his desk. "I have to put your answers into the system. You'll
be notified by mail."

Leaning back, not making eye contact—he was lying.
There was no need for the computer. He wasn't going to
pass me, and he wanted me out of here before I realized it.

"I need this," I said.

"Well, then, I wish you the best of luck," he said.

I stood up. "I want to serve my country."

The shrink had one hand under his desk. Like he was ready
to push an alarm button, or holding a gun.

"God bless you," he said. "Thanks for coming in."

With his free hand, he motioned to the door. For the first
time, I noticed that the stump of his missing finger was mangled, as though it had been chewed off.

I left.

For weeks after, I avoided my usual street corners. I kept my
back to alley walls, waiting for someone to come looking for

me. I thought the shrink had figured out what I was, and I had to assume he told somebody—his review board, the cops, both.

But no one came. I guess someone decided that a psychological profile isn't enough evidence for an arrest warrant. Or maybe when my residential address turned out to be fake, they decided they didn't have enough information to track me down.

Since then, I never tell people what happened to my parents. I don't discuss my eating habits. I can never forget how vulnerable I am—if someone guessed I was a cannibal, they wouldn't have much trouble proving it. The only thing that keeps me visiting death row rather than living there is that I haven't given anyone reason to suspect me.

But if Fallun figured it out based on a few simple answers, other people might figure it out too.

CHAPTER 14

WHY DIDN'T THE VAMPIRE ATTACK THE SNOWMAN?

ROBERT SHEA'S SCHOOL IS A BRICK BUILDING SO square it might be made out of Lego blocks. Decades' worth of graffiti splatter the walls, scrubbed enough to be illegible, but not enough to restore the building's original color, which I'm guessing was brown, like a seventies sofa.

There's a warden—a slender black woman in a high-visibility vest whose job is to report suspicious-looking strangers. She's looking at Thistle and me. Thistle pulls her jacket aside to reveal her badge, and the warden nods cautiously.

Every time Thistle looks at me, I worry that I missed something. A vein between my teeth, some viscera in my hair. I was late, because I scrubbed my skin raw in the shower for a straight half hour. Even so, it's impossible not to worry that she can tell.

Johnson used intravenous drugs, and he was sexually promiscuous. He probably had all sorts of diseases. The thought makes me feel a bit sick. I shouldn't have eaten his flesh raw, but I couldn't help myself.

The first few kids flood out of the school bus. Sixth graders, shrieking and laughing at one another, bouncing on their toes like boxers. The eighth graders are right behind them, mostly paired up, couples nipping at one another's ears and grabbing each other's butts.

It doesn't take me long to spot Jane Austin in the crowd. She's walking alone, backpack over one shoulder, her eyes on the school like she's not really seeing it. She looks right through me until I wave.

She stops dead. Looks at me, looks at Thistle, looks at the badge.

"Jane Austin?" Thistle says.

"Fuck," Austin says, looking at me. "You're a cop?"

I say, "Robert wasn't your boyfriend, was he?"

She half laughs. "What? What's that supposed to mean?"

"He was dating a girl named Portia," Thistle says. "She plays the guitar."

"Portia Gillies?" Austin glares at us. "She's a lying bitch. Robert would never be interested in her."

Her voice wavers. She's lying.

"That's what you told yourself," I say. "How could he be so obsessed with her, while you barely registered on his radar? What did she have that you didn't?"

"This is bullshit," she says, and turns away. "Get lost."

"Someone kidnapped Robert," I say.

Austin stops walking. Thistle gives me a sidelong glance.

"And his parents," I continue. "And then the kidnapper made sure no one would report them missing. He emailed Robert's mom's friends and his dad's boss, telling them the family was going to Chicago. He sent emails to the drummer in his band and to his girlfriend. He even canceled Robert's gym membership online.

"The only thing he missed was you. A girl who was sweet on Robert, but who never had the guts to talk to him. So the only photo she could get was one someone else took at a party. So she was never even close enough to him to call him Bobby like everyone else did. He never knew she existed, so the kidnapper never knew it either."

"Shut up!" There were tears in Austin's eyes. "You don't know anything!"

"Not for sure," I said. "But I'm real good at guessing."

She's wheezing, like a panic attack. I feel sorry for her—but if she'd told me the truth two days ago, I might have found the kid by now.

"Why?" she chokes. "Why would anyone want to kidnap Robert?"

"That's what we came here to ask you," Thistle says.

"I don't know!"

"Is he friends with anybody important? Someone who might tell him their secrets?"

"Robert's buddies are musicians!" Austin says. "What important secrets could they possibly have?"

"He got money? Does he do drugs?"

"No. He's good. A poor and decent guy. All he has is his looks."

I think of my new profile of the kidnapper—a rapist with a fetish for young blond boys.

"Yes," I say. "He has his looks."

Austin is rummaging through her bag. "I logged in to someone else's profile," she said. "Someone who was friends with him. I got some more pictures—I was gonna make more posters."

She hands me a crumpled envelope. The warden is looking at us. This probably looks like a drug deal to her. I stuff the envelope into my jacket pocket.

"What am I supposed to do?" Austin asks. She's sobbing, like it's only just hit her. "Can you help him?"

Hostages make terrible pets. Tough to keep them fed and quiet. You need somewhere they can go to the bathroom. Sometimes they need insulin, or asthma inhalers. Robert and his parents have been gone more than a week. Their chances aren't good.

"Don't worry," I say. "We'll find him." Maybe alive, maybe not.

Thistle hands her a business card. "If you think of anything," she says, "you call us. Got it?"

Austin nods miserably.

"Good. You should go to class."

She wipes her eyes with her sleeve and turns back to join the river of running kids.

When she's out of earshot, Thistle says, "You really believe the kidnapper took a whole family?"

"Do you?"

She watches Austin disappear through the doors of the school. "It fits the facts, but it's weird as hell."

"You got that right. I've never seen a case like this before. And I'm not sure how to solve it."

Thistle digs her phone out of her pocket, fiddles with it for a moment and hands it to me. "I've blocked the caller ID," she says. "Officially, I'm still sick."

I dial and press the phone to my ear.

"Hello?" Luzhin says.

"It's Blake," I say. "I'm calling about Cameron's look-alike."

It takes me a few minutes to explain everything I've learned over the past couple days, and my theory about what it all means.

"This is a lot of speculation," he says finally. "Even for you."

"What's the alternative?" I say. "A whole family moves from Houston to Chicago without telling a single friend or colleague in person? And leaves their cat to die?"

"Folks do everything online these days. I found out about my niece's engagement when she changed her Facebook status—that's just how people announce things now. The fact that no one's seen them in the flesh, that's lack of evidence, not evidence."

"You want evidence," I say, "then open an investigation."

"That's going to be hard with no one to file a missing person report."

"Jane Austin will."

"But she didn't even know the victim."

"Sounds like you don't think the Shea family is worth the FBI's time," I say. "Too poor, maybe? I'm sure CNN would be interested to hear about that."

I can hear the anger in Luzhin's voice. "You *know* that's not how it is."

"Prove me wrong. Open the case."

There's a long silence.

"Fine," he says.

I smile.

"Don't think this means you automatically get rewarded," he continues. "The legwork you've already done isn't enough. You have to actually find the kid."

"You're doing the right thing," I say.

"Don't you talk to me about right and wrong," he replies. "I know which is which."

He hangs up.

I pass the phone back to Thistle. "He's opening the investigation."

She looks like a shark that smells blood in the water—not exactly happy, but determined. "Then I should get over to the field office," she says.

"Good idea. Make some calls about flights to Chicago. Get someone to start canvasing near Shea's house."

"What are you going to do?"

"Think," I say. "I'm out of ideas, so I need to think up some more."

I'm in the kitchen, pulling on some pink dishwashing gloves, tucking the sleeves of my raincoat into the wrists. My vision is distorted by the old pair of swim goggles on my face. The hard white dust mask keeps a cocoon of hot air around my mouth and nose. Since John Johnson isn't around anymore, I'm naked from the waist down. It's liberating, though I haven't yet figured out what I'll do about rent. The cash hidden in Johnson's room won't last forever.

The safest way to get rid of a body is to buy some drain cleaner, or whatever else is available with a high concentration of sulfuric acid. Put the body in the bathtub and scrape the flesh off it with a hand plane, the same kind of tool used to smooth timber.

I swing a framing hammer against the Tanzanian's rib cage, shattering it into chunks that fall to the floor of the tub like fish sticks. Then I crack the sternum, the forehead, the pelvis. I keep on swinging until no part of him is bigger than a matchbox.

Bones aren't the only inedible bits of the human body. Skin, glands and tendons are too chewy, while some organs are toxic. I keep all these parts in a sealed bucket, which has been thawing for the past two hours and is now ready to be tipped into the tub like pig slop.

I pick up the jug of sulfuric acid. Very, very carefully, I pour it over the bone fragments. For a minute, nothing happens. Then they start to crackle and hiss like sausages on a low-heat barbecue.

When the jug is empty, I turn on the ventilation fan, which rattles and coughs like the oldest man on earth. I didn't want to turn it on earlier, just in case there was bone dust in the air that hadn't settled yet. Bone dust gives you lung cancer. I didn't want any to get stuck to the fan blades.

Even with the fan on, the fumes aren't pretty. I used to have to stand here in the stink with the door locked while the bodies gurgled and spat. Now that Johnson is gone I can sit on the couch and watch TV while I wait.

An hour later the bones and tendons have dissolved. I pick up a twisted wire coat hanger and dip the hook into the acid. After a bit of fumbling, I find the plug and pull it out.

I wonder if anyone misses him. Unlike the John Doe who

was cremated in his place, courtesy of Luzhin's wizardry with paperwork—one of a thousand unidentified black male corpses who lie on freezing slabs for months with no one to claim them—the Tanzanian had neighbors and friends. Plus, he was a bit famous during the trial.

As I watch the dead man disappear down the plug hole in a gray-brown whirlpool, like the Ambulance Killer before him, I feel like I should say something. A brief eulogy. A few kind words.

But when I eventually get caught and executed, no one will say anything nice about me.

I shower. First with the raincoat and gloves and goggles on, then naked while they drip dry on hooks above the tub.

Being poor has its benefits. After I've toweled off, it doesn't take me any time at all to decide what to wear to dinner tonight. I have only the two outfits, one of which is always either soaking in the sink or draining on the towel rack while the other is on my body.

I carry the day's clothes through the house and toss them into the sink. Then I lift the rest off the rack and pull them on. Done.

It's also easy to stay in shape, since the only food I can afford is fresh fruit and vegetables, plus the occasional death row playmate. But I'm rare—obesity can be a sign of poverty these days.

Mrs. Radfield explained that to me and the other kids at the group home once. "Iowa gets to vote first in the presidential caucuses," she said. "Can anyone tell me what the primary industry of Iowa is?"

Arty, the girl who stole my meat loaf, raised her hand. "Corn?"

"Correct. This means the candidates have to promise to continue subsidizing corn farmers, or else they don't get to be president. So the farmers end up growing more corn than the country needs, which means they need to find something to do with the excess. What they do is turn it into high-fructose corn syrup and sell it as a cheap sugar substitute. And what's the problem with that?"

"Gives you diabetes."

Mrs. Radfield nodded. "Plus heart and liver disease. Hence, fat poor people."

When I was homeless, I spent every donation on meat, not cheap candy. That was lucky; no one gives money to a fat beggar.

I'm also fortunate that I don't live in Mexico. All this cheap food gets trucked down there, putting local growers out of business, so they try to get to the USA to find work. And Mexico's collapsing economy has left the way open for drug cartels and corrupt police, causing even more Mexicans to flee up toward the border.

"Iowa has created a problem," Mrs. Radfield said, "that Texas has to solve."

A straight razor waits on the windowsill in the bathroom. I pick it up, splash some water on my face and scrape the stubble from my cheeks.

When I'm done, a single droplet of blood hangs from my jawline. I touch it and put my finger to my lips. Other people's blood always tastes better than my own. Don't know why.

I tear a square of toilet paper off the roll and stick it to the wound. Then I hold my head under the faucet and wet my hair before scrubbing it with a towel and slicking it back so it'll dry in that position.

Looking at myself in the mirror, I conclude that I look as good as I ever will. Why am I going to so much effort? Thistle has seen me on a regular day. She's not going to be fooled into thinking I'm handsome or even above average. Plus, why would I care if she did?

It's for the restaurant, I tell myself. *If it's someplace fancy, I don't want to attract attention by looking out of place.*

When I meet the gaze of the guy in the mirror, I get the sudden, unnerving sense that it's not me. *I'm* a rescuer of children, who likes puzzles, while *he's* a demon, hungry for human flesh. Any second now, the demon will smash his fist through the glass, grab me by the throat and pull me toward his unhinged jaws.

The illusion lasts only a moment. The man is nothing more than a reflection of me. Both a person and a monster.

The sun sits just atop the trees outside. It's time to leave. I lock up the house, get in the Chevy and drive.

The Hall residence isn't far out of my way. I have time to stop by and ask Cameron if he was molested. By the kidnapper, that is, not his mother.

When I get to the gated community, the old guard with the long teeth—the ex-cop—is on duty again.

"Mr. Blake," he says. "Different car?"

After seventeen years with the local cops, he probably knows what a stolen car looks like.

"I don't remember introducing myself," I say.

"The kid told me to let you through if you came back."

"Cameron Hall?"

"I guess so," the guard says. "Blond teenage boy? In the car with Ms. Hall?"

"That'd be him. He say what he wanted?"

"No. This was last week."

If Cameron wanted to talk to me last week, why hasn't he called me?

"Okay," I say. "Thanks."

The guard unlocks the gate. I drive through into the darkness of the gated community. The grounds are as quiet and perfect as a cemetery. A minute later I'm standing on the Halls' porch, ringing the bell. I don't hear movement inside.

I bang on the door. "Ms. Hall, Cameron, open up."

Nothing.

"It's Timothy Blake," I say. "I saved Cameron's life, the least you can do is let me in."

More silence. They're not home.

Maybe I don't need to talk to Cameron to get the information I need. Perhaps a quick look around his home would be enough.

I close my eyes and do a mental walk through the house, looking for easy access. The back door and the screen door covering it are both locked. The windows all have bolts on them, and I don't want to risk smashing one.

I try to remember the status of the windows in Annette Hall's room. Closed, yes. But locked? It didn't look like it.

I vault over the side gate and ascend the wrought-iron grid beside the back door, ivy sticky under my fingers. I'm in luck—Ms. Hall's bedroom window is stiff, but not locked. I pry it open and slip inside.

Once I'm in, I stand still for a few seconds, listening. The only sound is the beeping of the alarm downstairs. I trot down and turn it off, using Annette Hall's birthday. Silence falls.

The downstairs area looks just like it did when I last saw it. The same clothes fill the hamper in the laundry. The knife in the kitchen still has a drop of my blood on it.

Back upstairs, Annette Hall's bed is made, but otherwise the room is unchanged. The en suite is clean. The drugs are still in the cupboard behind the mirror. There are no extra loofahs in the shower, the soap doesn't appear to have decreased in size, the towels aren't bloody. No sign that someone's been in the shower for hours and hours, scrubbing themselves until they bleed, the way rape survivors sometimes do. But of course, I'll have to check Cameron's bathroom too.

I open Ms. Hall's wardrobe. Five or six outfits are missing.

And there's a spot on the top shelf where I think there was a suitcase before.

My blood runs cold. This is all starting to feel horribly familiar. Robert Shea's house was sanitized in exactly the same way.

Has the kidnapper been here a third time? Waited for the FBI to let Cameron and his mother go, and then dragged them both from their home?

There's no sign of forced entry or a struggle. I know I'm missing something; I just can't work out what.

If the Halls have been abducted again, I have to tell Luzhin—but I can't let him know that I'm breaking into houses.

I pick up the phone and hit the button marked *Block caller ID*. Then I dial Luzhin's office. It's almost six, but he's probably still there.

The phone rings three or four times before Luzhin picks up. "Who is this?"

"It's Blake."

"Where are you calling from?"

"A friend's house. Listen, I just drove out to the Hall place, and it doesn't look like anybody's home."

"Hey, you can't go hassling victims," Luzhin says. "That's the FBI's job."

Ha ha. "I just wanted to ask Cameron a couple questions," I say. "The car isn't in the drive. Have you seen Cameron since we rescued him, or Annette?"

"No," Luzhin says. "But I asked them if there was anybody they could stay with, and she said her folks lived nearby."

Cameron's grandparents. I remember seeing *Mom + Dad* in the list of recently dialed numbers.

"Oh," I say. "Well, maybe they're with them."

"I'll phone Annette's cell first thing tomorrow and check that they're okay. You just worry about finding Robert Shea. Got that?"

"Yes, sir," I say, and hang up. Then I scroll through the recent call list on the phone until I find the number for the grandparents, and hit Redial.

It seems likely that Luzhin is right and that's where Cameron and his mother have gone, but I have to know for sure.

The call goes to voice mail. I memorize the number so I can try again later.

I head down the hall to Cameron's room. A quick poke around doesn't reveal much. Some clothes missing. No bloody towels in the en suite. No used condoms among the trash.

This could be exactly what it looks like: the kid's gone off to stay with his grandma and grandpa.

Sometimes people send me Rubik's Cubes and, after a bit of fiddling, I realize that they've peeled the colored stickers off and rearranged them so it can't be solved. The feeling I get when I'm searching for the scratch marks, the ones that'll tell me which squares have been moved, that's the feeling I'm getting now, looking at this empty house.

I'm waiting on the sidewalk outside the restaurant, thinking about Dr. Fallun. About the questions he asked at the army interview, about the way he looked at me, the way he somehow knew what I was.

He's the reason I'm so nervous about meeting Thistle tonight. She's not a shrink, but she is a cop. I've never hung out with a cop in a social context, certainly never one as smart as Thistle. Surely she'd know a serial killer if she had dinner with one.

I watch the servers watching me through the double-glazed window. They're probably used to homeless people coming in, asking for a table and a menu, and then going to the restroom to wash themselves before walking out again. I haven't been a beggar for a few years now, but I still have the look—

hollow cheeks, faded clothes, rough skin. Servers are very perceptive. They need to be, since they live off tips.

I could go in, say Thistle's name and phone number, and wait for her inside. But they'll give a better table to her than to me.

And here she is anyway. She's dressed up—I can see a cream halter top under her coat, and a silky skirt that's dark red, almost black. Her high heels are a matching shade. Pear-shaped studs sparkle in her earlobes.

And she's smiling. That's what makes her truly beautiful, and I find myself off balance. This is a date with a woman who's both out of my league and very dangerous to me. I shouldn't be here.

"Timothy," she says. "Good to see you."

I nod and gesture toward the door. "After you."

We walk up the red carpet, which is a little too short and narrow to create the sense of luxury the owners probably hoped for. But the fact that it's a restaurant at all seems luxurious to me.

"You been here before?" Thistle asks.

I laugh.

"What?" she says.

Oh. She wasn't kidding. I'm used to Luzhin, Richmond and Johnson—it's weird to have a conversation where I'm not being looked down on.

"Nothing," I say. "I just don't get out much."

"Agoraphobia?" she asks.

"Poverty." It just slips out.

She laughs, although I think she's only pretending to believe I was kidding.

"Table for two?" the waiter says. He's white, tall, with hair gelled back to reveal a Dracula-style widow's peak. The doubtful glance he sends my way is quick, but I catch it.

"Reservation for RT," Thistle says. "For six-thirty."

"This way, ma'am," the waiter says. "And sir."

He leads us to a table in the corner with hard wooden chairs on either side of it and a candle burning in a glass on top. As we walk, we pass another couple who have just been presented with the check.

"Don't worry," the man is saying. "I got this."

The woman says, "You sure?"

"Of course." He gets out his American Express, but he looks unhappy—like he wanted her to fight harder. I wonder how Thistle will look when I don't offer to pay.

She takes off her coat and perches on the far side of the table. I like being able to see the door, but I don't want to make a big thing of it, so I just sit down.

Her top exposes a star-shaped scar on her shoulder. An old bullet wound. She sees me looking.

"My FBI star," she says.

"Sorry," I say, and look away.

I find myself staring at the other couple. I memorize the man's credit card number out of habit. It's not as hard as you'd think—the first six numbers on an Amex card are always the same, so I need to remember only thirteen digits including the verification number. Amex is the perfect card for fraud, partly because the verification number is on the front rather than the back, but mostly because Amex customers use their cards so often that they're less likely to notice a few stray charges on their statement.

In the USA, you're likely to get caught if you try to buy anything with a stolen card. But not in Egypt, Russia or Indonesia. That's why, if you can find the right online forum, you can sell a stolen card number for about fifty bucks. The minimum wage in Texas is $7.25 per hour, so the Amex number I just memorized would be worth almost a whole day's honest labor. If it weren't for this skill, I'd still be sleeping on dead grass under an overpass.

The waiter hands us wine lists. Thistle turns hers down, saying, "Just a diet soda for me, thanks. I'm driving."

I say, "Soda for me too."

"You sure?" Thistle asks. "I'm buying."

"Just soda."

The waiter picks up our wineglasses and goes away. He looks disappointed. Drunk patrons tip more.

"So," Thistle says.

"So."

She hesitates. "You, uh...wanna talk about the case?"

I'd be much more comfortable on familiar ground. "Sure."

"No record of the Sheas flying anywhere. But I dug up Robert's medical records. He had a renal cell carcinoma. Rare in kids."

I frown. "He had cancer?"

"Yep. But they treated it successfully—with a nephrectomy."

My feet have been twitching in my shoes. Now they stop. "He had a kidney removed? When?"

"Admitted to Park Plaza two weeks ago, discharged three days later," Thistle says. "The procedure was a success. Nothing else noteworthy."

"So Robert Shea needed a transplant."

"Well, he didn't *need* one, but you're better off with two functioning kidneys, yeah."

"And a week after he lost his, someone ripped one out of Cameron Hall."

"I know what you're thinking," Thistle says. "But it makes no sense. Cameron Hall's kidney wasn't given to Robert Shea. It was left in a car to rot."

Our sodas arrive. We fall silent.

"I want to know what's in Shea's sealed juvie record," I say.

"We'll need a warrant."

"Could you get Luzhin to arrange that? He likes you better than me."

"I already did," she says. "He's working on it. Why do you think he doesn't like you?"

Because he knows I eat people. "I'm not one of his agents. He's suspicious of outsiders."

"Bullshit. I think he's proud to have you on his team. And if he's not, he should be."

She's wrong, but the sentiment is touching. I stare down at the menu without really seeing it.

The waiter comes back. "Are you ready to order?"

Thistle gestures at me. *After you.*

"Porterhouse," I say. "Raw."

"Rare?"

"Yeah, that's what I meant. Really rare."

The waiter turns to Thistle. "Ma'am?"

"I'll have the lamb cutlets, thanks," she says. "With a side of Greek salad."

"You still okay for drinks?"

"Yep."

He leaves again.

"If it's the same kidnapper," Thistle asks, "why was there no ransom this time?"

"I'm thinking the ransom was a decoy," I say. "Or at least a side goal. The kidnapper wanted Cameron for his own reasons, probably sexual."

A woman at another table is glaring at us. I probably should talk quieter.

Thistle says, "Is there any evidence that Cameron was sexually assaulted?"

"No physical signs, according to the hospital exam. But I still want to ask him about it. And now he's left town to stay with his grandparents."

"I could probably get their number," Thistle says. "I'll give them a call tomorrow if you want."

"Thanks, but Luzhin said he'd do it." Plus, I already tried. "Did anyone do a profile while Cameron was missing?"

"Probably. Not that it'll do us much good."

I'm surprised. Most FBI agents aren't openly critical of profilers. "Why not?"

"Because profiling is mostly statistics," Thistle says. "If a profiler gets a case, let's say death by poison, she'll know that most poisonings are done by women, whereas male murderers use guns or brute force. So her profile will say we should be looking for a woman. Right?"

"Right."

"But that only works because she's got lots of other poisonings to compare the case to. A profiler's first step is to examine similar crimes and look for common features among the perps."

"And that won't work here," I say. "Because there are no similar cases."

"Exactly. Kid goes missing, ransom demand, kidney returned, ransom increased, consultant kidnapped…" She waves her diet soda at me. "Similar kid abducted, parents taken, photos stolen and so on. You won't find a single case that resembles this one."

She takes a sip from her straw. I scratch my chin.

"Well, that tells us something," I say. "We're looking for a perp who's nothing like anyone we've caught before. What's the exact opposite of a typical kidnapper?"

"Rich," Thistle says.

True. Most crime comes from necessity, so most criminals are poor.

"College educated," I say.

She nods. "Parents still happily married."

"Maybe with a family of his own."

"Middle-aged. Female?"

I think back to the man in the parking lot. I didn't get a

good look at him, but he was big. "No. The guy who took the ransom was definitely male."

"But that could've been an accomplice."

"A duo?"

"Maybe."

"Okay. A rich, smart, middle-aged duo, one of whom is male."

"Married to each other, maybe?" Thistle says.

"Husband and wife team?" I think it over. "Maybe they're looking to spice up their sex life and pay off their mortgage at the same time."

"This is good." Thistle smiles. Her teeth shine like piano keys. "We work well together."

"It's good if we're right," I say. "Otherwise we're just leading ourselves further off track."

Our meals arrive. Rare meat doesn't take long to cook. My steak is thick, bloody, alone in the center of the plate.

Thistle holds up her glass. "Cheers."

I clink mine against hers. "Cheers."

Thistle stabs a lump of lamb with her fork and swallows it. "So how did you end up consulting for the FBI?"

Well, Luzhin caught me eating a mugger, but I was able to black-mail him because of his cocaine addiction.

"I used to love *The X-Files* as a kid," I say.

She laughs. "Me too! I used to dye my hair to look like Scully."

I smile, picturing her as an ultraserious young black girl with dyed red hair. "Well, I dropped out of high school, and you can't join the FBI without a college degree. But I still wanted to help, so here I am."

"Why did you drop out of high school?"

This part's true, and therefore harder to explain. "I moved into a group home when I was one. But no foster family took me right away, and the older I got, the harder it was.

Eventually I was sixteen, old enough to look after myself, so I had to move out of there, but I had no home to move into. I was already flipping burgers at McDonald's on the weekends, but that wasn't enough to pay rent, so I had to leave school to work there full-time. That lasted until I turned twenty-one—because the minimum wage is higher for adults they had to let me go or pay me more, so they let me go. What?"

Thistle is staring at me. Her head is tilted slightly, like she's looking at one of those pictures that could be a vase or could be two faces.

Have I said too much? Has she realized what I am?

"Scary Timmy?" she says.

Suddenly I'm staring back at her. I can't believe this.

Reese Thistle. RT.

"Arty?" I say.

CHAPTER 15

**IF YOU HAVE ME, YOU WANT TO SHARE ME.
IF YOU SHARE ME, YOU DON'T HAVE ME.
WHAT AM I?**

ONLY ONCE BEFORE HAVE I MET SOMEONE WHO grew up in the group home alongside me. His name was Jared Carter. I didn't know him well—as a child he was always hovering at the edge of the game or the argument, listening but not engaging.

Unlike the rest of us, his parents weren't dead, as far as anyone knew. He'd been delivered to the home as a baby by someone who claimed to have found him in a shopping cart—hence his last name. The only time I remember speaking to him was after I'd found some undeveloped film in the trash, and he showed me how to make a pinhole camera out of a cardboard box. But we had no developing fluid, so we couldn't look at the pictures we took.

One time a bunch of us were playing tag and some kid tagged Jared and said, "You're it." Jared chased the others around in circles for a little while, but he'd never played before and wasn't very good. He didn't know how to corner a bunch of players so you could be sure to get one of them. He hadn't learned how to feint one way so his prey would dodge the other, into his waiting hands.

After a while the kids got bored of being chased so clumsily and decided that someone else should be "it." But no one volunteered, and an argument broke out. Eventually a kid named Stephen turned to Jared and said, "Just fucking run faster, faggot!" and punched him in the side of the head.

Another kid ran over, and I remember being surprised, him not seeming like the type to break up a fight—but he didn't; he just started hitting Jared as well. Soon a whole bunch of kids were beating on him.

He never fought back, but he never cried either. It was like his brain went somewhere else while his body was getting battered.

There were too many of them for me to intervene physically, and I couldn't afford to lose my whole social group by ratting them out to the staff. So I ran to my room and sat on my bunk, and waited for the noise to stop.

It took a long time.

As an adult, Jared Carter shot his wife six times, then ran out of bullets. When the police showed up twenty minutes later, they found him on his knees on the kitchen floor, fist clenched around the barrel of the gun, striking her corpse with the butt over and over and over. It was as if he'd stored up every punch anyone had ever landed on him, and now he was letting them all out again.

His baby daughter was crying in front of the TV. She ended up at the same group home he grew up in. And Jared ended up on death row, which was where I found him. His bones are buried in my backyard—this was before I discovered that you could use sulfuric acid to dissolve them.

And now I'm faced with Reese Thistle—or, as I used to know her, Arty.

"I can't believe this!" she's saying. "You're here!"

I know how she feels. The more I look at her face, the more I recognize the girl I used to know. The birthmark on her neck. The slight angle of her dark eyes.

"Arty," I say again, the name unfamiliar on my tongue after so long.

She giggles. "No one's called me that in years."

"You're a cop," I say.

"I know!" she says. "And you're…" She hesitates as she realizes there isn't a word for what I am. "You're you!"

"Can't argue with that."

Arty works for the FBI. It's weird enough seeing childhood acquaintances as adults. Weirder still to see them in positions of authority. Doctors, cops, politicians.

"What are the chances?" Thistle asks. "Of us running into one another again after all this time?"

"One in a million, probably," I say. "Although, we live in the same city, and we're about the same age, and—" Something she said before finally registers. "Wait, did you just call me 'Scary Timmy'?"

Thistle clears her throat. "Uh, yeah. Some of the other kids, they used to call you that."

That was surprisingly astute of them.

"God, I'm sorry," she says. "We were cruel to you, weren't we?"

I shrug. "I think everyone was cruel to everyone."

"That's no excuse. I shouldn't have stolen your meat loaf that time. You remember?"

"I shouldn't have beat you up after," I say.

"Hey, that's not how it was. I beat *you* up."

I frown. "That makes no sense. You stole my meat loaf, so I hit you—"

"And I hit you back, harder."

"Yeah, but then I pulled your hair and—"

She laughs. "I kicked your ass, that's what I did."

The woman from the next table is staring at us again. I clear my throat.

"Hey, do you remember Jared Carter?" Thistle asks.

I pretend to think about it. "Vaguely. Why?"

She tells me about the murder of his wife and his death

sentence. Then she asks me if I remember Buzz Ritchie. He'd owned the only complete deck of playing cards in the home, so he'd been popular. As an adult he moved to Miami and drank himself to death at a friend's thirtieth birthday party.

Do I remember Greta Chase? Little girl, obsessed with *Pocahontas*. She's in prison now. Got busted with almost twenty ounces of blow. The cops thought she was dealing, but could only prove possession.

How about Stephen Stattelis? He was the one who punched Jared in that game of tag. Two years ago he lost forty grand at a blackjack table in Atlantic City and tried to earn it back as a male prostitute before getting stabbed to death by a rival's pimp.

"Looks like we're the only ones who turned out okay," she says.

It's just you, I want to say. *I'm worse than all of them.*

"Why were you at the group home?" I ask. "What happened to your folks?"

She gives me that look that people get when they've explained something a thousand times before and know exactly what reaction they'll get. "They couldn't afford to keep me. So my father drove off a bridge. Killed himself, and my mom. Tried to kill me too—I was in the back seat."

My childhood doesn't sound so bad compared to that. I've always assumed that I was fated to be this way—a man turned me into a killer by slaughtering my parents in front of me. I had no choice. It's not my fault.

But Thistle isn't a killer. She had it equally tough, and she turned out fine.

"I'm sorry," I say, like you're supposed to.

"It's okay," she says. "I don't remember it. So, they were killed when the car hit the water. But I was fine. He put on my seat belt, can you believe that? Why would you put a seat belt on if you were going to— Anyway, the police boats got to the car less than a minute after it sank, and there was still air in the cabin, so they got me out. But there were no foster families with room for me, so I got dumped at the group home. I guess I'm lucky the cops didn't just leave me in the evidence locker."

I chuckle.

She smiles. "Thanks. People never laugh at that joke."

"Then why do you keep telling it?"

"I figured someday I'd meet someone who would. And here you are."

"Here I am. You left when you were eleven, right?"

"Ten. A couple adopted me, put me through school—they still live in Houston."

"Is your adopted dad a cop?"

She raises an eyebrow. "Why do you ask?"

"Most folks wouldn't let their only daughter join the force," I say. "They think it's too dangerous."

"Who says I'm their only daughter?"

"Most folks don't adopt if they already have kids."

She laughs. "You're just full of stats, aren't you?"

"But I'm right, right?"

"Half right. My adopted mom was a cop, not my dad. Houston PD."

"I don't suppose you asked her if she knew the guard on Annette Hall's gate? The ex-cop?"

She smiles. "Actually, yes. Couldn't help myself. According to the company that runs the gated community, his name is Morris Brattan. Mom says he was discharged in 2002 after one too many allegations of sexual harassment."

"Did she know him?"

"Not personally. It was a big department."

I've finished picking the last scraps of meat from my steak. The bone is as clean and white as an elephant's tusk.

"You want some of this?" Thistle asks, gesturing at the remains of her salad.

"Sure," I say. I never turn down free food.

She slides her plate across to me.

"Can I ask you something?"

"You can ask," she says. "I might not tell you."

"Why did you leave your husband?"

Her hand, which has been fiddling with one of her ear studs, pauses.

"Funny," she says. "People usually assume he left me, not the other way around."

That never even occurred to me. I can't imagine anyone leaving her. "Because he was a player?"

"Because he was handsome. He had options. But I was the one who left."

"So what went wrong?"

She stares down at the table, thinking. "This is going to sound awful, but he wasn't all that interesting."

"I've heard worse things."

"We met in college, and I fell in love with his arms, his cheekbones, his butt—and his wallet. It's embarrassing, but he tried to impress me with his money, and it worked. He bought me tickets to see all my favorite bands. Jewelry too, sometimes. And fancy food."

"Hell, I would have married him," I say. "How did he get rich?"

"His parents gave him a big allowance, and one year he gave most of it to a friend who was starting up a marketing company. When it took off, he sold his shares for about five times what he'd paid for them."

"Smart," I said.

"Lucky. It could easily have gone the other way, and he was honest enough to admit it. Anyway, by the time I realized that he talked a lot but didn't have much to say, we were already married."

A cherry tomato bursts in my mouth.

"I found myself working longer hours to avoid going home. Inviting friends over for dinner every single night so I didn't have to talk to him, but all *they* wanted to talk about was what a nice house we had. When no one was available, I'd turn on the TV. Didn't even matter what was on—I'd watch until he went to bed.

"For a long time, I planned on staying with him anyhow. I told myself I was lucky. But I just kept thinking that he'd had it so easy, with his rich parents and good looks and smart friends. He would never have survived what I went through. And that made it tough to respect him. To love him."

"I'm sorry," I say. I've heard enough divorce stories to know how the next few months must have gone.

"It's okay." She lifts her glass of soda. "I didn't want to hurt him—he was a nice guy—but I just couldn't keep going. So I moved out and lived with my folks for a bit, until I couldn't stand my dad's bitching about how I'd thrown my life away."

"Seems to me like you did the opposite."

"That's what I said, right before I moved out. So…" She leans back in her chair. "After McDonald's fired you, what did you do?"

I blink, startled by the segue. "Uh, nothing," I say. "Lived on the streets for a while."

"Shit, really?" Thistle says. "How long?"

"Three years. Felt like longer."

"How did you get out of that?"

By stealing things and selling them. Cars. Drugs. Guns. I decide to skip that bit.

"I went to the library and set up an online business," I say. "Solving puzzles for money."

"Puzzles?"

"Yeah. Riddles, Rubik's Cubes, jigsaws, whatever. People mail them to me, I solve them and send them back."

"And people pay you to do that?"

"Sure."

"Why?"

"When you say you can solve any puzzle, people want to prove you wrong. Some of them are willing to bet money on it."

"So you make enough to live off?"

Only because half the payments come from Nigerians—and they're really for credit card numbers, not puzzles. "Sure," I say again.

"But you're smart," she says. "You got skills. No offense, but isn't there something better you could be doing?"

"Ten million Americans are looking for work," I say. "Lots of them have college degrees and references. What chance have I got?"

"None, if you don't try," Thistle says. But she doesn't sound as if she likes my odds.

The waiter returns to take our plates away. "Can I get you the dessert menu?" he asks.

Thistle looks at me.

"I'm not hungry," I lie. Now that Thistle has turned her focus to my life, I'm keen for the meal to end. The less she knows about me, the better. Why was I so open? I've been careless.

"No, thanks," she tells the waiter.

"Coffee?" he presses.

"Just the check."

He nods and walks away, probably hoping the next occupants of this table will be less tight.

"I would like a coffee," Thistle whispers. "But it's so expensive here. How about we move on?"

I look out the window at the glimmering stars. "Will anywhere be open?"

Thistle shrugs. "Your place or mine?"

I should say no, thanks. Tell her I've got too many puzzles
to do. But the idea of her seeing my house, of having an FBI
agent drinking coffee in a kitchen in which a dead body is
currently concealed, is so alarming that I panic.

"Yours," I say immediately. It just slips out.

Thistle's house is even smaller than mine, but the neighborhood is better. I'm not seeing any bars on windows, and
none of the mailboxes bear dents from baseball bats.

"You live alone?" I ask as she pulls into the driveway.

"I have a roommate. She's in Florida visiting her mom."

I'm both relieved and worried. I don't like meeting new
people, but I don't like being alone with Thistle either. She's
dangerous to me, and I'm dangerous to her. Nothing good
can come of this.

She unlocks the front door. "Sorry about the mess," she
says as she pushes it open and flicks on the light.

There's no mess. She's just being modest. The table is bare
but for a weekend newspaper, there's only one CD on top of
the player while the rest are alphabetized on the rack.

In fact, I get a sense that this is cleaner than the place usually is. She expected me to come here.

A young Jack Russell terrier bounds up to us and barks at
me.

"Hello, Junie!" Thistle says, scratching the dog's ears. Then,
to me, "Don't mind her. She hasn't met anyone new in a long
time."

The dog sniffs my feet and then sprints away into another
room.

"See? She's bored of you already."

Thistle slips off her shoes and walks into the kitchen. I can make out a tattoo through her stocking—a ribbon of musical notes curled around her ankle.

She puts the kettle on the burner. "It's just instant, I'm sorry. Cream, three sugars and one salt, right?"

"Good memory."

"It's memorable." She gets the milk out of the fridge. "Make yourself at home."

I look around. "Where's your violin?"

She blinks. "What makes you think I play the violin?"

It might be rude to point out the callus on her neck. "Just guessing."

She shakes her head in disbelief. "Close. I play the viola."

I sit down on the sofa. "Are you in an orchestra?"

She laughs. "It's not that kind of music."

"What kind of music is it?"

She pours boiling water into two mismatched mugs. "It's, uh...modern."

"Let's hear it," I say.

"No way." Her dark skin makes it hard to tell, but I think she might be blushing.

"Yes way."

"I'm too embarrassed."

"The more you stall, the bigger a deal it is and the more embarrassing it will be."

She thinks about that, says, "Good point," and flees the room.

I'm just starting to wonder if she's climbed out her bedroom window when she comes back, holding what I guess must be a viola. It looks like a violin, but a little bigger—the body is maybe seventeen inches. Her left hand is curled around the frog of a bow.

"Promise not to laugh?" she says.

"Is it going to be funny?"

"I hope not."

"Then I won't laugh."

She sighs and presses the viola to her neck.

I wait.

I'm not sure what I was expecting—maybe the lonely cry of a sonata, perhaps the same amelodic stuff she was always humming as a child. But what she gives me is something altogether different.

She starts bouncing the bow on the strings, quickly, evenly, creating a sound like the strumming of an electric guitar. With every eighth beat she brings the bow down hard on the body of the viola and it cracks like a snare drum. Her tattooed foot stomps the ground, strengthening the beat, and suddenly I find my toes are tapping as well. And then Thistle is dragging the horsehair across three strings at once, making distorted sounds that Metallica would be proud of.

She *would* be out of place in an orchestra. This isn't classical music at all—this is rock and roll.

She's humming, maybe unconsciously, and suddenly I recognize the tune. It's "Baby, I Ain't Your Man" by Harry Crudup and the Smooth Candies. I like her version more than his.

Last week she said she hadn't heard of the band. She must have looked them up and learned this song.

Thistle and I had the same start in life—rescued by police from the clutches of our dead parents. But she's become a smart, tough FBI agent who can learn a new song on the viola in only a week or two. I'm a poor, unemployed cannibal. Where did our worlds diverge? Where did I go wrong?

Thistle strikes the final chord and leaves her bow raised, like a swordswoman rallying her troops.

"Holy shit," I say.

Thistle laughs. "You like it?"

"It's incredible. How did you teach yourself to do that?"

She doesn't ask how I know she's self-taught. Maybe she's getting used to me figuring things out.

"I found this in a pawnshop," she says, tapping the viola. "I just liked the look of the wood, and the shape, you know. I got a bow at a different pawnshop, then I played along to CDs at home. First just the bass lines, then, when I got a little better, the melodies and the chords. I've been playing for maybe eight years now. Never showed anyone before."

She sits down next to me on the couch. "Do you play anything?" she asks.

"Remember when we were kids," I say, "how there was a playground just up the street from the home? Sometimes I used to go there, pull sticks off dead branches and play the equipment like it was a giant drum kit."

"There's an elementary school just near here," Thistle says, deadpan. "We could go there together and jam."

I laugh, imagining what would happen if someone called the cops after seeing us beating on the play equipment. "We probably wouldn't get away with it," I say. "We're not as cute as we used to be."

"Sure you are," she says, and kisses me.

I'm paralyzed, like a cat who's spotted a rival. Her lips are touching mine as she waits for some kind of response.

She must think I'm deciding whether to kiss her back. In reality, I'm just trying to suppress my carnivorous instincts. My mouth has never been this close to someone without biting them.

And I'm failing. First I'm probing her upper lip with my tongue, tasting her. Then I'm sucking, then I'm nibbling gently.

Stop, I tell myself. *Stop this.*

But I can't.

Thistle slides across me, straddles my lap, rakes her fingers through my hair. I can smell her lime perfume. My hands creep around to her lower back, and I can feel the knobs of her vertebrae through her top. She has no idea of the danger she's in.

"What about the coffee?" I say. It's the best excuse I can come up with.

Her mouth brushes against my earlobe. I can see the veins pulsing in her neck. I can feel my lips pulling back, an involuntary reflex, exposing my canines.

"Fuck the coffee," she whispers.

"That doesn't sound sanitary."

She laughs and starts fumbling with the buttons on my shirt. I slide my hands up the soft skin of her thighs, under her skirt. I squeeze her butt cheeks—firm and smooth.

This is a crisis, and it could soon become a disaster.

She sighs as she pulls my shirt open. Her fingernails graze the hard flesh that's left when hunger has burned all the fat away. The scar tissue on my ribs, my belly, my hips.

"You're so tough," she whispers.

She thinks I'm the opposite of her rich, handsome ex-husband. And I am—in more ways than she knows.

Thistle grabs at my belt.

"We shouldn't do this," I say.

She slips the strap through the buckle. "No one at the Bureau has to know."

She's right, something in my head says. *You could devour her and get away with it. No one would guess, except maybe Luzhin, and he couldn't prove anything.*

Come on. You never turn down free food.

Thistle lifts her top over her head, revealing small, juicy breasts in a half-cup bra. I can see scars under her armpits, just like the ones that cover my arms. Old fleabites from our beds at the home. We're the same, her and me—except we're not.

She reaches behind her back to unclasp the bra.

"Stop. Please."

She pauses. "Why? What's wrong?"

"I can't do this," I say, partly to myself.

"Why not? Don't you want to?" She looks pointedly down at my crotch, where a bulge is visible under the zipper.

How could I possibly explain?

"Not before we're married," I say.

Her eyes bug out. "What?"

"I mean, I'm not proposing," I say hurriedly. "I didn't mean— I'm kind of religious, that's all. I can't do…this. Not before my wedding night."

She stares at me, like she can't decide if I'm serious.

"It's a sin," I add.

Thistle stands and picks up her top. "It's okay," she says. "I get it. If you're not interested in me—"

"No, I am," I say. "I am. I really like you. I just can't."

The words are out of my mouth before I realize that they're true. I *do* like Thistle. And the fact that she likes me too feels like the first good thing that's ever happened to me. I can't let myself hurt her.

"Please," I say. "I want to. But it's an affront to the Lord. And if I see any more of you, I don't think I'll be able to control myself."

This last part is pure truth, and she sees it. After a long moment, she sits back down on the couch next to me.

"So…you're a virgin?" she says.

I try to look embarrassed. It's not much of a stretch. "Yeah. I mean, I've done some stuff, but not the actual…you know."

"Penetration," Thistle says bluntly.

Her no-bullshit attitude is one of the many things I like about her. "Yeah. That."

"So which religion are you?"

I smile, stalling. "You must think I'm crazy."

She shakes her head. "No! Not at all. I'm just curious about your beliefs."

"I'm Catholic," I say.

"I didn't think anyone could stay Catholic after meeting Mrs. Radfield."

I shrug. "There was a church I used to go to most Sundays. The priest was really nice."

"So you don't go to church anymore?" she asks.

I don't like the idea of Thistle thinking that I believe in God. I wonder what the Bible says about cannibalism. *Eat this, for it is my body.* But even more, I hate the idea of her thinking I don't like her.

"I go at Christmas," I say. "And Easter. Do you?"

She shakes her head. "I'm an atheist. Does that bother you?"

"No. I'm not sure how much of the good book I believe, it's just…your virginity is something you can't get back, you know?"

"True."

"I'm sorry," I say. "I hate feeling like I let you down."

"It's okay," she says. She puts her arms around my neck. "In fact, I respect it. Celibacy must take a lot of willpower."

I think of all the times I've eaten someone and sworn I'll never do it again.

She kisses me on the cheek. "I shouldn't have come on so strong. Still interested in that coffee?"

I nod. She gets up and pads back over to the kitchen, still in her underwear. She's enjoying making me uncomfortable.

I pull my shirt back together and do up the buttons. Then I pull on my jacket.

Jane Austin's envelope falls out of my pocket. I hadn't gotten around to looking at the pictures yet. I open the flap and start flicking through them.

Suddenly I'm squeezing them so hard I'm crumpling the corners.

"Reese!" I yell.

She whirls around. "What?"

"Robert Shea and Cameron Hall don't just look alike," I

say, running over to her with the photos. "They're identical twins."

"That makes no sense," she says. But her eyes are widening as she shuffles through the photos. She's seeing what I saw—that the kid in the pictures looks exactly like the one I rescued from the warehouse, except for a different haircut and a couple more pounds.

"Annette Hall is Robert's mother," I say, figuring it out as I say the words. "She gave him up for adoption—maybe she could afford one kid but not two. Then the Sheas took him in. Now the same kidnapper has abducted him."

"Why couldn't it be the other way around?" Thistle asks. "Why couldn't Cameron be Celine and Larry Shea's son?"

"Because he looks too much like—"

Something snaps into place in my head. We're looking for someone the Halls know. Someone they might willingly go somewhere with. Someone with a motive to kidnap both Cameron Hall and Robert Shea.

Ninety percent of kidnappings are executed by relatives.

"I'm thinking we need to find the dad," I say.

CHAPTER 16

**I HAVE SIX FACES AND TWENTY-ONE EYES,
BUT I AM BLIND.
WHAT AM I?**

THE WOMAN IS A SHORT, SLIM FORTYSOMETHING with high-riding jeans and a well-polished belt buckle about three times the practical size. It makes up for her engagement and wedding rings, which are no bigger than a cop could afford. She makes it across the foyer to the FBI receptionist before I do, so I sit on the faux-leather sofa and wait.

"I'm here to see the field office director, thank you," the woman says, like she's ordering a sandwich.

"Sure thing, honey." The receptionist doesn't ask for her name. She just picks up the phone and dials. "Hi. Is the director available?"

There's a pause.

"Uh-huh," she says, answering a question.

Another pause.

"Uh-huh," she says again, meaning *I understand.*

Another pause.

"Thank you kindly. Bye." She hangs up. "I'm afraid he's not here."

"He's always here," the woman says. "He's been here for twenty years."

"Sorry, honey. Can I take a message for him?"

"Sure. Tell him not to push for joint custody."

She spins around and walks out without looking at me. I

don't look directly at her either, but even with my peripheral vision, I can tell it's the woman from Luzhin's family photo.

"Mr. Blake," the receptionist says.

I stand up and walk over. "Can I use your phone?"

"Sure thing." She holds up the receiver. I take it and dial.

The line chirps in my ear, five times, six times, seven. Somewhere, a hundred miles away from me, a phone is ringing.

"Come on, you old coot," I mutter. "Pick up." The phone rings five more times and then goes to voice mail. Cameron's grandparents are still not home. I'll have to try later.

Cameron's father is named Philip Hall. At this point, that's all I know about him. I don't have an age, an address or even a phone number. There's nothing I can do until I've spoken to Annette Hall—and every passing second takes Robert Shea farther away.

"Thanks," I tell the receptionist, handing the phone back.

"Anytime, honey," she says. "You don't want to try their cells?"

"I don't have—" Wait. After Cameron's kidnapping, the FBI would have bugged the landline at the Hall residence. That's standard. If I can get ahold of the records—or, better yet, the recordings—I wouldn't just find the grandparents' cell numbers. I would get the numbers of everyone else who's called them since. You never know where your next lead is going to come from.

"No, thanks," I tell the receptionist. "Just the visitors' log."

She slaps it down on the desk. "Sign here."

Once I'm in, I immediately start peering among the cubicles. It's Luzhin I'm here to see, and I don't believe for one minute that he isn't here, but I can't help looking for Thistle.

Last night, for the first time in many years, I fell asleep smiling. And after my shower this morning when I looked in the mirror like I always do—to check what other people will see when they look at me—I was thinking of one person in particular.

But she's not here, as far as I can see. I wonder where she is, and if she's thinking of me.

Luzhin's door is open. I step inside. "I have a lead."

Luzhin doesn't look up. He's writing something on a notepad. When I'm about to sit down, he says, "Close the door, please."

I go back and ease it shut.

"I've just spoken to Agent Thistle," Luzhin says. "She says you took her out to dinner last night."

"Well, that's a lie. She took *me* out to dinner."

His eyes are icy. "This isn't funny. What do you want with my agent?"

"Nothing. She invited me. I accepted. How is this your business?"

"Why did she invite you? Why did you accept?"

"She invited me because she likes me," I say. "And I accepted because I like her."

Luzhin's face stretches into a horrified mask as he realizes I'm telling the truth. "She likes you? Why?"

I echo Thistle's words from last night. "Because I'm smart. I have skills."

"No," he says. "It's because she doesn't know you're a monster."

A vision of the future flashes through my mind. The look on Thistle's face as Luzhin explains the terms of our arrangement. She'd probably laugh, at first. Then, when she realized he believed what he was saying, she'd assume he was crazy. Then she would start thinking about the way I eat rare steak and drink weird coffee, and what I said about not being able to control myself. Then she'd wonder if she was the one going crazy.

"You're not going to tell her," I say. Half statement, half plea.

He clenches his fists. "How can I? She'll rat us both out. But let me tell you something, Blake." His eyes are pink around the edges. "If anything—*anything*—happens to her, you're in deep shit. To hell with my career. I will go to the national director in Washington and tell him everything. I'll go to prison, but you'll get a goddamn lethal injection. You got that?"

I nod. It's sweet, in a way. Like a father lecturing his daughter's boyfriend before prom.

"I mean it," he says. "You don't touch her. Understood?"

"Understood."

We stare at each other for a minute, breathing heavy. Then he smooths down his tie and says, "What's your lead?"

"I need to see some phone records," I say.

He sighs. "Why?"

"Because I have a suspect in the kidnappings of Cameron Hall and Robert Shea."

That gets his attention. "Who?"

"Their father."

"Which one's father?"

"Both. They're identical twins." I take out the photos, pass them over. "This is Robert Shea. Once we get in contact with Annette Hall, she'll admit that Cameron had a twin brother who she gave up for adoption. And I'm hoping she'll give us some way to find the father."

Luzhin leans back in his chair. "Do you have any reason to suspect him, besides the fact he's related to both victims? Does he have priors or anything?"

I shrug. "I don't have his rap sheet, but there'll be something. People don't start out with abduction and organ theft—they do some petty stuff and work their way up to it."

Luzhin nods thoughtfully. "Sounds like a strong lead—but I can't let you follow it."

"What? Why?"

"Because we have no evidence against him except these."

He gestures at the photos. "Which I don't want to know how you got."

"But—"

"Relax. I said I can't let *you* do it, not that it wouldn't get done. No judge in Texas will release those kind of documents to a civilian with so little evidence. I'll get an agent to track down the dad and see if he has a record, okay?"

"So what do I do?"

"Something else. Which phone records were you looking for?"

"Annette Hall's. I'm guessing you tapped her phone?"

"Yeah. But the tech guys would've told someone if they heard anything significant."

My idea of "significant" might be different from theirs. "I want to check it out anyway."

He shrugs. "Vasquez was the one who planted the bug. He should be able to get you the recordings—I'll tell him you're coming."

"Waste of time," Maurice Vasquez says. "Period."

Vasquez is one of the most handsome men I've ever seen. His gold skin is marble-smooth, his nose straight, his eyes thick-lashed and dark. His muscular arms hang from broad shoulders, which are about my eye height. He hasn't told anyone that he's gay, but I'm pretty sure. It's something about the way he carries himself, and the way he talks to women—with both compassion and disinterest.

He's also whip smart. Sometimes I think going through life looking like a big, dumb jock is what made him that way. Like he had to study harder than anyone else to get himself listened to when he talked.

"Why is it a waste of time?" I ask.

"Because that bug didn't record a damn thing," he says.

I look around at the forest of desks, each with an old CRT

monitor and several circular stains from coffee cups. Head-phoned agents are reading computer-generated transcripts at the same time as they listen to the audio, and correcting any errors they hear.

"You remember it specifically?" I ask quietly. I always keep my voice down in here. I can't shake the fear that there's a listening device in Luzhin's office, and that even as I stand here, one of the agents is listening to a recording of us, rec-ognizing my voice and reaching for a gun in a desk drawer.

Ridiculous, I know. Luzhin commands so much respect here that no one would ever suspect him of a speeding ticket, let alone selling criminals as food in exchange for informa-tion. And no one could conceal a bug so well that he couldn't find it. His office is probably the safest place on earth to speak your mind, assuming your voice isn't as loud as that of his boss.

"I remember them all," Vasquez is saying, and even though he must hear a thousand recordings a day, I believe him. "And there's nothing on the one you're talking about."

"Can I listen to it anyway?"

"You're not hearing me. There's nothing on it. I don't mean no one said anything interesting—I mean the record-ing is just hour after hour of digital silence. The file size is less than ten kilobytes."

Oh. I probably don't need to listen to that.

If this were any other agent, I'd ask if he was sure he'd hooked the bug up to the phone right. But Vasquez doesn't make that sort of mistake.

Instead, I ask, "Is that rare?"

He shrugs. "Yeah, but it happens. Usually means no one's home. Other times, it just means no one ever called."

The Halls aren't home, but they were when the bug was installed. So no one called.

"How long do you leave the bugs active after a case is solved?"

"Depends if you're talking about a physical bug or not. In some cases, we think the house or office or whatever is being watched too closely for us to send in a technician, so we get the phone company to record the calls remotely and send us the data. They keep doing it right up until there's a verdict at the end of the trial—although any conversations with a suspect's lawyer or doctor get deleted before we can listen to them.

"But other times, we're less concerned about being spotted and more concerned about leaks at the phone company's end, which do happen from time to time. So we listen in directly by installing a telecoil and a voltage probe within the phone itself or on the telephone pole outside. It works fine, but there's no budget for making new bugs, so we need to take the existing ones away to put in other phones. We do it as soon as the case is closed."

"This case isn't exactly closed."

"I know," Vasquez says. "They got the kid but not the perp, right?"

"Right."

"So the bug will probably get left another week or so. When the trail's colder."

"If it picks anything up before then," I say, "will you call me?"

"No, but I'll call Luzhin and ask him to call you."

"Thanks."

"No problem," Vasquez says. "Someone told me the perp beat your ass and locked you in his trunk."

"Nope. He *drugged* me and locked me in his trunk. My ass remains unbeat."

"And they're still letting you work the case?"

"I don't work cases," I say. "I just help out, that's all."

"Uh-huh. You know what's the most common thing people say right before they die?"

"'Ouch'?"

"They say, 'I'm making a citizen's arrest.'"

I don't laugh. "Well, I wasn't trying to arrest anybody. The guy broke into my house."

"Because you were working the case. My point is, maybe you should leave the policing to the police." The computer monitors reflected in his black eyes glint like starlight. "Someday you're going to wind up dead."

"I'm thinking that's true of all of us," I say.

The spray paint was probably supposed to be red, but it's been applied so hastily that it looks pink. It reads *Fuck You peace off shit*. The letters get smaller and smaller as the vandal realized he was running out of room on my door, and then bigger again as he decided to put the last couple of words on my window.

I park my car in the driveway—this place has no garage—and turn off the headlights. It doesn't take long to figure out that the graffiti has nothing to do with me. It must be the work of one of my roommate's clients, looking for a fix and furious at his absence. I should have seen that coming.

I unlock the door and step inside. Fortunately, the addict wasn't desperate enough to break in—or maybe he didn't have the skills to pull it off.

Either way, this is something I'll have to deal with. I can't have users coming around searching for drugs. They might look in my freezer.

Speaking of which, I'm starving. I go to the kitchen and open the freezer.

John Johnson's body is gone.

I stare at the boxes of frozen hash browns for a few seconds, heart pounding. There should still be an arm and a chest filet left. I shift a bag of peas aside and find a human foot, but that's it. Not much meat on a foot. Where's the rest?

Someone has been here. But they didn't go for Johnson's stash. They went for mine.

If it was the kidnapper, this changes the game. Now that he knows I'm a cannibal, I can't let the cops capture him alive. But where did he take the meat? And why?

And what if he's still in the house?

The thought is terrifying, but encouraging at the same time. If he hasn't left yet, then my secret hasn't left with him.

I close the freezer as quietly as I can and tiptoe out of the kitchen. There's no sign that anything else has been moved. No room for anyone to hide behind the couch. There are no shadows between the vertical blinds.

Creeping down the corridor toward the bedrooms, I listen. Just distant dogs barking and sirens carrying on the breeze.

The trunk of a car slams shut outside. The noise makes me jump. I edge over to the window and peer between the blinds. No cars visible except mine. No pedestrians around. Whoever it was, they're gone.

Johnson's bedroom is unoccupied, his bookshelf untouched. I crouch to look under his bed. Nothing.

My room. I swing the door open quickly so the hinges don't squeak. Jigsaws, bits of paper, the mattress on the floor, nothing out of the ordina—

There's a red spot on my mattress, just visible under the corner of the blanket. More spray paint? Did the vandal get in after all?

I lift the blanket.

My mattress is covered in bloody smears and handprints. It looks like someone used my sheets to scrub an abattoir. In the midst of it all is a chain of bones: the innards of Johnson's arm. His skeletal hand, surprisingly small without the flesh, is curled up like a dead crab.

It looks like someone took the meat out of the freezer and ate it in my bed. I put my palm against one of the handprints and realize the someone was me.

I don't remember doing this. Am I losing my mind?

Sleep-snacking. I've heard it's common in compulsive eaters, which is a pretty mild description of what I am. It's never happened to me before, but it's the only explanation I can think of.

Thistle caused this, indirectly. When I come home, I usually have a bite of whatever meat I can find. But last night I didn't—I was too distracted. Too *happy*.

So my body just got up and did it anyway, after I was asleep. And this morning, I didn't notice the bloody sheets.

My bones feel like tubes of ice. I've known that I'm crazy since that first bite of the mugger. But now I know how little control I have.

I take my roommate's bones into the bathroom and toss them into the tub. Then I go out to the kitchen to get my rubber gloves and my sulfuric acid. It's going to be a long night.

I'm woken by the phone. I roll out of bed and stumble out into the kitchen, naked. Snatch the phone off the hook. "Yeah?"

"Where the fuck are you, man?"

"Who is this?" I say.

"It's Patrick. Who's this?"

"You got the wrong number."

"Like hell I have the wrong number!" the man yells.

Ah. Another junkie.

"Well, this is Timothy. I don't know any Patrick."

"Oh, wait. You— Oh. Is your roommate around?"

"No," I say. "I haven't seen him in a couple days. I can take a message if you want."

"Where's he gone?"

"Not sure. Some friends picked him up from the house."

"Which friends?" Patrick asks.

"No one I knew, but he didn't take a suitcase or anything. I'm sure he'll be back soon."

There's a pause. Drug dealers who get picked up by "friends" often don't return.

"What's your number, Patrick?" I say. "I'll get him to call you when he's back."

"Nah, that's okay. I'll, uh…I'll call back later."

"You sure? It's no trouble. What's your last name?"

The junkie hangs up.

Too easy. I go back to my bedroom, check the sheets for blood and bone, and fall back in.

The phone rings again.

Shit. Some people are so desperate for a fix that their survival instinct completely disappears. I climb out of bed, go back to the kitchen and pick up the phone. "Yes?"

"Blake." It's Luzhin. "You are a goddamn genius."

I press the phone a little harder against my ear. "You know something about Cameron's dad," I guess.

"Yep. Philip Hall did go to Pennsylvania, but he just moved back to Houston last month."

"He got a criminal record?"

"Grand theft auto, armed robbery and assault with a deadly weapon, all in the one night. Seems like he'd lost a shitload of someone else's money at a roulette table in Atlantic City and was trying to pay them back."

Compulsive gambler, violent criminal. Seems like a good fit for our kidnapper. "He do any time?"

"Therapy and a suspended sentence. Want to hear the best part?"

"What?"

"He's a nurse."

Access to drugs. Medical experience. But you wouldn't get enough anatomy training to remove a kidney in a nursing diploma. "He go to college?"

"Three years of med school," Luzhin says. "Then he dropped out."

"This is our guy."

"Yes, it is. I sent a patrol car to his house with a warrant."

"I want to meet him."

"If I get my way, you will. He'll be in the Death House in no time."

"No—I want to be in the car that picks him up."

There's a pause.

"Blake, you don't have to be there. This is the guy. If we catch him, you'll get your reward."

"Not if we don't find Robert Shea," I say. "Those are the rules."

"And you don't think we can find the kid once we have the perp?"

"He'll lie to you. And I'll be able to tell."

"Why are you arguing against yourself here?"

That's a good question. Why am I working harder than I have to for my meal?

Thistle, I realize. She was impressed when I rescued Cameron. She'll be even more impressed when I find Robert too.

"I'm a lot of things, but I'm not lazy," I say. "I want to be in the car."

He sighs. "You can meet him in the cell at the field office. Okay?"

Good enough. "Okay."

I hang up and go back to the bedroom. I didn't have time to wash my clothes last night, since the bathtub was otherwise occupied. But yesterday's clothes still smell okay, so I pull them on.

The phone rings again.

I storm back out into the kitchen. What now?

"Yes?"

"No need to come in," Luzhin says. "Philip wasn't at his house."

They need me after all. "Give me the address."

CHAPTER 17

I WEIGH ALMOST NOTHING AND I'M NOT HOT, BUT YOU CAN'T HOLD ME FOR LONG. WHAT AM I?

THE HOUSE IS A JUNK HEAP. THE FENCE HAS BEEN broken and mended in so many places that now it's made out of five different kinds of wood. The windows look like frosted glass, but they're not—that's just cobwebs. A rusty peg is nailed into the front lawn, like maybe a dog was tied up there once.

I drive past and leave the Chevy a block away. Parking a stolen car outside the FBI field office is one thing. Leaving it right outside a suspect's house during a police search is quite another. Cops will be running the plates of any car left nearby.

I jog back to the house, step onto the rickety wooden porch and knock on the door.

"Timothy Blake," I yell. "Luzhin sent me."

The door opens to reveal a woman in a white plastic suit that covers everything except her face and hands, which are gloved. It even covers her shoes. She looks like a giant baby in a onesie.

"You can't come in like that," she says, and closes the door.

I'm just about to knock again when she opens it and hands me a suit like the one she's wearing. I step into it and start pulling it up over my legs.

"Can I keep this?"

"Why?"

I shrug. "It's cool." It'd be better than my raincoat.

"No," she says. "We don't have the funding for replacements. I'm going to need it back. You can keep these, though." She smiles sweetly as she hands me a pair of latex gloves.

"Gee, thanks."

She steps aside, and I enter the house.

The inside isn't much of an improvement on the front. Nails protrude from the ceiling. The drafts have swept mouse droppings into crannies between bookshelves and walls. The shelves have no books on them—just shoeboxes and almost-empty coffee mugs.

"You find anything yet?" I ask the woman.

"Yep. Dust. Lots and lots of dust."

She looks stressed. It's probably harder to catalog a dirty house than a clean one.

"Anything that might tell you where he's taken his victims?"

"All I can tell you is that it's not here. No blood spatter, no powder residue."

"What about wear and tear on the pipes? Anybody been chained to them?"

"Nope. Just dust."

She walks away into another room, where I can hear cameras clicking and low voices.

I walk in the other direction, up the hallway to the two bedrooms. One has a bed that isn't much more than a stretcher and a lowboy with an ashtray on it. A mousetrap waits under the bed. No bait.

I open the top drawer of the lowboy and find two pairs of jeans and three T-shirts. The labels make them about the right size for the guy I saw stealing the ransom money.

In the second drawer I find a woolen coat and a hoodie. We can get Philip Hall's DNA from these, unless he washed them thoroughly. Judging by the rest of the house, he probably didn't.

The other bedroom has been converted into an office, sort

of. There's a plastic table covered with papers in the corner, next to a swivel chair with a missing wheel that looks like third-hand government surplus.

I start sifting through the papers. A property deed for the house, some electricity and gas bills, a bank statement. The statement has been used to flatten a spider.

"Be quick with them." The woman has sneaked up on me again. "We need to take them away."

"Any reference to Cameron Hall or Robert Shea in them?"

"Who?"

"The victims."

"Oh. We don't get told about the crimes. They send us a memo with the address, and we come in and turn the place upside down. But I don't remember seeing those names anywhere."

I grunt. I don't see them either, but something has caught my eye: another property deed. The address matches the warehouse where I found Cameron.

I hold it up. "Make sure Luzhin sees this."

"Sure," the woman says, but I can tell what she's thinking: *Don't tell me how to do my job.*

"Seriously," I say. "Out of all the evidence you got so far, this is the most important."

"I heard you," she says. "I'll do it."

Either she will or she won't—no point repeating myself. I go out to the living room, where a CSI tech is taking pictures while another scribbles on the labels of a sheaf of Ziploc bags.

A single wooden chair sits at an angle beside a dining table with an old TV on it. The only other furniture is a beanbag, but not much else would fit.

The room is joined to a kitchen, if you can call it that. There's kitchens, there's kitchenettes and then there's this. It's a stove, a sink and about two square feet of bench space.

"Find anything good?" I ask.

The photographer ignores me. The bagger says, "That's for someone else to decide."

"Have you run the black light over everything yet?"

"Yep. Nothing."

Interesting. Philip Hall can't go back to the warehouse, but he isn't keeping his victims here either. Only two property deeds. Where else could he have taken them?

"Do we know what kind of car Philip Hall drives?"

"Who?" the woman asks.

I can't believe this. "The guy whose house you're in."

"Like I said, we just get the addresses. I don't know about his car, I don't know about his victims, I don't know what his favorite kind of cereal is. It's not like the bullshit you see on TV—we don't solve crimes, we just collect data. Okay?"

"Okay. So I guess that data doesn't include the tire tracks in the driveway."

The techs look at one another.

"We're getting to that," the photographer says.

"Glad to hear it." I peel off my gloves as I walk to the front door, then throw them onto the porch. I leave my plastic suit in a pile and head back out to the car.

I look down as I pass the driveway. Thick tracks. Big tires. I'm thinking Philip Hall has a van. Windowless. Probably white. A Dodge Sprinter, maybe, with a turbo-diesel engine and room for three thousand pounds in cargo. Plenty of space for the three Sheas, if they're still alive.

Maybe I should go back inside and call Luzhin, tell him my theory. But I didn't see a landline in the house, and those CSI techs didn't seem likely to lend me a cell phone—

A thought almost trips me over as I walk back toward my car. Yesterday I called Luzhin from Cameron's house. Why didn't the bug Vasquez planted record the conversation?

He must have installed it wrong. But I've never known Vasquez to make a mistake.

The puzzle pieces rotate in my head, slotting into empty spaces, popping back out when they don't fit. I'm so pre-occupied that I don't notice the cop standing next to my stolen Chevy until I'm too close to turn away.

He's overweight, balding. Somewhere in his late thirties. What looks like a G17 on his hip—one of the two million Glock pistols that sit in glove compartments and in shoeboxes on top shelves of closets and in police armories all over the world, capable of shooting 9mm Parabellums at twelve hundred feet per second.

He's levering open the trunk of my car.

This is not standard procedure. You see a suspicious car, you run the plates. If it comes back as stolen, you call a tow truck. You don't break into the trunk unless you've had a tip-off that something is inside.

That tip-off can only have come from someone who had a reason to be nearby and saw me arrive. Someone who knows what I look like and has reason to sabotage my investigation. Someone like Philip Hall.

Just as I'm wondering why he would tell the cops to search my car, the trunk pops open.

The cop yelps and stumbles backward. The sour fumes of death spill out of the trunk. Flies materialize out of nowhere, buzzing in ever-tightening spirals toward the body inside.

I get a quick glimpse—enough to see that the dead man's T-shirt is soaked with blood, his chest slashed to ribbons but his face intact. He stares at me sadly. I don't recognize him.

I can't help but step closer. I'm just another fly, eager to take advantage of someone else's bad luck.

The cop sees me staring at the body. Not sickened, not horrified—hungry.

"Hey," he says, reaching for his gun. "Hey, you!"

His voice is like a defibrillator, shocking me back to consciousness. My brain switches on, and I realize how much trouble I'm in. I waste a split second wondering if I can convince him that I'm just a rubberneck who has nothing to do with the car or the body.

Then I turn and run.

I have a head start of about ten yards. The Glock's effective range is more like fifty. But this is a residential area, with plenty of cover. I swerve toward one of the houses before he can squeeze off a shot.

My feet slap against the driveway. A chain-link gate separates it from the backyard—I jump over it like an Olympic hurdler. Hopefully I'm in better shape than the cop is.

He's puffing into a radio behind me, "Ten ninety-six, we got a ten ninety-six, over." He's requesting backup. If I don't lose him soon, I'll get cornered.

The backyard has a small aluminum shed, which I quickly dismiss as a hiding place because of the padlock on the door. Instead, I run to the hedge at the rear of the property and hurl myself into it. The branches scrape at my cheeks and eyelids as I climb over the picket fence buried within it.

Another backyard. Scraggly garden. Swimming pool barely larger than a spa, covered by a tarpaulin. No chlorine smell, which usually means salted water.

The cop will expect me to go right, along the path. Instead, I go left, hop up onto the retaining wall and leap toward the high fence. Splinters dig into my palms as I scramble over it and drop onto the grass on the other side.

I crouch silently for a moment. The cop was still behind the hedge when I climbed over here, so he didn't see me do it. But if I move, he'll hear me and be back on my trail.

Over the pounding of my heart, I can just make out the sound of his shoes clacking against the path. "Goddamn it, where are you?" Can't tell if he's talking to me or his backup. But he's moving farther away.

A dog barks. I turn my head to see a huge brown poodle

bounding toward me, teeth bared. Shit. Even if I don't get maimed, the cop's likely to hear the racket.

The worst thing to do when a dog attacks is run away, even when there isn't a cop waiting with handcuffs at the ready. Dogs can run at thirty miles an hour. Even Olympic sprinters can't match that.

Instead, I move toward the dog, trying to confuse it, scare it, make it think I'm bigger and scarier than I am.

It doesn't work. The poodle is an eighty-pound monster, nothing but muscle and adrenaline. I'm running straight at it, making the fiercest face I can, but it just runs faster, and soon it's leaping through the air, flying at me, jaws first.

Fending off a stray dog was one of the first skills I learned when I was homeless. In a way, it's easier than fighting a man—a dog's only weapon is its teeth.

But it's like chess. I have to sacrifice something to win.

I hold up my forearm, and the poodle clamps onto it with its fangs. It's like sticking my arm into a rosebush filled with hornets. My blood leaks into the poodle's mouth, and for a moment it thinks it's won.

Then I shove my arm forward, choking it.

At this point, the dog has a choice—let go, or asphyxiate. Most dogs are too dumb to give up, and this one is no exception. It whines as I push it backward, eyes rolling in terror. Saliva gurgles in its windpipe. Its legs are quivering.

I don't want to kill the poodle. I don't even want it unconscious. So I curl my free hand into a fist and belt it in the side of the head, momentarily stunning it. Its jaws spring open and it staggers drunkenly sideways.

I run for the brick wall at the far end of the yard. I've reached it by the time the dog starts barking again—not at me, this time, but at the cop, who's climbing the fence. I clamber over the wall and sacrifice a precious second looking back.

The cop is halfway over the fence, but he's stopped. The

dog is snarling and snapping at his heel. Unlike me, his life isn't on the line, just his paycheck.

I've seen enough. I keep running, and running, and running. Soon I'm in someone's driveway, and then I'm out on another road again.

I pass an open garage. No one inside. I have no tools to steal the car, but a bicycle leans against the cinder-block wall. I run in, snatch it up and carry it back onto the road. Then I jump on and pedal my ass off. Soon I'm riding hands-free so I can squeeze the bite on my arm, stemming the blood flow.

Five minutes later a patrol car zooms past in the opposite direction, sirens shrieking. I'm outside the search radius.

But that cop knows what I look like. He knows what car I was driving. He knows I'm wounded, and he can get DNA from the blood I left on the fence. It won't take his colleagues long to track me down.

CHAPTER 18

**A MAN TAKES HIS SON TO A DOCTOR.
THE DOCTOR SAYS, "I CANNOT TREAT
THIS BOY—HE IS MY SON."
HOW IS THIS POSSIBLE?**

BY THE TIME I GET BACK TO MY HOUSE, THE bleeding has almost stopped, but my hand is stuck to my forearm. It's like peeling off a giant Band-Aid when I remove it so I can get to my keys.

I leave blood on the handle when I open the door, and on the dead bolts when I close it again. I go into the bathroom, flick on the light, twist the faucet and listen to the hot-water tank rattle as it heats up. When the water is warm enough, I stick my arm under it and rinse the wound.

The punctures are narrow enough to pinch closed, and they're not deep enough to reveal the yellowish fatty tissue. No need for stitches or staples. I lather my hands up with soap and start rubbing it into the holes in my arm. It burns as I push it in.

You're much better off getting bitten by a dog than by a person, I tell myself. The bacteria that lives in a dog's mouth is mostly the kind that doesn't affect humans. I'm sure I read that somewhere.

Once I'm done washing the wound, I check in the cabinet for some gauze. There's none.

I go to the line, where my other shirt was hung out to dry yesterday. It's probably the cleanest bit of fabric in the house, so I tear off the sleeve and pull it over my arm.

It's too loose. I get the stapler from my roommate's room—

he used it for sealing Ziploc bags so he could be sure they hadn't been opened. I pull the severed sleeve tight around my forearm and staple the fold shut. Then I jiggle my arm around, checking that the makeshift bandage doesn't move. Good enough.

I rummage through my roommate's wardrobe until I find a suitably generic sweater. Gray fabric, thin. It fits okay.

I wish Johnson had left some antibiotics behind, but I've looked through all his things—his filing cabinet, his address book, his drugs—and found nothing useful.

Right now, the cops will be scraping my blood off the fence and my hair off the headrest in the car. Soon they'll be searching databases for my DNA. I've been careful, so I'm hoping they won't find any matches. But you can only eat so many people before someone notices. Maybe I left a trace somewhere. Maybe some cop has been hunting me for years, and this is his big break.

I wiped down the steering wheel, the stick shift and the handle before I got out of the car. I always do. But they might still get lucky with a partial print or two. Those will match my civilian consultant file at the FBI.

I'm guessing that was Robert Shea's adoptive father in the trunk of my car. By dumping it there, Philip Hall has put me in the frame for Robert's disappearance, and therefore Cameron's abduction. No one saw Philip Hall abduct me from my home. No one saw his car as he took me to the warehouse where Cameron was imprisoned. The cops saw another man take the bag of cash outside the Walmart, but they'll say he was my accomplice. And Philip Hall doesn't know this, but when forensics search my house, they'll find human remains. I'll get the needle, and Philip will go free.

But it will take them three days to get the results from the print and DNA search. If I can find Philip Hall, Robert Shea and his adoptive mother before then, the cops will stop circling me. Luzhin can use his paperwork wizardry to keep me in the clear.

First things first. The cop could provide a decent description of me to a sketch artist. I need a makeover.

I take a pair of scissors from the kitchen, return to the bathroom mirror and start hacking off my hair. Thick clumps fall between the blood droplets on the floor. It looks like a cat attacked a bird in here.

I consider going all the way to the skin but decide it's not a good idea. Short hair just means a haircut. If I go bald, those who know me might wonder why.

I remove a bottle of hydrogen peroxide from the cupboard under the sink, squeeze my eyes shut and pour some over my scalp. When it starts to burn, I splash water on my hair and rub it with soapy hands until the peroxide is gone.

I towel my head dry and look in the mirror again. My hair's a little lighter, but not so much that you'd assume I'd bleached it. Perfect. If this cannibal-detective thing doesn't work out, I could become a hairdresser.

Three days to find Philip Hall. I have no idea where he is. There's someone who might be able to help, but it's risky. I might get killed just for asking.

I'm waiting at a bus stop, sweating under the sun. If it were summer, you'd be able to smell the asphalt. One time I saw some out-of-towners—cameras on straps around their necks, brand-new souvenir T-shirts with the Texas Longhorns logo—standing around a local woman as she poured some bottled pancake mix onto the sidewalk, just to show them how it hissed and bubbled. I hung around long enough to eat the pancake after they'd gone, closing my eyes and trying to imagine the grit was cracked pepper.

Lobbyists for the auto industry have ensured that buses are rare in Houston, and not cheap. But the cops will be looking at all car thefts near the scene of my almost-arrest. If I steal some wheels now, I'll have to ditch them again almost straightaway.

A bus squeaks to a halt by the curb, and I get on. The driver is a male fortysomething who looks like a sixtysomething. Like me, he has aged in dog years. I feed a couple of my room-mate's bills into the ticket machine, and it slurps them up.

When it's a short ride, I always take a seat near the front so I don't have to walk past as many people who might remember me later. When it's a long ride, I take a seat near the back to reduce the number of people who can casually stare at me while I'm sitting down. But today there are only two free seats, and one of them is next to a woman so fat that there isn't much of the seat left empty anyway. The other is near the back, and I take it.

"Howdy," says the man I'm sitting next to. Shaved head, short beard. Tracksuit.

"Howdy," I say without making eye contact. There's something sticky under my shoes, like a recently evaporated puddle of Coke. Looking down, I see a line of ants looping through the stain, scraping it up with their pincers. It occurs to me that their nest must be miles and miles away, and they'll probably never see it again. That is, unless they climbed on at the depot, in which case they might eventually climb off again when the bus is parked there and not even realize they'd moved.

"Real hot for fall," says the guy.

In the same library book that taught me about Theia and how the moon was made, I read that Earth travels two hundred million miles around the sun between fall and spring. Some people die without ever having left their hometown, and yet they could be ninety million miles from where they were born.

We're all just ants, riding a bus on a highway too long to comprehend.

"Yes, sir," I say. "That it is."

★ ★ ★

I ride the bus past a row of bars before getting off at a stop near a convenience store. A long-lashed woman in fishnet stockings is leaning against a nearby streetlight pole, sucking a cigarette. She smiles at me and says, "Hey, baby. Want to have a little fun?"

Real sex workers pay no mind to poor people. "No, thanks, Officer," I say.

The fake hooker glances around to see if anyone heard. By the time she looks back, I'm already gone.

Houston has real streetwalkers on Hillcroft Avenue and the 610 South Loop, but here all the women are cops. The nearest strip club is actually a brothel, and the police don't have enough evidence to raid it, so they plant undercover operatives around it to catch the dumber clients. They make enough arrests to fill their quotas, leaving the brothel with enough customers to stay in business. Everybody wins.

The humming neon reads *The Noir*, which stands for Nightclub of Ill Repute. The curtains, red and velvety, are all drawn. A statue is poised out front—a naked woman bending down to pick some flowers, legs straight, ass out. A fountain bubbles around her ankles.

Two burly doormen look me up and down as I approach. Each one is a head taller and thirty pounds heavier than me. A feast.

"Cover," one grunts. "Three dollars."

I hand over three of Johnson's crumpled bills and they stand aside.

Like its name, the Noir is dark. The maroon carpet is thin underfoot. I hover in the antechamber until the fake potted plants and fleshy posters come into focus, and then I step through into the gloom of the main chamber.

It's early, so the stage is empty. The pole gleams in a spotlight someone left on. But the strippers are here, writhing weightlessly around the armchairs as if underwater. The men, little more than silhouettes, are perfectly still but for the reptilian eyes that follow nipples and ass cracks around the room.

I avert my gaze. Too much skin. It's like a meat market in here. My palms are itchy.

Part of me is jealous of these women. If I could earn two hundred bucks an hour by taking my clothes off and letting strangers invade my personal space, I would. Assuming I could do it without accidentally tearing anybody's throat out. But Texas doesn't take kindly to loose women. These girls probably tried every other profession before this one. Like me, they're here because they have nowhere else to go.

The liquors glitter like a waterfall behind the bar. A young white woman—clothed—with a vineyard of tattoos up her arms is standing behind it, fiddling with her cell phone. She looks up as I approach and flashes a practiced grin. It's probably typical for nervous patrons to drink before they approach the dancers.

"What can I get you?"

"Nothing just yet," I say. "I'm here for a meeting with Charlie."

"Charlie who?"

"Charlie Warner."

The smile evaporates. "Sorry," the bartender says. "I don't know anyone by that name."

I wanted to fool her into thinking Warner sent for me. Evidently I failed. I don't want to get anyone else involved—Luzhin has been chasing Warner for his entire career, so I don't want him to hear that I was at the Noir—but I don't have much choice. "Your boss probably does," I say. "Maybe you could get him?"

She looks at my tattered shirt and my bandaged arm.

"It'll only take a minute," I add.

The woman reaches underneath the bar and I tense up, in

case she's going for a gun. But her hand comes back empty, and a second later, a door opens behind her.

A narrow-shouldered man with thinning hair comes through, looks at me and says, "Can I help you, sir?" He says *sir* very doubtfully.

"I'm here to see Charlie."

"Which Charlie?"

"Charlie Warner. It won't take long."

The boss looks at the bartender before turning back to me. "Not here right now, I'm afraid."

"I can wait." I sit down on a bar stool. "You're open all night, right?"

"Maybe I can pass on a message for you."

"Maybe you can. Tell Charlie that one of the…uh, retailers has given notice and might have been acquired by a competitor." In other words, a rival drug lord has taken one of your dealers.

"Which retailer?"

"I only know the trading name, I'm afraid," I say. "John Johnson."

"And what did you say your name was?"

"Timothy Blake."

The manager touches the bartender on the upper arm. "Get Mr. Blake a drink," he tells her. "I'll be right back."

He disappears back the way he came, and the bartender says, "So. *Now* what can I get you?"

Deciding to make the most of the free drink, I order the most expensive cocktail on the menu. The bartender chops some strawberries and tosses them into a glass with a scoop of ice cream. She drizzles in some mango schnapps, pineapple juice and Midori. Then she sticks two sparklers into the top and ignites them with a cigarette lighter before sliding the glass over to me.

I stare at the sizzling tower of brightly colored sugar for a moment before plucking a bendy straw from a dispenser and taking a sip. It's too cold and too sweet to be enjoyable.

"Is it your birthday, sweetie?"

I turn around to see a stripper leaning against the bar. She's black and thin, her painted nails tugging at the shoulder strap of her bra.

"How about a private dance?" she says. "Thigh meat."

My heart is pounding. "I'm sorry?"

"My treat," she says again, with a wink. "For the birthday boy."

I must be losing my mind. She's trying to turn a free lap dance into an expensive fuck. It's more likely to become a bloodbath.

"No, thanks," I say.

"You sure?" She slides an arm around my shoulders and leans in for a sip of my drink. Her tongue probes the tip of the straw before it disappears between her lips. The veins are pulsing in her neck, inches from my teeth.

"Alabama," the boss says from the doorway.

The stripper looks up at him.

"Take a hike. Mr. Blake's leaving."

"I am?" I say.

"You are," he says, and then the world vanishes as a cloth bag swallows my head.

It takes only a fragment of a second for me to react, but it's a fragment of a second too long. One of the big doormen has already grabbed my forearms and is holding them behind my back. I try to kick him in the shins, but he dodges easily, and then there's a click and something hard presses against my jaw.

"Stay still or you get a hole in the head," the boss says.

I stop struggling. I think of all the dancers, and the men. They must be seeing this, but they won't intervene.

"We don't mean you any harm," the boss continues. "But if you want a meeting with Warner, this is how you get it."

The doorman pushes me out of the room, not the way I came in. We move through a cold area with something humming—a fridge, I guess, in a kitchen. Someone pats me down, searching my legs and arms and crotch for weapons. They reach up under my shirt, looking for a microphone. The whole search takes less than thirty seconds, and then we barge through what sounds like a fire door into the alley behind the club.

I can hear a car engine idling. Doors unlock and open. A palm holds my head down as I'm pushed onto the creaking leather of the back seat, and then the door is closed behind me. A seat belt zips across my chest. Plastic cuffs are tightened around my wrists.

My captors say nothing, so neither do I. My breaths are hot against the cloth bag. Every instinct screams to *get it off get it off get it off*, but I fight the urge to struggle and, instead, start memorizing the movements of the car as it grumbles away from the curb.

We turn right at the end of the alley. Then five minutes of stopping and starting in traffic before we turn left somewhere else. Onto a highway, I'm guessing, since the car rises a bit and then spends twenty minutes going fast and straight. I can sometimes hear trucks roaring past.

We turn right onto a loop and then stop and start and turn a few more times. Right. Left. Left. The car slows down incrementally and then stops, brakes hissing.

The other occupants of the car don't move, but someone opens my door from the outside and unbuckles my seat belt.

"Get out," someone says. A new voice. Rugged, male.

Still blind, I fumble halfway out of the car before someone pulls me the rest of the way. I'm shoved across some blacktop, some cement, some tiles and finally carpet before the bag is pulled off my head. I suck in an enormous gulp of air, blinking as my eyes adjust to the sudden brightness.

I'm in a doctor's waiting room.

At least, it looks like one. I see old magazines. A reception desk, unoccupied. A fish tank in which a neon tetra chases its own tail incorrigibly. A man in a suit looms beside the door I apparently just stumbled through. Another guy waits in front of the door at the other end of the room. Big, impassive, crew cuts—the two men aren't twins, but they may as well be.

A backless sofa, the sort built for ten people, takes up the corner of the room. Neither man moves to stop me as I wander over to it and flop down.

Alongside the magazines on the coffee table, I notice a smattering of white dust, scraped into a narrow line. A short straw sits beside it.

"That's for you," the big man blocking the exit says.

"No, thanks," I say.

"It's not optional."

They have checked that I'm not wearing a wire, but they want me to do something illegal. To prove I'm not a cop, or compromise me if I am.

It's unlikely that they brought me all this way to poison me. I put the straw in my nostril and lean forward. It's surprisingly hard to line it up with the powder, having never done this before. When I sniff it up, half the cocaine stays on the table, but I get enough to sting the inside of my nose. That seems to be the only effect the drug has on me. I don't feel any different.

The two men look at the remains of the line, and then they look at me expectantly. The expressions on their faces strike me as hilarious, and I feel a giggle bubbling up from my chest. I swallow it back down again.

"Okay," one of them says. "You can come through now."

I stand up. My dog bite has already stopped aching, and my toes are fidgeting inside my shoes. I watched John Johnson do coke a few times; based on what I saw, I probably have half an hour before I start imagining bugs crawling under my skin. Then again, maybe that's a symptom of long-term use.

The man near the exit stays where he is. The other man opens his door and steps inside. I follow him in.

I know the FBI has someone in Charlie Warner's inner circle. That person is likely to be fit, because undercover cops have to be, but thin, because it's a stressful job. They will have piercings, because those are less permanent than tattoos, and nothing says *cop* like an inkless, unpierced criminal. They'll look bored, because that's the exact opposite of nervous.

There are four people in the room. Three of them are pudgy, tattooed and very interested in me. Not bored. Not cops. The last one is a middle-aged woman with perfect teeth. Her arms, curved with the muscles you get from a rowing machine, stretch out from a sleeveless blouse made of red satin. Her legs are holstered in a pair of white jeans, which stretch down to a pair of cowboy boots with not much sign of wear.

"I'm Charlie," she says. "And just who might you be?"

CHAPTER 19

MY MAKER HAS NEVER USED ME.
MY BUYER WILL NOT USE ME.
WHEN YOU USE ME, YOU WILL NOT SEE ME,
SMELL ME OR HEAR ME.
WHAT AM I?

"TIMOTHY BLAKE," I SAY. "THANKS FOR, YOU know, taking the time to see me." I sniff and lick my teeth. The coke is kicking in.

The room is more like a library than an office. Floor-to-ceiling bookshelves, stacked with hardbacks, are deadening the air. Warner's voice sounds much closer than she is.

"You're welcome," she says dryly. "How much more time you get depends a lot on the next few words that come out of your mouth."

"Fair enough," I say. "My roommate is one of your dealers. Two days ago he got picked up by somebody, and I haven't seen him since." After a pause, I tell her my address, since I don't know John Johnson's real name.

"Uh-huh. And what do you expect me to do about this?"

"Nothing. I just thought, since his abductors were probably rivals of yours, you might be interested in knowing what they looked like and what car they drove before I mention it to the cops."

She leans back in her chair, which tilts without so much as a squeak. "I don't have any real rivals. Whoever picked up your friend, they're no threat."

"Not a threat. An opportunity."

I'm getting a sense of the hierarchy in the room. The three other people look at Warner whenever she's talking, and they keep glancing at her when it's my turn, to see how she reacts. But two of them occasionally glance at the other one—a bearded, glasses-wearing guy who's built like a wrestler. He must be Warner's second-in-command.

"I know you have a trial coming up," I say. "The FBI's making a case against you."

She doesn't look worried. "Something tells me their witnesses aren't going to testify."

"You have people inside the FBI, I get it," I say. I can't stop myself from talking faster and faster. "Probably the DOJ too, federal marshals, whatever. But I heard some pricey security firm has gotten involved. All the state's witnesses are gonna be surrounded by high-end bodyguards from out of town. People you don't know and can't buy."

Her expression is hard to read. "Where'd you hear that?"

I can't tell her that I saw the security van turn up at the FBI field office. "My roommate told me before he left. So it seems like what you need is a patsy."

"Ah," she says. "I get it. You give me enough info to track down this rival distributor, and I frame them for everything I'm charged with. Clever. And I imagine you'll want something in return?"

"I'm trying to find somebody," I say. "A guy named Philip Hall."

Her face shows no recognition. Any remaining suspicions I have of her involvement with the kidnappings trickle away.

I wonder what Luzhin would do if he were here. Warner has used her wealth to stay out of his reach for years. She had his friend murdered. Would he try to kill her, knowing he would die too?

"He buys drugs," I continue. "He gambles. I thought you might be able to point me in the right direction."

"I see."

Her henchmen watch her. She doesn't look at them.

"Why you want to find this Philip Hall?"

"He owes me thirty-five thousand dollars," I say. "But he's also a wanted man. There isn't much chance of getting paid back unless I find him before the cops do."

"What's he wanted for?"

"Kidnapping."

"Uh-huh. How are you going to make him pay?"

"That's between me and him."

"Wrong." Warner takes a cigarette from her desk and twirls it between her fingers. "If I help you find him, it's between you, him and me."

A crime boss with a conscience? "If you have ethical concerns—"

She laughs. After a fraction of a second, so do her employees.

"If his body shows up," she says, "and word gets out that my boys were looking for him…" She puts the cigarette back in the drawer, unlit. "You see my problem?"

"He'll come to no harm," I say. "I was going to take the money without him knowing."

"A thief, huh?"

"No. It's my money."

"Right," Warner says. "Well, I can't guarantee that I'll be able to track him down."

"That's okay," I say. "I can't guarantee that you'll be able to track down the guys who took my roommate either. I just want to share information."

She takes out the cigarette again. Sees me looking. "I'm trying to quit," she says. "Some folks tell you to throw every pack in the trash, put them down the garbage disposal, whatever. But then you're not kicking the habit—you're running from it." She returns the cigarette to the desk. "Me, I'm practicing having it in my hand without putting it in my mouth."

I say nothing.

"What do you do for a living, Mr. Blake?" she asks.

"I sell card numbers," I say.

"If you're looking for a raise, I have a vacancy in retail."

Drug dealing is dangerous work. "After what happened to your last guy? Thanks, but no, thanks."

She nods, and I realize that her offer wasn't genuine. If I'd said yes, she might have thought I killed John Johnson to get his job, or at least his stash. I inadvertently passed the test.

"Okay," she says. "I'll ask around about Philip Hall in exchange for everything you know about the guys who took your roommate. Deal?"

"Deal," I say.

She holds out her hand to shake—and then withdraws it. "I'm a woman of my word," she says. "This is your last chance to back out. You better take it, if you have nothing good to give me. Or else there will be hell to pay. Got that?"

I hold out my hand. She shakes it.

Her second-in-command, the bearded guy, speaks. "I should get started, I guess."

"You should," Warner says. "Call me when you've found Philip Hall."

He leaves, and she turns back to me. "Tell me what you know."

"There were two of them," I say. "Male. Both in gray suits. One about a hundred seventy pounds and six-one, Caucasian, black hair. The other only five-eleven, but more like a hundred eighty pounds. Also Caucasian, but with brown hair and a silver stud in his right ear. They drove a white 1983 Chevrolet Malibu."

This sounds like a lot of information, but it's not. Those are common heights and weights, which is why I chose them. But Warner will want something more concrete. "You got a pen?" I ask.

She's already taking one from her desk. "Go ahead."

I give her the plate numbers of the car I stole—the one with the body in the trunk. But I give her the numbers it had before I switched the plates. That way, when she gets her mole inside the police to look it up, she'll discover the car was reported stolen days before John Johnson went missing, giving my story some credibility.

"That all you got?" she says.

"Sorry. I didn't hear anything they said, and I didn't follow the car."

"Your roommate—he go with them willingly?"

"That's what it looked like. Maybe he thought they worked for you."

"Maybe. Maybe not." She looks at her watch. "I have another appointment."

Before I realize what this means, the black bag covers my head again. Someone has crept up behind me.

"Thanks for your help," I say as someone hauls me out the door.

When I'm in the car again, I ask the driver if he can drop me off at my house rather than taking me back to the Noir. He or she doesn't reply, so it's not until I feel the vehicle come to a stop twenty minutes later and the bag is pulled off my head that I realize I'm at home.

The other passenger unlocks the door and uncuffs me. I've barely climbed out onto the curb before the car zooms off into the night.

I take a deep, shaky breath. I'm not dead. But I feel like Adam, right after taking a bite from the snake's apple.

I unlock my front door, step inside and walk straight over to the telephone. I start dialing Luzhin and then change my mind and call Thistle instead.

I am expecting her answering machine, but she picks up on the second ring. "Thistle."

"I have an anonymous tip for you," I say.

"Blake? Is that you?"

"Wouldn't be very anonymous if I told you, would it?"

She laughs. "I guess not. What can I do for you?"

"You got a pen?"

"Sure."

I give her the same license plate number I gave Warner. "Sometime within the next couple of days, someone is going to search the police database for those numbers. That someone is working for Charlie Warner."

"You're kidding."

"Nope."

Her voice goes serious. "How could you possibly know that?"

"Officially, I don't know it, because knowing it could get me killed. That's why this is an anonymous tip. And it's why you'll have to get some other evidence against the mole before charging them."

"Got it. Are you okay?"

"Why?"

"Because people who run into Charlie Warner tend to wind up feeding alligators."

"Don't worry about me," I say. "Just find that mole."

"Sure thing. Call me if there's anything else you need."

I hang up. I've just framed a nonexistent drug lord for my roommate's murder, exposed a mole in the police force and arranged for the kidnapper of two teenage boys and their families to be tracked down.

All things considered, not a bad night out.

The next afternoon, I find Maurice Vasquez at the field office hunched over a transcript, scribbling on it with a ball-point pen.

"Goddamn typists," he says. "Can't spell for shit. How hard is it to work out an apostrophe?"

"I'd have thought grammar would be the least of your worries," I say.

"Wrong. A misplaced apostrophe can change the whole meaning of a sentence. Sometimes it's enough for a defense attorney to get reasonable doubt." He looks up. "Did you want something?"

"That bug I was asking about. You sure you installed it right?"

"I didn't install it. But it was hooked up in all the right places. Why?"

If it wasn't Vasquez, that makes mechanical failure a whole lot more likely. "Luzhin said he told you to install it."

"He did. But one of the other techs got around to it first."

"Do you know which one?"

He sighs. "No. I just opened the phone, found the bug already inside, checked it was connected properly and closed it again. Why?"

A flame is taking hold in my stomach. "No reason," I say. "Just seems weird, days and days of recorded silence."

"I know it's frustrating," Vasquez replies, "but like I said, I'll ask Luzhin to call you if I find anything at all. Okay?"

"Okay," I say. "Later."

He picks up his pen and resumes his apostrophe-adding. I walk away, looking for Thistle.

There haven't been a lot of lucky breaks in this case, so I'm trying not to get my hopes up. But this feels like the lead that could unravel the whole thing and bring Philip Hall into my reach.

I find Thistle in her cubicle, typing an email. I knock on the wall to get her attention.

She spins around in her chair. Her mouth pulls into a smile. "Timothy! You've changed your hair. I like it."

Her lips are the prettiest thing in this world, and for a second I almost forget what I came here to tell her. "Thanks. You got a minute?"

"Sure."

"I just spoke to Maurice Vasquez. He says that the bug he put in Annette Hall's phone never recorded anything except silence. But—"

"What happened to your arm?"

I look down and see that a corner of my makeshift bandage is poking out from under my sleeve.

"Got bit by a dog," I say. "A poodle, believe it or not."

"Jesus," she says, and then slaps her hand across her mouth, horrified. It takes me a moment to remember that she thinks I'm Catholic.

"Don't worry about it," I say.

"Did you go to the doctor?"

"I'm fine."

"You need antibiotics. If that gets infected—"

"I can't afford a doctor."

I regret the words as soon as I've said them. I don't want Thistle to know how poor I am. But she barely blinks.

"I've got a friend who's an ophthalmologist," she says. "She owes me a favor."

"My eyes are fine."

"She can prescribe something. For free."

"Fine, sure. Can I speak my piece now?"

She nods.

"Vasquez says he never installed the bug—he opened the phone and it was already there. He thinks one of the other FBI techs planted it first. I think it was someone else, and that's why nothing is getting recorded."

"Someone else like who?"

"Like Child Protective Services."

"You think someone noticed Annette Hall's racism and called the CPS?" she says, deadpan.

This is risky. I have to hint at what I know without explaining how I know it.

"I have a hunch," I say. "Do you trust me?"

"Yes," she says. No hesitation.

"You remember how weird Jim Epps acted when we talked to him?"

"Cameron's friend? Yeah."

"I think he suspected Annette Hall of molesting her son, and I think he—or maybe someone else with similar suspicions—called CPS. Then I think they got a warrant to bug Cameron's home."

Thistle stares at me. "You got any evidence for this?" she asks finally. "It's a long shot."

Not as long as she thinks. "Other than a general feeling from Jim, Annette and Cameron," I say, "I have nothing."

"Feelings aren't worth much in court," Thistle says, considering the idea. The fingers of her right hand are twitching, as though she's playing the viola again.

"No," I say. "But if I'm right, then the CPS bug would have got the original call."

"And we could get the techs on to it." Thistle's eyes have started to sparkle. "They could work out where the ransom demand was recorded."

"I have no official power," I say. "You'd have to make the call to CPS."

"I'll get a phone number," she says. "But I doubt it'll belong to anyone important. We might have to fire escape somebody."

I don't know what that means, but it sounds like she's on board. "No problem."

When I worked the grill at McDonald's as a teenager, there was a vegetarian girl who took orders out front. It was the manager's policy to have female staff using the registers and male staff doing the cooking and cleaning. "Tits behind the counter," he said, more than once. "Tits sell burgers."

I never spoke to the girl, but that didn't stop her talking to me, mostly about her pet rabbit. "Last night I let Hedges out of her cage," she said, grinning, "and she ran under my bed. By the time I found her this morning, she'd eaten my diary." Or: "You know, when she was just a baby, she used to sleep in my shoe."

It wasn't just the rabbit. She'd inquire about other people's pets too. If someone told her about a kitten attacking a shoe-lace, she'd laugh and laugh.

I hadn't been there long when she quit. Rosy-cheeked, she told us she was going to work full-time for PETA. "As an un-paid volunteer," she said, "at first. But hopefully later they'll start paying me. And it isn't about the money, of course."

It struck me at the time how different our lives must be if she could afford to increase her hours *and* reduce her paycheck. But I didn't say anything, and then she was gone.

I kept flipping patties, week after week, watching the meat bubble and hiss. The manager hired a new young woman who kept a blob of gum stuck under the counter and put it in her mouth when he wasn't watching.

Fourteen months later, the vegetarian came back as a cus-tomer. None of the other staff had been working there long enough to remember her, and she didn't see me—I just rec-ognized her voice.

"I used to work here," she told the man she'd come in with. "Before I volunteered at PETA."

"You were in PETA?"

She snorted. "They had me doing lethal injections on dogs with bad backs and killing mice so they could feed them to snakes and birds. I lasted three weeks."

When she got to the front of the line, she ordered a Quarter Pounder.

This Child Protective Services agent reminds me of her. Not visually—he's thirtyish, white and slender, with eyes as dark as gutter puddles. It's more how he sounds than how he looks.

"I'd like to help," he says, as though he's said those words a thousand times before and means them a little less each time. His voice is thick and hoarse, like he's been coughing. "But I can't give out the details of ongoing investigations."

People join the CPS because they like kids. Then they spend every day taking them away from their parents while they scream and cry. Idealism to nihilism in a few short years.

"We're not interested in the kid's personal history," Thistle says. "Or what it was that made you concerned for his welfare, or who you suspect of doing whatever it is you think they've done. We just need to know if you bugged his phone."

"That would be a detail of an ongoing investigation. I can't give that information out."

"To the public, sure. But we're the FBI." Thistle touches the badge on her belt, as if the guy might have forgotten it was there. "Anything you tell us stays a secret."

My stomach is roaring like the engine room of a cruise ship. The CPS agent wouldn't make much of a meal, but I want him anyway. I haven't eaten in too long. John Johnson was a skinny drug addict. Not like those big, soft death row inmates. The hunger is making it hard to focus.

"It's not about who you are," he says. "And it's not about secrets. There are rules, and I have to follow them."

"Well, we have rules too. They say that if we don't get an answer today, we come back tomorrow with a subpoena. That subpoena comes with its own set of rules, which says that when we give it to you, you have to drop everything and go looking for the information we need. Not one of your subordinates—*you*."

She looks around the room, at the papers smeared across his desk, the calendar with scribbles on every square. "And I'm guessing you're too busy to want that. You're also not going to want Cameron Hall's information spread around any further than it has to be. But requesting subpoenas is a fairly noisy process."

"I'm sure that won't be necessary," the guy says. "If you'll just give me some contact information—"

"What for?" I put in. "We're right here."

"What I mean is, so someone can call you with a solution to the problem."

"We're on the clock here," Thistle says. "There's a kid missing. We can't afford to be sitting by the phone."

"It won't take long," the guy says. "I just need to make a few calls."

"Oh, okay." Thistle looks at me. "So we'll just wait outside, then?"

"Sure," I say.

We step out onto the blue-green-gray-checkered carpet of the hall and pull the door shut behind us. Under the chatter of the TV hanging from the wall, I can hear an indistinct mumbling as the guy calls his boss.

It's the same as calling a phone company, Thistle explained to me in the car on the way here. If you want to talk to the operations manager, the worst thing you can do is ask for them. Whoever picks up the phone will block you, because they know their place: a buffer between the public and anyone important.

"What you gotta do instead," Thistle said, "is make a request that the person you're talking to has no power to grant, like a refund. Make enough of a fuss that they'll be desperate

to palm you off onto their superior. It's a sneaky way to the
top—I call it 'fire escaping.'"

"It's taking a while," I say. "That's a bad sign."

"Not necessarily," Thistle replies. "The boss could already
be off looking for the answers we need."

"But we don't just need to know about the bugged phone.
We need to hear the recording."

"One thing at a time, Scary Tim," she says.

My stomach gurgles. I can still taste Thistle's lips on mine
from the other night. I shut my eyes.

"You okay?" she asks.

Before I can reply, a woman with a pearl necklace walks
down the corridor toward us. A firm smile is fixed on her
round face. "Agent Thistle?" she says. "Mr. Blake?"

"That would be us," Thistle says.

"I'm Georgia Palenna," she says. "I'm the assistant director. Sorry about the confusion."

She seems to be pretending that the guy we've been talking to just didn't understand what we wanted.

"No problem," Thistle says, playing along.

"I gather you need approval to see some case notes?"

"Yes. Cameron Hall. You have them?"

Palenna laughs politely. "Not on me. But I can confirm,
in confidence, that a listening device was installed in his residence by a CPS operative."

Thistle shoots an impressed glance my way, before saying,
"Thanks. Did it record anything?"

"I'm not aware of its activity. We don't have enough active
devices to justify a twenty-four-hour surveillance team—the
recordings are listened to only when the agent in charge of
the case checks it."

"We're going to need to hear everything that was recorded." She's telling, not asking. Trying to make it impossible for Palenna to say no.

It doesn't work. "I'm afraid that won't be possible. That sort of material—"

"Would already be in our possession," I say, "if you hadn't stopped the FBI from bugging the phone."

"The CPS can hardly be held responsible for an FBI agent mistaking a wiretap for one of their own."

"You can be held responsible for what happens to the kidnapped kid, since sharing the recordings could save him."

"The bug thing would be embarrassing for the FBI," Thistle says. "But a dead child would be worse for CPS."

"For everybody," I say.

"Especially the child," Thistle adds.

Palenna's smile has been replaced by an equally practiced look of concern.

"Of course I will do everything I can to help any child," she says, "within the bounds of the law. It's the latter part that's problematic."

"We are the law," Thistle says, as though she's always wanted to speak those words. "Like I told your colleague, I'm happy to get a subpoena—but that wipes out our chance of getting this done quickly and quietly."

Palenna looks at us for a long time and then nods. "Wait here." She walks away, pulling out her cell and dialing.

"Fire escaping really works," I whisper to Thistle.

"I know, right?"

We watch Palenna talking in the distance, her eyes to the ceiling, one hand on her hip.

"So which church do you go to?" Thistle asks.

"The priest moved north six months back," I say. "Seemed like a good excuse to find one closer to home. So you could say I'm between churches right now."

"I could help you pick."

"That's kind," I say. "I'll think about it."

We stand in silence for a while.

"I'm sorry about the other night," she says.

"Don't be," I say. "Getting jumped by you was the best surprise I've had in a long time."

She grins. "In that case, how about a movie next weekend?"

I haven't been to the movies since group trips at the home. "Is there anything good out?"

"Probably not. We could rent one, watch it at my place."

"I'd like that."

"You could show me some of that 'other stuff' you've done."

I didn't expect this problem to surface quite so soon. How close can I get to Thistle without my killer instincts kicking in? Nudity is out of the question. Even kissing might be too much. But it will be hard to convince her that my religion forbids all physical contact. Maybe I can pretend to be into S & M. Like, I need to wear a muzzle to get off.

"Isn't that supposed to wait until the third date?" I ask.

"Well, we've already had one." She nudges me. "We could rent two movies."

I'm about to reply when I see something on the TV. It's footage of cops disassembling my Malibu.

"...found in the trunk of the vehicle," the news anchor is saying. "When asked if the body had been identified, the police offered no comment."

"What's this?" Thistle says, turning to the TV.

"Nothing," I say.

"But," the anchor continues, "they did release this sketch of the driver."

I lunge forward and kiss Thistle.

"Mmmph!" she says.

I'm watching the TV with one eye. The sketch makes me look like I'm made of Plasticine, but otherwise it's pretty good. Cops make better witnesses than civilians.

Thistle pushes me away. "Someone will see," she says, suppressing a smile.

"Sorry," I say. "I'm just looking forward to that date. Those *dates*."

She shakes her head. "You're full of surprises, Scary Tim."

I am. But some of them she won't like. I'm now the subject of a statewide manhunt; Thistle is bound to see the sketch eventually. Will she recognize me?

Palenna is coming back. "Just what the hell is this?" she demands.

Whoops. She must have seen the kiss. "What's what?" I ask.

"No more bullshit." Her face is white. "The recording. How did you know about it, and why the fuck didn't you tell us sooner?"

"I don't know what you think we're hiding from you," Thistle says, "but you're wrong. We don't know anything about the recording. That's why we need to hear it."

"If that's true," Palenna says, "then we're all in deep shit." She turns, walks away, realizes we're not following and says, "Come on!"

We follow her to an AV room. The two TVs seem excessive, given that the room is barely bigger than a closet. The PC between them has a monitor as deep as it is wide.

Palenna picks up a cable and plugs it into the headphone jack on her phone. Taps the touch screen.

"You want to tell us what we should be listening for?" Thistle asks.

"It'll be pretty goddamn obvious." Palenna cranks the volume on a dusty pair of speakers.

"Hello?" It's Annette Hall's voice. Shaky.

"You called the fucking *cops."*

It's the same voice we heard before. A distorted growl, made crackly by the speakers. This time he sounds angry.

"No!" Annette says. *"No, I did just what you told me to!"*

"I saw you do it."

Is that possible? Could Philip Hall have been watching through the window as his ex-wife dialed 911?

"Lie to me again and your son dies," he continues. *"You called the cops, and now you're going to pay for it."*

"Please. Please don't do this."

"Here's what we're going to do. Are you listening?"

Annette is hyperventilating.

"Answer me or he dies."

"I'm…I'm listening."

It's not a recorded message this time. Philip is interacting with Annette, which probably means Cameron was elsewhere at the time.

"This afternoon you're going to proceed with the drop. You're only going to bring twenty thousand dollars, not four million. And your kid won't be there. But tonight, the cops are going to tell you they found your son."

"I don't understand."

"Shut up. You're going to go to the hospital. They'll show you a young blond boy. You're going to act like he's your son. You can act, can't you?"

Thistle and I look at each other.

"Holy shit," she says.

"I don't understand," Annette is whimpering.

"He'll pretend you're his mother, or his real mother dies. You'll pretend he's Cameron, or the real Cameron dies."

The break-in at my house. The ride in the trunk of the kidnapper's car. The warehouse. He *wanted* me to find and rescue Cameron—because it wasn't Cameron.

"Then who was it you saved?" Thistle demands.

"It was Robert Shea." I'm realizing the truth as I'm saying the words. "That's why they looked the same. They *were* the same."

"When they release him from the hospital," Philip says, *"the*

two of you are going to go home and wait for my instructions. This time, you'd better fucking do what I tell you."

"I'm sorry," Annette cries. *"I'll do everything you say. Just, please, don't—"*

Philip hangs up.

CHAPTER 20

MY LIFE CAN BE MEASURED IN HOURS.
I SERVE BY BEING DEVOURED.
THIN, I AM QUICK. FAT, I AM SLOW.
THE OLDER I GET, THE SHORTER I GROW.
THE DARK IS MY FRIEND, THE WIND IS MY FOE.
WHAT AM I?

"I HAVE A PROPOSITION."

"Who is this?"

"I'm the guy who saw you two years ago."

"You got the wrong number, pal."

"I saw you eating raw meat. Self-defense—so you said."

Even through the phone, Luzhin's voice was sharper than before. He was off the coke, and no longer afraid.

I peeked out the window, expecting the house to be surrounded by cops. But the alley was empty except for puddles and rain-shredded missing person posters.

"How did you find me?"

"It was easy. These days I'm in a position of responsibility. I have access to things. So I wondered if you wanted more."

"More what?"

"More meat."

If this was a trap, he wouldn't be speaking so ambiguously.

"How?" I sounded more desperate than I intended.

"It's like playing hangman, but in reverse. When you solve the puzzle, you get the guy on the gallows."

There was a whining in my ears, like a hand grenade had gone off near my head. It was as though I could actually *hear*

my mind spinning. My heart beat faster and faster. My lungs
were tight.

I'd been using stolen credit cards to buy steak at the supermarket and eat it raw. When that didn't quiet my hunger, I'd
been catching rats in homemade traps and taking bites out of
them while they were still breathing. But it wasn't enough.
I was desperate for exactly what the man on the phone was
offering: a fresh human.

"Blake," Thistle is saying, "Luzhin wants to talk to you."

I snap back to the present. Thistle is holding out her phone.
Palenna is yelling something. I'm barely aware of her.

Three years of working for Luzhin and I've never had a
case like this. I've never been so wrong.

Philip Hall's plan is like a crossword puzzle in my brain.
Every time I fill in a blank, the answer to another becomes
obvious.

He went to Cameron's house after school. Picked him up
in his van. Took his backpack, left his cell phone and parked
the van near a pay phone to make the ransom call when Annette got home. He distorted his voice so that she wouldn't
recognize it.

And then what? Did he drive back to the house in time to
watch her call the police? Was there enough time for that?

"People are going to lose their jobs over this," Palenna is
saying, "and none of them will be me." She says this as though
sheer determination will make it true.

When Philip found out that Annette had contacted the
cops, he called her again, threatened her and then went looking for a kid who looked a bit like his son. He found one:
Robert Shea. That's why he took the photos from Cameron's
house. He didn't want the police seeing what the real Cameron looked like, in case we realized what he'd done. When
he discovered that Robert Shea had undergone a nephrectomy,
Philip was forced to set up the stunt with the mannequin and

the kidney. If only I'd looked at the photos from Cameron's social media. Then I would have realized the kid in the warehouse wasn't him.

Now four people are missing. Annette, Cameron, Robert and Robert's mother, Celine. That's a lot of people to keep in one van. The chances that they're still alive are close to zero.

"Luzhin wants to speak to you," Thistle says, and hands me the cell phone.

I hold it to my ear. "Yeah?"

Luzhin's voice is thick with rage. "How long did you think you could keep this going?"

"I beg your pardon?"

"You bring me the wrong kid and you think I won't find out?"

A sick feeling is growing in my gut. "If you're suggesting that I could have known Shea was lying—"

"Known? You *told* him to lie! You drugged him, broke his hand, threatened him, convinced everyone he was Cameron Hall just so you'd get your goddamn reward!"

"That makes no sense," I say.

He doesn't seem to hear me. "You're finished, Blake," he shouts. "I'll lock you up until Judgment Day!"

"Okay, sure," I say. "I'll tell her."

"Tell her what? I'm talking to *you*, asshole!"

"No problem. See you soon." I hang up and casually put the phone on flight mode before I toss it back to Thistle. She drops it into her pocket without noticing.

"Director wants us back at the office," I say.

"Got it," Thistle says. "Let's go."

Luzhin knows I'm a killer. I have no hope of convincing him that I didn't threaten Robert Shea and his family. Right now he will be calling a judge to arrange an arrest warrant, and listing my offenses as kidnapping, assault, extortion and drug possession. Perhaps, in a crisis of conscience, he will add the names of the inmates I've eaten.

Or maybe there will be no warrant, because I know too much. Maybe it will be a quiet word to a dirty cop who owes him a favor, followed by a bullet to the back of my head.

Will Thistle believe I'm innocent? Not once she sees the sketch of me. Not once she shows a photo of me to the cop I fled from yesterday.

"I need the bathroom first," I say, and look at Palenna. "Where is it?"

Palenna leads us out of the AV room and up the corridor to a men's room door.

"Give us a minute," I say.

Palenna nods. "All right. Tell your boss I'll help with the investigation in any way I can." She's making it clear that this is the FBI's problem, not the CPS's.

As she walks away, I lean in close to whisper in Thistle's ear. "I'm sorry," I say. "I really screwed this up."

She doesn't notice as I dip my hand into her jacket pocket.

"We'll deal with it," Thistle says. "Don't worry."

I walk into the men's room without looking back, her keys clenched in my fist.

Inside, I open a stall and kick up the lid of the toilet so Thistle will hear the *clack* as it hits the porcelain.

In most offices, the bathroom is the best-ventilated room in the building. The cheapest ventilation method is a great big hole in the wall, and that's exactly what I find—about six square feet of frosted glass with a square foot of wire mesh above it, through which I can feel a cool breeze. The window is locked.

Years ago I had a nightmare. I was a dog galloping through a Vietnamese jungle with flames singeing my fur as army choppers whined above, splashing more and more napalm onto the tree branches. I woke to discover that my house was on fire.

Jesse, my roommate before Johnson, later claimed that he had left a candle burning on the kitchen bench and that the flame on the gas stove had gone out when he wasn't looking. A gas cloud had expanded in the kitchen until the candle ignited it, setting the curtains and cupboards alight. I believed him, all except for the part about it being an accident. I think he just wanted to see what would happen. If the candle hadn't been in the same room as the stove, the whole house could have exploded.

Fortunately, back then I had a hammer to break a window and a heavy blanket to protect me from the broken glass as I climbed out. I don't have either of those now.

I bunch the sleeves of my jacket into my fists so my knuckles are covered. I flush the toilet to cover the sound, then slam my fist into the glass.

Windows are fragile, but not as fragile as Hollywood makes them look. It takes three tries to smash the glass, which jingles down onto the sidewalk below.

I kick out some stray shards, scramble through the frame and drop to the ground. One of my feet twists as I hit the concrete, and I stagger to the right as I stifle a groan. Running from the law isn't easy with a broken ankle—but it's not broken. A sprain, maybe. I can put some weight on it.

No time to lose. Thistle and Palenna may have heard my exit over the flushing toilet. I have to get as far away from here as possible. I jump in Thistle's Crown Vic, start the engine and pull out onto the road, driving into the setting sun.

Getting across the border into Louisiana or Arkansas won't be enough to put me out of Luzhin's reach. I have to get to Monterrey or Chihuahua—somewhere in Mexico, where he has no power and where the local cops won't care enough to go looking for me.

The hundred and fifty dollars in my pockets won't get me far. I should have taken all the cash hidden in John Johnson's room, but I didn't want to be carrying thousands of dollars around in case I got mugged. Stupid. I eat muggers for breakfast. Maybe I could go back and get the money?

If I do, getting out of the USA will take twice as long. If I don't, it'll be twice as hard.

Five minutes later I hear sirens on the wind. No time to get off the road. A patrol car sweeps past without pausing, headed for CPS. Thistle must know that I'm missing but hasn't yet realized her car is gone.

The fading sirens make me think of the Ambulance Killer, which makes me think of the Death House, which makes me regret that I'll never get to meet Philip Hall. Not only will he never end up on my dinner plate, but I'm getting chased out of Houston for a crime he committed. Of all the reasons I imagined I'd have to leave Texas, I never thought it would be because of something I didn't do.

More to the point, I never expected to be outwitted by a divorced problem gambler. How did he get the better of me? And what will he do once I'm gone?

If the cops catch Philip Hall, I would be exonerated. They're pretty lenient on resisting arrest when it turns out you were innocent. But Philip Hall is smarter than Thistle or Luzhin have given him credit for. Without my help, he might get away with all of it. Forever.

Even if I escape to Mexico, the only woman who ever respected me will live out the rest of her life thinking I betrayed her.

It's getting dark by the time I reach what used to be my house. I have no friends and no family, so as far as the cops are concerned, this house is the only place worth staking out. Once I've left it, I'm practically safe—but what if they are already here?

I park Thistle's car about six houses up from mine. No cars on the street, patrol or otherwise. No twitching curtains in any of the nearby houses. No dog walkers with earpieces— no pedestrians at all. But if the police aren't here, they're on their way. I have to move.

I hop over the fence into the backyard instead of opening the squeaky gate and slide my key into the back door. The wood isn't cracked, and the hinges are dirty as ever. No sign that it's been forced. This is good. If the cops had been here, they wouldn't have picked the lock. They would have knocked and then, when no one answered, broken the door off its hinges.

Just the same, I'm silent as a ghost as I slip inside.

I go into my room first. It's not where the cash is, but Thistle will know what I'm wearing, so I grab my bloodied shirt and stuff it into a plastic bag. I wish I had time to wipe down this room, erasing the prints and DNA. But once I'm in Mexico, it won't matter.

I go into Johnson's bedroom, pick up one of his hollow books and take out two bricks of cash. A couple of thousand dollars. Enough to get me to safety, I hope.

I stuff the first bundle into my pocket, turn around to leave—

And someone punches me in the face.

I'm on the floor before I know what's happened, my nose sizzling like it's been electrified. A blizzard of hundred-dollar bills fills the air like in an old rap video. The thought that my roommate has caught me stealing his stuff whips through my head before I have time to remember that he's dead.

Suddenly my ribs are crushed. A pair of hands close around my throat. I claw at them, but they just get tighter. My eyes feel like they're swelling up in their sockets as the blood flow to my brain stops and the cartilage of my Adam's apple creaks.

For the first time, I see my assailant's face. It's not my room-mate's ghost, and it's not a cop. It's one of Charlie Warner's bodyguards.

I let go of his hands and brace myself against the floor, pushing up against his weight, unbalancing him. He could stop me from getting my arms out from under him, but he'd have to let go of my throat, so he doesn't.

Mistake. I pull my hands loose and punch him in both ears simultaneously. He yelps, and his palms spring off my neck. I use this opportunity to head-butt him, my forehead crushing his nose like a crabapple under a motorcycle boot.

He rolls off me, and even as I'm coughing and splutter-ing against the sudden oxygen overdose, I roll onto him and pin down his wrists, one with my hand, one with my knee.

Then someone else grabs the back of my shirt and hauls me off him. The other bodyguard, perhaps. I try to wriggle free, but something hard hits me in the back of the head, and then I'm too dizzy to struggle.

"Quit squirming, Blake," someone says. "You're coming with us."

As the bodyguard picks himself up off the floor, his col-league drags me out of the bedroom.

"You know I found a human foot in this psycho's freezer?" one of the bodyguards says.

"Holy shit! You, uh, better bag it, I guess. Warner doesn't want anything illegal left behind."

"That'll take a while. Did you see all the pills in that bedroom?"

The first bodyguard walks into the kitchen while the sec-ond drags me into the living area. A plastic bag rustles as one of them wraps up John Johnson's foot.

Someone pounds on the door, and everyone freezes.

"Police!" A woman's voice, but not Thistle. "Open up!"

Warner's goons look at each other. One of them claps a

sweaty palm over my mouth, putting enough pressure on my chin to keep my jaw closed. I swallow the rising tide of vomit.

"Leave the pills," one bodyguard whispers. "Go!"

The bodyguards pull me through the kitchen, out the back door and onto the back porch. A smart cop would have sent her partner around the back to see if I'm running. But no one's out here.

The goons haul me over the knots of weeds in the tiny backyard and through the gap in the rear neighbor's fence. Somewhere behind us, I can hear wood snapping as the cops break down my door.

I'm dragged through the neighbor's carport and out onto the sidewalk. A van pulls up alongside us, the door slides open and I see a thick-necked guy with a goatee cradling a shotgun.

The bodyguards push me into the back. One of them climbs in after me, while the other gets into the cabin with the driver. The guy with the shotgun slams the door, and the van lurches into motion.

"What's this about?" I ask.

"Shut up," says the guy with the gun.

I do. Blood trickles down the back of my neck, making my shirt collar sticky.

The bodyguards looked surprised when the cops showed up, which means that Warner sent them before she knew I was a fugitive. Why? What does she want with me?

The van trundles along for maybe twenty minutes, out of the suburbs and onto a disused highway. We pass a bullet-spattered sign that says WELCOME TO SALVATION HILL. Salvation Hill is one of seven ghost towns scattered around Houston County, abandoned for more than a hundred years. My heart goes a little quicker.

The van pulls over near a Baptist church, the windows missing, the crucifix on the roof knobby with dried bird shit.

Other than the church and an empty sawmill, there's nothing but flat scrubland all the way to the horizon.

The shotgun guy's finger is on the trigger, so I don't move as someone opens the door from the outside.

It's another guy, with another shotgun.

"Get out," he says.

I clamber out of the van. Charlie Warner is holding a spiral-bound notebook and looking at me with bored contempt.

"Mr. Blake," she says. "We need to talk."

"You could have just called me," I say. "There's no need for this." I gesture at the two guys with shotguns, the two bodyguards and the driver, who is getting out of the van and drawing a pistol. He's left the keys in the ignition. We must not be staying long.

"I thought about that," Warner says. "But I couldn't decide whether to call your home number or your office at the FBI."

I don't have an office, but I get her meaning.

Warner beckons to her goons. One of them presses his shotgun to my spine. If he pulls the trigger, my intestines will burst out like the monster in *Alien*.

"Move," he says.

We all walk over to the sawmill. There aren't many of these in Houston anymore—a lot of them went out of business when it became cheaper to import lumber from Belize, and a couple were destroyed in accidental explosions. This one is still in good condition. The floor is polished, gleaming in the setting sun. The glass in the windows is intact. Someone is still using it for something.

As I'm frog-marched through the front door, I see plank after plank of cedar, hickory and mesquite. But my eye is drawn to all the saws. Hacksaws, drag saws, ripsaws, teeth glinting in the reflected moonlight.

My skin is crawling. I know why we're here now.

"I'm not a cop," I say. "I helped the FBI out on some kid-napping cases. That's all."

"In what way did you help?"

"The cops are idiots," I say, hoping this will please her. "I look at the evidence, I tell them who did it. It's not hard."

The driver is unfolding a sheet of plastic on the floor, like the kind painters use. He weighs down one corner with a plastic jug. Yellowish fluid sloshes around inside.

The preparations made, he puts a cigarette in his mouth and fumbles with a lighter. Warner's eye twitches, but she doesn't tell him not to light it. She's practicing her self-control.

"And this role," she says. "Did it require you to steal a car, or was that your own idea?"

My heart beats a little faster. "What car?"

"The car you sent my boys out to find. The car that turned up with switched plates and Philip Hall's body in the trunk."

CHAPTER 21

**IRENE DIED IN VERMONT. IKE DIED IN CANADA.
NOBODY MOURNED THEM—
IN FACT, PEOPLE REJOICED.
WHY?**

NO.

No *way*.

She cannot be saying what I think she's saying, or else I truly have gone mad.

"Philip Hall is dead?" I ask.

"Don't you dare pretend you don't know what I'm talking about," Charlie Warner says. "Would you care to tell me why you sent me to look for a guy you already killed?"

"I didn't kill him," I say. "I didn't even know he was dead."

"I'm confused," Warner says. "I don't like being confused."

I barely hear her. A dead man can't confess. A dead man can't exonerate me.

But that barely matters, since I'm about to die. One of the shotgun guys has propped his gun up against the wall and is plugging a circular saw into a wall outlet.

"I'm as confused as you," I say. "More so. But we can figure this out."

"My theory is that you just can't help yourself," Warner says. "You killed Philip Hall for fun, and you tried to set me up to take the blame."

"I didn't. I swear to you."

But at the same time, I'm remembering how my roommate's arm disappeared. Later I found blood all over my bed.

I know I'm a cannibal, I know I'm a sleepwalker, I know I was hunting Philip Hall, and I know he's turned up dead. In my car.

I know that I'm crazy. But what if I'm crazier than I thought? What if I *did* do this?

"Thirty-five years ago, a young couple moved from Philly to Houston, Texas. Soon the woman fell pregnant, and not long after that they had a baby boy. One night they were watching TV with the sound off when—"

She's done some research. "This isn't about my parents," I say.

"—someone broke into their house. When he discovered the owners were home, he shot the man in the face and the woman in the chest. If the bullet had been an inch lower, it would have hit the baby she was feeding."

The saw blade starts whirling. The shotgun guy walks toward me, gripping the handles. My stomach churns.

"This is not about my parents," I say again.

"The robber fled," Warner continues, "but no one heard the gunfire. The baby should have starved to death. Yet a week later, the mailman heard him crying. When the cops broke down the door, they found that the baby had eaten most of his mother's breast—"

"This isn't about my fucking parents!" I scream, and throw myself at her. My heart feels like a flaming trash can. My teeth seem too big for my mouth, as though I'm turning into a werewolf.

One of the bodyguards trips me up, and I land face-first in the sawdust. It burns my nostrils and makes my eyes water.

"You're a mad dog," Warner says. "And you gotta be put down."

I can hear the snarling teeth of the saw edging closer.

"You should have just shot me," I whisper.

"Sorry. But it has to be a painful death. I need people to be afraid of lying to me."

I scoop up a handful of sawdust.

Warner is quicker than her men. Even as I'm throwing the sawdust at the driver's face, she's yelling, "Shoot him!" and throwing herself facedown on the floor, but no one pulls the trigger fast enough. The cloud of sawdust reaches the blazing end of the driver's cigarette first.

The explosion sucks all the air out of the room with a dark *whumph*. Even with my eyes squeezed shut and my arms over my face, I can see the light and feel the heat. A hurricane of grit scrapes my skin. Everyone is screaming, except the driver, who probably died instantly.

There's no time to be dazzled. The others will recover soon, and for all I know, I've lit a fuse that will send the whole building up in flames. Sawdust is incredibly flammable.

I scramble out the door and head for the van, tripping and sliding in the dirt. Halfway there, I hear Warner's voice: "Freeze, asshole!"

I keep running. A shotgun booms out across the plains. No dust kicks up, so she must have aimed high. I collide with the van, yank open the door and jump in.

The second shotgun blast hits the van. It sounds like a sudden hailstorm against the paneling. I twist the key, shove my foot down on the accelerator, and then the van is zooming back out onto the road. It's a full minute before I start breathing again and realize that I have no clue where I'm going.

Philip Hall is dead. I'm wanted for his murder.

But I didn't do it. The more I think about it, the more impossible it seems. I might be a killer, and I might be losing my mind, but there's no way I tracked down a wanted fugitive in my sleep, murdered him and concealed his body without knowing about it. I've been too goddamn busy.

So how did he get into the trunk of my car?

The body looked very fresh, but I doubt someone put him there in broad daylight while my car was parked near Philip Hall's house. It must have happened the night before last, while I was destroying Johnson's bones and cleaning my bed. Someone broke into my trunk and put Hall's body inside while the car was in my driveway.

Philip Hall wasn't the kidnapper. Nor was he Robert's father—Robert's picture seemed to resemble Cameron only because the boy I met was Robert, not Cameron. But Philip is sure to be blamed for the kidnappings, since the property deed for the warehouse was found conveniently on his desk.

A police helicopter thunders past overhead, the searchlight cutting through the darkness below. The FBI knows I'm nearby, but they must think that I'm on foot. The light sweeps over the van and keeps moving through the shadows on the other side of the highway.

I need to decide. Do I exit the USA, leaving Thistle behind thinking I did something I didn't do? Or do I stay, and search for the real culprit, risking my freedom and my life?

Houston is as dark as the night sky. Knowing that a killer is out there, somewhere, gives this city a sense of menace. Two killers, actually. Him and me, circling one another in the gloom, like Earth and Theia, headed for a collision that will obliterate one of us.

Blood is running down my lip; my nose was broken when the bodyguard punched me. I bang my fist on the steering wheel, and the keys jingle under the ignition. This would be so much easier if only I knew the identity of the real kidnapper—

And suddenly I do.

Someone who might have met both Robert and Cameron and noticed the resemblance. Someone who seemed more interested in the FBI's investigation than any of the other witnesses. Someone whose best years are over, leaving him with money troubles and an addiction to feed. Someone who's been to my house. Knows where I live.

I take the next exit off the highway, humming "Baby, I Ain't Your Man."

A light is on behind the window.

The apartment block is even worse than I expected. Bricks exposed by peeling paint, roof tiles chipped. Windows graffitied and close enough together that the apartments are either pretty big and have two windows each or really small with only one. I'm guessing it's the latter.

You can't hide two teenage boys and their parents in a space like that. I'm now pretty sure that Robert, Cameron and both their families are dead.

Anger burns behind my jaw. But I can't tell if it's for what the killer did to them, or what he's done to me.

I climb the stairs. It's tough, with my twisted ankle and my shredded arm. Every step makes my broken nose throb. But I have both my fists and most of my teeth.

The apartment I want is on the first floor. There are two brass locks on the door. Picking them would give him time to hear me, grab a gun and shoot me as I came in. There's a good chance there's a spare key in the dead potted plant by the door, but even if there is, opening the door the usual way poses the same risk, especially if he's got a chain.

I can hear the thickest strings of an acoustic guitar chiming inside. Doesn't sound like a recording. The bastard has no idea that I'm coming.

I raise my foot and aim for the hinges. No second chances—I have to give this all I've got.

The plan is to storm in, grab him and make him tell me where the bodies are. If they're on the premises, then I'll drag him to the lockup. If they're not, I'll beat some other proof of his guilt out of him and drag him just the same.

I was scared of him before. Not now. Now it's just me and another dead man walking. His fists against mine—assuming I don't give him time to get to his gun.

The door makes a sound like a thunderclap as it splinters and falls through its frame. I storm in just in time to see Harry Crudup's head whirl toward the sound, eyes wide. Incredibly, rather than just dropping the guitar, he tries to balance it back on its rubber stand as I run forward and grab him by the throat. The guitar hits the floor with a *boom*.

"Found you," I say.

"What the fuck?" he rasps. He doesn't know how I tracked him down. He doesn't know about Johnson's address book. He doesn't know that I finally figured out the connection between the two kids: their music teacher.

He swings a fist at me. I weave around it, get behind him, put my free hand on the back of his bald head and slam his face down against a nearby table. His heel springs backward toward my crotch. I snap my knees together to block it, then put my forearm across the back of his neck.

I can't let myself bite him. Not if he's going to prove my innocence to Thistle.

"I've got the money," he says.

I figured he'd have spent it by now—junkies don't have much self-restraint. The money is all the evidence I need.

"Where?"

"Just don't hurt me, man," he says. "Please."

"Where?"

He points. I drag him through the door he pointed to and find myself in a tiny bedroom. There's no sheet on the mattress, nothing but a rusty alarm clock on his bookshelf. I wonder if he rents this place, or if he's squatting.

Crudup moves toward the bed. I pull him back like a dog on a leash. "Just tell me."

"Beneath the carpet," he says. "Under the bed."

I lift up the mattress with my free hand. Through the chicken-wire bedframe, I can see a lump under the carpet. Too flat for a gun. But it looks too flat for twenty thousand dollars too.

"Get it," I say.

He crawls under the bed, slips his hand through a slit in the carpet and digs out a bundle of notes. Thrusts it at me. I don't take it. It can't be more than five hundred bucks.

He presses it into my hand. "That's more than I owe," he says. "And it's all I got. I swear."

"Owe?"

There's terror in his eyes. "You tell Mr. Johnson that's everything I got!"

Does he seriously think I'm here as an enforcer for my ex-roommate?

"I'm not here about that," I say.

He looks baffled.

"Where did you hide the bodies?"

You could put a billiard ball in his mouth without touching his lips. "What bodies?"

"Cameron Hall! Robert Shea! Larry—"

"No, Cameron's alive!" he says. "Some guy found him in a warehouse."

"That was Robert Shea!"

"Okay, Robert Shea found him. Whoever."

I raise my fist, and he cowers. And that's when I really know I've got the wrong guy. If he had the stomach to kill six people and remove a kidney, he wouldn't be this scared of a guy like me. And if he wasn't afraid, he couldn't make it look that real.

Crudup is innocent, and I've run out of suspects. The cops will catch me soon, if Warner's people don't first. My life is over.

Crudup is blubbering on the ground, his brown skin

gleaming with sweat. It looks almost like pork crackling. This could be my last chance for a decent meal.

"Please don't hurt me," he sobs.

I crouch down next to him. He's a big guy, and not too fit. Lots of delicious flab.

"Please," he says again.

I take about two hundred dollars from Johnson's stash and hand it to him. "That's to fix your door," I say. "John Johnson is dead. You don't owe him anything anymore."

He thinks it's a trick. The money falls to the floor.

An apology wouldn't do much good at this point. Wouldn't lessen his fear, nor the guilt in my stomach. But maybe there's something else I can give him.

"But if you're not in rehab in two days," I say, "then I'm coming back for you. Got that?"

He just looks at me. I leave.

I dream that I'm in the execution chamber at Huntsville. I'm wearing my school clothes, with their tarnished buttons and patched knees. My upper lip is crusted with snot.

A severed arm is lying on the gurney, fat and juicy. The wrist is hooked through a handcuff.

A puddle of blood surrounds the broken elbow joint. The bone glistens like a freshly glazed pastry. I walk over, pick up the arm and take a bite out of the hand.

It rears up like an eel, tendons bulging, nails scratching at my eyes. I scream and wrestle with it, tumbling to the floor. It grabs for my throat but gets my jaw instead, and I clamp my teeth down on the fingers. An electric shock stutters through my body as my mouth fills up with blood.

I jolt awake and bump my knee on the steering wheel.

I'm sitting in Warner's van in the parking lot near Crudup's house. The engine is off. I had intended to close my eyes for only a minute. It's still dark. I can't have slept for long.

The taste of human flesh is still on my tongue. Too salty to be just part of the dream. I open the door, and the interior light clicks on.

My left hand is dark and sticky. There are tooth-shaped gouges all over it. I've been chewing my own hand in my sleep. Moaning, I pull off my shirt and wrap it around my hand. There's no pain, but I can already feel a tingling as the limb wakes up. It's going to be agonizing in a few minutes.

I catch a glimpse of my reflection in the rear-view mirror. Blood is crusted around my mouth, my nose is crooked, sawdust is caked in my hair. My cheeks are singed pink from the explosion.

On the plus side, I no longer look much like the sketch artist's depiction of me.

I reach for the key to start the engine. Then I stop. There's nowhere in the world to go.

It's too late to leave Houston. There will be roadblocks on every highway out of town. I risked everything to track down the kidnapper, and I failed.

Nothing to do but wait for the FBI to find me and lock me up. There's a certain peace in this. For the first time in days, in months, in years, I don't have to do anything. I can just sit here, and soon I'll be in prison. They'll give me a bed to sleep in and three meals per day, at least until they execute me. They are supposed to give you anything you want for your last meal—I wonder if they'll let me have one of the other inmates.

I rub one of the scars on my leg through my jeans with my good hand, out of habit. The playing field behind the group home where I grew up looked lush and soft from a distance, but actually the grass was just tufts of weeds exploding out from between rocks and grit. While playing games, I often fell over onto the stony dirt, and one time I fell hard enough to scrape some skin off my knee. It was a minor wound and would have healed up within a week, except that I kept scratching off the scab before it hardened. Now I've got this scar, a daily reminder of my poor impulse control and my constant need to see what's beneath the surface.

Spending the rest of my days behind bars is something I can live with. But not knowing where those five people went and who took them, *that's* too much to bear.

Still, it's not like I have a choice. I'm one guy, wanted by the law, with nothing but a stolen van and a dwindling bundle of cash.

I consider going to Thistle's house and waiting for her to come home. But I'd never convince her that I'm innocent— because I'm not.

I didn't kill Robert Shea, I'd say. *Or Cameron Hall, or their families.*

Then why'd you run? she'll ask.

Because I ate a bunch of other people, and I was worried Luzhin was going to reveal it.

At that point, she'd probably just shoot me.

As I watch a bat flutter overhead, I think of another conversation with Thistle. One she might be having right now.

I've sealed off all the roads out of town. It's only a matter of time before we catch him.

No point, Luzhin will say. *He's long gone.*

But I'm not.

A guilty man would have fled, but I stayed to try to find the real killer. Luzhin won't expect that.

He hates me because he knows I'm a monster. But if I turned up on his doorstep, he might just believe me.

I start the van and pull out of the lot.

CHAPTER 22

WHY DO YOU ALWAYS FIND ME IN THE LAST PLACE YOU LOOK?

THE HOUSE IS BIG, BUT BADLY MAINTAINED. Paint eaten away by the springtime rains. The planks that make up the porch are rotting near the edges, where they weren't oiled properly. Signs of more recent neglect too—a bunch of cling-wrapped newspapers buried among the shrubbery.

The first time Luzhin offered me a condemned man to eat, I drove to the field office and waited for him to leave. Then I followed him home. I crouched in the garden and watched through the window as he greeted his wife and his daughters and started frying schnitzels for their dinner. The next morning, when he left for work and his wife took their kids to school, I broke in and had a look around. The house looked nicer then.

I don't slow down as I cruise past in the van. If he sees me coming, he'll assume I'm here to silence him. Sneaking up on him won't be easy, but getting to him before he reaches his gun safe is my best chance of survival.

I turn a corner and park the van in a side street under a big tree so Luzhin won't see it if he happens to be upstairs and looks out the window.

His driveway is empty, but he has a two-car garage, and the roller doors are shut. No way to tell if he's home or not.

His neighbor, on the other hand, is definitely not around. No lights on in the house, no car in the carport. The mailbox slot is blocked by a soggy wad of junk mail. I run through the carport, climb over the rusty gate leading to the yard and peep over the fence at Luzhin's house.

No lights on there either. Maybe Luzhin is asleep upstairs— or out looking for me. Probably worrying that someone will catch me before he does, and I'll spill the beans about our arrangement.

I clamber over the fence and drop into Luzhin's yard. The weeds rustle as they cushion my fall. My chewed-up hand is burning, and the dog bite feels almost as bad. Maybe Luzhin will have some alcohol I can pour on my wounds to steril- ize them.

I tiptoe through the darkness, past a rickety shed, up a path of chipped paving stones, all the way to the back door of the house.

Locked and dead-bolted. I have nothing to pick the lock with, and kicking the door in would make too much noise. Luzhin will hear it if he's home, and the neighbors will hear it if he's not.

I go back down the path to the shed. The door is sealed by a fat padlock, but the shed itself is thin aluminum, bolted to the ground only at the corners. I grab a corner of the door and bend it outward, making a gap just big enough to crawl through.

The shed holds a few tarpaulins, a neatly folded tent under a layer of dust and a toolbox in which I find some screwdrivers and pliers and wrenches. These would be useful if the door was only single-locked, but since there are two keyholes, I'll need a more precise instrument. I take a flat-head screwdriver and close the box.

As my eyes adjust to the darkness, I see two fishing rods propped up in the corner. Where there are rods, there are hooks—I find them in a small plastic container on the ground. These should do.

I crawl back out of the shed and head for the back door,

twisting one of the hooks into a straight line. I jam the screw-driver into one of the locks and turn it, maintaining pressure, like it's a torsion wrench. Then I start fiddling with the fish hook, trying to find the pins.

It would normally take me about nine minutes to pick a lock like this. Tonight it takes almost fifteen, because I'm working in the dark, with a mangled hand, and I'm trying to be completely silent in case Luzhin is inside.

The second lock clicks, and the door swings open. I find myself in a kitchen, grimy linoleum under my feet. There's a gas stove, a knife block and a thin filmy curtain hanging over the window.

In case I need to leave in a hurry, I pull back the dead bolt before closing the door so it doesn't lock behind me. I walk slowly, wary of creaking boards underfoot.

If Luzhin is here, he's probably upstairs, asleep. Just in case, I examine every shadow as I cross the living room. The couch is splitting at the seams. The TV is small, with an old-fashioned semi-round screen. Probably used for information rather than entertainment; I can imagine Luzhin switching on the news if he heard sirens, but not under many other circumstances.

A door in the wall must lead to the garage. I try the handle. Locked.

A soft scuffle from behind me.

I whirl around to face the stairs. A door is set under the staircase, leading to a cupboard, or maybe a basement. The noise came from in there.

Slow, silent, I move toward the door. Put my hand on the handle, and my ear to the wood.

Breathing, fast and ragged. He's in there.

The gasp means he already knows I'm here. No chance of sneaking up on him. So I call out, "It's me."

No answer.

"Don't shoot me or anything. Not until you've heard what I have to say."

The breathing continues. Dark and heavy. For a moment I wonder if he might be keeping a dog down there.

"Hello?"

Still no answer.

I slide back the bolt, without pausing to wonder how he got in there if it's locked from the outside. Slowly, I pull open the door. More stairs are revealed, leading down into the darkness.

The breathing is louder now. It bounces around the blackness so that it sounds like a hundred lungs rather than just two.

Again, I say, "Hello?"

Nothing. The door swings closed behind me.

I step down. Two steps. Three. The shadows are swallowing me up.

Something hits me in the face, gently. I hiccup with surprise—but it's just a bead, hanging from a string. A light switch.

I pull the string, and a neon light clicks on.

The basement has a concrete floor, brick walls and a low ceiling. Woodworking tools hang on metal hooks. Foam rubber mattresses are propped up against the walls. A gas can stands in the corner. It's a typical basement—

Except for the woman. She's chained to the wall by her raw wrists, a black bag over her head.

As if in a dream, I walk the rest of the way down the stairs, and the rest of the room is revealed. Four more prisoners are manacled to the other walls, all limp and pale.

Two adults.

Two teenage boys.

CHAPTER 23

IS A CLOCK THAT LOSES A MINUTE PER DAY BETTER THAN ONE THAT HAS STOPPED?

MY FIRST THOUGHT IS THAT THE HOODED FIG-
ures are Luzhin and his family, kept prisoner by a maniac.
But his wife and kids left him. I saw her—*Tell him not to push
for joint custody*, she said.

My second thought is that Luzhin has some kind of sex
dungeon. But that doesn't seem to fit, since everyone is fully
clothed, and while I've never been to a sex dungeon, I'm
pretty sure there would be whips and dildos.

I pull the hood off the nearest prisoner. Annette Hall gasps
through her nose. Tape is stretched over her mouth. Her eyes,
twitchy with terror, lock onto mine.

I stumble backward. No. This can't be right.

Luzhin isn't the kidnapper. He's one of the good guys. Determined, brave…

And willing to let me eat people if it helps close cases.

I scrunch my eyes shut. It's impossible. Luzhin was in an
FBI van behind the Walmart while the kidnapper was picking up the ransom—

Or he said he was. But when the kidnapper vanished after I
chased him around the corner, Luzhin was already there. He
could have just taken off his disguise, thrown it behind the
dumpster and pretended that he'd left the van to give chase.

But why would he do this?

"Mmmph!" Annette Hall says.

"Shhhh." I need to think.

I pull the hoods off the other prisoners. Robert Shea, then a kid who looks a bit like him—the real Cameron Hall, I guess—and two people who must be Larry and Celine Shea. The parents give me pleading looks, while the two kids stare at the floor, as if eye contact might trigger a beating.

If Luzhin is the kidnapper, that would explain how easily a look-alike for Cameron Hall was found. It would have been as simple as typing *male, 14, Caucasian, brown eyes, blond hair* into the search fields of the police database. Robert would have come up because of his sealed juvie record.

Luzhin doesn't own a van—but he could easily have gotten one from the police impound. In fact, he could have taken Nigel Boyd's ambulance. An unconscious person getting loaded into an ambulance is much less suspect than one getting put into a van. He could have borrowed a human kidney from the morgue and reprinted some test results from a different case so it appeared to be a DNA match with Annette Hall's blood. I never saw the photos he supposedly pulled from Cameron's social media profiles, but I bet they were actually photos of Robert Shea.

When Luzhin first gave me the case, I told him Charlie Warner was the kidnapper. He knew she wasn't, so I guessed that he had someone in her inner circle. Then I saw her inner circle, and none of them looked like a cop. There was no undercover agent. He knew Charlie Warner wasn't the kidnapper—because he was.

The doctors found Rohypnol in Cameron's bloodstream. You wouldn't happen to know anything about that, would you, Blake?

He knew I'd doped Robert up, because he knew he hadn't. It all fits.

Except for one thing. Why? Can his cocaine addiction have gotten so bad that this is the only way he can finance it? Why not just steal cash from the evidence locker, like the other corrupt agents do?

Maybe it's been him stealing from the evidence locker all this time.

Annette is staring at me, horror in her gaze.

No—not at me. Behind me.

Something whistles through the darkness and slams into the side of my skull. It's like falling headfirst into a volcano. I plummet to the floor, my ears whining, and look up in time to see Luzhin—two of him, because my eyes won't focus— raising a baseball bat to strike again.

His face is the same, yet different. It's like looking at a statue of him. He looks neither pleased nor horrified to find me down here. He may as well be a robot.

I throw my hands up to protect my head, but not quick enough. The remaining cartilage in my nose snaps under the blow. My brain quivers like Jell-O under the battering.

I'm going to die down here. This is the last thought that enters my head before I black out.

I wake up reluctantly, with the sense that I'll regret it. My shoulders are in agony, all the ligaments stretched. My face is a mess of tender flesh. My wrists, hot and swollen, are chained to the wall above my head. Now I'm just another of Luzhin's trophies.

When I try to breathe, an involuntary groan comes out.

"Quiet."

My vision is still a supernova of shattered focus, but I don't need to see to know who's talking. His voice is flat. Colder than I've ever heard it. All pretense stripped away.

"Why did come here, you stupid son of a bitch?" he mutters.

"*I'm* stupid?" I spit out some blood and mumble through split lips. "This whole time I thought the kidnapper was some kind of mastermind. But you're just making it up as you go along, aren't you?"

It's probably not smart to piss him off. But how much worse could things get? He's won.

I can hear him fiddling with some more shackles to go around my ankles. The other prisoners weren't wearing anything like that. I'm getting special treatment.

"You didn't think Annette would call the cops," I continue. "But you needed the money, so you couldn't return Cameron. Instead, you abducted Robert Shea. You took his parents too, for leverage. But you didn't know they had a cat, or a would-be girlfriend keeping tabs on him."

Luzhin tightens the chains, ignoring me.

"Worse still," I say, "you didn't know Robert Shea had cancer. He'd had a kidney removed the week before. You had to pretend to steal Cameron's kidney just so no one would realize you'd released the wrong kid. I guess your plan was to make Annette empty out her bank account, now that the case was officially closed and no one was paying attention. But when you saw that I was getting too close, you had to frame Philip Hall, kill him—"

Annette gasps. She didn't know Philip was dead.

"—and frame me for his murder," I finish. "Then kill me too, I guess. Shoot me, and claim I resisted arrest. Now you have six prisoners you don't know what to do with. All this trouble, just so you can feed your goddamn drug habit."

There's a pause.

"I've been sober since the night we met," he says.

Out of everything I just said, *that's* the part he objects to. I try to shrug, but with my arms bound above my head, it doesn't really work.

"Fine," I say. "Gambling debt, brothel bills, whatever."

"That money is saving lives."

"Whose?"

He just looks at me.

I remember seeing the van outside the field office, loaded up with expensive out-of-town bodyguards.

"The witnesses," I say, finally seeing it. "For Charlie Warner's trial."

"She kills people, Blake." Obsession lights up his eyes. "Dozens directly, thousands indirectly. She fed my friend to a fucking alligator. And she has people in every government department. There was no chance of convicting her. The DOJ couldn't be trusted to protect the witnesses and the jurors. But four million dollars buys some pretty damn good private security." He nods to himself, satisfied. "Just one conviction, and half the crime in Texas will be wiped out."

He picks up a roll of duct tape and peels off a strip.

"I get it," I say. "You're insane, but I get it. Except for one thing."

He doesn't even pause. "Yeah?"

"Kidnapping, extortion, murder—what makes you any better than Warner?"

"You're an animal, Blake. I wouldn't expect you to understand."

"Try me."

"Seven dead," he says, "to save hundreds. Thousands over the long-term. That's the difference." Then he slaps the piece of tape over my mouth, puts the roll back on the shelf and clomps up the stairs.

He's out the door before I register what he's said. Philip Hall. Plus me. Plus the five other prisoners.

Seven dead. He's decided to kill us all.

I hear his car start in the garage. The automatic door rolls up and closes again once he's left.

I don't know where he's going, or why, or how long he'll be gone. I'm certain of only two things. One: I have to be gone before he gets back. And two: there's no way out of here.

The handcuffs are too tight to slip out of. I've been pull-ing constantly since I woke up, but each one gets jammed up against my thumb and the other side of my wrist, where they cut deep grooves into my flesh. My feet are a similar story. I have no hope of getting either fetter past my ankle.

I could use the tools hanging from the walls to break the chains. A power drill, a hacksaw, a pair of pliers. But Luzhin isn't stupid. They are placed well out of reach. No objects of any kind are within range of my clutching hands or kick-ing feet.

I'm useless now. My skills are noticing things and reading people. I'm not an escape artist or a strongman. Now that I know Luzhin is the killer, my abilities are redundant.

Not that they did me much good. I never suspected Luzhin, not even a little. Even Thistle trusted him, and she's at least as smart as me. No one else will have figured out the truth.

Perhaps I can engineer a rescue. There's tape over my mouth, but Luzhin made a crucial mistake. If I stretch my face upward and my hands downward, I can grab the cor-ner of the tape. My hand is sweaty, so it takes a while to get a good grip—but once I've got it, the tape tears off quickly and easily.

"Help!" I scream. "Somebody help us! *Help!*"

I listen. At first there's nothing. And then a distant muf-fled mumbling sound. For a joyous moment I think I've succeeded—and then I realize it's one of the other prison-ers sobbing.

They've tried this before, and it didn't work.

"Help!" I yell again. "Please! Somebody!"

The house I shared with John Johnson was never truly si-lent. It was quiet, sometimes, but I could always hear the dis-tant roar of traffic or the soft mutterings of the neighbor's TV.

This isn't like that. There is a complete absence of noise

from outside. The foam mattresses suck up all sound. Shouting will do nothing.

I'm a death row inmate. Not here by choice, yet because of my choices. I'm waiting for a visitor who will kill me and then secretly dispose of my body.

How long will Thistle look for me? A month, maybe, before she decides that the trail has gone cold. She might believe I'm living in hiding somewhere, but most cops know that no one ever really gets away with anything, long-term. Eventually she'll assume that I got what I deserved, and she'll be right.

I bang my wrists against the wall and my ankles against the floor and roar through clenched teeth until the whole mess sounds like a chain saw going through a chain-link fence. I didn't live through my parents' murders and the group home and sleeping under a bridge and the pyromaniac roommate and the drug-dealing roommate and everything else that happened to me just to wind up here.

I look up at my hands.

They're good hands. They've served me well until now.

Before I have time to change my mind, I put my left thumb into my mouth and bite down, just past the biggest knuckle.

Hot blood rushes down my throat as the skin and muscle split, sending a shock of agony spiraling up my arm. Soon my teeth hit the metacarpal, bone on bone, and I try to chomp through it. But the skeleton is too strong.

I relax my jaw and release my mangled thumb. If I don't get free and find something to stem the blood flow in the next few minutes, I'm going to go into hypovolemic shock. So I grab the thumb with my other hand and bend it until I feel the bone snap. A jagged shard erupts through the skin, and I put the whole mess back in my mouth and keep chewing and tearing.

With one last crunch, the thumb finally pops loose from

the rest of my hand. I swallow without thinking, and it goes down my esophagus like a gristly cocktail weenie.

I pull.

My thumbless hand still won't fit through the cuff.

I moan with horror as I realize that I've mutilated myself for no reason, and that I'll be dead before Luzhin even returns.

I pull again, harder.

My hand slips out with a slick rattle.

It takes a second for me to realize I'm giggling. My mad chuckles echo through the dark. I tell myself that I'm just relieved, but maybe it's more than that. Maybe I've completely lost my mind. The nine-fingered cannibal, laughing at himself in the shadows.

With my left arm free, I have more reach. Stretching out sideways, I grab the leg of Luzhin's workbench. My hand slips off the first time, because my thumb isn't there to grip one side. But the second time I get a better hold of it. It's fixed to the wall, but not well. I can shake it.

I pull and push and pull and push until something jangles to the floor. A monkey wrench. No good—not unless I want to smash all the bones in my feet to get them out of the fetters. I keep shaking the bench.

Thunk. The power drill falls to the floor. I drag it over.

I check that the bit is in and switch it to counterclockwise mode. My cuffs are welded to a steel plate above my head, which is attached to the wall by four fat screws. I jam the bit into one of the screw tops and pull the trigger.

Blood dribbles onto my forehead as the drill whirs. Soon the screw is loose enough to yank out and toss away. I get started on the second screw, already feeling a little dizzy.

As a little boy, I wondered if dying people could keep themselves alive with sheer willpower. I never seemed to fall asleep against my will, no matter how tired I was, so I couldn't see why death would be any different.

Screw number three comes loose. I struggle to line up the bit with the last one.

It seemed like if my parents had loved me enough, mere bullets shouldn't have stopped them from staying with me.

I'm regressing. I'm begging myself to stay alive, like it's a choice.

Screw number four is out. I tear the plate off the wall. With both arms free, I can take off my shirt and wrap it around my crippled hand. The fabric flushes red instantly. I hold it in place with my armpit while I drill the screws that bind my fetters to the floor.

Maybe it's for the best that I swallowed my thumb. Without it I might not have the energy to keep going.

One screw loose, one to go. I keep drilling, the tool trembling in my grasp, until the last one is out. I'm free.

I climb to my feet and stagger over to Annette Hall, loose chains jingling. Pale, no shirt, covered in blood—I must not look like much of a rescuer.

"Stay quiet," I tell her hoarsely. She makes no sign that she's heard or understood.

I tear the tape off her mouth. It comes easily, and there's a lipstick kiss on the sticky side—he must have used the same strip of tape over and over.

"Where does he keep the key?" I ask.

She gags, and I realize there's still something in her mouth. I put my fingers between her lips and pull out a wadded-up tube sock.

"You've got to get us out of here," she says. Her voice has an early-morning croak to it. She hasn't spoken in days.

"Where's the key to your cuffs?"

"He keeps it on him."

That's when I hear the garage door winding upward, and she screams.

CHAPTER 24

WHAT CRIME IS PUNISHED IF ATTEMPTED, BUT NOT IF COMMITTED?

I SLAP MY HAND OVER ANNETTE'S MOUTH. LU-zhin is probably coming down here either way, but I'd pre-fer it happened later rather than sooner. He's still in his car at the moment—I can faintly hear the engine noise, the squeak-ing brakes.

If I run, I could probably make it out of the house before Luzhin comes inside. I didn't hear him lock the basement door. Then I could call Thistle from a neighbor's phone and summon backup. But when he sees the police coming, Lu-zhin might kill his prisoners to keep them quiet.

If I stay, and Luzhin comes down here, I won't be able to fight him. I'm already bleeding to death. He'll kill me, and the prisoners won't be any better off. No one will know they're down here. And without a key, it's not like I can get them out, can I?

You could bite off all their thumbs, says the crazy, hungry part of my brain.

Remembering the sledgehammer I used to free Robert the first time around, I quickly scan the room. Some regular-size hammers, some wrenches. No sledges.

One day, no matter what, my life will end. At least today I have the opportunity to get killed trying to do something good.

"I'm getting you all out of here," I whisper. "But you gotta stay quiet."

I take my hand off Annette's mouth. She shrinks away while I jam the drill bit into the screw top and pull the trigger.

The drill squeals, and the screw comes out surprisingly fast. The old brickwork crumbles around it. I tell myself the mattresses will stop Luzhin from hearing us.

"Can you walk?" I ask.

She nods. "He takes us up to the bathroom every day."

I unwind all four screws, and the metal plate clangs to the floor. Next in line is Robert Shea. I start drilling again. "He won't want to kill us in his regular clothes," I whisper. "He'll go upstairs to change into something disposable. When he does, we can sneak out the front door together. Then we're gonna run like hell. Got it?"

Robert's plate falls off the wall, and I catch it. "By the way, tell Jane Austin she saved your life," I say. I might not make it out of here alive, and she deserves to know.

I start unscrewing Larry Shea. He's a big guy, but not as big as Luzhin, and he looks hungry and frail. He won't be much help if Luzhin comes down here. The screws are taking longer than they should—I have to pull the trigger of the drill with my mangled hand and steady it with the other. Larry mumbles something through his tape.

I peel it off and pull out another sock. "What?"

"Let my wife go first," he gasps.

"Shut up," I tell him. If I had time to think about that sort of decision, I wouldn't have released the child molester first. I yank the last screw out and the plate falls off the wall.

"Wait at the top of the stairs," I tell him as I start working on Celine's chains.

"Not without my wife," he says, but with less conviction.

"Standing here won't get her out any faster," I grunt. I could add that Robert is better off with one parent than none at all, but I'm already undoing the last screw. Husband and wife run up the stairs and huddle by the door with Robert.

Last is Cameron Hall. Photographer, trumpeter, friendless. The boy I've been hunting for weeks now. The one who was screwed up by his mother, literally. The one I was so sure would be dead. I start working on his chains.

"You're gonna get us all killed," Annette Hall says.

I keep drilling.

"Listen to me," Annette says. "That front door is loud. Two dead bolts and a chain. We can get it open, but it'll take a minute, and he'll hear us. He'll just come down the stairs and shoot us."

"I left the back door unlocked," I say. But it's hard to imagine all six of us clambering over that fence, silently, in our condition. And I know from my previous visit that Luzhin's bedroom window overlooks the backyard. If he sees us while he's getting changed…

"I have a better plan," Annette says.

I yank Cameron's plate free. "I'm listening."

"Cam and the others can hide in the guest bedroom on the ground floor. I'll pretend to be still chained to the wall in here. When the son of a bitch opens the basement door, he'll see me. He won't realize the others are gone until he comes down the stairs. You can hide under the stairs and trip him when he's halfway down. Then we'll overpower him together while the others open the front door and run for help."

"Mom," Cameron says uncertainly, "you gotta come with me."

"I can't," she says. "He'll open the door expecting to see me right there. I have to stay."

I hesitate. It's a good plan. Annette has had a few days to observe Luzhin's house and his movements. In a way, she knows him better than I do.

She's effectively risking her own life—and mine—to save her son and three other people. I wouldn't have thought she was the type.

"Trust me," she says. "This will work."

I'm too dizzy to argue. I've lost a lot of blood.

"Okay," I say.

"Go," Annette tells Cameron. "Hide in the guest bedroom and don't make a sound. Okay, baby? Not a sound until you hear us yelling. Then you run. Out the front door."

Cameron's eyes fill with tears. "I can't."

"You can," she says, and kisses him on the cheek. "Go. Now!"

Still Cameron hesitates. She pushes him away. "Go!"

He runs up the stairs to the others. They disappear through the basement door. Cameron closes it behind him.

Annette and I stare one another down in the dark. She doesn't know that I know the truth. She raped her son—but now she's putting her life on the line to save him and five other people.

Children fear that monsters exist. Adults fear that they don't—that the world is just a jigsaw of screwed-up people with good qualities as well as bad.

"Did you have sex with Cameron?" I ask.

She looks at me for a long time. Too long to be innocent.

"No," she says finally.

"I don't believe you."

"He asked me." Her voice is quiet. Worn down. "The fucked-up thing is, I wanted to say yes. But once you open a door like that, you can't close it again."

I don't know what to say to that.

"Don't screw this up," she says, and puts the black hood back on her head. She holds the metal plate against the wall as though it's still bolted in.

"Do I look okay?" she asks.

I don't have time to respond. Quiet footsteps approach the basement door. Luzhin is coming.

The power drill is still by Annette's feet. I snatch it up and scramble out of sight under the stairs just in time. Luzhin opens the door above my head, casting a rectangle of light across Annette. I can see her through the gaps between the stairs.

I wait for him to walk down the stairs.

He doesn't.

A gunshot rings out.

Brain matter explodes out of Annette's hooded head. Her whole body goes limp in an instant. She slumps to the floor. The metal plate lands on her, and she doesn't react.

Luzhin storms halfway down the stairs, ready to shoot the other prisoners—he must have decided to do us all quickly, like pulling off a Band-Aid—but he hesitates when he sees the fallen plate.

I don't give him time to figure it out. I pull the trigger on the power drill and shove it between the steps.

Luzhin shrieks as the drill pierces his ankle. The spinning bit turns his skin to ribbons and punches a neat hole into the bone.

Luzhin's ankle collapses under him and he tumbles down the stairs, still screaming. I hear his forearm crunch as he hits the floor, but Annette Hall's corpse cushions the blow to his head. He's still holding the gun.

I scramble around the corner and run up the stairs, but Luzhin recovers quickly. The bullet travels faster than the speed of sound, so I see the blood burst from my chest before I hear the shot. I trip on the last step and land half in, half out of the basement.

My pectoral muscle feels like it's filled with razor blades. Shredded flesh rubs against a shattered rib as I drag myself through the basement door and kick it closed behind me.

The front door is wide-open. The other prisoners must have fled when they heard the first shot. I should run too, but I can't even stand up. I've lost too much blood.

I can hear Luzhin limping up the stairs. I can't drag my-self away from the door. But I have just enough strength to reach up and slide the bolt across, trapping Luzhin in his own dungeon.

Luzhin fumbles with the door. It stays closed.

There's a thud as he kicks the door from the other side. It stays shut.

He kicks again, but not hard enough. I guess he can't put any weight on his ruined ankle. He's trapped.

So get the fuck up, Timothy.

Instead, I let my eyelids flutter closed.

Silence. Long enough for Luzhin to realize that his other prisoners are long gone. It's over.

I drift off to sleep for a moment before another gunshot wakes me up. I look up at the bolt sealing the door. Intact.

A thud from inside the basement.

My eyes drift closed again.

It's impossible to tell how much later I feel rough hands rolling me over. I want to tell whoever it is to go away, but I'm too tired even to open my mouth. Someone is calling my name, but I'm not sure if they're real or if they're part of the dream world that's pulling me in, as slow and strong as a coastal tide.

Hands roam across my chest, strong palms finding their mark, and it's only now that I realize I'm not breathing. I try to start again, but it's like I've forgotten how. I'm dizzy. I'm dying.

Thump! The first shove of the CPR cracks another rib, but the pain is on the other side of aquarium-thick glass. After an-other whack, there's nothing. Maybe my rescuer has spotted the bullet wound. Or maybe he's still going, but I can't feel it anymore. I'm no longer half-dead—closer to three-quarters.

A mouth covers my own and air rushes into my lungs, so

much that I feel like I might burst. I'm getting CPR from someone who learned it the old way. Who learned mouth-to-mouth as well as compressions.

The lips are soft, full. I recognize them. The woman who's trying to save me—the woman who, for some reason, thinks I'm worth saving—is Agent Reese Thistle. Bringing me back to life with a kiss.

I black out.

CHAPTER 25

WHAT ANNIVERSARY PRESENT DID THE HANGMAN BUY HIS WIFE?

THE PAIN THAT PUT ME TO SLEEP IS THE SAME pain that wakes me up. When I open my eyes, the brightness is agony, so I shut them again. I tilt my head on what feels like a pillow, and the movement sticks tiny knives into my chest.

But I can hear a little better. The beeping of the machines is clear enough. I'm in a hospital. The smell reminds me of two-star motel carpet, recently scrubbed with cheap cleaner.

"You're in a lot of trouble," someone says.

I open my eyes again and squint at the woman who's spoken. Caucasian. Dark clothes. Red hair. Choker necklace. The rest is too fuzzy to make out.

"I'm not dead," I croak. "So not as much trouble as I expected."

She doesn't laugh. "Kidnapping, false imprisonment, assault and murder. You know what the penalty for all that is in Texas?"

"How long have I been unconscious?"

"That's not important."

"Who are you?"

"What matters is who *you* are. An ugly, poor drug dealer. There's not a jury in the state that won't find you guilty."

I can see her a bit better now. Freckles, rimless glasses. A young woman with an old woman's voice. No anger in her expression, but no sympathy either.

Looking down, I see that my chest is all taped up. My

thumbless hand is wrapped in so much gauze that it looks like cotton candy on a stick.

Thistle must have kept me alive somehow. What about Luzhin's four hostages? Did they all make it to safety?

"Are you my lawyer?" I ask.

"*Your* lawyer? No."

"Well, I'm no drug dealer."

"Addict, then. We found all kinds of narcotics in your house."

"Not mine."

"Good luck proving that."

My back is killing me. "Shouldn't you tell a nurse that I'm awake?"

"No," she says. "You can't talk to anyone until you've heard what I have to say."

"So say it."

"If you don't go down for the drugs, you'll go down for the kidnappings. If not for them, then for the murder of Philip Hall and Peter Luzhin."

"Luzhin's dead?"

"Whichever way you look at it, you're spending the rest of your life behind bars. And depending on how many counts you're found guilty of, the rest of your life might not be very long."

"It was Luzhin who kidnapped all those people," I say. "Not me."

She registers no surprise. And finally I realize why she's here—to sweep this whole mess under the rug.

"No one will believe that," she says. "The man spent fifteen years serving and protecting, whereas you're just another broke junkie who needs to be put down."

"If a jury got a look at his basement, that might show them the kind of man he was."

"Nothing illegal down there. And I've got a military psychologist who'll testify as to the kind of man you are."

I thought I'd heard the last of Fallun, the doctor who kept me out of the army. Apparently not.

"The Sheas will back me up," I say. "I saved them."

"They won't be saying anything to anybody, not after the nondisclosure agreements they signed, or they'll find themselves in prison right alongside you."

"I want to see them," I say.

"They've moved to Connecticut, where they can get the best medical care for Robert. They wanted to put all this behind them."

All except the government hush money—Connecticut has the highest cost of living of any state in the USA.

"And Cameron Hall?" I ask.

"With his grandparents. A long, long way from here."

I know their phone number. But even if I contact Cameron, the government will use every trick they know to stop him from helping me.

"I'd like to spare the taxpayer the cost of a trial," the woman continues, "along with the expense of incarcerating you and possibly the even higher price of your execution. Perhaps we can come to some agreement."

She puts a two-page document on the bedside table. "This grants you immunity from prosecution, provided that you maintain absolute silence on the facts of this case until such time as the federal government declassifies it." She places a pen beside it. "Sign it when you're ready."

I exhale. "So Luzhin gets to die a hero, the Sheas get paid a fortune and I get to not be executed for something you know I didn't do. Is that about it?"

"Don't waste my time, Mr. Blake," the woman says. "Just sign the NDA."

Part of me wants to tear up the piece of paper and throw it

at her. But I'm not sure I have the strength. And she's right—what good would it do? Luzhin's already dead. No one is out there hankering for justice. And I don't doubt that she can get me thrown in prison if she wants to. I'm lucky she didn't just put a pillow over my face while I was unconscious.

I pick up the pen and sign the piece of paper. The drugs make it hard—it's like trying to write in cursive with a paintbrush. Trying not to look relieved, she takes it and points to a spot on the second page. "And here, please."

I scrawl my name on that page too. "Are you going to cover my hospital bill?"

"Are you kidding?" she says, taking the second page. "Do you know what health care costs in this country? Fortunately for you, someone else already paid on your behalf."

She points at my bedside table, which holds some flowers and a greeting card. The front of the card says *Thanks a bunch!*

Angling my head, I can see a handwritten message on the inside: *You solved a problem I didn't know I had. We're even. Charlie.*

With Luzhin out of the way, Warner gets to bribe, threaten or kill all those witnesses and jurors. Soon she'll be free.

The redhead has already walked out the door. Her heels are clicking away down the corridor as she heads for wherever it is these people hide in between crises.

"Hello?" I call out. "Nurse?"

No answer.

There should be a call button somewhere. I run my hands along the sides of the bed until I find a cable on my right, and then I follow it to a plastic bulb. I squeeze it. Nothing happens.

I start tugging at the sheets, trying to loosen them enough to climb out and go looking for someone. It's slow work. Before I can make any real progress, a nurse walks in. He's short, black, square-chinned and chewing gum that smells like nicotine.

"You're awake," he says. "Good morning." He starts tucking the sheets back in where I loosened them.

"How bad am I hurt?" I say.

"You'd better discuss that with the doctor," he says.

"So where's the doctor?"

"She'll be here soon."

"How soon?"

"Soon."

He glances at the IV solution bags hanging from a pole next to the bed.

"What am I on?" I ask.

He seems uncertain whether or not to answer. Finally he says, "Painkillers."

"What kind?"

"Morphine."

"Not enough. I feel like shit."

"You'll feel worse if you get hooked on morphine."

"Only when I can't get it."

He gives me a sharp look, like he's not sure if I'm joking. Then he smiles.

"You could switch me to something less addictive," I say.

"Ask the doctor."

"When's the doctor coming?"

"Soon."

I laugh, and there's a tightness in my chest. I feel a hundred years old.

"Try not to move," the nurse says. "You'll tear your stitches."

"How many have I got?"

"If the bullet had been an inch lower, you wouldn't have any at all."

That's twice that I've been saved by a high bullet. The nurse leaves. I resume trying to unfasten the sheets.

I don't realize I've fallen asleep until I hear the doctor come in. She's a meaty Native American with graying hair who barely looks up from her clipboard.

"You're a real lucky guy, Mr. Blake," she says, as if to herself. "How do you feel?"

"Like I've been bitten and shot."

"The bullet hit your right lung, but in the big scheme of things, that isn't bad—it missed your heart and your spine. It looks like someone got to you pretty quick."

"It didn't feel quick," I say.

"I'll bet. But a few minutes longer and we wouldn't be having this conversation. You'll be good as new in three weeks or so."

"Good as new?" I ask doubtfully.

"I mean you'll have some scars and a missing thumb, but you shouldn't have any trouble moving."

"How long do I have to stay here?"

"Assuming nothing drastic happens, I'll discharge you tomorrow."

"How long have I been here already?"

She glances back down at the chart. "Three days."

"Anyone come to ask about me in that time?"

"I wasn't here yesterday," she says, "so maybe, but I haven't seen anyone except your wife."

The redhead must have told them I was her husband to get access to me. Classy.

"She's been asleep in the waiting room since I got here," the doctor says. "Want me to send her in?"

Not the redhead. "Sure," I say, just to see what happens.

What happens is the doctor walks out and soon comes back with a rumpled-looking Reese Thistle.

"Hi, honey," I say, because the doctor is looking at her suspiciously.

"Sweetie," Thistle says, and takes my hand.

Apparently satisfied, the doctor leaves.

"Did you take me to Vegas while I was unconscious?" I say. "Make an honest man out of me?"

She looks embarrassed. "Sorry. They wouldn't let me see you otherwise."

We're silent for a while.

"You can't tell me what happened, can you?" she asks.

I shake my head.

"They made you sign something?"

I nod.

"Sons of bitches."

She's staring at my EKG, but she's not really seeing it. She's seeing all the things she should have seen before. Things we both should have.

"You already know what happened," I say.

"After you ran, Luzhin presented me with DNA and finger-print evidence that proved you were the kidnapper," she says.

"But I trusted you. I knew you wouldn't do something like that. So I figured there was only one person the real culprit could be. I was already on my way to Luzhin's house to arrest him when Cameron Hall made the 911 call. That's how come I got to you so quick."

"I'm sorry I ran."

"I would have too."

Would she, though? If it had been her, framed for mur-der, would she have turned herself in and trusted the cops to prove her innocence? If it had been me in the back of a car as it went over a bridge, and her suckling at her dead mother's breast, would she be the cannibal and me the FBI agent? Who am I? Who is she?

"You can stay at my place." She takes my hand. "Until you're back on your feet."

I want so badly to say yes. To wake up in Thistle's bed and make her a cup of coffee each day. To sit side by side on a park bench in the sun and eat normal food together for lunch.

To kiss, and have sex, and share secrets, and do all the things that regular people do.

But without Luzhin, I have no one to eat. Over the next few months, the hunger is going to drive me crazy. Eventually I'll lose control. And then Thistle, the only person I've ever cared about, will get hurt.

The Greek soldier from the book of myths, the one exiled because of his wounded foot—he won the war, but he never got to marry the Spartan princess.

"I'm not religious," I say.

She looks puzzled.

"I didn't want to hurt your feelings, so I told a stupid lie."

I say, "You're just not my type."

She looks at me for a long moment. Her eyes go flat as she realizes I'm not kidding. She lets go of my hand.

"That's okay," she says finally. "I understand. You can stay with me anyway, if you want."

"No, thanks."

She nods stiffly. Then she walks out without looking back.

CHAPTER 26

SOME PEOPLE FEAR ME.
OTHERS LONG FOR ME.
NO ONE HAS EVER SEEN ME—
IN FACT, I NEVER EXISTED—
BUT YOU SPEAK MY NAME EVERY DAY.
WHAT AM I?

THE COYWOLVES HOWL OUTSIDE MY WINDOW. Long and low. Lonely, or hungry, or both.

The toy in my hands is a complicated wooden thing. I've been at it for hours, and I'm starting to think it might be my favorite kind of puzzle—unsolvable. The sort that keeps my thoughts on a tight loop. The sort that doesn't release me to my memories, and wishes.

The phone rings. I ignore it, as I've ignored every call for three weeks. I don't want to hear from Thistle or to discover that it's not her calling. I don't want to talk to anyone else at the FBI. I don't want to chat with John Johnson's desperate ex-clients. I just want to be alone with my hunger.

A knock at the door.

I ignore it, twisting the components of the puzzle, looking for the path that will break them apart.

Another knock, and a voice. Female. "Blake, I know you're in there."

Not Thistle. Not a junkie.

I shuffle through the fingerprint dust—I never bothered to clean it up after I was exonerated—and open the door a crack.

Charlie Warner is on the doorstep, shielded from the rain by an expensive umbrella. Two bodyguards—new ones—stand on either side of her. She wears a subtle and probably expensive shade of lipstick, and a woolen coat that reaches her knees.

"I don't like being kept waiting," she says.

"Congratulations," I say. "I hear you're a free woman."

She bows slightly. "The trial went well. Can I come in?"

The worst she can do is kill me. I stand aside.

She walks in cautiously. It's like she worries that the floor will leave marks on her shoes. One of the bodyguards stays outside, the other follows her in. I shut my eyes. Too much meat in this room.

"I owe you an apology," Warner says. "You were telling the truth. You didn't kill Philip Hall."

"The flowers were sufficient," I say. "Are we done?"

"The man you did kill," she says. "With the sawdust and the cigarette. He wasn't just my driver. He performed a valuable service for me, and now he needs to be replaced."

I open my eyes and gesture at my crappy living room. "If you're after money..."

"I'm not." She looks at a folding chair and decides not to sit. "When my boys were here picking you up, they found something in your freezer. A human foot. Chewed."

I should be scared of her, but at this point it's hard to care. I make a half-assed excuse: "I think you mean John Johnson's freezer."

"What impresses me most is that's all they found," Warner says. "They took another look around while you were in the hospital. The rest of the body was gone. No trace at all. The cops didn't find anything either."

"There's nothing in the freezer now," I say. "You can check."

"I'm not here to blackmail you, Blake. I came to offer you a job."

"What kind of job?"

"Body disposal. One per week, guaranteed." She smiles, showing whitened teeth. "Interested?"

* * * * *

ACKNOWLEDGMENTS

THANKS TO THE WISE AND HARDWORKING TEAM at Allen & Unwin who took a chance on this book and made it much more palatable. I'm especially grateful to Jane Palfreyman, Genevieve Buzo, Hilary Reynolds, Deb Stevens, Andy Palmer and the terrific freelancer Ali Lavau for their tasty suggestions.

Thanks to my bold and eagle-eyed friends at Hanover Square Press who devoured *Hangman* and requested dessert— the forthcoming sequel is thanks to them. Special thanks to Peter Joseph, Natalie Hallak, Libby Sternberg, Bonnie Lo and cover designer Kathleen Oudit.

Thanks to my determined and loyal mates at Curtis Brown, especially Luke Speed, Benjamin Stevenson, Kate Cooper, Stephanie Thwaites—and most of all, Clare Forster, who believed in this book from day one and spent years trying to find the right home for it. Thanks also to Daniel Kirschen at ICM for bringing *Hangman* to the American market.

Thanks to Adam Giagni, Michael Offer, Maisha Closson and all the others using their formidable talents to bring *Hangman* to the screen.

Thanks to the generous crime writers who shared morsels of wisdom with me over the years, especially those who knew how to dish up a repulsive character in an appealing way: Paolo Bacigalupi, Bret Easton Ellis, Andrew Hutchinson, Jeff Lindsay, Tara Moss, L.J.M. Owen, Michael Robotham and Emma Viskic. Thank you also to Joyce Carol Oates and Paul

Cleave, whose novels—*Zombie* and *The Cleaner* respectively—inspired this one.

Thanks to all the people who shared infuriating riddles with me.

Thank you to Ken and Trish Spoor, who let me stay at their home in Texas and shared some gruesome stories from their time in law enforcement. Thanks also to the staff, guards and inmates of the Belconnen Remand Centre, the Alexander Maconochie Centre and the Texas Prison Museum. Mistakes are my own. Thanks also to my scary but medically knowledgeable friends Maria Bernardi, Anne Douglas, Nick Earls, Katherine Howell, Tom Rowell and Jessi Thomson, who unflinchingly answered questions like, "What could I use to poison somebody if I wanted to eat the body after?"

Thanks to my strong-stomached Mum and Dad, who provided valuable feedback on tasteless drafts and who picked up a lot of the slack while I was writing and editing this book.

Thanks to the following people who digested versions of the manuscript and provided useful feedback: Ashley Arthur, Lisa Berryman, Claire Craig, Andrew Croome, Adam Keighley, Paul Kopetko, Jesse Parker and Sam McGregor.

Thanks to all my friends and family, who've tolerated the unusual demands of my unusual job for a long time now.

Biggest thanks of all to Venetia Major, who put up with me while I was working on the book, who read it many, many times and who always had a new insight to share. She also gave Reese Thistle her name, to which I've become very attached. Venetia, I love you—I'm so glad your patience is finally paying off.